*T*HE WINNERS OF NINE BOOK AWARDS transcending the genres of science fiction, environmental fiction, and action-adventure, *The Girl Who Rode Dolphins* and *Dolphin Riders* have proven themselves thrillers with a labyrinth of spellbinding twists, turns, and thunderous action that takes readers on a roller coaster ride of nail-biting suspense and explosive adventure.

Upon its original debut, *The Girl Who Rode Dolphins* received the following multiple awards:

- *Winner of Best Epic Adventure of 2008*
  BooksandAuthors.net

- *Winner of Best Science Fiction Epic Adventure of 2008*
  BooksandAuthors.net

- *Winner of Science Fiction Genre*
  2009 Green Book Festival

- *Finalist in Action Adventure Category*
  2009 National Indie Book Excellence Awards

- *Winner of Environmental/Green Fiction Category*
  2010 International Book Awards Competition

- *Winner of the Talking Category*
  2015 Animals, Animals, Animals Book Festival

- *Honorable Mention Awardee in Science Fiction Category*
  2015 London Book Festival

Dolphin Riders, the sequel to *The Girl Who Rode Dolphins*, is an ensuing adventure combined with political intrigue that promises to captivate readers with enthralling action and mysticism on a scale every bit as intense if not greater than the first book.

- *Official Selection Winner of Action/Adventure Category*
  2016 New Apple Summer eBook Awards

- *Finalist In Action/Adventure Category*
  2016 Beverly Hills Book Awards

Following their original debuts, both books were re-released in 2023 by Seaworthy Publications, Inc. as a five-part cliff-hanger series as follows:

The Girl Who Rode Dolphins, 2nd Edition

- Part One - Gaia's Intervention
- Part Two - Gaia's Heartbeat
- Part Three - Retribution

Dolphin Riders, 2nd Edition

- Part Four - Creation
- Part Five - Survival

Gaia's Intervention

Part One
of
The Dolphin Riders Series

The Girl Who Rode Dolphins
2nd Edition

Gaia's Intervention

Part One
of
The Dolphin Riders Series

The Girl Who Rode Dolphins
2nd Edition

by

Michael J. Ganas

SEAWORTHY PUBLICATIONS, INC. • MELBOURNE, FLORIDA

Gaia's Intervention
Part One of the Dolphin Riders Series
The Girl Who Rode Dolphins, 2nd Edition
Copyright ©2023 by Michael J. Ganas
ISBN 978-1-948494-67-0

Published in the USA by:
Seaworthy Publications, Inc.
6300 N Wickham Rd.
Unit #130-416
Melbourne, FL 32940
E-mail orders@seaworthy.com
www.seaworthy.com

Library of Congress Cataloging-in-Publication Data

Names: Ganas, Michael J., 1946- author. | Ganas, Michael J., 1946- Girl who rode dolphins.
Title: Gaia's intervention / by Michael J. Ganas.
Description: Melbourne, Florida : Seaworthy Publications, Inc., 2023. | Series: The dolphin riders series ; part 1 | "The girl who rode dolphins 2nd edition." | Summary: "Former Navy Seal Jake Javolyn, a part-time smuggler by necessity and dive boat operator by profession, has come to Haiti in search of something. Hiring his boat out to Dr. Franklin Grahm, a renowned marine zoologist, Javolyn sets course for Navassa Island, only to stumble across a beautiful girl in the open sea. Encircled by a pod of six white bottlenose dolphins, the girl is found riding a seventh much larger but similar creature. Upon rescuing the girl from the nets of a tuna trawler crewed by vicious members of a drug cartel, Javolyn soon discovers the girl has strange and unusual powers. Even more amazing are her companions, for they are unlike any sea mammals he has ever encountered. They possess forelimbs with hands, super-intelligence, and are able to speak in human languages. From then on, he is plunged into a world of the supernatural and confrontation with iniquitous forces bent on vengeance and the capture of nature's most recent miracles. A stunning rollercoaster ride of epic adventure, Gaia's Intervention is the first book in this blockbuster series, an ecological saga that will leave readers spellbound and enthralled with its superb mix of intense action, environmental issues, and mysticism"-- Provided by publisher.
Identifiers: LCCN 2023020774 (print) | LCCN 2023020775 (ebook) | ISBN 9781948494670 (paperback) | ISBN 9781948494687 (epub)
Subjects: LCSH: Dolphins--Fiction. | LCGFT: Ecofiction. | Action and adventure fiction. | Fantasy fiction. | Novels.
Classification: LCC PS3607.A4385 G35 2023 (print) | LCC PS3607.A4385 (ebook) | DDC 813/.6--dc23/eng/20230804
LC record available at https://lccn.loc.gov/2023020774
LC ebook record available at https://lccn.loc.gov/2023020775

Dedication

To my gemstone, Harriet.

Facts

*H*aiti is currently the poorest country in the Western Hemisphere, a Caribbean nation beleaguered by economic strife, dismal squalor, and political instability, a land of defoliation and ecological ruin. It is a place with a violent past, punctuated by a succession of bloody rebellions and previously governed by an extensive line of statesmen and dictators whose policies were either inept, ineffectual, unpopular, corrupt, or oppressive. The Duvalier dictatorships of father and son, however, proved to be the most corrupt, oppressive and violent, and under their brutal regimes Haiti suffered deeply.

Francois "Papa Doc" Duvalier ruled Haiti from 1963 until his death in 1971 when his son Jean-Claude "Baby Doc" Duvalier took over the reins of power. Under the Duvalier governments, the population was kept in a state of fear, terrorized by the regime's secret police force, the Tonton Makout. They were also known as the VNS, Volunteers of National Security, and Papa Doc referred to them as his "civilian" military, while the citizens called them "the bogeymen." They were recruited mostly from Haiti's slums and were used to crush all opposition, often imprisoning without trial, torturing, and even killing individuals considered enemies of the state.

An estimated 60,000 Haitians were murdered at the hands of the Tonton Makout, which had a standing force of roughly 10,000 loyalists. Papa Doc made sure his secret police outnumbered the Haitian army by a factor of two in order to assure that he did not get overthrown in a coup. Both Francois Duvalier and his son also took advantage of the people's strong belief in voodoo to control the population. Consequently, much of the citizenry believed them to be voodoo spirits. To this day, voodoo, merged with Catholicism, is the religion of choice embraced by most Haitians.

Misappropriation of government funds amounting to hundreds of millions was common practice under Baby Doc's tyrannical rule, and in the wake of intense political unrest and pressure from the United States to step down, he was finally forced from power in February of 1986, whereupon he fled to France. A wealth of evidence shows various drug cartels to be firmly entrenched in present-day Haiti, where the political climate, endemic poverty and a breakdown in civil rule makes it an ideal staging area for the transshipment of illegal contraband, where public officials are often threatened or corrupted by bribery to keep a blind eye to drug trafficking.

Navassa Island is a small, uninhabited island, which lies in the Caribbean Sea between Haiti and Jamaica. The island originally belonged to Haiti before being claimed in 1801 as an unorganized, unincorporated territory of the United States, which currently administers it through the U.S. Fish and Wildlife Service.

Malique is a fictitious fishing village that lies roughly midway between the real cities of Saint-Marc and Gonaives along Haiti's western coastline. It has been created solely for the purpose of this novel.

Al Qaeda is an actual present-day organization of Islamic extremists bent on the destruction of the United States and its allies. To this day this terrorist group continues to flourish despite the loss of its originator and leader, Osama Bin Laden, who was killed by a team of U.S. Navy Seals when they stormed his hideout in Pakistan during a bold raid that occurred in 2011.

All mention of Haiti's former leadership and historical events, both past and modern day, are based on documented history and are used as a backdrop for the writing of this novel. In this way, history has been merged with fiction.

All characters, creatures and unusual settings that play a key role within the novel's plot are entirely fictitious and have been created solely for the reader's intrigue and entertainment.

Michael J. Ganas

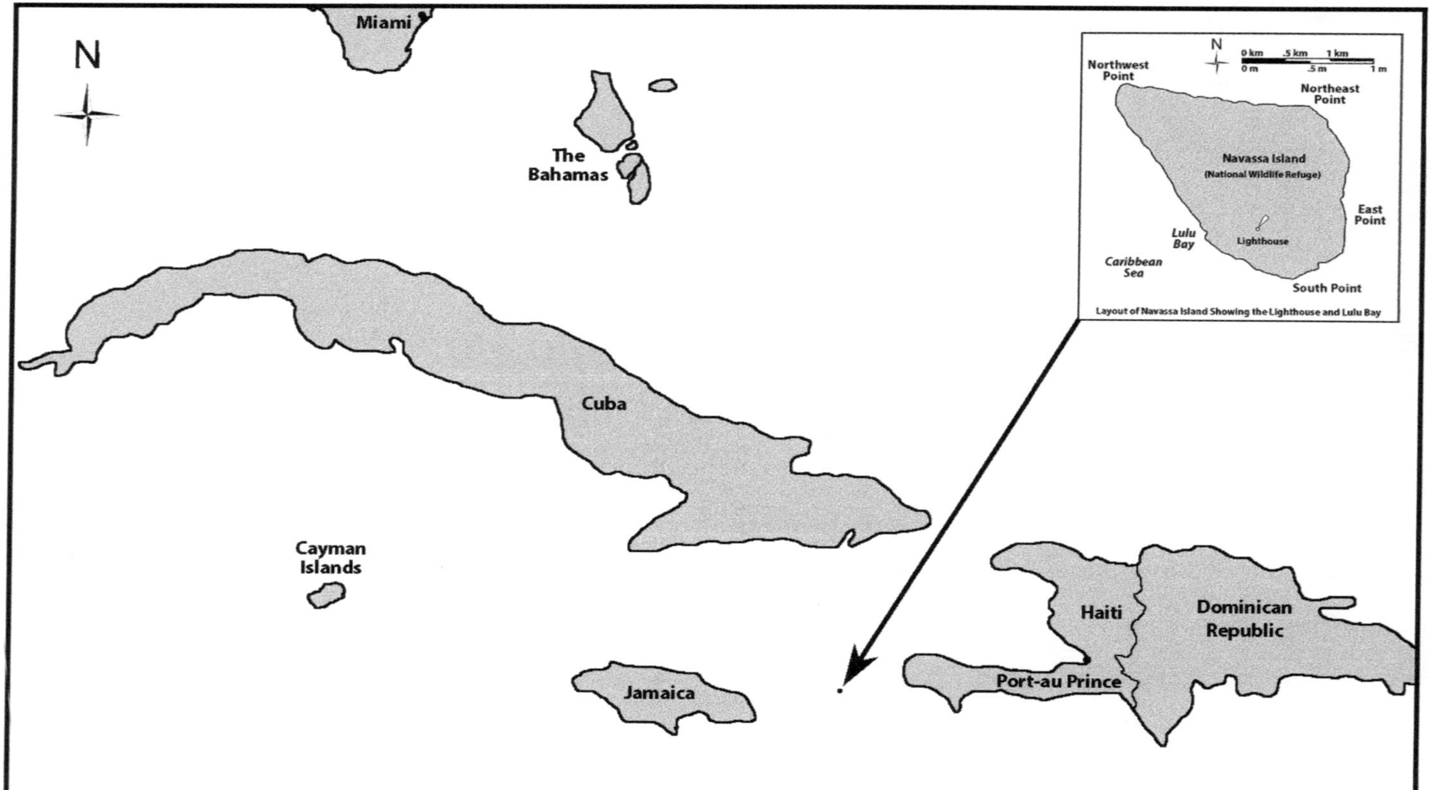
Miami
N
The Bahamas
Cuba
Cayman Islands
Jamaica
Haiti
Dominican Republic
Port-au Prince
N
0 km .5 km 1 km
0 m .5 m 1 m
Northwest Point
Northeast Point
Navassa Island
(National Wildlife Refuge)
East Point
Lulu Bay
Lighthouse
Caribbean Sea
South Point
Layout of Navassa Island Showing the Lighthouse and Lulu Bay

Navassa Island in Relation to the Western Coast of Haiti

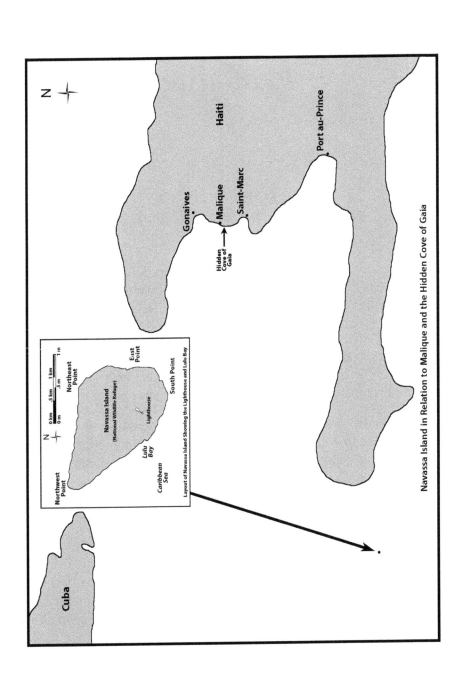

Navassa Island in Relation to Malique and the Hidden Cove of Gaia

Prologue

November 4, 1985
Somewhere in the Caribbean Sea

*T*he woman clung helplessly but with grim determination to the piece of flotsam, the final remnant of the sailboat that had borne her along the West Indies Archipelago over the last several weeks. The irate sea had become a brutal tormentor, lashing her face and eyes incessantly with brine that now burned like acid. She was exhausted, feeling her remaining strength rapidly ebbing by the constant buffeting. In spite of this, she stubbornly hung on, wondering how much longer the storm would last. If anything, it had gotten worse, much worse.

The pervading ebony blackness that had ravaged her throughout the night had now given way to a fierce mournful gray, and she knew that dawn had come. With wanton hands, the pounding gloom pressed itself upon her like a pillaging marauder caught in the throes of lust, every so often thrusting downward with a clumsy errant spike of searing white light and unleashing a harsh crackling outburst that merged with the cacophony of an excited sea. It tossed and jostled her violently, seemingly intent on ransacking her very will.

As another swell lifted her high, she pushed herself up as best she could from the meager panel of wood, careful not to unbalance it. The flotation it gave her was scant, and she wanted to avoid upending it again. Craning her head and reducing her eyes to mere slits against the onslaught of wind and driving rain, she glanced about hopefully. The sea remained desolate, with neither watercraft nor land in sight. Only a bleak wash of huge marching whitecaps and foam, raging and turbulent, lay beneath a low-slung formation of angry dark clouds that clung to the ocean like an impenetrable blanket of destruction. The dreary view disappeared as the wave bearing her suddenly swept away, and as she dropped down into another churning canyon she felt her spirits plunge.

But she was not ready to give up. Withdrawing into herself once again, she sought to escape the immensity and loneliness of it all. It was an old trick she had learned during her days of competition, a way of distancing herself from the pain. And now she would use it to hold at bay the demons of despondency that sought to pull her hope of survival into the dismal depths. Bolstered by this state of mind, she hung on, unwilling to quit.

As if adding to her misery, the wind abruptly swirled, howling madly, and whipping up a frothing spate that dashed her without warning. Temporarily blinded, she failed to prepare herself for the next towering wave that sought to devour. She became aware of the danger only at the last instant, and when she did, her pulse quickened. It was a white water monster of colossal size, far bigger than anything that had come before it. Cresting to a dizzying height, it hung momentarily as though it would swamp the earth. And then it descended, hammering down on her with such savageness that she thought she was being crushed. A torrent of water tore into her, viciously battering and tumultuous, seeking to find entrance into her mouth, throat, and lungs. Smothered to near suffocation, she was tumbled and pulled down yet again, much deeper this time. Inwardly, she screamed, but it was not a cry of panic, for she would not let herself yield to such primitive emotion. Rather it was a cry of defiance against the seemingly endless chain of crashing water that had pummeled her mercilessly and relentlessly throughout the night.

With gritty determination, she somehow found the strength to kick her way free of the ocean's death grip, desperate to capture another morsel of life-sustaining breath amid the wild turbulence. Reaching the atmosphere, she was immediately racked by a seizure of fractious coughing and gagging as she strained air into heaving lungs. Squinting through eyes swollen and scalded red, she caught fleeting glimpses of electrical discharges that danced in jagged streaks over the wind-whipped froth, contributing immeasurably to the hellish synergy of a sky and sea gone mad.

The wind suddenly shifted and intensified, coming around as if to challenge the very waves it had spawned, shrieking like an angry falcon set on drowning out the sea's pervasive roar. It slammed into the next rising swell, pushing back with a raw belligerency as though determined to destroy the wave's impetus. But the wave was not to be stopped, and it rose mightily like a rearing warhorse, building upon itself in preparation to trample and crush all that opposed it. Caught in its grip, the woman felt her stomach lodge in her throat as the mountainous swell catapulted her upward with explosive force. Flung to a seemingly impossible height, she glimpsed the sheer precipice of water that fell away, a giddy drop that shocked her to the very core. She remembered to inhale only at the last possible moment, filling her lungs as a massive sheet of water licked out to take her. The wave curled sharply, and she found herself hurled roughly into the abysmal trough far below. The water felt like granite as she struck, and the panel of teak to which she clung bucked up into her like a rodeo bull, driving the wind from her lungs, and for one fleeting moment she had the sensation of being smitten by the hand of an angry god. Tons of water pushed her deep as the wave collapsed on top of her, and it took all her strength to battle her way back to the surface above. Almost losing her grip on the hatch cover, she kicked insanely to keep her head above the surge, giving succor to the floundering buoyancy of her makeshift float. The wind blasted her, digging its fingers into the rampaging sea, roiling and aerating the water into a foaming maelstrom, and it was only an act of will that made her fight on.

Once again, she managed to find purchase in an atmosphere without pity, and she gulped greedily in an effort to trap air into starving lungs. Almost immediately, another furious jumble of white water engulfed her, tumbling and dragging her under like the claws of an avenging demon.

It was then that her will began to flag. She had been in the storm-tossed sea for what seemed like an eternity, although only fifteen hours had passed since her vessel had suddenly taken on water. Subsequent to a horrendous pounding lasting most of the previous day, the severely battered 50-foot sloop had finally succumbed to a watery grave despite its tenacious attempt to remain afloat.

For what was perhaps the thousandth time, she fought her way to the surface in the ragged buoyancy. The realization that she was no longer clutching the hatch cover only added to her torment, underscoring the utter hopelessness of her predicament. And for the first time since her nightmare had begun, she began to welcome the prospect of death. The fight within her was now gone, replaced by a budding eagerness for the sea to finally take her. It would be so easy. The ill-defined vortex that existed somewhere between a churning ocean and whirling wind seemed to suddenly diminish in its ferocity, and it beckoned her downward into the serene depths with a strange enfolding comfort. She hesitated, wondering why she had resisted the sea's promise so savagely and for so long.

With a detached awareness she puzzled over the luminescent oblates floating languidly below her, perhaps twenty in all pulsing in a silent synchronized dance as they bobbed in the surge, and she marveled at the multitude of iridescent strands that trailed behind each. She was familiar with all the known variations of such life forms, coelenterates that had flourished and evolved throughout the earth's oceans over the last 650 million years, but she had never seen a species such as this. She looked on, watching the silhouette of her physical body eclipse the soft glow of shimmering light. Vaguely she became aware of her own form, the outline of limbs, torso, and bloated abdomen, and with it a surge of guilt.

Startled, she was reminded why she had fought so hard to survive and suddenly the depths were no longer inviting, the wavering iridescence now suffused with the burning embers of hell as thread-like wisps embraced her like vines of searing fire. Fully galvanized back to consciousness, she began to scream in response to the intense pain rapidly consuming her, but the crushing burden of the sea would not allow this, threatening to inundate throat and lungs with liquid death. Steeling herself against the pain and the temptation to inhale, she fought back the rising panic that was like a convulsing rhino in her chest, one that was quickly gathering momentum in a headlong charge toward oblivion.

Trying to orient herself to the roiling surface, she glanced wildly about. It was the fading afterglow of lightning bolts acting like beacons from far above that gave her a sense of direction, but at the same time their remoteness drove home the overwhelming futility of her plight. With a feeling of total failure, she realized she was now too deep and too exhausted to reach atmosphere before blacking out. As darkness began to flood the fringes of her consciousness, she cursed her own weakness and the men who had brought this upon her. She would perish without a trace, lost at sea like the others who had accompanied her. Even worse, her potential offspring would be denied the life that awaited it, and instinctively she embraced her swollen womb protectively in an act of forlorn sympathy.

The movement increased her agony as more painful welts erupted along her belly, a severe reminder that she was still entangled among the strange life forms. But the pain also told her that she was still among the living, and it gave her a temporary respite against the blackness that was slowly eating its way toward the center of her awareness.

The pain became her universe, predominating all her other senses, and she did not notice the gentle nudge that came from behind. Looking up in a final farewell to the world above, she became mildly aware that the surface was much closer, the flickering discharges of electrical energy seemingly directly overhead. Perceiving she had transcended into a state of delirium she suddenly felt herself lifted into the explosive interface between sea and air, and she automatically inhaled deeply, simultaneously swallowing choking mouthfuls of water as an avalanching wave slammed into her. She didn't care, managing to get yet more air into aching lungs, coughing wildly in the process.

Encouraged, she could feel a residue of her former strength returning, and with it a shred of optimism. Something seemed to be keeping her up, stabilizing her against the turbulence. Yes, it was directly under her, alternately nudging and bumping her anatomy with a precision that was both gentle and yet strong enough to counter the violent surges that threatened to take her back under.

With considerable effort, she managed to glance behind her and was immediately stricken with terror. A dorsal fin poked above the rolling foam. Abruptly, the small spark of hope that had touched her vanished with the speed of a tiny comet plummeting into a black hole. She stared in horror as the creature rose higher, continuing to nudge her. It's dark back glistened, aglow in the faint luminescence cast by the mass of thread-like tentacles draped over it.

In that moment of despair, she lifted an arm inundated in the jelly-like strands towards the heavens and cried out to God to give her a quick and merciful end. Almost instantly and in answer to her plea, the clouds responded with a crackling burst of light that streaked down upon her, sizzling the water with a flaring brightness so intense that she was certain the gates of paradise had opened to receive her. All at once, both her plight and misery dissolved, replaced by strange images and thoughts that thundered through her mind with the grace of stampeding elephants. Then all sense of consciousness deserted her.

Chapter 1

May 23, 2008
Port-au-Prince, Haiti

*T*he two men looked glum as they drank thirstily from frosty mugs in a dingy corner of the dimly lit bar, one of many such watering holes situated along the shabby harbor. Speaking in hushed, guarded tones, they glanced warily at the occasional patron that drifted into the grimy establishment. Though seated, one of the men appeared to be a hulking giant, possessing wide bulky shoulders that ballooned from his tightly fitting tank top and leaned over the table like massive obsidian cliffs. The bright red bandanna that encircled his forehead seemed to be in a losing battle at stemming the flow of perspiration that emanated from the glistening dome of his cranium, an aftereffect of the muggy confines of the tavern, which provided little respite from the steaming tropical heat outside.

The black goliath listened intently to the quiet comments of his companion sitting across from him, a white man with riveting green eyes, intense and penetrating like those of a timber wolf on the hunt. Though physically dwarfed by his associate, he was by no means diminutive in size, displaying a hard lean torso to which his damp T-shirt clung and well-defined muscular arms that hinted of explosive strength and athletic prowess.

"It doesn't make sense. We should've found something by now," the smaller man whispered with exasperation.

The larger man gave a sympathetic nod. "Maybe so, but we have not yet completed all the possibilities. The area to the north may prove to be more fruitful. Perhaps tomorrow will bring us good fortune." Zimbola

1

sipped the cold ale, his expression distant. "Perhaps some spiritual guidance from Bon Dieu will put us on the right track."

Jake eyed his partner with skepticism. "You're not going to start with that voodoo malarkey again, are you, Zimby?"

Zimbola scowled, a rather frightening visage to those unfamiliar with the man's quirks. Leaning his bulk farther forward, he hissed, "Tis Obeah. I've told you before, in the English-speaking Caribbean we call it Obeah," pronouncing it "oh bee ah" and emphasizing the "ah."

Jake shifted closer. "Well, it was your oh bee ah," he mimicked, "that almost got me killed near Anse. Remember?"

The larger man's scowl vanished like a squall scudding over the horizon. Zimbola shrugged. "A dream spirit seduced me into believing we would find that for which we have been searching if we looked there. But the Loa was not an evil one, not an eater of men's souls."

Jake held up his left forearm, displaying the jagged puckered scar. "No, it was an eater of flesh… my flesh. That Mako nearly had me for dinner."

"That Mako got us the equivalent of fifteen hundred U.S. dollars at the Hilton in Anse," Zimbola countered. "At a dollar fifty a pound, it became dinner for the rich hotel guests who think they are eating swordfish."

"We didn't find anything, did we?" Jake reminded him.

"Loas come in many forms and their motives are not always understood by the living. Yes, it may have appeared to mislead us but it nevertheless brought us good fortune. Did it not?"

Jake waved a disparaging hand. Zimby, as he affectionately called his oversized friend, had grown up in Jamaica and had been indoctrinated into the islanders' beliefs from a very early age. Zimby's faith was unshakable, and sometimes a nuisance. To Jake, the worship of voodoo was primitive and barbaric, based on superstition and spectacle that overlapped the realm of black magic and witchcraft. But he had no desire to offend Zimbola by telling him that, although he suspected his friend sensed this. Zimbola had often tried to explain the fundamentals of this animist religion in which objects and natural phenomena are believed to have holy significance, to possess a soul or Loa. The Loa formed a pantheon of deities that included hundreds of spirits. Although Jake had been raised in a Christian family, his convictions were inherently temporal-based, instinctively rooted in the pragmatic: if you couldn't see, hear, touch, taste, or smell it, then it didn't exist. Unlike his Jamaican counterpart, Jake shied away from the notion that good fortune was the result of divine intervention, holding steadfast to the premise that you made your own luck. As of late, unfortunately, their luck had been anything but good.

As if reading his thoughts, Zimbola said, "We must take the necessary steps to turn the bad luck into good. I have heard of a most powerful Maman who lives on Tortuga Island." Zimbola ignored the frown that abruptly clouded Jake's face. A Maman was a high priestess of the Jamaican version of voodoo. "Perhaps if we went to her, she could provide us with the spiritual guidance to help with our search. If we sailed tomorrow, we-"

"Mr. Javolyn, I knew I'd find you here." The voice cut off Zimbola's discourse like a finely honed sword lopping off a head. The man behind it was short, dumpy, and walked with a pronounced limp. Chester Hennington hobbled over and sat down in the chair nearest Jake. Hennington claimed an eclectic lineage of English and Black African, with a smattering of French and other extractions introduced into his family tree at some point or other in generations past. Native to Port-au-Prince, he was a full-time broker by profession, typically intervening as agent to a variety of legitimate ventures but more often acting as a go-between for unsavory parties engaged in illicit activities. As usual, Hennington was clad in his customary three-piece suit of white linen, which although quite expensive by Haitian standards, never quite succeeded in producing the image of a successful businessman, a status he had actually achieved within both the rich and infamous circles of island culture. Beyond an air-conditioned environment, the ravages of oppressive heat and humidity were ever present throughout the sweltering city, causing even the most freshly laundered and pressed fabrics to hang limply on sweat-dampened bodies, particularly on individuals who were foolish enough to embellish themselves with formal attire that was further adorned with a wide-brimmed white fedora and tightly cinched necktie of glossy white silk, as did Hennington.

"I trust you gentlemen are having a pleasant day," Hennington said in nearly flawless, unaccented English, displaying a smile fringed with crooked, tobacco-stained teeth.

Jake kept his expression somber. "We were until you got here."

"Oh, come now, Mr. Javolyn, you're not going to keep blaming me for that little mishap that occurred last month, are you?" Hennington objected wearily as he removed the fedora to expose a flattened mat of thinning silver-streaked hair. He placed the hat on the table and began to dab away at the sweat that beaded on his honey-colored but deeply furrowed brow with a handkerchief. The remnants of what must have been a nasty bruise marred his right cheek, and the flesh below his left eye appeared to have developed a line of scar tissue since the last time Jake had seen him.

Jake slugged down some more ale, taking the opportunity to take inventory of the three black men that had accompanied Hennington into the tavern and who were currently lingering at the bar, watching the conversation with quiet interest. They seemed to be paying special attention to Zimbola's imposing presence and the menacing scowl he focused in their direction.

Jake couldn't fault Hennington for his precautionary measures at self-preservation. In a country with a minimum wage of less than $2 a day, personal bodyguards were cheap. In Haiti, the Western Hemisphere's poorest nation, guys like Hennington were prime targets for roaming thugs, called "zenglendoes" in the native Creole, who mugged and killed for money. Rampant violent crime had been plaguing the country's capital, an overcrowded and crumbling city of two million inhabitants, for several decades now, and it seemed to be getting worse. Just last week, a well-known businessman was gunned down in broad daylight on a thoroughfare in one of Port-au-Prince's "safer" neighborhoods when three cars blocked his vehicle in traffic and an assailant shot him five times. In another recent incident at a local cockfight arena, a guy named Junior went into the ring to cash in on his winnings only to be gunned down. Stray bullets from the gunmen also killed two security guards and a bystander, while another innocent onlooker was severely injured. Political unrest accounted for a significant amount of the crime. A month earlier, four pipe bombs were thrown at the residence of a U.S. Embassy official. Jake recalled the rise in violence that seemed to accompany every presidential and legislative election, underscored by politically motivated killings and indiscriminate gunfire directed at pedestrians. All of these occurrences tended to create an overall environment of fear in which no citizen felt safe. With armed robberies, break-ins, murders, and carjackings becoming commonplace, criminals were operating with near impunity. Trying to impose law and order in the impoverished Caribbean nation was a challenging undertaking, particularly in light of the legal system that was both inefficient and infested with corruption. Understaffed with some 3,000 officers in a country of nearly nine million people, the Haitian National Police force was extremely limited in its enforcement capabilities, with bribery being epidemic among its constituents and some of the officers being worse than the vilest of criminals. The bottom line was that the more affluent members of Haitian society could ill afford not to pay the expense of personal security if they wanted to survive.

Jake slammed his stein onto the table with more force than intended and affixed Hennington with a hostile glare. Out of the corner of his eye, he spied the man's retinue stiffen in readiness. Hennington waved them off.

"You told me the Kingston run would be a cakewalk, that there'd be no risk. Just a simple load of bootleg CDs and DVDs, that's what you told me. Well, somebody wanted that shipment pretty badly, enough to wager having a running gun battle at sea and shooting up my vessel."

Several customers at nearby tables were beginning to stare, and Jake realized he was starting to shout. He made a conscious effort to lower his voice and eyed Hennington intently. "Somehow we managed to get away, but I couldn't help being suspicious about what I was carrying, so I decided to have a look inside those crates. And do you know what I found?" Jake paused for effect. "Military grade weapons, AK-47s, land mines, and RPGs."

Hennington looked unperturbed. "You have to understand, I'm just a simple middleman. Clients come to me all the time seeking a runner, and I arrange it. I'm rarely informed about the true nature of the contraband."

Javolyn wasn't convinced if this was true or not. He and Zimbola only occasionally resorted to smuggling, and only when they were in desperate need of cash. In conducting such work, it was a normal rule of the trade not to be too concerned about what one transported, only that you moved it from point A to point B, with no questions asked. With smuggling, there was always the risk of being boarded by authorities, or even worse, by being ambushed by pirates. Whenever a smuggler was captured by authorities, penalties were subject to the type of illegal cargo he was caught hauling. But more often than not, you could bribe your way out of such a predicament. When such an option failed to work, long-term incarceration was usually the inevitable result of being caught with shipments that involved drugs or weapons, since such contraband invoked the most severe punishments. However, in the event one was unfortunate enough to be waylaid by pirates, you could easily find yourself thrown into the briny depths as shark bait. And many smugglers could not discount the possibility that a gunboat captain operating under the flag of an island nation would resort to piracy for personal gain. All in all, any self-respecting individual engaged in the clandestine trade of smuggling understood that the level of monetary compensation for services rendered should be based on the degree of risk one undertook.

"I should have been paid three times more than what I received," Jake snarled.

"I'm sorry, but the deal was consummated when you made the delivery. My client will not agree to dispersing additional compensation."

"Then I should have deep-sixed the cargo when I had the chance," Jake said with annoyance, fighting back a strong inclination to cinch the tie surrounding Hennington's bloated neck a few inches tighter. Unfortunately, he still needed the man, for better or worse, and had no desire to terminate the relationship as yet.

An uncomfortable silence followed before Hennington said, "I have another job for you, actually two...that is, if you're still interested," his tone conciliatory.

"What is it this time, nuclear bombs?" Jake replied hotly.

Hennington ignored the sarcasm. "I think I can get you $50,000 for the next run."

Even Zimbola, who had been keeping a wary eye on Hennington's entourage, turned to look at the broker. The most they had previously been paid was $15,000. The blatant anger that had characterized Jake's foul mood a moment earlier subsided into a mask of impassivity. Something extremely valuable had to be at stake to be offered a sum of that magnitude, but this time he would not be duped.

"I have to know what I'll actually be hauling before I can accept," Jake said.

"I'm not at liberty to divulge that."

Jake studied Hennington shrewdly. "Operating expenses have escalated considerably as of late and my boat sustained quite a bit of damage on that last run. The repairs were exceptionally expensive." In actuality, he and Zimby had patched all the bullet holes themselves with nothing more than epoxy, paint, and gel coat. "On top of that, not knowing the disposition of the cargo will cost extra. Make it one hundred and you have a deal."

For the first time in their mutually beneficial relationship, a relationship that had up to now favored the fat businessman, Hennington failed to maintain a poker face. In fact, he appeared quite aghast. "If time were not of the essence in this matter, I'd take my business elsewhere," he bristled in outrage. "Seventy-five!"

Jake remained adamant, sensing he had the upper hand. "No way. It's one hundred or I pass on this one."

Hennington gathered in his dignity. "Very well. But don't expect me to throw any more work your way once you complete the run."

Jake ignored the threat. He was now convinced that the man needed his services more than he needed Hennington. "When and where do I make the pickup?" he asked.

"You'll be notified of that as soon as the client gives me that information," Hennington said, once again assuming a businesslike demeanor.

Javolyn leaned back in his chair. "You mentioned two jobs?"

Hennington sighed. "I have a small party from the states who are looking to charter a dive boat – marine zoologists from the University of Miami. Their spokesman made a point of telling me how limited their funds are. Fellow by the name of Grahm." Hennington had arranged charters for Javolyn on numerous occasions in the past, most of them sport diving excursions in which Jake had played host to wealthy vacationers.

"By any chance, his first name didn't happen to be Franklin?"

"Why yes, I believe it was. Do you know him?"

Jake shook his head. "I never met the man, but I've read some of his work. He's an eminent scientist within his field. Can he afford twelve hundred a day?" Twelve hundred was his minimum going rate, otherwise he was losing money.

Hennington's fingers played with the brim of the fedora lying on the table. "One thousand dollars for each day's leasing of your boat was the most he was willing to offer. However, he did agree to pay the cost of any fuel expended that exceeded five-hundred gallons during the trip. He mentioned he needed a vessel of sufficient size to accommodate three people on an outing lasting two, maybe three days."

"Did he have any particular destination in mind?"

"He said he'd disclose that once his party boarded your vessel. He'd like to sail tomorrow. Do you want the job?" Hennington seemed to be growing impatient.

Jake hesitated, strongly tempted to turn down such a meager offer. If he hadn't been so desperately strapped for cash, he would have. "Yeah, I'll take it," he said begrudgingly, casting morose eyes on the stein of ale in front of him. Have him meet us at the usual place, oh six hundred." As an afterthought, he added, "I assume this trip will not conflict in any way with our first item of business."

"The shipment won't be ready for at least one week, that much I know," Hennington answered testily. "Please make sure you and your vessel are available at that time."

"You don't have to worry about that." Jake scrutinized the broker's face. "By the way, Hennington, you don't look so good. You have an accident or something?"

"I fell off a ladder," Hennington muttered. He stood up and placed the hat back on his head."Gentlemen."

Zimbola watched as Chester Hennington's escort followed their benefactor from the premises. "You constantly surprise me, Jay Jay. First you agree to ferry cargo without knowing what we be carrying or where we be goin'. Then you go against your own policy of never taking a party sailing for less than your normal fee." He looked lugubrious. "My father used to say, 'A fool is the man who sells himself too cheaply, but the biggest fool of all is the man who is easily lured by the promise of wealth, for he unwittingly takes the devil along for the ride.'"

Jake merely smiled at the metaphor. There would always be risks.

Chapter 2

*A*lmost four weeks prior to having met with Jake Javolyn and Zimbola in the waterfront tavern, Hennington sat meekly, hat in hand, before Colonel Henri Ternier at the Port-au-Prince Headquarters of the Haitian National Police. Ternier's office, though neat, orderly, and modestly furnished, gave no hint of the brutality of the man, with the walls lined with a multitude of framed photographs predominantly depicting a smiling Ternier shaking the hand of various important government officials. The largest picture, strategically hung behind his desk so as not to be missed by anyone visiting him in his inner sanctum, showed Ternier standing tall and proud next to President-elect Rene Preval, the current leader of the Haitian government. Less obvious and positioned in a far corner of the room, another picture displayed the Colonel with Preval's predecessor, President Jean Bertrand Aristide, removed from power by the U.S. in February of 2004 in the midst of a rebellious uprising.

Henri Ternier had good reason to smile, Hennington thought grimly, having amassed a considerable amount of wealth in connection with narcotics and weapons trafficking over the last several years. Following the ouster of "Baby Doc" Duvalier in 1986, Haiti's government had been notoriously unstable, drawing the attention of rich Colombian drug lords who had immediately taken advantage of the complete breakdown of bureaucratic institutions during that period. Haiti was particularly appealing because of its geographic location, offering the most direct route - barring transit of Cuba - from Colombia to the United States. In addition, the Island of Hispaniola on which Haiti is situated had a wide variety of harbors and inlets that provided ideal protection to drug smuggling vessels. Moreover, the Haitian Air Force had no radar facilities and did not routinely patrol Haitian airspace. Planes laden with drugs could take off and land freely at any of the island's numerous secondary airstrips. The country offered many ideal staging areas where large quantities of drugs from the cartels could be stored prior to shipment to the states. By first buying up legitimate businesses to serve as front companies for their smuggling operations and gaining access to local commerce, the Colombians then focused on recruiting and corrupting public officials to protect their interests. Key military officers such as Ternier were ideal candidates for recruitment since they were in a position to assure noninterference in drug operations.

Command of the Dessalines Barracks had allowed Colonel Ternier to play a pivotal role in Haitian politics, mainly because his unit was responsible for safeguarding the Presidential Palace. One particularly powerful drug lord, Rafael Cardoza, had established a working relationship with Ternier by using Hennington as a go-between. Payoffs to the Colonel to look the other way were made on a shipment-by-shipment basis. As of late, unfortunately for Hennington, Colonel Ternier had been growing increasingly dissatisfied with the amount of money he had been receiving and seized a shipment of drugs in protest, re-selling the load through his personal connections at a substantial profit. When Cardoza investigated the impoundment, he discovered that Hennington had been pocketing most of what should have gone to Ternier. Hennington's left kneecap still throbbed painfully at the memory of the beating he had received at the hands of Cardoza's ruffians for his transgression.

Cardoza had sent his chief lieutenant, Sebastian Ortega, with two other hooligans to administer the punishment and to make sure Hennington was to right the wrongs he had committed against Ternier. Ortega let it be known in no uncertain terms what the outcome would be if Hennington did not get back in the good graces of the Colonel. Ternier was too valuable a resource to lose at this point in time and they had an aggressive schedule of shipments to maintain, most of which would make their way through Haitian territory. Upon being kicked and punched just short of having severe bodily damage inflicted on him, Hennington was given a final reminder. The heavy blow to the kneecap had left him a hobbling cripple during the last month, and walking had been especially painful.

Hennington remembered the intense agony of the baseball bat bashing his patella as he lay crumpled on the floor and the final instruction mouthed by a snarling Ortega standing over him. He was to meet with Ternier as soon as possible. He was to get back into the Colonel's good graces by making concessions with his own funds. The Colonel would be expecting him.

Ternier appeared to be concluding some paperwork as he sat behind his desk, completely ignoring Hennington ever since he had limped painfully into the office and been offered a chair by one of the colonel's adjutants. After what seemed like several minutes of prolonged, unbearable silence following the aide's exit from the room, the barracks commander finally looked up, locking dark baleful eyes onto him. The abysmal loathing lurking deep within those hellish orbs was hypnotic, like vicious monsters rising to the surface to devour prey, and Hennington suddenly found himself paralyzed with fear. Unlike the congenially smiling man in the photographs decorating the office walls, the feral grin displayed on Ternier's face was so far removed from a state of benignity that it could only be described as malevolent and foreboding. Here was a side of the man he hadn't seen before. Hennington felt a chill knife through his body, realizing that up to now he had severely misjudged the true nature of the man seated across from him. The amiable benevolence Ternier had shown him on previous occasions had been a skillfully erected façade, designed to deceive by masking the intrinsic profundity of underlying cruelty that was now revealed in one fleeting moment, mainly through those terrifying eyes. Clearly Ternier was not a man to be trifled with.

"So, Mr. Hennington, I am told you have been cheating me," Ternier said in mock joviality, speaking in the native Creole.

Hennington swallowed hard, unable to conceal his growing fright. "It was all a misunderstanding, I can assure you." He was aware of his own quavering voice.

"Yes, I'm sure it was," Ternier said softly, rising from his chair and calmly walking around the side of the desk. "How foolish of me for thinking a man such as yourself would let greed get the better of him."

Ternier began a slow circuit of the room, hands clasped behind his back, his bearing rigid and aristocratic. He was a tall man, clean-shaven and possessing a light-brown complexion complemented by a closely trimmed mat of tightly curled black hair capping his head. Sporting a crisply starched and pressed uniform that molded snugly to a brawny, evenly proportioned body, Ternier presented a striking figure.

Stopping with his back to Hennington, he stared at the wall as if looking through it. "How despicable of me for considering the supposition that you were withholding the remainder of my gratuities for yourself when I should have known all along that you were merely keeping those monies in escrow on my behalf," he said evenly, reverting to English that held a slight French accent.

Hennington sat transfixed, galvanized with dread. "Yes, yes, I was going to turn it all over to you at the conclusion of the next shipment… as a token of my, uh, appreciation." The reply came out in a sputter.

Henri turned around, directing rabid eyes at the fat broker. "I am too cynical to be worthy of your friendship," almost sighing as he said it. He walked behind Hennington who sat as if electrified.

"Can you ever forgive a man like me for his lack of good faith?"

Hennington nodded vigorously, too fearful to speak or look behind him.

Ternier eyed the back of Hennington's head, a myriad of gruesome possibilities flashing through his psychotic brain. "You do me honor," he said. "But perhaps I can atone for my mistake by giving you a tour of our humble facilities here."

Ternier nearly crept as he came around the chair to loom over Hennington, who appeared as if he were on the verge of a stroke. "Come," Ternier said in a barely audible whisper, smiling without humor. "I have some things you may be interested in seeing."

Fifteen minutes later, Chester Hennington, escorted by Colonel Henri Ternier and three policemen, was led down a poorly lit, squalid corridor, one of many such hallways in the National Penitentiary adjoining the Dessalines Barracks. The three plainclothes police officers worked directly for Ternier and were the same three men that Jake Javolyn would later assume to be Hennington's personal bodyguards. In a way they were, for they had been assigned the arduous task of keeping Hennington alive and safe on the crime-ridden streets of the city. This arrangement had come about shortly after Ternier was contacted by Cardoza's chief lieutenant. Ortega had apologized for Hennington's greed. He had also informed the Colonel about the nature of the punishment Hennington had received and that the broker had some amends to make. Restitution would be forthcoming. Greenbacks previously pocketed by the broker were to be immediately turned over to Ternier. Ortega further told Ternier that in Hennington's present condition, however, the broker would fall easy victim to the "zenglendoes" prowling the waterfront since that was where Hennington conducted most of his business. Upon hearing this, Ternier had quickly dispatched the three undercover policemen, making it clear that while they were to protect him, they were also to obey the broker's directives until further notice.

As the five men proceeded down the corridor, the air became rank with the smell of unwashed bodies. Human sweat and excrement seemed to hang in the air, making Hennington almost gag. As they came around a bend, a holding cell reminiscent of a slave ship appeared before them. Within the cell's dark confines, Hennington could just make out a horde of black bodies crammed into a space no more than twelve by fifteen feet. The overpowering stench of biodegrading urine assaulted his nostrils like a heavy blow, and he nearly collapsed from dizziness in the 105-degree Fahrenheit temperature.

About forty-five men sat on the cement floor, one behind the other in tight rows, knees to chins. Most were scrawny, and a profusion of interminable sweat plastered their tattered, soiled clothing to their bodies. Beyond the bars there was no toilet or sink with running water. The entire floor was jammed with inmates, with no room available to lie down anywhere. Even worse, there were no fans, air-conditioning, or ventilation of any kind to reduce the buildup of stifling heat and foul odors. Such amenities would have required electricity to power them, a relatively expensive commodity in the poverty-stricken nation. The broker was appalled at the sight of a communal bucket caked with feces sitting in one corner of the cell where prisoners could defecate or urinate. To Hennington, the overall scene was horrifying. He had heard rumors about these conditions, but one had to actually see it to believe that such an environment of human misery existed.

Ternier broke the spell of revulsion. "These men are criminal detainees. They get one meal a day, and it is not very much. Malnutrition is common here because we can only afford to feed our prisoners 1,300 calories per day. Most people require 2,000 calories if they are to survive. As a result, a few of these men will ultimately die of starvation before they are released." The Colonel was speaking English again. He seemed to be enjoying himself immensely at the sight of such abject suffering. The wretched conditions did not seem to invoke any repugnance from him whatsoever.

Ternier continued with his rhetoric. "These men are kept here in pretrial detention. They have not yet had the opportunity to go before a judge. With our inefficient judicial system and without the posting of bail, some of these detainees will be here for years, even if their offenses are very minor."

The Colonel directed the beam of the flashlight he carried at a pathetic, emaciated wreck of a human being at the rear of the cell. "That one there has been in here for nearly three years awaiting trial for the theft of a tape recorder. Such an offense would normally get him a maximum sentence of thirty days jail time, but he will most likely starve to death before he goes to trial."

At that moment, Hennington could no longer restrain the rising nausea overwhelming him. He let fly, grabbing hold of the holding cell's slime-ridden bars to keep from collapsing, while vomiting copiously onto the filthy floor. When he finally lifted his head, he appeared quite sick.

Ternier and the three officers laughed loudly at this. "Surely the sight of these inmates does not make you ill," he chortled. "But I do not advise touching these bars. Fungus and parasitic infections are quite common down here."

With a start, Hennington let go of the bars and wiped his hands vigorously against his trousers.

"And unfortunately, nothing can be done for these poor souls if they should get an infection. You see, there are no doctors available to diagnose or treat sick detainees. There is no medicine at this facility," Ternier said without sympathy, once again exhibiting that insane grin of his. "Come now, we have more to see."

A tremulous Hennington was led to a heavy steel doorway where two uniformed guards armed with shotguns were stationed. At seeing

Ternier, they came to rigid attention and saluted. The Colonel did not reciprocate, flouting the military custom. Obsequiously, one of the guards pulled open the bolt on the door to let Ternier and the others pass. They came into a hallway where the lighting was much better. A succession of rooms with wire-reinforced glass windows lined one side of the corridor.

"It is inside this sector of the building where detainees who cause trouble are brought," Ternier said as he walked past the first two rooms, both of which were unoccupied. He stopped at the third cell and looked inside. Beyond the window, two guards were pummeling an inmate with batons while the man was strapped helplessly to a chair. Although the man was bloodied from a heavy gash in his forehead and appeared to be unconscious, the guards continued to enthusiastically beat him about the shoulders, arms, and knees.

Ternier turned to Hennington. "This man complained too much about the length of his pretrial incarceration."

At the next window, two other guards were casually inflicting serious pain on another inmate. One guard wielded a cattle prod while the other held a lit cigar. They took turns, alternately electro-shocking and burning the victim, targeting various places on his naked black body while he hung upside down, suspended from the ankles by a chain attached to a ceiling hook. A slow trickle of blood oozed from a deep abrasion where the chain, wrapped tightly about the man's ankles, had chafed the flesh raw. The guards seemed to focus most of their efforts on the man's genitals. A mass of ugly blisters covered the man's body, giving him the look of a diseased leper. The man's agonized suffering must have been going on for some time now from the way some of the blisters were beginning to suppurate. With his hands cuffed behind his back and a cloth hood tied over his head, the detainee was totally defenseless. Though somewhat muffled by the hood, the man's piercing screams could be heard quite loudly through the glass window, eliciting a wave of involuntary shivering in Hennington.

Hennington could not bear to watch such torture and glanced over at Ternier who took in the scene with glazed eyes. "This man struck a guard yesterday," the Colonel said slowly. "He will be subjected to this kind of punishment continuously for the remainder of the day. I have seen only two criminals survive such disciplinary action over a prolonged session such as you see here. But they are like walking dead men now."

Ternier savored the fact that prisoners under his control perished on a frequent basis. He had established a fairly thriving business in the sale of Haitian cadavers to foreign medical schools. He had originally been indoctrinated about the merits of such an enterprise during the reign of Jean-Claude Duvalier, popularly called "Baby Doc" by the masses, when he had functioned as one of Duvalier's secret police. During that period, Jean-Claude's wife, Michele Bennet, had indulged in such a practice, which was found to be repugnant by many high-ranking officials in the Duvalier administration. In keeping such a ghoulish tradition alive, Ternier had no doubts that this side venture would continue to bring in ballooning revenues as time went on. Periodic uprisings and revolts among the oppressed minions meant a growing supply of dissenters against government authority would be available for arrest and detention. Growing crime and increased political unrest were the progeny of abject poverty, and both were the main driving forces of an escalating detainee population, which had quadrupled in the last six years in the face of a virtually unchanged prison budget.

The new government was making extremely slow headway in implementing reforms, and little had changed in the ways of incarceration and the treatment of prisoners in spite of the outcries from humanitarian activists. Truth be told, most of the day-to-day power rested in the hands of ranking police officials such as the Colonel. Such thoughts gave Ternier much pleasure. But he had much bigger plans than the mere sale of corpses.

The Colonel gazed fixedly at Hennington. The fear written on the broker's face was as palpable as the wounds being wreaked on the man hanging inverted in the room before them. Fear was a viable and most effective method of control. Like a weapon, it could be pointed at any target of choice. It provided a perverted type of incentive for bending people to one's will. Instinctively, Ternier knew that every ounce of human activity could be traced back to this common denominator of all human emotions. Fear equated to survival. Primordial to human nature, it could govern anything as minute as a thought or as cumbersome as a choice. Fear could knock the person down who allows it, or destroy the individual who forgets it. All modern dictators used fear as a mechanism for motivating the actions of the people they ruled. Lenin, Stalin, Hitler, Mao, Pol Pot, Idi Amin, and Saddam Hussein – Ternier had studied them all – had created a climate of fear through killing, torture, and imprisonment of enough of the masses to convince the others that submission was the most efficient technique of survival. By terrifying the population of a country, the ruling government could do as it pleased.

Ternier smiled at Hennington's emotional state. The tour of the prison was having the desired effect. Only one more stop was necessary to ensure unwavering cooperation from the man. Leading him to an unguarded but battered steel door located at the far end of the hallway, Ternier stopped short of the closed entrance. His face revealed a dark, rancorous smirk that seemed to harbor knowledge of something even more frightening than the horrors to which the broker had already been shown.

The other members of the party stood frozen and the Colonel sensed their uneasiness. They had all been here before, but even they could not get used to the secret that lurked on the other side of the doorway.

Creaking on rusted hinges, the door swung slowly outward until it clanged with finality against the sidewall, the sound of the contact echoing dully down the corridor and unnerving everyone except Ternier. The entrance was vacant. Watching Hennington closely, Ternier could see the confusion registering on his persona, the result of wondering who had opened the door.

With a firm grip on Hennington's elbow, the Colonel guided him into the room beyond. The glow of burning candles danced eerily along the back wall, doing little to penetrate the darkness that dominated the closer reaches of the low-ceilinged chamber. Hennington looked sharply to each side of the entrance but failed to detect anyone standing in the shadows. Glancing apprehensively behind him, he realized the other three men in his escort were holding back, refraining from entering the poorly lit room. A chill raced up his spine. From the look on their faces and the way they fidgeted, he knew that whatever the chamber held could not be good.

As Ternier continued to lead him forward, Hennington felt the dark presence even before discerning its form, a tenebrous malevolence that blended in with the flickering candlelight as if it consisted of inky mist. A cloaked figure sat quietly, a hood concealing its head.

It was then that Hennington became aware of the multitude of human skulls grinning hideously at him from behind the silent figure, hundreds of them stacked one upon the other and lining the rear wall of the chamber. As if anticipating Hennington's reaction, Ternier tightened his grip on the broker's forearm and drew him still closer to the hooded apparition. Hennington's legs began to tremble uncontrollably, and it was all he could do to prevent his bladder from emptying at that moment. The evil that emanated from the personage before him was almost tangible, like the stench of a decaying corpse.

All at once, the figure rose, lifting the cowl from its head. A pair of eyes glimmered in the semi-darkness, mesmeric orbs that held the same ominous stare as did Ternier. Even before the old woman opened her mouth to speak, Hennington somehow sensed who she was.

The woman directed her gaze momentarily on Ternier. "I am pleased you have come, my son," she rasped before bringing those crazed, penetrating eyes to bear on Hennington once again. "Do you wish this man to receive the punishment he deserves?"

Staring at Hennington, Ternier knew the man was now his, another addition to his already substantial cadre of acolytes who would be useful in helping him attain his ultimate goal. Yes, he thought, the dysfunctional mud hole known as Haiti was possibly a step closer to changing forever.

Chapter 3

The reddish-gold afterglow of sunset cast the avenue in an eerie shadow as Phillipe made his way toward the pub known as Dante's Cavern, one of the classier dives lining Port-au-Prince's waterfront. Dark complexioned and slight of build, some might easily have confused him for one of the city's countless street waifs if not for the state of his apparel. In sharp contrast to the other orphans who went about barefoot and barely clad in the remnants of grimy rags that passed for clothing, Phillipe appeared relatively clean and unscathed by the hardships the streets presented. And for that reason alone, his safety was always at risk, a fact that he well understood.

Garbed in unsullied shorts and T-shirt complemented by a pair of fairly new sneakers made in Taiwan, he knew he was a tempting target to the other urchins who infested the back alleyways, having been one of them during the first fifteen of his sixteen-year life. Extremely astute in the ways of the street, he moved along with an outward confidence that belied his inner caution, a trait inherent to him. In the dismal slums, peril hung inexorably like the sharp blade of a guillotine, always ready to descend, and constant vigilance was key to keeping one's neck clear of it. With nightfall now upon him, the potential dangers he sensed lurking about were made all the more palpable and he quickened his pace.

The door of a nearby tavern unexpectedly flew open, throwing a feeble light from within onto the darkened pavement. A sudden burst of rhythmic reggae blaring, and laced with the sound of laughter, it assaulted Phillipe's ears as it poured from the entrance like a gust of wind, wafting off into the placid night air as if to cleanse it of all iniquities. Phillipe kept walking as four men trooped out, their silhouettes eclipsing the pub's lit interior.

As the tavern door slammed shut behind the trailing member of the group, the din of festive gaiety abated abruptly, allowing the dispirited pall of Haiti to come flooding back like a dark, towering tsunami surging over a headland, turbulent and irrepressible. A vague sense of foreboding presentiment suddenly blossomed within Phillipe, making him shudder involuntarily.

"A donde vas mi cachorito?" one of the men called loudly, his tone guttural and ostensibly slurred.

Phillipe stopped momentarily, realizing he was being addressed. The man staggered forward in the classic reel of the drunk, repeating the question even louder than before. Phillipe spoke French, English, and the native Creole fluently, including smidgens of several other languages, and knew the man's utterance was an idiom of Spanish, the kind typically spoken by Colombians and Venezuelans who were often seen along the waterfront. Although he rarely conversed in such a dialect, he clearly understood the words. Where are you going, my young pup?

One of the other men guffawed rambunctiously, throwing a bantering taunt in the same tongue as his inebriated associate. Phillipe translated the implication of the shouted jest. "You walk like you fly, Pedro…all over the place!"

With the exception of Pedro, an eruption of howling mirth ensued.

Pedro advanced on unsteady legs, ignoring his companion's gibe or the jeering repartee of the other two. "Come here, my young tuna," he grunted, his glazed eyes fixed implacably on Phillipe like those of a drugged cobra. "I'm going to carve a fillet from you."

As the man drew closer, Phillipe recognized him as a crew member of the *San Carlo*, a Colombian tuna trawler currently berthed in the harbor. The men that worked aboard her were notorious bullies, having gained a reputation among the locals for inflicting excessive brutality and cruelty on anyone unfortunate to cross their path. Colombian fishermen, he knew, always had money in their pockets, enough to easily convince any policeman chancing upon their forays of violence to look the other way. After all, another orphan lying dead in the street, mutilated, and discarded like so much trash, was actually acceptable to most Haitian police patrolling the area. They looked upon such deeds not as a crime but as a solution to eliminating the street rabble, a growing problem within the Haitian capital where petty thefts, robberies, and muggings flourished with a growing frequency.

The man approaching him was perhaps the worst of the Colombian lot, having left at least one dead Haitian in his wake whenever his ship was in port. A sadistic killer by nature, he used the waterfront as if it were his own personal hunting ground, a place where he could satisfy his lust for blood with impunity.

Phillipe cursed himself for having hesitated and turned to leave, but the possibility of escape dimmed as the other three men scurried with surprising speed to cut off all retreat, surrounding him like a pack of hyena closing in on prey.

Not liking the manner in which his situation was developing, Phillipe tried darting between two of the bullies and would have succeeded if not for a foot extended by one of the men. He went sprawling chest-first onto the hard pavement as his assailants hooted loudly. Phillipe knew these hooligans were seeking some form of entertainment, and for the time being he was to be the center of their amusement.

Looking behind him, Phillipe caught the glint of metal in the hand of the one called Pedro. He had seen how alcohol consumed in quantity could cause even intrinsically good-natured people to become ignoble, but he perceived the man hovering above him to be the foulest type of drunk, ruthlessly dangerous and capable of any heinous act. Once the effects of his liquor-induced fugue wore off, such an individual would remember little of any atrocity he carried out. Even in sobriety, the man would likely harbor a nasty mean streak.

Phillipe endeavored to scramble to his feet, but a booted foot caught him in the side of the temple, knocking him onto his back.

"Hold the little tuna down so I can gut him!" Pedro ordered, lurching above Phillipe like a malicious beast.

Panic-stricken, Phillipe brought knees to chest and kicked upward, slamming his heels squarely into Pedro's stomach. The big man let out a grunt, teetering backward but managing to keep his feet.

"The tuna has spirit," one of the ruffians snarled as Pedro stumbled forward again. "Perhaps he is too much for Pedro to reel in."

"Shut your fucking mouth, Vargas!" Pedro screamed, brandishing the knife threateningly. "Maybe you'd like some of this."

A charged silence descended. The jovial mood of Pedro's companions dissipated like windswept fog, a capitulation born of fear rather than respect. That Pedro was the recognized leader of the group, Phillipe had no doubts, and his apprehension increased.

Getting his legs under him, Phillipe dodged beyond the grasp of the closest man, only to be seized from behind by two others.

"You little street scum!" Pedro bellowed. "I'm going to cut you good."

Mortified, Phillipe recoiled as though bitten by a snake. The blade wielded by Pedro gleamed malevolently in the moonlight as the big man swayed drunkenly before him. Phillipe stared dully, now unable to move or cry out.

A hand suddenly appeared out of the gloom and latched onto Pedro's wrist, immobilizing any further movement of the weapon it guided. Another hand girded Pedro's throat, easily enfolding it like a black python. The Colombian's eyes bulged in disbelieving shock as his body was lifted from the ground, feet dangling like those of a man hung from a gallows.

"I don't think you want to do that, mon," Zimbola hissed, his massive frame dwarfing the suspended man.

Phillipe gaped in amazement as something thumped heavily from behind. No longer restrained, he turned in bafflement as several more thuds resounded. One of Pedro's cohorts lay motionless at his feet while another was in the process of pitching face-first toward the ground in the aftermath of a vicious right cross that collided with authority against the man's jaw.

In comparison to the swiftly moving interloper who had delivered the knockout punches, the last of Phillipe's standing attackers moved sluggishly, launching a desperate but lackluster blow at the intruder's head. Gracefully and almost too quick to follow by eye, the intruder ducked under the punch, digging a hard left into the bully's ribs and following it up with a powerful right that nearly dislodged head from torso. Phillipe could not help but wince as the man's head snapped back from the impact, his body slumping in a heap as if his legs had been abruptly chopped off at the knee.

Phillipe glanced back over his shoulder. Pedro was still held aloft, his legs doing a crazy jig as they kicked wildly in the air. An expression of intense pain mingled with fear began to register on the Colombian's face as Zimbola gradually increased the pressure to both neck and wrist, cords of muscle slowly rising like heated dough in his forearms. All at once, the knife dropped silently from Pedro's hand to go clattering on the pavement.

Still clutching the man by the throat with his left hand, Zimbola raised his right, balling his huge fist and dropping it like a club. As if it were a sledgehammer striking an anvil, it slammed into the top of Pedro's skull. The Colombian's body immediately went slack, drooping like a wet dishrag, and Zimbola lowered him to the ground.

With the threat eradicated, Phillipe let out a long, slow breath, viewing his rescuers with a detached surrealistic awareness.

"I thought I told you to stay off the streets at night," Jay Jay scolded. "Had we not happened along when we did, you'd be fish chum."

The anger displayed by Jay Jay caused Phillipe to look away. "I...," he started to say.

"They clocked you pretty good," Jay Jay said, his ire replaced by concern. He stepped forward and, with a finger, gently explored the region behind Phillipe's right eye. The skin was noticeably swollen and Phillipe grimaced when Jay Jay touched it. His head suddenly throbbed miserably.

Zimbola stood over the fallen men, eyeing them with disdain. He spat contemptuously. His expression suddenly clouded and he looked around searchingly, his large, flat nostrils flaring wide like that of a bloodhound on the trail of a scent. He lifted his hands and sniffed them carefully, contemplatively.

Jake could not help but notice his companion's behavior. He had seen him do this before. "What? What is it?"

"These men, they have the reek of albacore rotting in the sun."

Jake tested the air. The usual blend of odors that pervaded Port-au-Prince's waterfront were all there, some of them quite pungent, including the unpleasant smell of decaying fish flesh. But Jake could not discern any trace aroma that would indicate tuna. He didn't have the finely tuned olfactory equipment that Zimby possessed.

"So? What of it?"

"They are tuna fishermen. Colombians."

Jake studied Zimbola questioningly. "How do you know that?"

"There is only one tuna trawler in the harbor, and it flies the Colombian flag."

"He is right," Phillipe chirped in. He pointed to Pedro's inert form. "That one there, he is an evil man. He has murdered many of the orphans who live in the streets. Killing gives him pleasure."

"All the more reason to keep off the street at night," Jake fumed.

"I had to come," Phillipe protested. "That boat that attacked us at sea, it came nosing around the *Angel*. Hector thought you should know right away."

"Are you sure it was the same vessel?"

"I am sure."

Zimbola took stock of the area all around them. "It would be wise for us not to remain here any longer," the black giant urged. "Come! Let us return to the *Angel*."

Jake nodded in agreement. And with the possibility of both zenglendoes and corrupt Haitian police lurking about, or even worse, the shipmates of the unconscious men coming upon them, it would be prudent on their part to vacate the vicinity as quickly as possible.

Chapter 4

*T*he moon hung peacefully in the star-rich heavens, bright and full, casting pale beams through the window of a simple thatched cottage. Small wavelets from a calm sea lapped softly like caressing fingers on the white sandy beach of the cove, no more than seventy feet from the modest structure which overlooked the water. Every so often, the tranquil atmosphere was punctuated by a low moan, a sound discordant with the pervading serenity. The noise grew more strident, more persistent, rising in volume. Within the cottage, a young woman tossed in troubled sleep, her forehead glistening with sweat in the subdued light, her wails of anguish incoherent and reaching a fever pitch.

Suddenly she sat bolt upright. "No!" she cried shrilly, her scream piercing the night with all the potency of a dagger thrust into living flesh.

A cacophony of chirps and twitters reverberated from somewhere nearby, as if in empathic response to the girl's distress.

With her eyes now fully open, the vision in the nightmare continued to haunt her much like the ache of a recent injury that, although mostly healed, keeps its victim in lingering pain, a pain which fades all too slowly. Restless, the girl shook off the final tendrils of sleep and arose to stare out the window.

The water shimmered quietly, its surface broken by several forms drifting languidly near the shoreline. As if aware of the girl's presence, the forms stirred in animated salutation, beckoning to her in a comforting lilt of low chittering. They were always there for her, affectionate companions whose very lives seemed to vacillate around the core of her existence. Their trust in her was implicit and unwavering. Whereas she hardly knew herself, they appeared to understand her completely.

She perceived that an outsider witnessing such interplay would have considered it to be nothing more than the equivalent of puppies displaying fawning adoration toward a revered master. But the bond went way beyond that. In stark contrast to a puppy, which had little insight about the world around it, the wisdom of the creatures in the cove transcended anything on a human scale.

In a convoluted way she was their nurturing sister, dispersing emotional nourishment, which they readily consumed and then channeled back to her many times magnified. Diametrically counter to the condemning nature that was indigenous to her own species, the creatures roaming the cove evinced an infinite capacity for compassion, and with it, unconditional forgiveness. Such noble qualities would normally preclude any desire for retribution, but she now sensed a subtle change in their attitudes. Whereas they were still averse to acts of reprisal, they were no longer willing to remain completely pacifistic, forever predisposed to accept the abuses cast upon them. This new perspective, she was certain, did not hinge on a desire for vengeance. Rather it was born of a need to defend, to survive. She could not fault them for it, for she too, was changing.

She could no longer sit idle. Passivity, she realized, was a philosophical dead end, a path which was becoming increasingly illogical to follow if she wanted to see her friends flourish and propagate. There was so much to be learned from the new breed, newcomers to an already evolved species that viewed the universe around them with an awareness that differed markedly from humanity's. They were smarter than their genetic predecessors, possessing an elevated clarity of thought. Their numbers, however, were dwindling and they urged her to act, to lend them the assistance they so desperately required of her.

Again, the vision tugged at her, pulling her spirits into a quagmire of despondency into which she was slowly sinking. She knew the creatures would have seen the vision. They always saw through her eyes, through her mind, and she through theirs. They were forever psychically linked to her, heart and soul.

The girl looked up at the moon, as if seeking an answer to her dilemma, wiping away the tears that flowed down alabaster cheeks. But she already knew what she must do. Jacob would help her. He always did. Mother, on the other hand, would not approve.

There were forces at work, ominous and powerful, of magnitudes far-reaching and which she could not fully fathom, but she knew that destinies would change monumentally for the worse as a result of them. A sense of urgency overcame her as the inner voices beckoned like strands of silk gossamer, pulling gently but firmly. If she went to Jacob now and they sailed within the hour, it was still possible they could prevent a terrible calamity from occurring.

The girl dressed quickly and left the cottage, her dark glossy hair streaming behind her and reflecting moonlight like polished ebony as she ran along the sandy beach.

Chapter 5

*L*ights flickered over the water beyond the shipping berths, indicating the presence of various watercraft floating at anchor within the harbor. From the shadows, Jake, Zimbola, and Phillipe studied a particular vessel at a distance of no more than 300 feet, and noting another boat that was tied up alongside.

"I smell trouble!" Jake whispered.

Zimbola glanced up at the sky and scowled. "I do not advise rowing the skiff out under such a moonlit night."

Jake was already slipping off his shoes. "Give me ten minutes, then follow me out in the skiff."

Zimbola grabbed Jake's arm. "We do this together."

Jake hesitated, looking solemnly at his friend for several seconds, then nodded. He turned to Phillipe who stood impassively, handing the boy his shoes. "Hold onto these and wait here. If we need you, we'll signal you by turning the deck lights on and off three times."

Zimbola shed his bulky clodhoppers and also left them with the boy. Both men crept out onto a nearby pier, darting behind pilings and keeping to the shadows. It was late and the immediate area was absent of any pedestrians. Jake spied a mooring line hanging loosely from a deck cleat and latched onto it, lowering himself effortlessly until he was fully immersed in the brine without making a splash. Less graceful than his companion, Zimbola followed.

A sudden bout of luck aided the men's stealth as the umbra of a cloud cluster slid across the lunar disk, shrouding the harbor in a tenebrous gloom. Abruptly, the silvery iridescence of the water fell into darkness.

Jake kicked smoothly along in a silent breaststroke with Zimbola dog paddling beside him like a ponderous black walrus, each man careful not to swash the water's surface lest they be heard as they approached the tethered vessels.

As both men got closer, Jake noticed the abutting boat to be at least thirty feet shorter in length than his own 65-foot, 70-ton North Sea trawler. With the moon still obscured in cloud, it was difficult for him to detect any movement along the deck of the intruding craft, which was positioned with its starboard side against the trawler's larboard. He could just make out the outline of a dive platform jutting from the intruder's stern.

Fifty feet from the intruder, the vessel closest to them, Jake stopped, and treading water, faced Zimbola. Keeping his voice low, he said, "Let's split up! See if you can get aboard their boat, whoever they are." He turned and indicated the back end of the vessel. "Climb onto that stern platform. I'll go up the *Angel's* anchor line. Keep low until you hear something."

Zimbola acknowledged Jake's rudimentary plan with a nod, then swam away. It took Jake another two minutes before his hands clasped the coarse hemp of the trawler's anchor line, and he began his hand over hand ascent toward the *Angel's* bow looming forty feet away.

Displaying the agility and supple strength of a spider monkey, Jake traversed the length of taut rope in a matter of moments. At the top he hooked a hand over the bow rail and with a final powerful heave, launched himself up and over the bar to land in a catlike crouch on the deck. As if sculpted in stone he remained in that position, watching and listening, until he was satisfied that he went unobserved. All was quiet except for the normal creak and groan of the hull timbers resounding softly through the vessel as it rocked gently in the slight tropical breeze, giving Jake the impression the trawler was deserted.

He crept forward on bare feet, peering up at the wheelhouse in anticipation of discovering trespassers, but there was nothing to suggest the presence of a boarding party other than the strange vessel reeved to the trawler. As Jake skulked along the starboard walkway adjacent to the galley, the faint sound of voices drifted over to him. Cautiously he moved forward.

The voices were coming from the aft deckhouse which served as a salon. Leaning with his back against the outer wall of the cabin, he sidled along it until he was even with the edge of its forward window. Someone was talking, the tone unmistakably accusatory.

"-arms to terrorists jeopardizes the security of the United States." The speaker sounded gruff, masculine.

"The captain did not sell military weapons to terrorists!" a second voice replied angrily. The voice was Hector's. "This vessel does not smuggle arms."

"You and the rest of the crew can be classified as enemy combatants by virtue of aiding and abetting Islamic extremists."

Jake listened in astonishment. What the hell!?

"This vessel can be impounded and its crew shipped off to Guantanamo Bay for indefinite detention and interrogation," the same speaker went on. "Unless you cooperate, that's what you can look forward to."

Something stirred in Jake's memory, vague and fleeting, then vanished just as quickly. He pivoted his head enough to peek through the Plexiglas. Hector was seated at the teak dining table looking more recalcitrant than cowed. Four men stood hovering over him in a belligerent phalanx, the spokesman with his back to Jake. He could see that all of them had handguns strapped snugly in shoulder harnesses and that one of the men held a shotgun pointing idly at the deck. The faces of the strangers visible to him had the gravity of authority etched onto them.

Hector spoke defiantly. "You have no jurisdiction here. Haiti is a sovereign nation."

"This vessel flies the American flag, and as such is under the official registry of the United States government. The Haitian government is lending their full cooperation in countering any potential threats by terrorists."

Jake listened intently to the man's words, a sharp twinge of anxiety gnawing away at the pit of his stomach like a rodent scavenging for food. He hated terrorists and all they stood for. The very thought that he may have inadvertently assisted in the political objectives of Islamic radicals made his head reel.

The speaker of the boarding party continued to press Hector. "I ask you again, where is the captain of this vessel?"

Hector folded his thick arms stubbornly. "And I tell you once more, I do not know!"

"You don't know or you aren't saying?"

Hector remained mute.

Strangely, the inflection of the man's speech triggered some distant memento of past experience, but Jake had no time to mull over its significance. Before he even realized what he was doing, he walked through the open cabin door.

Jake kept his voice calm and level. "He doesn't know."

All four men were clearly startled, the shotgun wielder raising the weapon sharply to bear on Jake while the other two reached for their side arms. The leader of the group, however, reacted the fastest, spinning in a lightning manner to face the sudden intrusion, his gun drawn and leveled with the quickness of a mamba prepared to strike. A look of stunned amazement slowly flooded his expression as he regarded Jake.

Jake was equally stunned, and he stared at the man dazedly. "Mat? Is that really you?"

The weapon in the man's hand was instantly lowered. "By all that's holy, I can't believe what I'm seeing," he said jubilantly as he holstered the gun.

The two men came towards one another and embraced like long lost brothers, and in a way it wasn't far from the truth. Mat Daniels had been a brother in arms along with Jake in the U.S. Navy Seals. They had worked closely together on numerous missions with Seal Team Six, most of them classified and highly dangerous. Jake had saved Mat's life on more than one occasion when they had made intelligence-gathering excursions into Somalia, Afghanistan, Pakistan, and Iraq. They had been together during several firefights during the toppling of Saddam Hussein's regime, and Jake remembered vividly how he had slung Mat over his shoulder, all 195 pounds of him, and carried him for more than two miles along the banks of the Tigris River in southern Iraq in order to avoid capture. An errant artillery round from an Iraqi tank had left Mat with a jagged four-inch chunk of shrapnel lodged just above his right knee, reducing him to a hobbling cripple during the mission.

"You're a sight for sore eyes, buddy," Mat effused breathlessly, the air driven from his chest by Jake's powerful hug.

Ignoring the bewilderment of Daniels' companions, Jake broke from his friend's embrace and asked, "So what's this all about, Mat?"

Daniels suddenly appeared embarrassed and he looked away, avoiding Jake's eyes. "I think we have some talking to do," he said, obviously flustered.

Composing himself swiftly, Mat glanced at his associates. "Guys, meet Jake Javolyn, the most incorrigible bad ass this side of damnation."

The men continued to look befuddled, fidgeting nervously.

"He's all right, trust me. Jake hates terrorists more than I do."

Daniels turned back to Jake. "I have some things to discuss with Mr. Javolyn. Why don't the three of you go back aboard our boat and wait for me there." The men still looked uncertain, and in a placating tone, Mat added, "Don't worry, I'll explain later."

All three men filed past Jake, measuring him with appraising eyes and shaking their heads in exasperation.

Jake grinned back like a sated falcon that had just had its fill of carrion. "Oh, and by the way, guys, I strongly advise you to keep clear of the big black man sitting on your stern platform," he said, tongue in cheek. "He gets awful crotchety when he hasn't eaten."

Mat rolled his eyes, shaking his head. "Always the comedian."

Jake faced Hector. The Creole seemed unperturbed by his recent ordeal, and not the least surprised by this fresh turn of events. With Jake, nothing ever seemed to surprise him. "Hector, let Zimby know what's going on and that I'll be indisposed for a while."

Hector remained stoic, closing the door behind him as he stepped from the room. He was a short, blocky man, a head smaller in stature than Jake.

Taking a seat at the teak table, Jake scrutinized his old friend. All previous traces of humor on Mat's face were now replaced by a weighty graveness.

"So that was you a month ago," Daniels said. It was more of a statement than a question.

Jake nodded slowly. "I had no idea it was you. At the time, I assumed I was being dogged by pirates looking to take the *Angel*."

Mat sucked in a prolonged breath. "I'm with the Department of Homeland Security now. Those men with me, we're part of a special counterterrorism task force assigned to the Caribbean."

"I couldn't help overhear you grilling Hector," Jake said. "Did I understand you to say Islamic extremists are operating here in Haiti?"

Mat hesitated, deciding how much information he should reveal. "Yes!" he finally offered. "Our intelligence gatherers have intercepted an inordinate amount of chatter emanating from terror cells affiliated with Al Qaeda. Much of that chatter alludes to this region. We don't as yet know precisely what, but it appears something big is coming down."

To Jake, such a possibility made little sense. As far as he could gauge, Haiti, one of the poorest nations on earth, presented few, if any, targets that would attract terrorists. While it was true that the more radical elements of Islam had fanned the flames of an intense anti-Western hatred within the Middle East, particularly against Americans, they sought to disrupt such cultures in any way that would impact those economies in a negative way. Haiti, however, was far beyond the mainstream of Western economic well-being.

The number of Muslim fundamentalists joining the ranks of Islamic militants had grown dramatically over the last decade and was now reaching epidemic proportions, threatening Westerners on a global scale with their radical religious views. What had originally been confined to the Middle East had now spilled over to the rest of the world, spearheaded by overzealous and frenzied fanatics who used terror to further their goals.

Jake had lost one of his closest friends to Islamic fanaticism during the destruction of the World Trade Towers and had come to hate extremists. To Jake's way of thinking, religious fanatics mistakenly saw themselves as the spokesmen for mankind, stubbornly shoving their dogma down humanity's gullet. Islam, in particular, seemed to be more prone to violent fanaticism than other faiths with its extreme intolerance of non-Muslim cultures and viewpoints, often targeting Westerners for death in the form of spectacular strikes such as what occurred on 9-11.

Deep down, Jake did not buy the chief justification used by Islamic militants for such mayhem against Americans, and that was his country's support of Israel. He considered such rationality to be nothing more than a sham, a moral guise behind which they hid. Intuitively, he believed that abject poverty was the primary driving force behind their attacks, the actual mechanism that fueled their hatred. Although rich in oil, the wealth of Middle Eastern nations was predominantly controlled by the royal families who lived in lavish comfort in stark contrast to the overwhelming majority of their countrymen. Within such cultures, amenities produced by petroleum-induced wealth rarely made its way to the common man whose standard of living was far below that of the West. And with mushrooming Muslim populations spiraling out of control in combination with limited and continually strained resources, it was only natural that the poorer classes would turn to Islam as if it were a precious asset.

As Jake saw it, the present religious strife between Muslims and non-Muslims was simply a belated replay of the religious wars that had plagued the tail end of the European Middle Ages. Unfortunately, he knew that conflict, prolonged over an extended period, tended to be self-perpetuating, often plunging out of control and overshadowing all sense of reason. And with fanaticism, the original tenets of the religion itself would somehow get lost in the midst of the rabid fervor that was rapidly taking hold.

The bottom line was that militant radicals within the Muslim culture were abusing their faith for religious and national causes. Members of the ultra-extremist Wahhabi sect of Islam were breeding the next generation of mass murderers through clandestine funding in conjunction with an international network of mosques and religious schools located not only in the Middle East, but in Asia and Africa, as well.

And although the more moderate constituents of Islam claimed that their religion was essentially gentle and non-violent at its core, Islamic fundamentalists continually urged their brothers to align themselves against nonbelievers of the Muslim faith, claiming it was their religious obligation. Regardless of whether their political goals were justified, to extinguish all Western influences in the Middle East and to exterminate Israel, their means of accomplishing those objectives were certainly not. Political suicide bombers, being trained by Hamas, Hezbollah, and other groups on an on-going basis, were being taught that success would grant them a special place in heaven. Jake abhorred such acts. The horror of blowing up a busload of children could not, and should not, be rationalized under any agenda.

Far worse than the Third Reich had been, and much more dangerous in their potentially destructive capability, Islamic militancy advocates sought to destroy any last vestige of any culture or religion other than that which they practiced. Their ultimate goal was to establish a theocratic dictatorship throughout the world, much like the rule of the Taliban, which flourished in Afghanistan for a short period before the U.S. toppled the cruelest of all governments ever known to exist.

Jake assessed many of the Islamic states to essentially be loathocracies, with their faiths based on an extreme hatred of anything non-Muslim, most particularly Western cultures. And while he understood that you could not condemn a people or faith simply on the actions of its more extreme elements, history had shown that men never carried out evil so completely and cheerfully as when they did it out of religious conviction. In fact, more wars were fought in the name of religion than for any other cause throughout human history.

While in the Seals, both Jake and Mat had received extensive training in counterterrorism, not only learning techniques aimed at thwarting the ambitions of terrorists, but getting insight into their way of thinking and their underlying motives as well. Islamic fundamentalism was a subject they were well-acquainted with and a topic on which they had had ample time to discuss on many occasions. Mat had often listened with rapt attentiveness as Jake espoused his philosophical views regarding religious extremists and knew that Jake had only one solution for dealing with such people. And that was to contain them at every opportunity. As Jake had often said, religious militants were unreachable on a rational level, for such individuals harbored deeply rooted and twisted ideologies that deviated substantially from the true tenets of their faith. Focused on killing and destroying in an effort to maximize body counts, their mind-set was of a single purpose and they would not be denied their fixation. And Jake well knew that it was so much easier to destroy than to create or construct. Overall, such religious fanaticism presented enormous setbacks to the advancement of the human race.

Jake had nothing personal against practitioners of Islam, nor the true doctrines of the religion itself. In fact, direct experience with most Muslims he had come across during assignments in predominantly Islamic countries had shown the people to be warm and courteous toward foreigners, providing hospitality to strangers whenever it was warranted.

Choosing his words carefully, Mat said, "Look, Jake, for whatever it's worth, I think you've been pulled into something much bigger than you bargained for. Knowing you the way I do; you probably had no idea what you were hauling at the time." Mat eyed his friend shrewdly. "Can I assume that to be the case?"

Jake weighed the question conscientiously. In a way he couldn't explain, he felt like a traitor, not only to his country of origin but to himself as well. "Yes…yes you can," he said slowly.

Both men understood that if Jake admitted outright knowledge of the cargo, Mat's position as a United States counterterrorism agent would not only be compromised, but potentially put in jeopardy if Mat did not carry out his responsibilities by arresting his longtime pal. And Jake knew that was something Mat would never do, no matter what the circumstances. The bond of trust that had developed between them was strong enough to outweigh any sense of duty on Mat's part, and he was certain Mat would never betray that trust. Mat owed Jake his life, plain and simple. It was basically a thing of honor and obligation.

"We've been tracking the people who received that shipment," Mat said. "It turns out the contraband ultimately reached a Yemeni national who runs an import-export business here in the city."

"And no doubt a Muslim!" Jake interposed without speculation. He had already done business with that same Yemeni, giving him cause to examine his dealings with the man under a new light.

Mat smiled, measuring Jake with a knowing look. "His business is relatively new, established within the last six months."

Jake found himself growing uneasy with the turn the conversation had taken. "So what's your take on all this? Why would Muslim extremists be interested in the Caribbean Basin? This region offers no economic importance of any significance worth disrupting, no target-rich environment."

Mat shrugged tiredly. "Maybe they see it as a useful staging area from which to launch attacks, a place within striking distance of American soil."

Jake thought this over. It made sense. Haiti reeked with political turmoil. While the new government was currently receptive to aiding the U.S. in curtailing the ever-present drug trade which was firmly entrenched in Haitian affairs, the fledgling regime had by no means given stability to the island nation. And although such cooperation was proving to be a thorn in the side of Colombian drug lords, making it much more difficult for them to conduct their operations and eroding their influence on the country, the cartels had counterattacked with resiliency. Battling back in a desperate bid to reassert indirect control of the nation, they deliberately incited various political factions in an effort to keep the region unstable. Political unrest equated to easier drug trafficking. One major drawback in creating such an environment, however, was that it inadvertently provided an inviting haven for terrorists, allowing them to go relatively unnoticed.

"You look like you could use some shut-eye," Jake said, suddenly aware of Mat's weariness. It was apparent Mat had gotten little sleep in the past several days as evidenced by a dark growth of stubble dominating his lower face in concert with bag-ridden, bloodshot eyes. "This assignment wearing you down, old buddy? You always were one who never knew when to stop and rest."

Mat scrutinized Jake oddly. "That sounds rather strange coming from you. I've often wondered how you managed to carry my sorry ass all that distance back in Iraq. The doctors pried more steel out of you than they did me. You took down seven of Saddam's Elite Guard firing from the hip as you ran with me like a sack of useless baggage slung over your shoulder."

"Strong body, weak mind," Jake replied flippantly. "I've told you before, pain doesn't register on a small brain like mine." As soon as he uttered the words he grew serious. "The way I remember it, you were far from useless. You held onto your weapon and waxed at least three others yourself as I carried you."

"There's a subtle difference between compulsive valor and unavoidable discretion," Mat countered. "And it's usually fatal."

"So you've often said."

The grin on Mat's face fell away abruptly like a load of stone into a ravine. "You always enjoyed walking the edge, the thrill of the chase. To you, it never mattered much whether you were the pursuer or the pursued, the hunter or the hunted. Unnecessary risk and danger are like aphrodisiacs to you. You eat them like candy. But some day they're gonna be your undoing. You keep prodding the devil and he's gonna stick that pitchfork of his where the sun don't shine."

"I'll keep that in mind."

Mat's expression remained stony. "Same old Jake. I should have known that was you when our paths crossed a month ago. I must say, your use of that waverunner was admirable, the kind of tactics only you would think of employing. Very innovative and enlightening."

Jake could not help but chortle. "I would rather you use the word effective."

Jake recalled the incident lucidly. He always made it a practice to conceal his vessel's identity during a smuggling gig, flying a false flag to indicate a bogus country of origin and draping the boat's name and serial numbers with canvas. Such precautions made it difficult for potential boarders to trace the registry of his craft.

The pickup had gone fairly smooth. Jake and his crew had just completed stowing the contraband after having made the rendezvous at the designated transfer point at the east end of Montego Bay. The five large crates that had come off the beat-up fishing boat were bulky and heavy, and it had taken the combined strength of the *Angel's* four crew members with the help of the five nondescript occupants of the transfer vessel to move the cargo aboard the North Sea trawler.

It was less than a minute after the two boats had pulled apart and the *Angel* was steering a course back to Haiti when Jake realized something was amiss. The intruder had been spotted on radar long before it got near enough to hear, a shadowy wraith closing rapidly on an intercept course as it sped over the dark, moonless ocean. Four times Jake had altered the trawler's direction, and each time the intruder had changed course to follow, dogging the *Angel* with the tenacious intent of a rapacious shark on the hunt and eliminating any possibility that they were not being pursued.

That was when Jake had resorted to a Code One. Hector and Phillipe immediately sprang into action and began prepping the waverunner, a Kawasaki STX-12F. The small craft sat perched above the vessel's fantail on the aft-most section of the *Angel's* superstructure, all portions of its surface painted a non-reflective charcoal black. At a distance of twenty meters on a moonless night at sea, even Phillipe's sharp young eyes could not discern it after it was launched.

A customized heavy-duty inflatable chute assisted in the launching and could be rapidly unfurled with the flip of an air valve, causing it to extend at an angle to the water directly astern of the trawler. An air-filled tube, eighteen inches in diameter, formed each side of the chute, providing it with a certain amount of rigidity. The device was similar in construction to those used by commercial airlines for fast exiting of passengers following emergency landings. Four lengths of stainless steel cable rail connected the air tubes to an elevated boom, two per tube, giving additional support to the structure, much like the cables supporting a suspension bridge. The chute was made all the more accommodating for launching the waverunner by a stream of water flowing down its surface. Water was supplied by a centrifugal pump, which automatically kicked in upon extension of the ramp, turning the chute into a veritable water slide. Incorporated into the system were two vacuum pumps devoted to sucking air from each tube. The pumps were automatically engaged by dual hydraulically driven reels mounted to the superstructure on opposite sides of the chute. The reels provided the means to retract the makeshift ramp and had the capacity to furl the contrivance within twenty seconds after full deployment. The entire setup had been rigged months earlier, primarily for discouraging pirates and other unsavory parties from attempting to hijack the *Angel* on the open sea. So far, this was the first opportunity Jake had to use it.

Jake had carried out at least a dozen drills with the ship's crew in launching the STX-12F, springing the procedure on them without warning at randomly chosen intervals, day or night. Each man in the crew had a specific assignment to carry out during the operation. Flaws in the procedure had been discovered and perfected, and gradually their response times had improved to the point where Jake would be hitting the water within fifty-eight seconds of a Code One alert. This did not include the time it took for Jake to don his shorty wetsuit with the Farmer John top which left his muscular arms exposed, nor the effort of securing the additional gear strapped to his body. Jake had made it standard operating procedure to be fully outfitted in such dress at the start of each smuggling run. He was a firm believer in preparedness, something drummed into him while in the Seals, and the Seven Ps were solidly ingrained into his thinking: Prior Proper Planning Prevented Piss Poor Performance.

With ship's radar showing the intruder to be lagging just beyond one nautical mile astern of the *Angel*, Zimbola had laid back on the variable pitch control lever in the pilothouse, feathering the trawler's three propeller blades into a near-neutral angle of attack. Such a feature caused the vessel's forward speed to drop off quickly from its previous twenty-two knots in spite of the constant engine rpm.

Jake bounded rearward from the pilothouse and leapt onto the waverunner, now fully prepped and armed, as the launching ramp cascaded open to touch the sea twelve feet below him. In unison, Hector, Phillipe, and Zimbola gave the tiny craft a mighty shove and the Kawasaki lurched forward like a bull out of a rodeo gate, sliding onto the chute's nylon surface. Strands of muscle stood out in Jake's shoulders and forearms as he gripped the craft's handlebars tightly, bracing himself in anticipation of the impending impact as the waverunner gained momentum on the slippery ramp. The Kawasaki rushed down and slammed into the ocean with all the ferocity of an orca looking to feed, and it was all Jake could do to keep himself from being catapulted forward. A curtain of spray immediately erupted as the craft's nose momentarily submerged and struggled to assert buoyancy. The Kawasaki wallowed crazily, teetering to one side as the trawler's wake caught it, but then righted itself and quickly stabilized.

Jake turned to watch as the *Angel* picked up speed again, its hulking silhouette shrinking as it receded into the night. The thrum of the trawler's Swedish Penta MD-96 diesel engine began to fade with distance as he engaged the Kawasaki's ignition and felt the 1,199cc, 4-stroke marine motor come alive in a quiet purr. He turned the throttle halfway and veered laterally away from the *Angel's* course, bumping lightly over the leading edge of the trawler's port side wake and skimming perhaps 200 meters before shutting down the craft's engine.

Checking the luminous dial on his Caravel dive watch, Jake confirmed that approximately 110 seconds, give or take a second, had elapsed since he had initiated the Code One. Not bad. The STX-12F was perfectly suited for the course of action he planned to undertake. With a vertical profile extending no more than twenty-six inches above the water, the small craft would be nearly undetectable on radar. And that -included the special accessories Jake had retrofitted to the body of the Kawasaki just forward of the console. Most of the time, the unique accoutrements were kept hidden in a secret compartment aboard the trawler and could readily be retrieved and snapped into place on the waverunner in a matter of moments. In addition, the engine that powered the craft was one of the quietest in its class and would be almost impossible to hear over the drone of most powerboats plowing the sea.

Jake glanced around, trying to get his bearings. Except for the stars glittering overhead like bright jewels scattered over a black carpet, the ocean was a mass of gently heaving darkness, ominous and foreboding to those less familiar with it. Polaris, the North Star, winked like a comforting beacon, low in the darkness and directly forward of the tiny craft. A quick check of the console-mounted compass told Jake he was indeed facing north when looking over the handlebars.

The *Angel's* familiar but slowly dwindling thrum finally abated completely and Jake sat still, listening intently as the Kawasaki pitched sluggishly among the low, silent swells. All was quiet, black, and lonely, as if Jake had been cast into deep space between galaxies. Several moments passed before the faint sound of another vessel reached his ears, progressively growing louder as it approached.

The intruder was running without lights and remained virtually invisible within the cloak of darkness as it swept along the same course as the *Angel*. The noise level grew rapid in intensity, reaching a deafening roar that dominated all Jake's senses, and for one fleeting instant, with heart pounding and pulse racing, Jake expected to be crushed by the passing boat. But then a noticeable shift in the frequency of the sound suddenly occurred, the telltale sign of the Doppler Effect, indicating the vessel was now traveling away from his position.

With great relief, Jake expelled the lungful of air he hadn't realized he'd been holding and strained his eyes in a futile attempt to locate the intruder. An indistinct eidolon seemed to momentarily materialize before him, then vanish just as quickly, a dark shadow on an even blacker backdrop, but he couldn't be sure. He rotated on the seat he straddled and pulled the combination earpiece-mouth mike from the Kawasaki's rear storage compartment, plugging it into the waterproof Motorola radio attached to the console.

"This is Arrow," Jake said calmly. "You read me, Goliath."

Zimbola's deep voice rumbled back in Jake's ear. "This is Goliath. I read you loud and clear, Arrow."

By prearrangement, Jake had instructed Zimbola to keep radio chatter to a minimum lest their pursuers intercept their transmission. He knew, however, that such a possibility was quite remote.

Satisfied, Jake reached behind him again, this time retrieving the AN/PVS-7 night vision goggles which he hurriedly strapped on. Both shock resistant and sealed from the environment, the unit was indispensable to the task at hand.

The ocean surface abruptly blossomed into view before him, the intruder charging away at what he perceived to be nearly twice the speed of the *Angel*. Jake started the 140-horsepower engine and engaged the drive, accelerating rapidly over the calm sea and steering a course parallel to the pursuing vessel. He estimated the intruder to be half a mile behind the *Angel*. Pulling to within 100 meters of the intruder, he let up on the throttle by a quarter turn and kept pace with the pursuing boat, maintaining a fixed position relative to the craft while holding the Kawasaki astern and to its port side just beyond its wake.

Jake decided to refrain from any action until he was certain of the intruder's intentions. The vessel chasing the *Angel* did not possess the classical lines of a U.S. Coast Guard Cutter. He studied it carefully, the NV goggles revealing it to have the configuration of a modern-type cabin cruiser, the kind with a swept-back, streamlined bridge. The vessel was sleek and fast and was swiftly overtaking the *Angel* dead ahead of it.

"Arrow, here!" Jake blurted. "I am fixed on the tango. Let's see what he wants."

"I hear you, Arrow. Goliath out!"

Jake kept the NV goggles trained on the intruder, looking closely for signs of potential hostility as it bore down on the *Angel*. He reached forward with his left hand and groped the two securely fastened objects centered directly over the bow of the Kawasaki, an over-under weapons combination. They were locked, loaded and, if need be, ready to strike with the deadliness of poisonous serpents. But Jake's primary objective was not to wound or kill, only to defend and dishearten. Given a choice, he would much rather prefer to strike fear into possible assailants instead of injury. And though it was true that he had killed on several prior occasions in the midst of fierce firefights while in the Navy Seals, he was not a killer by nature.

The lower weapon was an M-60 machine gun, the kind that could be side-mounted to light military helicopters, particularly LOHs, and aimed by lining up the aircraft with a target during a strafing run. A box-like magazine configured to the gun currently held 1,000 rounds of belted 7.62mm ammunition, with every fifth round a tracer. The M-60 could spit 550 rounds per minute and had an effective range of 1,100 meters.

Fixed in place above the M-60 was an MK-23 Stoner, another rapid-fire weapon that had been popular with the Seals during the Vietnam War. Manufactured by Cadillac Gage, its magazine could hold 150 rounds of 5.56mm ammo that belt-fed at a rate of 850 per minute. Praised by the Vietnam-era Seals for its overwhelming suppressive firepower, the weapon had one major drawback, and that was its proneness to jamming unless kept immaculately clean. Mounted immovably to a special rack, each weapon could be brought to bear on a chosen object by aligning the longitudinal axis of the Kawasaki toward the target.

Jake controlled the elevation of the guns by changing the pitch orientation of the waverunner. By shifting his weight forward or backward and either gunning or laying back on the throttle, the nose of the craft could be elevated or lowered at will. Accuracy of the guns was a matter of skill and dexterity on the part of the driver.

The actual arming and firing of each weapon, however, was another matter. The M-60 had an electronic safety and could only be armed by lifting a swivel-guard cap located on the lower console and flicking a toggle switch housed beneath it. A thumb button situated on the left handlebar of the craft could then be depressed to fire the gun.

Operation of the Stoner, by contrast, was all manual. A cable guide connecting a lever at the left hand grip to a sleeve on the Stoner's trigger provided the mechanism by which the lighter machine gun was able to discharge. The lever was similar to the braking device used on multi-speed bicycles, and in fact, was actually taken from one. By squeezing the lever against the Kawasaki handle grip, the Stoner could be fired.

Both machine guns and ammunition had been purchased illicitly through a bootleg weapons dealer operating within the heart of Port-au-Prince, the same Yemeni national Mat had mentioned. While perusing the dealer's extensive inventory, Jake had come upon the Stoner and had been immediately drawn to it like a moth to a lit candle. Unlike the stockless, aviation-version M-60 which was not intended for use by the foot soldier, the Stoner could be quickly detached from its mount and hand-held, allowing its wielder to fire it from the shoulder or hip. And although the Stoner could be a most effective weapon because of its extraordinary discharge rate, its magazine could be expended in slightly over ten seconds if fired continuously.

The Kawasaki STX-12F carried one more customized feature, which further enhanced its formidable disposition. It packed two 40mm torpedoes, also compliments of the Port-au-Prince arms dealer. Jake had learned that the dealer had obtained the torpedoes discretely from Rosoboronexport, a maker of Small Class submarines. The torpedoes could be launched from firing tubes retrofitted to each side of the Kawasaki hull.

The torpedoes were armed and fired via an electronic system similar to the M-60. Two pre-launch swivel guards protected arming toggle switches, one for each firing tube. The guards were essential in preventing accidental arming during rough, bumpy rides over an uncooperative sea. Another thumb button just to the left of the right hand throttle triggered the designated torpedo, depending on which toggle switch happened to be in the on position. If both switches were activated, then both the right and left side torpedoes could be launched simultaneously. To ensure that no significant deviation occurred along a torpedo's alignment path following launch, the manufacturer recommended the water-based projectile be fired from no more than sixty meters away from its intended target, and never in a choppy sea when launched from the surface.

Although Jake had previously test-fired both machine guns at floating targets during practice drills and was confident in his skill at hitting any object within their immediate range, the torpedoes were as yet untested.

Other than a sheathed survival knife secured to a calf, one additional weapon resided with Jake. A suppressed Heckler & Koch USP-9 semi-automatic submachine pistol rode his right thigh, held firmly in place by a ballistic nylon holster that descended from a tactical pistol belt and strapped snugly to his leg. The belt held five spare 15-round magazines. Jake had grown accustomed to such a weapon from his days in the Seals, and the feel of it always gave him great comfort whenever he was subjected to potentially dangerous situations. The USP-9 along with its associated ammunition had also been supplied by the same Haitian arms dealer.

Jake watched as the intruder got to within fifty meters of the *Angel*, then was nearly blinded as a brilliant flash of light, greatly intensified by the night vision goggles, lit up the night like a miniature sun. He quickly lifted the goggles to his forehead and blinked away the spots dancing before his eyes. A marine flare arced lazily high above, its dazzling glare giving definition to the two vessels churning the water beyond him. As the flare descended, two figures could be seen scurrying out onto the bow of the pursuing craft, and in their hands the protruding muzzles of assault weapons coming to bear upon the *Angel*.

All at once, Jake lifted the swivel guard from the M-60's arming switch and flicked the toggle, steering wide of the intruder's prow before angling in on it. Leaning back in his seat, he maxed out the throttle so that the Kawasaki's nose rose up. At the correct moment, he thumbed the firing button. The waverunner vibrated in protest as the M-60 chattered deafeningly under the short 12-round burst suddenly unleashed, then settled back into an easy glide as Jake eased off the trigger. Several tracers defined the trajectory of the enfilade, streaking over the heads of the individuals perched on the intruder's bow and sizzling off into the distance like tiny shooting stars, red and fiery. The men immediately hunkered down in confusion, completely caught off guard by this unexpected threat.

Jake leaned the Kawasaki over sharply, veering back toward the intruder's stern and building distance from it. With all surfaces of his craft and weaponry cloaked in a non-reflective coating of black, his wetsuit and accessories black, and all of his exposed skin smeared in lampblack, Jake was certain the crew members aboard the intruder would have trouble spotting him on the dark ocean. That is, unless they possessed night vision equipment as he did. However, it was a consideration he didn't have time to worry about.

Jake spoke curtly into his lip mike. "Arrow to Goliath. Please give our uninvited guests the welcome they deserve."

Zimbola's voice reverberated in Jake's ears like a bass drum. "It shall be my pleasure, Arrow. Goliath out."

Several seconds passed before a flight of red tracers erupted from the *Angel's* stern, spewing angrily above the intruder like a swath of broken laser beams. As pre-arranged, Hector was giving his pursuers something to think about.

The ocean receded into darkness once again as the flare faded and finally winked out. Jake's last glimpse of the armed men showed them to be sprawled face down on the bow of their vessel, now thoroughly discouraged from rising into a possible fusillade of shots coming from nearly opposing directions.

Lowering the NV unit to his eyes once more, Jake noted the relative positions of the pursued and pursuing vessels, careful to keep clear of the *Angel's* field of fire. Like Jake, both Zimbola and Hector were currently outfitted with similar night vision capability and were also tracking the movements of the intruder within the veil of darkness.

A sudden burst of return fire ensued from the pursuing vessel as the weapon bearers aboard her overcame their surprise. Muzzle flashes from their guns flickered brightly, stabbing into the surrounding pall of night with the urgency of a blind man poking away attackers with a cane.

Something pinged loudly in Jake's ear and Zimbola's voice came back at him in a bellow of surprise. "Jeez mon, that was close! Arrow, we are taking fire! We are being hit!"

"You don't have to be nice anymore, Goliath," Jake growled testily. "Give 'em hell!"

Zimbola did not bother to answer, and within moments the *Angel* sent a stream of tracers swarming low over the water. Through the NV goggles, Jake could just make out the barrel of the infantry-version M-60 aboard the *Angel* as it swiveled on its mount, its muzzle belching spurts of reddish-orange hell while it protruded menacingly from the opening in the inch-thick bulletproof Plexiglas behind which Hector stood. The intense exchange of gunfire persisted as the intruder's gunmen homed in on the tracers' origination point at the *Angel's* stern, the occasional glint of ricochets caroming off Hector's shield attesting to the accuracy of their marksmanship.

It was becoming apparent to Jake that the intruder had no intention of backing off as it continued to dog the *Angel* like a hound on the scent. In spite of Hector's withering spray, the pursuing vessel kept coming, and Jake surmised that it was only a matter of time before a well-placed round found its way through the opening in Hector's Plexiglas shield. And he could only imagine what the sporadic peppering of incoming automatic small arms fire was doing to his beloved vessel.

Circling back into the fray, Jake made the decision to end the conflict. As a measure of damage control, he had to disable the intruder as quickly as possible. Reaching down, he activated his right-side torpedo. Several days earlier, he had tampered with the weapon, unscrewing the nose cap, and reducing the amount of explosive powder within by two-thirds. The torpedo he was about to launch was now limited in its destructive capability, presently rigged only to blow a hole of sufficient size at the waterline of an unsuspecting watercraft to possibly sink it. If the vessel before him was equipped with a heavy-duty bilge pump, then it might possibly be able to limp into the nearest port to effect repairs.

Jake opened the throttle all the way. The Kawasaki picked up speed rapidly as another discharge from the *Angel's* M-60 lanced out over the water and reached for the intruder. From Jake's perspective, it appeared as if the pursuing vessel was taking more than it was giving, but he couldn't be sure. The intruder was running a zigzag course, challenging Hector's skill, which was marginal at best.

Once again Jake charged in on the intruder's port side, quickly converging on it like a guided missile. Leaning the Kawasaki precariously to the right, he steered for a point seven feet forward from amidships on the vessel. He would make a sincere effort to avoid hitting the intruder's left fuel tank, which would normally be stationed more toward the stern on most modern cabin cruisers.

In its bid to remain elusive from the *Angel's* machine gun fire, the intruder unexpectedly veered back in Jake's direction and the gap between their relative positions closed even faster. In moments he was eighty meters from his target, then seventy. As he closed within sixty meters, the intruder shifted away abruptly, almost as if the boat driver was aware of Jake's presence. Muzzle flashes continuing to thrust forward toward the *Angel* from the intruder's bow told Jake otherwise, however, and he tilted the Kawasaki to starboard to match the course change of his target, gambling that the gunfire would not be diverted in his direction.

In less than a second, Jake adjusted his attack run and quickly homed in on the pursuing vessel until he was certain he couldn't miss. He thumbed the launch button and the Kawasaki yawed slightly to the right in reaction to the 40-mm torpedo that shot away. Partially submerged, it raced across the gap of water separating the two watercraft.

Turning the waverunner hard to port, Jake angled off on a course parallel to the intruder with no more than thirty meters between them. When nothing immediately happened, he thought the projectile had either gone wide of its target or failed to detonate. But then an orange coruscation of fire flared up briefly from the intruder's side as the small missile punched through its hull. A plume of water flew skyward a half second ahead of the hydrostatic pressure wave that radiated outward from the small explosion and caught up to the Kawasaki. The force of it jolted the STX-12F and Jake had to hold on tight as it passed.

The effect of the blast was almost instantaneous. As if suddenly dragging a huge anchor, the pursuing vessel rapidly slowed, its bow rising sharply as its hull came off plane. The flicker of discharging weapons immediately ceased as those aboard her were rocked by the impact.

Jake knew the torpedo had done its job. With the integrity of the vessel's hull compromised, the bilge pump would be taxed to its limit. The rampant inflow of seawater gushing into the vessel would substantially add to its weight and pull the hull deeper, increasing its drag characteristics. With such a condition, the craft's powerful engines could not possibly propel it with the same impressive speed as before, and further pursuit would only exacerbate the rate at which water entered through the hole in its side.

As Jake sped away from the damaged vessel, he noticed it was beginning to take on a slight list as its gun bearers scrambled below decks to investigate the cause of the problem. He smiled knowingly, self-assured that its crew would be occupied with stemming the rush of seawater into the hold.

Speaking into his lip mike, Jake summoned the *Angel*. "Arrow to Goliath."

"Goliath here." There was an edge to Zimbola's voice.

"Cease fire! It's over!"

Relief showed in the black giant's tone. "I am most happy to hear that, Arrow. We will forever be in Agwe's debt."

Jake rolled his eyes. It seemed that whenever they survived a tight situation, Zimby never failed to credit some divinity within the pantheon of voodoo spirits. From what Zimbola had told him, he knew that Agwe was the spirit responsible for the sea, including organisms and other things residing in and above it. Water-based flora, fauna, ships, and even hurricanes fell into its domain.

"Lower the ramp, Goliath. Arrow is now inbound for docking."

"I read you Arrow."

Less than a minute later, Jake gave the Kawasaki just enough throttle to make it back up the launching ramp. The maneuver never ceased to exhilarate him. With too little speed, the waverunner would fall short of its cradle immediately beyond the ramp's apex, only to slide listlessly backwards into the ocean like a salmon failing to make the next level in a steep cataract. With too much momentum, the STX-12F would invariably rocket up the ramp and slam into the cushioned bumpers within its crib like a runaway train, more often than not jettisoning Jake over the handlebars into the padded backstop. The docking procedure was best carried out under mild sea conditions, and always with the *Angel* cruising along into the wind at the same constant speed - 12 knots - which allowed Jake to perfect his skill. Strong gusting winds and choppy or rolling seas always compounded the difficulty, and if too severe, made such a maneuver nearly impossible to execute. On this particular occasion, though, the Kawasaki slid smoothly into the awaiting cradle with nary a jolt.

A grumbling voice pulled Jake from his reverie. "We barely made it back to Kingston that night. You almost sank us."

The vivid memory melted away like ice over a hot stove as Jake suddenly became aware of his friend studying him intently. "You gave me little choice. My crew and I tried to discourage you, but you refused to back off. You should've followed your own advice." He sighed, then cracked a smile. "What was that you said about discretion?"

Mat remained somber. "Tell me, Jake, why are you here in this shit hole of a country?"

Jake continued to smile but kept silent.

"I've looked this vessel over," Mat went on. "With it, you could probably make yourself a nice lucrative, and I might add, honest living in the more upscale tourist havens that abound in the Caribbean." He paused for effect. "But not in this godforsaken place. Something's keeping you here, Jake, and it ain't the smuggling trade. You're too smart for that. Care to tell your old pal what it is?"

A full ten seconds elapsed before Jake responded. "When the time is right, you'll be the first to know."

Exasperation scudded across Mat's face like a storm cloud. "God damn you, Jake! You're putting me in a very awkward position."

"I don't recall asking for any favors."

An uncomfortable quiescence began filling the room like fog sweeping in from the sea, and Jake thought it best to change the subject. "Tell me Mat, why did you try to stop me that night without any backup? It doesn't fit your style."

"I did have backup, but they went after the vessel you rendezvoused with," Mat replied brusquely.

Jake nodded. He could see that Mat was under a lot of stress.

"Listen, Jake, why don't you join DHS. They need guys like you. I can pull a few strings and have you on their payroll within a week."

When Jake did not immediately reply, Mat sweetened the pot further. "Your crew also. Hell, I'll even get them to lease this vessel at a more than fair price. It can be your base of operations. We've always worked great together, you and me. Whaddaya say?"

Jake sighed deeply. "I appreciate the offer, it's most generous. But I just can't do that at this time."

A volatile mixture of disappointment, frustration, and annoyance sparked fleetingly in Mat's eyes, but he managed to hold back the flood of invectives that rose in his throat like superheated magma seeking escape. Jake had always been stubborn.

For a long moment Mat just stared back, perplexed by Jake's answer. "Not at this time?" he echoed in a pained tone, his bearing suddenly growing stiff. "Does that mean you'll reconsider it later on?"

"Yeah…I just may take you up on it, but not right now," Jake said, trying his best to mollify his friend.

This seemed to satisfy Mat and his manner loosened a bit. He reached into a pocket and scribbled on the back of a card. "This is my mobile phone number. You should be able to reach me most hours of the day. Call me if you change your mind. I'll keep the offer open long as I'm able to."

Jake took the proffered business card, his eyes roaming over the emblazoned bold letters: Mat Daniels, Director of Special Operations, Caribbean Counterterrorism Task Force, Department of Homeland Security.

"Impressive!" Jake said, taking in the information.

Mat appeared a trifle chagrined, shrugging disparagingly over the importance of his post. "Don't let the title fool you, titles mean nothing out here. Stopping the bad guys is the only thing that counts for anything."

"I assume your superiors have given you a certain amount of latitude in how you use your budget," Jake speculated. He was thinking back to his days in the Seals when constraining budgets could sometimes negatively impact the outcome of a mission.

Mat shook his head dismally. "Unfortunately, I have to account for every dime spent. Formal requisitioning is a way of life in the DHS."

Jake found it hard to keep the bitterness out of his tone. "Some things never change when you work for Uncle Sam."

"You can say that again," Mat agreed. "It was like pulling teeth getting the funds approved to have my boat repaired. The damage you caused Relentless was quite costly."

His expression hardened again. "Thanks to you I've been filling out forms for the last month."

"Sorry about that, old friend, but you should know better than to drop in on someone unannounced the way you did. One can never be too careful when sailing these waters, especially at night. We live in dangerous times."

"Just one more reason to consider joining up with me. Between us, we could do some serious ass-kicking, keeping terrorists and the people who aid them off balance. Together we just might make a difference."

"Forever the idealist, the visionary."

"If we're going to win this war, we need hard-nosed warriors, men like yourself who are both tough and devious. You were one of the best to ever serve in the Seals. You owe it to your country."

The words hit a sensitive spot and Jake suddenly snarled. "Don't lay that patriotic rhetoric on me! I think I did more than my share for God and country. Unfortunately, there's too many so-called leaders who ultimately control the destinies of men like us, many of them either so incompetent that they are truly dangerous or so dishonest that they should be dismissed."

The severity of Jake's contempt stunned Mat as if he were forcefully slapped. "You're still stewing over Myers, aren't you?" he said softly.

"Yeah."

Mat well understood Jake's pain. He felt it too. It was like a persistent virus that wouldn't go away. Continuing to keep his voice gentle, he said, "Myers knew the risks same as us. You've got to let it go, Jake…let it go."

"I can't."

Dave Myers had also been a Navy Seal, a comrade-in-arms along with Mat and Jake, but had been killed in Afghanistan, the victim of an abominable betrayal within Jake's unit. A soldier turned traitor by the name of Yeslam Omar Raduyev had murdered him, shooting him in the back just before bolting off like a thief in the night.

Jake had first run into Raduyev during BUD/S training. BUD/S was a Navy acronym that stood for Basic Underwater Demolition/SEAL (Sea, Air, Land), and much of the training had taken place at the U.S. Naval Amphibious Base in Coronado, California. A Chechen by birth, Raduyev had immigrated to the United States in 1992 at the age of sixteen to attend college. Four years later, after having received a Bachelor of Science in Nuclear Engineering from Cornell University, he had enlisted in the U.S. Navy as a pre-condition for achieving American citizenship. Upon attaining the rank of ensign, he had applied for admission to BUD/S and was accepted.

From the onset, Raduyev had been a loner, absorbing all aspects of the training with ardent eagerness despite the brutality of the indoctrination. So physically and emotionally demanding was the six-month program that by the end of Hell Week, the third week of training, the original class of 180 physically fit young men had been pared down to 56. While all of them had been driven well beyond the endurance limits of even gifted athletes, three standouts began to emerge as the most promising of the elite warrior force – Jake Javolyn, Mat Daniels and Yeslam Omar Raduyev. Time and again, however, Jake had proven himself to be the toughest of the three, consistently besting his closest challengers as the training wore on and intensified.

To Jake the intense training rigors had been perversely enjoyable. Hard fought competition was nothing new to him. For most of his life he had thrived on it. In high school he had been the New Jersey State wrestling champ in his weight class during his junior and senior years. Such outstanding performance had won him an athletic scholarship to the University of Michigan where he had distinguished himself as a fierce competitor not only on the wrestling mat, but also on the football field as a defensive safety. In his third year at Michigan, he had led the nation in tackles, pass interceptions, and return touchdowns, causing him to come under heavy scrutiny by professional football scouts who sought solid prospects. By his final year, he had captured the NCAA wrestling crown in the 189-pound weight class and was considered an Olympic hopeful. In the midst of his athletic prominence at Michigan, Jake had managed to earn himself a degree in mechanical engineering. But upon graduation, he had declined his invite to the Olympic tryouts and had opted for the military instead. The lore of mortal combat had always fascinated him and there was something that automatically drew him to the Seals, considered to be the world's toughest soldiers.

During his indoctrination at BUD/S, Mat had never let his rivalry with Jake get out of hand, always accepting lost battles with good grace. They soon became close friends and had been paired up as swim buddies during the grueling drills. Yeslam, on the other hand, quickly became embittered when he failed to outperform Jake during the training exercises, seeming to take it as a personal affront.

Early in the training Raduyev had kept a low profile, drawing little attention to himself. Whenever Jake would glance in his direction, he could not help but notice the Chechen's beady dark eyes darting about like those of a pernicious serpent, deceptively cunning and cruel, always seeming to search for signs of weakness in the other trainees. And like a serpent, Raduyev somehow gave Jake the eerie impression that the Chechen was gauging the ideal time to strike venom into some unsuspecting victim. Nonetheless, as the program advanced, the drill instructors began to take notice of Raduyev's physical attributes. He was exceptionally strong and only seemed to tire under the most taxing hardships. His body was lean, hard, and muscular, exhibiting wide flat pectorals, chiseled abs, and broad shoulders. At six feet two inches, he was a fairly large man, standing an inch taller than Jake and outweighing him by a good fifteen pounds. Whenever Raduyev would outdistance his classmates in a grueling long-distance run or swim, his dark eyebrows would arch triumphantly over malicious eyes, giving him a malevolent, satanic look. But this only occurred when Jake was not immediately involved in such competition. Jake was the one man among the trainees who always seemed to outlast or finish ahead of the pack, including Raduyev, no matter what the exercise entailed. Jake particularly thrived on obstacle courses, blowing through them with relative ease. For all of Raduyev's speed and quickness, Jake was always faster. For all of Raduyev's exceptional stamina, Jake's endurance proved better.

As the weeks of training continued, Raduyev's bitterness towards Jake mushroomed into full-blown hatred, and the Chechen's quiet aloofness gradually transformed into overt contempt. The drill instructors noted Yeslam's growing discontent and his intense desire to be the top trainee among his peers. They saw the heated rivalry as a useful tool in raising the performance of the other students to new heights, and as a result both Jake and Raduyev were each designated as a team leader. With the entire trainee class divided into teams, a battle of wills quickly evolved between groups as to which one would be the best.

Mat Daniels was assigned to Jake's team, and it was Mat who put things in perspective one day during a brief respite between exercises. "I think Yeslam sees this as a contest between Islam and infidels," Mat muttered jokingly.

Jake looked surprised. He stared over at the Chechen and took stock of the way Raduyev glared back at him. "You think he's turning this into some kind of holy crusade?"

"Absolutely! There are six other trainees here that are Muslims and they're all in his crew. The drill instructors set it up this way to add fuel to the competition between teams. I overheard them talking about it."

Jake almost laughed. "So, he wants to use this training program to make a religious statement."

"Yep." Mat spoke glibly. "And if his team succeeds in being the best under his leadership, then he'll prove that God is on his side and the rest of us infidels just can't cut the mustard."

Jake grinned fiendishly, setting his shoulders and thrusting out his jaw. "Well, we'll just see about that."

Shortly after, each team was issued an IBS – Inflatable Boat Small – and made to race one another over distances covering anywhere from five to twenty miles or more. The courses varied and spanned stretches of sandy beach and open water, with lots of obstacles in between. Boat crews were forced to alternately carry the heavy boats over deep sand and paddle through rough seas, frequently having to lift the bulky vessels over fences and other obstructing barriers and launch them in rough surf. Capsizes were commonplace, and very often crews had to beach their ponderous IBS while bucking awesome riptides. The races were always physically draining and the instructors did their utmost to ensure that crew members suffered as much discomfort as possible, keeping them constantly cold, wet, sandy, blistered, bruised, and most of all, exhausted. But Jake's calming presence and iron will to keep plodding along in the face of brutal conditions became a rallying point of inspiration for team members, and his crew easily succeeded in winning each race. There was a payoff to winning those competitions, too. The first crew to finish ahead of the others got to rest while awaiting the remaining crews to complete the course before the start of the next exercise. And nearly every time the boat crews concluded the final leg of a five, eight or ten-mile trek, they'd be instructed to carry the IBS back to the starting point, at which point they'd fight their way back through the surf, only to repeat the course.

With each new race the intensity of competition would climb to a new height, and each time Raduyev's crew managed to come in a close second. Although the instructors hollered incessantly at the trainees that they were slow, worthless pukes, they were inwardly pleased. They realized they were witnessing the best times ever recorded in the history of the Coronado training facility. Even boat crews finishing third and fourth had faster times than those of top crews in years past. Those who were making it through the training walked proud. They were being tempered by extreme hardship and persevering. As they continued to be put through the fires of hell their confidence in themselves grew, and they started to believe there was virtually no physical demand they couldn't overcome.

It didn't take long for everyone, both trainees and instructors, to comprehend that Jake's determination to set the standard was ultimately responsible for elevating everyone's performance in the spirit of competition. As a result, a reluctant admiration towards him began to unfold from all the members of his training class – that is, all except Raduyev. With each loss to Jake's team, Raduyev's frustration continued to mount and fester. He began to grow increasingly irritable with other members of his team over their inability to win a single race. It did not take very long for him to become abusive and bullying, and the respect his crew had shown him early on began to dwindle. Near the end of the

IBS exercises, a breakdown in the morale of his team caused them to lag behind the other crews, and a short time thereafter the instructors replaced Raduyev as team leader.

During a forced hasty meal at the facility's mess hall one afternoon, Raduyev's anger could be contained no longer. It boiled over into a silent, seething rage and he leered unwaveringly at Jake from two tables away with murder in his eyes. Several other trainees noticed the simmering hostility, and a member of Yeslam's crew sitting opposite from the Chechen, a trainee by the name of Myers, glared at Yeslam reproachfully. "What'd you want him to do, throw a race just to appease your bloated ego?" he openly admonished, his Kentuckian twang just loud enough for those closest to overhear.

Slowly, Raduyev turned his head and set his gaze on Myers, his face contorted grotesquely as if he was seeing something repugnant. His rancor suddenly faded into a harsh grin, though it clung to his face precariously. Keeping his voice low, he said, "Ah, the Jew speaks, the little pig-swine who caused us to lose all the races."

Mat grabbed Jake's arm to keep him from interceding. It was not considered acceptable practice in the Seals to interfere in the disputes of others. Such a breach of etiquette could bring disgrace to the one you were attempting to defend. It was an unwritten code of honor. In the Seals a man took care of his own problems. Seals were expected to be tough enough to settle their own quarrels man to man without anyone's assistance.

"I should smash your face for that remark," Myers snapped between clenched teeth, managing to hold his voice to a whisper.

Raduyev's expression changed again, this time to bemusement. "Ha, I will give you this opportunity," he shot back, continuing with the whispered exchange. He glanced surreptitiously at two of the instructors who were out of earshot and busy in conversation. "Tonight, behind the barracks just after dark…you can try to smash my face there. From what I have seen of you so far, it would not surprise me if you failed to show, little pig-swine."

At a wiry 140 pounds, Myers was no match for the much larger Chechen, but he had spunk and there was no way he'd even consider backing down. "Screw you, maggot. You can bet I'll be there."

Word of the impending fight spread rapidly, and immediately following sunset the majority of Seal candidates were gathered behind the barracks to bear witness. For the most part, the soft-spoken, perpetually calm Myers was well-liked among his peers. Though he was one of the smallest men currently undergoing training, he was one of the most cheerful, never complaining about the exhaustive regimen he was subjected to, always making a joke of something even to the point of collapse.

As the crowd gathered, Myers stood stone-faced, his features revealing no emotion as he awaited the arrival of Raduyev. Finally, the Chechen showed up, an arrogant smile plastered on his face as he stepped through the mass of trainees. He swaggered up to Myers and stared scornfully down on him as though he were some repulsive life form that had just crawled out of a sewer. The size disparity between the two men was suddenly apparent to everyone watching.

"Come, my little pig-swine," Raduyev growled. "Try smashing my face now. I will even let you take the first punch."

Myers met his stare evenly, his face breaking into a rueful grin. "I never touch pig shit unless I get it on me first."

The Chechen's eyes flared at the insult and his right fist shot out in a blur. Myers was ready for it and he slipped the intended blow with surprising speed, catching his opponent with a lightning counter punch that caught Raduyev just below the right eye. Yeslam staggered back, bringing a hand to his cheek. Astonishment flooded his expression as he pulled the hand away and noticed a heavy smear of blood. Those closest to him could clearly see the flesh below his eye laid open to the bone.

Yeslam scowled back at his opponent in disbelief, the hate pent up like a keg of dynamite about to ignite. Instantly, his eyes turned red, and within them was the look of murder. With the grace of a seasoned matador, Myers sidestepped as the bigger man charged straight at him, landing a solid roundhouse kick to Raduyev's ribcage as he stormed past. The Chechen spun and charged again, seeking to land a blow of his own but missing. Myers landed two more punches to Raduyev's body before sliding smoothly away, making his adversary appear clumsy. It quickly became evident that Myers was an accomplished martial artist. Nevertheless, Raduyev kept pursuing with unabated intensity. Myers' blows were more humiliating than incapacitating, only serving to enrage the bigger man all the more.

Then it happened. The Chechen managed to wrap an arm around the much lighter man, and in spite of taking three more blows to the head, pulled Myers into a crushing bear hug. Myers was then flung down savagely in a crunching body slam, and before he could scramble away Raduyev used his superior weight and strength to pin him to the ground. Sadistic pleasure gleamed in the Chechen's eyes as Yeslam clutched Myers' throat in a vice-like grip with his left hand. Jake watched helplessly as Raduyev raised his right into a balled fist, ready to strike.

"What in blazes is going on here?" a stern authoritative voice suddenly bellowed. "I don't recall giving anyone permission to play."

Startled, Raduyev froze as if splashed with liquid nitrogen.

Instructor Cunningham pushed his way through the throng and glared menacingly at the two combatants. From the look on his face, both men were already in the brig doing hard time. "Raduyev and Myers, get your sorry asses off the ground!" he yelled belligerently. Stonily, he spun to address the onlookers. "Everyone drop and give me fifty."

Other instructors seemed to materialize out of nowhere, and following set after set of agonizing push-ups, the entire class was ordered to get their worthless, no load, good-for-nothing carcasses back to the beach. As expected, they had been hollered back into the cold surf fully clothed for the sixth time that day, unceremoniously forced to endure the Pacific's chilling turbulence for the next fifteen minutes.

"You want entertainment," Cunningham excoriated, "let's see how much fun you have rolling around in the sand again." Plastered with sand and grit, the class was taken on another four-mile run along the beach, water slogging in their boots as always. Covering that distance in anything more than thirty-two minutes was unacceptable, and any trainee taking longer than that to complete the run was ordered back into the surf.

Jake and Mat would eventually learn that the drill instructors had gotten wind of the impending fight and decided to let it take place, at least in part, before breaking it up. Raduyev had ended up in the infirmary with eight stitches and ultimately a prominent scar that memorialized the incident. His classmates would always remember him as the one who had gotten the worst of the encounter. His esteem rapidly plummeted and he became the butt of mocking jokes.

By contrast, Myers' popularity had risen sharply. He was the ideal representation of what a true Seal should be, fearless under any circumstances, no matter what the odds. In the Seals the fortitude of a man mattered most. Physical size and strength were always secondary. Jake knew from firsthand experience that Seals came in all sizes and shapes, and that those who completed the training were all equally deadly under combat conditions.

He also learned that Raduyev would have been drummed out of BUD/S altogether except for one redeeming quality, one the military considered to be highly valuable – he spoke fluent Arabic. Such an asset would prove indispensable on missions in the Middle East, which were becoming more and more frequent as of late.

Shortly after the fight, Raduyev's attitude changed markedly. As the stitched laceration on his cheek began to heal, his mannerism became more tolerant and less hostile. Even the drill instructors noticed the metamorphosis. But as Jake and Mat would learn, it was all a sham.

For the next several months, Jake and the rest of the surviving trainees had learned how to dive, plant and detonate explosives, and make parachute jumps from altitude. High altitude parachute openings, commonly referred to as HAHOs in military jargon, became commonplace, with the skill of the men quickly escalating. Jake discovered that HAHOs were routinely used in infiltrating enemy territory covertly. A Seal team could deploy their chutes and glide in formation over a distance of twenty or more miles undetected to reach an objective.

As the jump training advanced, the Seals were then taught how to properly execute the more dangerous HALO, or High Altitude Low Opening maneuver. These took even greater skill to effectively carry out, not to mention nerves of steel, for a trainee would experience free falling for 35,000 feet or more before initiating a chute opening, often less than a thousand feet above land or sea. HALOs were designed for dropping in rapidly and silently on an unsuspecting enemy, giving a foe only a very limited time in which to spot you, and even less of an opportunity in which to pick you off while still in the air. A soldier was less of a target free falling than while drifting lazily over someone with gun sights locked on you. In completing the jump portion of his training, Jake became expert in packing a chute and the intricacies of plotting a jump so that he could account for wind shear, thermals, and downdrafts and still land exactly where he wanted.

After several weeks of intensive jump training, it was during a practice HALO that Jake had almost bought the farm. He had leapt from a Hercules C-130 at an altitude of 26,000 feet, fully equipped for underwater diving exercises. Along with a dozen other trainees, including Mat, Myers, and Yeslam, everyone had been instructed to open their chute 2,500 feet above the Pacific, then drift down to the sea and regroup. Spread-eagled and reaching velocities of 120 miles per hour, the team had fallen swiftly toward the deployment zone.

Having been the last of the group to depart the aircraft, Jake watched the canopies of the others mushroom open below him, one after the other. His heart seemed to skip a beat when he noticed one of the jumpers continuing to plummet. It was Myers. Horror-stricken, he looked on as Myers tugged frantically on his ripcord, but nothing happened.

Without even realizing what he was doing, Jake withdrew his hand from his own ripcord and, holding his arms stiffly at his sides, arrowed his body headlong towards the waiting sea below. The maneuver minimized air resistance and accelerated his rate of fall. Within seconds he was gaining rapidly on the struggling Myers. By the time he had caught up to his classmate, he was less than a thousand feet above the water, and in that moment Jake knew this would be a one-shot attempt at saving his friend's life.

With perfect timing he changed the attitude of his body as he was about to hurtle past. Letting the air cushion his glide, he changed his angle of attack through atmosphere. Myers was suddenly before him, and steering himself closer, he drifted in on his target. In some respects, the maneuver wasn't much different than trying to close on an offensive running back on the football field, and he threw his arms wide a split second before making the tackle. Like a colliding meteor, Jake slammed into Myers with jarring impact, feeling the wind knocked from the smaller man. Managing to clamp both arms, then legs around his dazed friend, he groped for his own ripcord and found it. Yanking hard, he heard the familiar sound of his chute ruffle, then pop just before the ocean rushed up to meet them.

Both he and Myers had hit the water with jolting force, but miraculously the two of them had survived without sustaining any serious injury. Later on, a close examination of Myers' primary and reserve chute showed both had been tampered with.

Even though Raduyev showed concern over the incident, Jake refused to let the man's air of innocence fool him. Contrary to his nature, he had taken his suspicions to the commanding officer of the training facility, a captain by the name of Walter McPherson.

"Do you have any proof of this?" McPherson asked sternly.

"None sir, but I think Raduyev is the only one among us who would want Myers dead." Jake knew McPherson was privy to the fight that had taken place between the two men.

An angry scowl creased McPherson's face as Jake stood at attention before him. "Here at Coronado, Seal candidates do not accuse their classmates of anything unless they have actual proof to support it. Mere speculation is not sufficient grounds to incriminate someone. Do I make myself clear, Mr. Javolyn?"

"Yes sir."

"Up to now, your training record has been quite admirable. Don't blow it with any unfounded accusations." The captain pulled his glare from Jake and fixed his attention on some papers sitting atop his desk. "Dismissed!"

Jake didn't like McPherson. His initial impression of the base commander was not a good one, but having stood before him had only served to reinforce this opinion. He considered himself a pretty sharp judge of people, and McPherson in his judgement lacked the character and qualities befitting a captain in the U.S. Navy. It was not so much that McPherson refused to do something about Raduyev. The captain was correct in telling him he needed concrete proof in order to incriminate the Chechen. No, Jake couldn't fault him for that. And although he would be the first to agree that one shouldn't evaluate a book by its cover, McPherson just didn't exemplify the kind of attributes a person in charge of an elite combat training facility should project.

For one thing, the captain appeared flabby and out of shape, looking nothing like a warrior. But even worse, he could sense that McPherson was not remotely the warrior-type and would always lack the heart of one. No matter how hard the captain was to train, and that would be never, he could not be considered a warrior by any stretch of the imagination. In fact, he was certain the man would fold under the slightest physical hardship. Jake just could not picture McPherson ever leading a combat mission.

Based on what he had heard about the captain, he knew that McPherson was highly ambitious, having advanced relatively quickly through the Navy's ranks. It was primarily political clout that had advanced him, though to a lesser degree the man was also responsible for bringing innovative ideas to the attention of the Navy high command. It was McPherson who had pressed to have more Third World Muslims seeking U.S. citizenship go through Seal training, considering those with fluency in Arabic and in-depth understandings of Islamic cultures to be military assets. After all, it stood to reason that such individuals, with the proper training, would be extremely useful on missions in the Middle East, Northern Africa, and Western Asia where Muslim cultures predominated and where an American presence was growing more and more these days. McPherson saw such men not so much as elite fighting soldiers but as diplomats to the U.S. cause. Because of McPherson's relentless efforts and his father's connections with several rear admirals in Washington, he had pushed such a concept up through the chain of command where his vision had gained the support of influential Pentagon officials. Eventually it came under the scrutiny of the Joint Chiefs of Staff who had endorsed this fresh new perspective, rewarding McPherson with a promotion to the rank of captain and installing him as the current Coronado facility commander to oversee the training of Muslims into Seals.

In view of this, Jake had anticipated that McPherson would be unduly biased and unyielding to his concerns about Raduyev, but he felt it necessary to bring the matter before him anyway. It was quite clear now where Jake stood. No way was McPherson going to let his program get undermined by this upstart lieutenant. The captain was a stuffed-shirt bureaucrat, a bean counter, completely out of sync with anything remotely connected with war. The man hadn't been aboard a ship in ten years and surrounded himself with several lower-grade officers essentially made in his own image because true warriors made him uncomfortable. Jake could see it in his eyes. This was how the military seemed to operate these days, led by a bloated, top-heavy bureaucracy of flag-rank officers like McPherson who were armchair commanders at best, incapable of leading from the front and earning the respect of the men who usually did the dying under their inept commands.

Jake had learned that McPherson came from a wealthy affluent family. In fact, McPherson's father was a retired rear admiral. And like his dad before him, McPherson was an Annapolis graduate. The Naval Academy class ring adorning one of his fingers had laid stark testament to this, an insignia for success within the Navy's caste system, reputed to be one of the most inflexible in the world.

Although incredibly stimulating and always challenging, the remainder of Jake's training passed without further incident. By the time graduation arrived, a strong camaraderie had developed between Daniels, Myers, and Jake, and the three of them were nearly inseparable. Each of them knew they had formed a lasting friendship, something they would share for the rest of their lives. There was something about sweating, bleeding, and hurting together when striving for the same goal, a bond forged in the fires of physical pain between men.

Because the three of them worked well together and were exceptionally adroit at the special tasks they had been trained to carry out, one of the power brokers up the chain of command had recognized the wisdom in teaming them on one particular clandestine mission. That assignment had taken them into the remote reaches of Afghanistan. By that time, Jake, Mat, and Myers had more than a half dozen missions under their belts, and each of them had been decorated for combat valor several times over. Jake alone had already distinguished himself with two Silver Stars, three Bronze Stars, and two Purple Hearts. Four other Seals, including Yeslam Raduyev, had formed the remainder of the team, with three of the others being older warriors with considerably more experience under their belts.

Executing a HAHO from a Hercules C-130 at an altitude of 32,000 feet on a moonless night, they had glided in single file behind their team leader over a distance of twenty-two miles, sighting in on the infrared strobe lights strapped to his ankles. The jump had taken them into the craggy ravines and obscure trails bordering the Hindu Kush mountain range, a fortress-like maze of geography better known as Tora Bora.

As the team homed in on the designated rendezvous point using their Magellan GPS modules, the flashing blue strobe of a portable beacon winked up at them from below, and they spiraled in one by one in a corkscrew descent. The ground was reasonably level and relatively clear of boulders and ankle-twisting rubble at the small landing site, and each man floated in without mishap in the windless air.

They had met with a Pashtun local by the name of Gullu Sherkhan, an Afghan militiaman and spymaster on the CIA payroll. Sherkhan had identified himself with the appropriate password. The team's objective had been a formidable one, to gather as much information as possible about the Al Qaeda presence in the immediate area, including the whereabouts of their exulted leader, Osama Bin Laden.

With an AK-47 held at the ready in his right hand, Sherkhan had led them silently up a boulder-strewn hill. The team had followed him over the darkened landscape, each man wearing a set of Night Vision goggles to make the going less perilous over the rugged terrain. Carefully skirting a bomb crater fifteen feet deep without the use of such modern gadgetry, Sherkhan had groped his way through the darkness, eventually bringing the team to the mouth of a cave. Well back from the entrance, the interior of the cavern had been dimly lit by a series of lanterns strung out at intervals into the recesses of the chamber. The cave had twisted back into the hillside where it branched off into an array of honeycombed mazes. The memory was clearly etched in Jake's mind, and as he recalled it, he began to relive every facet of the experience.

Deep within one of the tunnels, Sherkhan felt it safe enough to address the team leader, Captain Jim Sheridan. "It was here among these hills and caves that we fought the Arabs for several weeks in the snow," Sherkhan said in near perfect, unaccented English. He was a sad-eyed man with a soft lulling voice. White-turbaned and wearing a ragged tan coat over U.S. Army-issue camouflage trousers, Gullu's manner was balanced between equal doses of battle-hardened bravado and guarded trepidation. His striking blue eyes took in every member of the team with mild interest, as if trying to gauge the true grit of each individual. Jake noticed that his gaze lingered a full second longer on Raduyev than on the others.

"Osama, himself, had holed up in this very cave," Sherkhan continued, his eyes taking on an awe-inspired glint under the glow of the lanterns.

"All the caves in the immediate area are empty now. It is rumored that the Kuchis have taken Bin Laden under their protection."

Prior to the mission, Jake and the others had been briefed about the inhabitants of the region and their customs. The Kuchis were Pashtun nomads who drifted around Afghanistan and Pakistan and occasionally into Iran. More than a million strong in numbers and spread out over numerous tribes, they were reputed to have a spy network that was the envy of any Western intelligence agency. With their herds of sheep, goats, and camels, these wanderers generally avoided towns and villages as they followed timeworn footpaths through the hills and deserts.

If passed on from tribe to tribe, it would be easy for Bin Laden and his cadre to remain hidden, particularly in view of the ancient but strange Pashtun code of honor called nanawateh. Translated into its English equivalent, nanawateh meant sanctuary, an often troublesome and paradoxical tenet to the hunters of Bin Laden. Along the Afghanistan-Pakistan border, the custom was almost never violated among the bewildering array of clans and tribes that inhabited the region. Collectively known as the Pashtun, the people were duty-bound to assist anyone who came knocking on their door seeking refuge, and that could include total strangers or even their worst enemies. A Pashtun was expected to defend his guest with his life if the situation demanded it. For any fugitive or outlaw, the part of the world where the Pashtun lived presented the perfect hiding place.

"Do the Kuchis know of the twenty-five-million-dollar bounty the U.S. has placed on Bin Laden's head?" Captain Sheridan asked.

Sherkhan stroked the close-cropped beard darkening his chin and upper lip, reflecting on Sheridan's question as if trying to make sense of it. "The Kuchis are aware of such a reward, yes. They are a treacherous lot and can often be untrustworthy, especially to outsiders to whom they look upon with deep suspicion. But once they give someone sanctuary they will fight to their last breath in protecting that person rather than betray him for the mere sake of money. To do so would bring disgrace to their tribe, one that would hang over them for many generations to come."

Sheridan nodded at this. "It seems that Bin Laden and his constituents have taken full advantage of such unique hospitality."

"We must not remain here too long," Sherkhan advised. "The night before, some Taliban led by a few Arab fighters attacked the nearby Afghan militia with rocket-propelled grenades and light machine guns. They are probably still lurking in these hills and watching for infiltrators. I am told that they have spies everywhere." His voice was so dull and devoid of emotion that he might have been warning them about the weather.

"Is it true that the enemy comes from the Pakistani side of these mountains?" Sheridan questioned.

"Yes. The Taliban and their Al Qaeda mentors move along trails that were once used by the mujahideen when they had fought against the Soviets. Several times each month they launch cross-border raids against American-led coalition forces, then retreat back into Pakistan's tribal region beyond the reach of U.S. warplanes."

Sheridan studied Sherkhan for several moments, then said, "Can you take us to Noor Ghani?" Noor Ghani was a local Wazir chieftain that the Seal team had been instructed to contact.

From the look on Sherkhan's face, the request did not sit well with him. "The man is not to be trusted. There is talk that he has been consorting with the Arabs. I must advise against it."

Sheridan was adamant. "Can you take us there?" he hissed.

Sherkhan sighed with deep resignation. "Yes, but we must move quickly. Dawn will be upon us in four hours and it is a long trip on foot."

Before leaving the cave, Sherkhan provided each member of the team with clothing typifying Pashtun dress, insisting that they would be less noticed and better received by the locals if they wore such garb. Various articles of clothing were stored in one corner of the cavern, some of the items in fairly good condition while others were worn, faded and stained with what Jake perceived to be dried blood. Sherkhan indicated that some of the garments had been taken from the bodies of Taliban and Al Qaeda warriors killed in battle. At first Captain Sheridan resisted Sherkhan's ardent recommendation, but after examining the clothing he decided it might be a good idea. With deft sweeps of his arms, Sherkhan wrapped a long, broad flag of ash-colored cloth in the Wazir fashion around the head of each Seal, all except Raduyev who was already skilled in the rudiments of donning a turban. After each man had finished dressing, Sherkhan gave a final inspection of the complete attire, looking over the baggy shalwar or kameez of each individual with a critical eye and making some final adjustments. Hidden beneath their loose clothing the men would still carry their utility belts and other Seal accoutrements, weapons, and ammunition. In addition, each man would continue to carry his bulky backpack.

Upon leaving the cave, Sherkhan guided the team in single file through the dark unlit hills as if he had built-in radar. Several times during the journey, Jake could not shake the feeling they were being watched, and with senses heightened he had scanned the surrounding terrain through the NV goggles he had strapped firmly over his eyes.

After several hours of trekking along antediluvian goat trails, Sherkhan brought the team to a village just before sunup. As Jake looked around him in the rapidly advancing twilight of dawn, he noticed that almost every house was built on steeples of rock. The silhouettes of turbaned men with rifles strapped to their backs could be seen beginning their morning chores in an adjacent poppy field. As soon as they became aware of the approach of the eight-man party they unslung their weapons. Half a dozen Wazirs strode forward with Kalashnikov AK-47s nonchalantly aimed at Jake and the others. Out of the corner of his mouth, Sherkhan told Captain Sheridan to keep his team's weapons lowered and to remain where they now stood. With a hand raised high in a universal gesture of peace, Sherkhan walked calmly toward the armed group, greeting them in Pashtu, their spoken tongue.

A lengthy parley ensued during which one of the Wazirs turned and ran in the direction of the largest nearby dwelling, a castle-like structure with high watchtowers and twenty-foot walls. Sherkhan continued his discussion, which from a distance seemed to grow heated at times. Finally, the man who had run off earlier returned to the group and more words were exchanged, upon which Sherkhan nodded and walked back to the Seal team.

"It is all arranged. Noor Ghani invites us to his home for lunch," Sherkhan stated, looking somewhat uncomfortable.

Later that afternoon, Jake and four of his teammates rested leisurely on rope-strung cots set out in a courtyard under the shade of a thriving grapevine pergola, having had their fill of roasted goat and okra.

Apparently the hospitality accorded by nanawateh still applied, and Noor Ghani proved to be a most polite and convivial host. Sitting cross-legged in conversation with Captain Sheridan and Gulu Sherkhan, Noor Ghani was a gaunt man with searching pale eyes and a bush of a beard that had the texture of steel wool.

With bees droning lazily above him, Jake rose and stretched his legs, moving close enough to overhear tidbits of the conversation. Like most Pashtuns, Noor Ghani could speak several languages. As a courtesy to his guests, he spoke to Sheridan in English.

Sipping green tea, Sheridan looked over his cup and said, "You have to understand, Osama Bin Laden is responsible for killing over three thousand innocent American civilians. By committing such an act, he has declared war on the United States."

"I am told you Americans hate Muslims," Noor Ghani replied, taking another sip of tea and glancing over at Jake offhandedly. Twelve of Noor Ghani's men sitting nearby along a stonewall situated to one side of the courtyard eyed Jake coldly, and Jake had to force a congenial smile as he looked their way. Noor Ghani turned back to face Sheridan. "Is this true?"

"The American presence here has nothing to do with religion," Sheridan answered, a tinge of frustration evident in his tone. "We are not in your land to fight some kind of holy war the way Bin Laden makes it out to be. No, Americans do not hate Muslims."

"Then perhaps your government does."

Sheridan shook his head. "My government only seeks to protect its citizens from further attacks by Al Qaeda. By taking offensive measures, we are able to contain him."

"Ah," Noor Ghani said, smiling broadly. "You do not demand badal?"

Sheridan looked confused and Sherkhan translated. "Our host is asking if you want to exact vengeance."

The Seal team leader thought this over carefully, then gazed back at Noor Ghani and nodded. "Yes. Bin Laden and his followers must pay for one of the greatest mass murders in history. Do you have any knowledge of his whereabouts?"

Noor Ghani's expression darkened and a stony silence fell over the courtyard. Something made Jake turn in Raduyev's direction at that moment. The Chechen's expression was left unguarded as he looked over at Sheridan, and in his eyes Jake was certain he saw the fire of pure hatred. Raduyev suddenly became aware of Jake's penetrating stare and abruptly glanced away, quickly hiding his emotions behind an exaggerated yawn and stretch.

Sheridan's frustration became more apparent. Though only a gap of less than four feet separated him and Noor Ghani, it might as well have been as wide as the gulf between galaxies and as deep as the chasm of hell. In spite of the rift, Sheridan was not about to give up.

"You seem like a reasonable man." he said, "a man of intelligence and compassion who is not fearful of speaking out. Yet I find it difficult to believe you would protect a man who seeks to brutalize people in the name of religion, an enemy of human rights and a threat to all those who do not agree with his philosophies. This man believes it's righteous to use any weapon at his disposal to kill anyone he sees as not following his distorted view of Islam. He has meticulously woven an elaborate curtain of deceit behind which he hides in order to create a climate of fear, chaos, and death. He is a man who expects others to do his bidding and, even worse, dying. Is he not a man who has boasted on numerous occasions that he looks forward to martyrdom, that he seeks a noble and honorable death during a head-to-head fight with American forces? If this is so, why does he continue to run and hide while he encourages others to do the dying for him?"

Sheridan eyed Noor Ghani coldly, waiting for him to respond, but the Wazir chief sat in brooding silence. "Bin Laden hopes to destroy people of different religions," Sheridan went on, "or even those Muslims who cling to divergent theological interpretations of Islam. His primary targets are all nations that are free in government, mind, and religion. Surely you must see the divisiveness he represents."

The darkness faded from Noor Ghani's demeanor, replaced slowly by a budding smile. He seemed to be enjoying this exchange of views. "Many Muslims see Bin Laden as a cohesive force, keeping people united in situations where they would otherwise fall apart. They believe he and his followers are virtuous, devout men, holy warriors who have offered their money, blood, and very lives to the almighty Allah in fighting for the downtrodden Islamic nations against the western cultures, which they perceive as being obscene and contradictory to the tenets of Islam. Most Muslims are likely to support Bin Laden."

Sheridan appeared bemused. "Until they feel the heel of oppression grinding into their necks, hearts, and dignity," he countered. Pausing, he assessed Noor Ghani carefully. "Do you share this belief? Are you a supporter of Bin Laden?"

Noor Ghani's smile vanished. "What I believe holds little value in this part of the world. Most Westerners have great difficulty understanding Pashtun customs. The Pashtun have a complex weave of loyalties and vendettas that goes well beyond politics and religion. Our people are divided into dozens of tribes and hundreds of clans. Disagreements between neighbors are common and often escalate into wars. Outsiders to our land are usually looked upon with deep suspicion. The presence of an invader has a tendency to unite the people, but as soon as the invader is driven out the tribes will go back to feuding among themselves. It is said that war against a common enemy is the only time the Pashtun are truly at peace with each other."

Captain Sheridan narrowed his eyes, trying to size up Noor Ghani as the Pashtun warlord went back to sipping tea. "I assume you are referring to the Soviet invasion of Afghanistan."

Noor Ghani lowered his cup and nodded mildly. "That was one such enemy, yes. But other would-be conquerors also learned about the Pashtun resolve the hard way. Alexander the Great and the British were other invaders who tried to subdue this land, ultimately finding the Pashtun to be ungovernable."

"The U.S. helped your people expel the Soviets," Sheridan pointed out. "With the aid of the Pakistani intelligence services, my government secretly supplied Afghan rebels with guns and Stinger missiles, valuable weapons which contributed immeasurably to the expulsion of the Soviets from your land."

An ironic smirk formed on Noor Ghani's lips, partially hidden under his heavy growth of beard. "That is true. But so did the Arabs who saw the struggle with the Soviets as a jihad, a holy war. Many Arabs came into the Pashtun tribal regions during that time to join our cause, including Bin Laden, volunteering to fight the Soviets. But such an alliance created problems within our tribes. Pakistani intelligence wanted to disrupt the Pashtun social order by assassinating Afghan leaders who resisted Pakistani control of the war. Various elements within the Pakistani government supported the Muslim clerics from Saudi Arabia who established numerous religious schools in Pakistan. These schools were funded entirely by the Saudis and were used to indoctrinate many Pashtuns with Islamic fundamentalism. The students at these schools became the Taliban and seized control of the Afghan government five years ago."

"Yeah, brainwashed zealots who were taught to hate," Sheridan retorted, finding it difficult not to let his anger show. "Puppets of Bin Laden who saw justification in brutalizing people by imposing a barbaric, if not moronic, code of conduct on those Afghans that were not caught up in such extreme fanaticism. Under Taliban rule, the views of Bin Laden were propagated and enforced. Torture and public executions for even petty infractions became commonplace. The way I see it, Bin Laden hijacked both a religion and then a nation to serve him in reaching his perverted goals. Establishing such a sovereign regime made it convenient for him to plan attacks against America with near impunity. In Afghanistan, he could openly recruit people into Al Qaeda, set up terrorist training camps, and experiment in developing chemical and biological weapons. Through covert affiliations with Pakistani scientists sympathetic to his cause he could garner the necessary resources to produce a nuclear capability."

"Yet he underestimated the resolve of your president," Noor Ghani interposed calmly, smiling at Sheridan's show of surprise over such a comment. "Bin Laden never expected your government to respond the way it did to the threat he posed. I think he was even more amazed when the Pakistani government allied itself with the U.S. against him. Within the protective curtain of Afghanistan, Bin Laden felt he was beyond the reach of foreign governments who were out to get him, safe and untouchable and surrounded by the Taliban who continue to see him as an exulted hero of Islam."

"Yeah, his colossal arrogance led to the downfall of the Taliban government," Sheridan agreed. "The Taliban would still be in power if not for him. Had they heeded the U.S. demand to turn him over they would have avoided much bloodshed. I seem to recall one of the Taliban mullahs claiming that Allah would protect the Taliban from attack by the U.S. It was as if they were goading us to invade and fight a drawn-out war similar to what the Soviets endured. That was just before we blew all their military installations to dust from the air. As observers, we had learned much about the way the Soviets had handled their war, and because of it we were not about to make the same mistakes. With the Taliban now ousted from power, Bin Laden has been uprooted from his Afghan stronghold and forced to flee from cave to cave. He is a man who appears to avoid a fight with American troops at all costs, a man who is obviously fearful of getting caught."

Sheridan stopped talking momentarily to study Noor Ghani's reaction, but the Wazir leader only continued to wear a congenial smile. "If you give us information leading to Bin Laden's capture, you will be twenty-five million richer in American greenbacks," Sheridan stressed.

Noor Ghani looked down and poured himself some more green tea, his expression suddenly pensive. "You have to understand," he said regretfully, "such a large sum of money would be useless to me. My life and the lives of everyone in this village wouldn't be worth a goat's eye if I did what you ask. The disgrace would hang over the Wazir for many generations to come."

Sheridan gave Noor Ghani an icy stare. "You have given Bin Laden refuge?"

Noor Ghani ignored the question. "I would be accountable to the jirga if I accommodated your offer. They would see it as a violation of the Pashtun code and gather a lashkar to destroy our homes, kill our livestock, and burn our crops."

From where Jake stood, he could read the confusion on Sheridan's face. There was something in what Noor Ghani just said that the Seal team commander hadn't been briefed on.

Sherkhan saw the look too and took the initiative. "The jirga are the supreme interpreters of Pashtunwali, the Pashtun ancient code of honor. The name refers to a tribal council of elders who are chosen by their respective clans. They are incredibly wise men; and their collective judgements are final and binding. They are the only men that a Pashtun will accept as his superior. They have been known to settle blood vendettas and land disputes. They are particularly harsh with violators of nanawateh and will assemble an army or lashkar from the other tribes and clans to punish anyone breaking the code."

Sheridan nodded with sudden understanding as he mulled the impasse thwarting him. From his expression, the cultural divide was stark and difficult for him to negotiate. "I gather this has nothing to do with Islam then."

Sherkhan looked solemnly at Noor Ghani before placing his gaze back on Sheridan. "Our host is bound by a strict code of honor which prevents him from helping you."

"We hold no particular allegiance to Bin Laden, nor the Taliban, for that matter," Noor Ghani stated glibly. "While it is true that Al Qaeda has been recruiting many Pashtuns to their cause by offering them large sums of money, the Arabs are still regarded as foreigners here even though their religion gives them a common bond with the people of this region. But I must admit there have been times when the Wazirs have sided with the Arabs or the Taliban if only to use them to fight against the Kharotis, a neighboring tribe with whom we have been warring for many years now. It is the Kharotis who are our real enemy."

"Why do you fight them?" Sheridan asked.

Noor Ghani shrugged, letting out a small laugh. "What is the cause of most wars? Land. For centuries, we Wazirs have been locked in a struggle over land with the Kharotis. They are treacherous rascals and will even betray their own fathers if it meant putting more money in their pockets. They cleverly sided with you Americans when you first came here, handing over an Uzbek terrorist to curry favor with your military. The Kharotis then coaxed the Americans into believing all Wazirs were allied with the Arabs, using your troops to harass and attack my people who resent being searched for weapons. When this happened, we had no choice but to side with the Arabs and the Taliban. They gave us weapons to fight against the Kharotis, but in so doing they wanted us to kill U.S. soldiers as well."

"It seems to me that both Al Qaeda and the Taliban have taken full advantage of your hospitality, what you call nanawateh," Sheridan said sourly.

Noor Ghani shrugged again. "It is our way."

Sheridan appeared uncomfortable. "You realize your people will remain in harm's way as long as Bin Laden or his followers stay holed up in this region."

A sly grin crept onto Noor Ghani's face, his eyes glinting diabolically. "Perhaps there is a way for me to help you without breaking the code."

This sudden shift in dialogue made Sheridan sit up straighter. "What might that be?"

"My daughter was kidnapped by the Kharotis," Noor Ghani said, his manner suddenly sullen. "This happened four days ago. She is the reason I have arranged this meeting." He fell into a gloomy silence and looked expectantly at Sheridan.

Sheridan was nearly speechless as he pondered the implications of this new development. "You want us to get her back for you, is that it?" he uttered in disbelief.

Noor Ghani nodded slowly, almost as if embarrassed by the unusual request. "Yes."

"And if we were to do you this favor, you would help us?" Sheridan pressed, folding his arms adamantly.

Sherkhan jumped to Noor Ghani's defense, seemingly grasping what the Wazir leader was offering. "He has already told us he cannot break nanawateh." Looking at Noor Ghani for his concurrence, he turned back to Sheridan and articulated what had been left unsaid. "Perhaps you will find the answers you are looking for if you rescue his daughter. Perhaps the whereabouts of Bin Laden will become apparent through such an attempt."

Sheridan dropped his gaze from Sherkhan and searched Noor Ghani's face to see if this was the actual offer. "Is this a pretext for shifting alliances?"

Noor Ghani smiled coyly. "While it is true my people resent an American presence in our land, there are some among us who have come to dislike the Arabs even more," he conceded. "They have brought us nothing but problems."

"What kind of problems?"

"By various unscrupulous means, they are slowly gaining control of our poppy trade."

Jake was well aware of Sheridan's deep-seated revulsion over heroin trafficking. It was an indisputable fact that the production of heroin was a cornerstone of the Afghan and Pakistan economies, and growing poppy was the first step in producing the addictive drug. He was therefore amazed when the Seal captain managed to keep his disgust from showing on his face.

"Would ransom be one of those means?" Sheridan asked dryly.

Noor Ghani drew back almost imperceptivity and stared at Sheridan in admiration. "You Americans are very perceptive."

"I'll accept that as a compliment," Sheridan muttered without humor. "But wasn't it the Kharotis who kidnapped your daughter?"

"Yes."

"And are they demanding a ransom for her?"

"They will only release her in exchange for a third of our farmland," Noor Ghani spat.

Sheridan remained silent for a long moment, tacitly inviting Noor Ghani to elaborate further. Something between confusion and exasperation began to manifest itself in his expression when the Wazir chieftain failed to offer additional information. "So where do the Arabs fit into all of this?" he coaxed, trying hard to keep his tone calm.

"For some time now, Bin Laden has been recruiting some Kharotis to be used as spies against American troops, bribing them with money and weapons. Through spies of our own, it has come to my attention that a neighboring Kharotis warlord by the name of Guz Khalil has taken them up on this offer. Khalil has been promised a portion of all the profits arising from the sale of poppy harvested on land controlled by Al Qaeda. It was Khalil who had my daughter kidnapped."

"Can I assume it was the Arabs who planted the idea of kidnapping your daughter in Khalil's head in order to gain control of your land?"

When Noor Ghani shrugged noncommittally, Sheridan's growing frustration became more evident. "Yeah, I know, nanawateh." Lapsing into silent contemplation for several seconds, he finally recapped the rudiments of the discussion. "So, through our intervention, you feel you can kill two birds with one stone. If we succeed in rescuing your daughter, you keep your land. In the process an opportunity may arise that pinpoints the location of Bin Laden and his cohorts, allowing us to remove Al Qaeda from this region. Is all of this correct?"

A shrewd smile sprouted on Noor Ghani's face. "You will do it?"

"You'll tell me where I can find this Khalil character?"

"I believe Sherkhan knows the way," Noor Ghani said, looking to the Seal team guide.

"Just one other thing," Sheridan said, seemingly eager to end the discussion.

"Yes."

"What's your daughter's name and what does she look like?"

"She is called Tesha. She is a beautiful child, just short of her thirteenth year. Sherkhan knows her by sight."

The Seal team rested for the remainder of the day, planning a night excursion that would take them to a remote location near Dandar Kili, a small Pakistani village situated close to the Afghanistan border. Sitting in the shade, Daniels, Myers, and Jake lounged comfortably, enjoying their special camaraderie, and entertaining each other by exchanging stories about their lives before the Seals. It was Myers who had spun the most unusual tale between the three of them.

"Haiti, you say," Daniels said. "Sounds very exotic. How long were you there?"

"Just long enough to get a taste of extreme poverty," Myers replied. "My grandfather, Mercades Myers, was a treasure hunter who ran a boat in the Caribbean. I spent a few summers with him salvaging what we could from sunken vessels."

"I take it that's where you developed your love of diving," Jake speculated.

Myers grinned enthusiastically. "Yep. Learned a lot from the old man. Taught me things you don't learn in the Seals."

"So, how'd you end up in Haiti?" Daniels asked.

Myers looked away, shifting his gaze to some distant mountains, his manner suddenly remote and reflective. "The last summer I spent with my grandfather was in Haiti, a place called Saint-Marc. I was sixteen years old." Pausing briefly, he seemed to explore something in the back of his memory before continuing. "Each day we'd take the boat outside the harbor, working the remains of an old Spanish galleon."

Jake's interest immediately perked. "You find anything of value?" The thought of finding sunken treasure had always intrigued him.

"Not at first," Myers said. "But towards the end of the summer, we started bringing up gold doubloons dating back to the sixteenth century. Let me tell you, it was one hell of a rush."

Jake had trouble containing himself. "So how much did you find?"

"Maybe a hundred coins. September was practically upon us by the time the venture began to pay off and, unfortunately for me, I had to get back to the states to finish my senior year of high school."

Still fascinated, Jake asked, "So was your grandfather still pulling up gold after you left?"

"Oh, yeah. About a week after I flew back, he hit the mother lode."

"You mean more coins."

"Coins and a lot of other things. Ingots were found, silver as well as gold, several tons of it. Jewelry and other types of valuable artifacts too, but mostly coins. Mercades called me a month after I got home to let me know the extent of the find. Claimed he had brought up close to twenty thousand doubloons. Said the haul was valued at somewhere between eighty and one hundred million dollars."

Daniels let out a loud whistle, prompting several Wazirs to look in their direction. "Good god, I had no idea we were speaking to the heir of a vast fortune."

"Hardly," Myers intoned, his demeanor suddenly turning rueful. "That phone call was the last time I ever spoke to my grandfather. He disappeared shortly after that."

The glint of something in Myers' eyes caused Jake and Mat to study him a little more closely. Lingering within them was a deep pool of anguish time had failed to erase.

Myers took hold of himself and forced a smile, realizing how melancholy he'd become. "Sorry about going wuss on you guys," he apologized, "but Mercades was special to me. I think I was closer to him than my own father."

"Did you ever learn what happened to him?" Jake prodded gently.

"Not right away, but give me a minute and I'll get to that. The whole time we were working that galleon, I had the feeling we were always being watched. Haiti is a poor, unstable country where government officials and the police are especially prone to corruption. I suppose there were a lot of people who would have happily slit our throats if they knew what we were bringing up."

"I don't claim to know much about treasure salvaging," Mat interjected delicately, "but doesn't one have to petition the local government to get salvage rights in waters under their jurisdiction? Wouldn't Haitian officials have known in advance what your grandfather was doing?"

Myers elicited an impish smile. "My grandfather was never one to follow the rules. Mercades had his own way of doing things, always skirting the law. He was always slipping money under the table to manipulate the system."

"So you think he bribed some of the local authorities to look the other way and leave his operation alone, no questions asked?" Mat pressed.

A short laugh left Myers' lips. "This I know for a fact."

"So what did you do when you didn't hear from him again?" Jake asked.

"About a month after I spoke to him, I received another phone call. One of Mercades' crew, a sidekick of his, notified me that the treasure had been impounded by the Haitian government and that Mercades and a partner of his, a man by the name of Frank Jameison had vanished. He had called from Kingston, Jamaica, telling me my grandfather's boat was berthed there at the time and that I should come pick it up. Said he'd managed to get the boat out of Haiti before the authorities could impound it."

"So what did you do?"

"Against the wishes of my parents, I left school and hopped a flight to Jamaica."

"You sailed his boat back to the states?"

Myers shook his head. "No. I ended up leaving the boat in Kingston with my grandfather's friend. We had an understanding that he'd take care of the vessel while I was gone."

A cynical frown formed on Mat's face. "Did it ever cross your mind that he might have done away with your grandfather and his partner in order to keep the treasure for himself?"

"Never. He had been with Mercades for a good ten years and was a trusted friend. He's Jamaican, a giant of a man with a normally gentle nature…well, that is if you don't piss him off. My grandfather had often told me not to judge a man solely by his outward appearance, because sometimes a huge heart lay hidden beneath a rough exterior, and that this particular man was a perfect example of that. I had come to know this individual pretty well during the summers I had spent with Mercades. If you knew this man the way I do, you would know that such a thing was not possible. He's probably the most loyal person I've ever known, the kind you'd like standing behind you in a bad situation. As a matter of fact, this fellow gave me an envelope containing one hundred thousand dollars, saying Mercades wanted me to have it if anything ever happened to him."

Mat was astounded. "Wow! Now that's trust."

Jake wanted to know more. "Did you ever go back to Haiti to find out what happened?"

"Yes I did. Before I got there I informed the U.S. State Department about what had happened. They said they'd get back to me but they never did. Haiti was in turmoil at the time, with rebellions and anarchy the law of the land. The year was 1985, just before Haiti's dictator, Baby Doc Duvalier, was ousted under pressure from our government. At great risk, Mercades' friend and I along with another man sailed the boat back to Haiti and slipped quietly into Saint-Marc harbor one night. He insisted on coming ashore with me, refusing to let me go alone. That was the type of guy he was, always protecting your back. Anyway, we touched bases with some of the locals we knew, trying to gather information on what had become of my grandfather. There was a girl there I had taken up with that last summer. Her name was Veresa. Her uncle owned a tavern in Saint-Marc. Through him she had heard rumors that Mercades and Jameison had been tortured and killed by members of Baby Doc's secret police."

Myers' voice stiffened as he uttered the last sentence, unable to speak for the moment. Mat gave him a few seconds to gather himself before pushing the conversation further. "I'd heard about the kind of men that worked for the Duvalier regime. They were mean bastards. Were you able to get any names?"

Myers' eyes narrowed darkly. "Only one name, but one I'll never forget. A man named Henri Ternier murdered my grandfather." He paused momentarily to take a deep breath. "When my stint in the Seals is over, I have a debt to settle."

Jake thought he caught something in the way Myers said this. "Is that why you joined the Seals, Flash?" he asked curiously, using the nickname Myers had acquired during Seal training. "You wanted to learn how to kill in order to even the score?"

The question seemed to catch Myers off guard for one brief moment. Apparently he hadn't expected such frank probing from his best friend. "Does that surprise you?"

It was Mat who broke the interlude of stunned silence that followed. "Revenge won't bring your grandfather back," he said softly.

Myers gave Mat a wry look. "You're throwing an overused cliché at me, something we've all heard in too many movies. This goes much deeper than vengeance. Justice has to be served. You think I should just forget about such a cowardly, despicable act? Isn't this very mission aimed at serving justice?"

"You're talking about going into a foreign country and executing a man you've never seen based on mere scuttlebutt," Mat argued. "To begin with, how do you know the rumor is true? How do you know that such a person even exists?"

"That's what I plan to find out," Myers insisted. His manner seemed to lighten as he leaned back, locking his hands behind his head as if to nap. "In any event, I'll be going back to Haiti, one way or the other." He expelled a deep sigh. "I have a son there."

"You're putting us on," Mat shot back.

"Nope."

"I take it you put Veresa in a family way," Jake deduced, smiling as he said it. "If my guess is correct, your son would be about sixteen or seventeen by now."

"He's almost eleven," Myers corrected. "But you're right about Veresa being the mother."

"So I take it you made other trips to Haiti."

"Yes, my last visit occurred in 1991, twelve years ago."

"When did you find out you had a son?" Mat asked. "I mean did you know Veresa was pregnant the last time you were in Haiti?"

Myers continued to loll reflectively. "It wasn't until two months ago I found out," he said. "Although Veresa and I kept in touch by mail, she never told me she had my kid. In the beginning, we wrote often, but then about seven years ago I stopped hearing from her."

"So how'd you find this out?"

"I received a letter from Veresa's aunt. In the letter she informed me Veresa had been killed some years earlier while visiting her in Port-au-Prince. She thought I should know I had a son."

"But how do you know it's your kid?" Mat reasoned.

"Oh, it's my kid, all right," Mat answered. Reaching under his kameez, he pulled a photo from a pocket and handed it to Mat. The photo was not recent, depicting a boy that was perhaps eight years old at most. "His name is Phillipe."

Mat scrutinized the photo carefully before handing it over to Jake. "Sorry for doubting you, old buddy, but having another with your DNA running loose on this planet is more than this world can bear, I'm afraid."

"Ha ha, very funny. You're a regular riot, Alice."

There was no mistaking the resemblance as Jake inspected the photograph. Though the boy's skin was a few shades darker than Myers', the facial features were a close enough match to suppress any doubts that the child was his friend's genetic offspring.

"Once I'm finished with the Seals, I'm going back to find him," Myers vowed, taking back the photo from Jake's outstretched hand.

Jake's eyebrows rose up. "You mean you don't know where he's living?"

"Unfortunately, no. Veresa's aunt was extremely ill when she wrote the letter. She told me she'd been shot and was trying to recover. She caught a bullet while crossing the street in one of Port-au-Prince's slums, an innocent victim of a gun battle between rival factions. In the letter, she indicated she might not survive the wound and that she feared for Phillipe's safety because there was no one else to take care of him. From the gist of the letter, outbreaks of violence are common on the streets, with crime spiraling out of control there mainly due to squalor and political unrest. That's how Veresa died. She, too, was a victim of such violence, caught up in a deadly crossfire in the wrong place at the wrong time. Anyway, since receiving that letter I've tried writing the aunt, but so far she hasn't answered my letters."

"She most likely expired," Jake said.

"It's a strong possibility. I–"

Captain Sheridan suddenly loomed above all three men. "We'll be saddling up just before sundown," he informed them. "Be ready to go as soon as it's dark." He glanced at Mat. "Would you mind taking a look at my Magellan unit, Mr. Daniels? I don't think it's currently functional." Each member of the team had unique skills, and Mat was the designated expert when it came to portable GPS systems.

After Mat got up and moved away, Myers looked at Jake strangely. "There's this thing I've been wanting to discuss with you," he confided softly, his tone oddly somber.

Jake had never seen his friend so serious. He immediately understood that whatever was sitting on Myers mind, it was a private matter meant for him, and him alone. "I'm ready to listen," he said, shifting closer in a show of confidence.

For the next five minutes, Myers went on to disclose something that had left Jake stunned, something that would ultimately determine the course of his life. By the time the team had set out in the direction of Dandar Kili, Jake was still sifting over the unusual disclosure Myers had revealed to him, all of it hinging on a promise he hadn't yet made, one he wasn't sure he could keep.

With Sherkhan leading the way, they traveled half the night through a mélange of ravines, ridges, and nameless trails. Two hours before dawn, they came upon the glow of campfires in a valley below them. It was then that Sherkhan called a halt to the expedition. Turning to Sheridan, he stepped close to the captain, keeping his voice low. "For us to proceed any farther would be unwise until we learn who burns those fires. I suggest you and your team remain here while I go on ahead to investigate."

Jake was close enough to the team leader to hear what was being said. Though each member of the team wore a radio with wire lip mikes and earpieces so they could communicate quietly and securely, Sheridan had insisted on maintaining strict radio silence during the mission unless it was absolutely necessary to break it. It was a standard precautionary measure used by Seal teams. From experience, Jake knew that radios had a tendency to develop static, sometimes spouting loud feedback and crackling at the most inappropriate times. And if the enemy happened to be close by and was similarly equipped with radios, a transmission had the potential of printing on another unit and giving your presence away.

Still wearing his NV goggles, Sheridan was able to locate Myers crouching further back behind him in the unlit terrain. Motioning the smaller man to his side through established hand signals, he redirected his gaze at Sherkhan's dark form. "This man will accompany you."

A moment of hesitation ensued before Sherkhan said anything. "Perhaps the soldier who speaks fluent Arabic should go with me. I do not speak the Arab language. If those fires belong to the Arabs, then such a man might overhear conversations that may prove valuable."

"That assumes you can get within earshot of their campsite," Sheridan whispered back skeptically. "It's probable they have sentries posted."

"I know this valley well," Sherkhan replied. "With the moon below the ridgeline, the darkness is our friend. It will give me enough cover to practically reach out and touch them. They will not even know I am there. Your Arabic translator will be especially useful under such conditions."

Sheridan hesitated with indecision. "Okay," he finally muttered. Though his tone was kept barely audible, Jake detected a faint trace of irritability in the captain's voice. "You can have both Raduyev and Myers, but I want you back here in twenty minutes. If you're not back by then, I'll assume all three of you have been captured."

Sheridan motioned Raduyev to join them before giving final instructions. "Twenty minutes is all I'm giving the three of you, otherwise the remainder of this team will be moving in on the people down there." He shifted his gaze between Myers and Raduyev. "One other thing," he stressed. "Unless you get into trouble or all hell breaks loose, I want you to continue maintaining radio silence. Is that understood?"

"Yes, sir," both men replied.

Sheridan set the timer on his luminous wristwatch. "Mark your watches starting...now!"

In the darkness, Jake could see Sherkhan nod in acceptance. "We will be back before then," Sherkhan murmured calmly. "You have my word."

"I hope so," Sheridan mumbled. "Now get moving!"

Within moments, all three men disappeared into the night.

This change of circumstance made Jake extremely uneasy. Sheridan's selection of Myers to accompany Sherkhan was a good one from a logical perspective. Myers was the smallest team member and probably the lightest on his feet among them, a man well suited for carrying out stealthy encroachments on an unsuspecting enemy. If any of them could breach the perimeter of an enemy base camp undetected, it was Myers. But he didn't trust Raduyev, plain and simple. With the Chechen at Myers back under the cloak of darkness, various possibilities came to mind, all of them iniquitous in nature. Certain that nothing good could come of this, a premonition of disaster began to take hold of him, escalating his anxiety with each passing minute. Unable to sit still any longer, he found himself sidling up to Sheridan.

"Permission to speak privately, captain?" Jake whispered.

Sheridan continued to keep his eyes trained on the fires below, but shifted away from the nearest man in consideration of Jake's request. "What's on your mind, lieutenant?"

"Begging your pardon, sir, but I have a bad feeling about this."

"Your concerns are duly noted, but we have a job to do."

From the captain's tone, Jake could tell he was annoyed, that he didn't want this operation complicated any more than it now was. "You don't understand, sir. I believe Raduyev has a vendetta against Myers. If they run into trouble, I don't think he'd go out of his way to protect Myers' back. Out there anything can happen. I'd like your permission to go on ahead as an added measure of safety."

"Permission denied," Sheridan hissed angrily. "You'll remain right here with the rest of the team. Now get back to your position."

Frustrated close to the point of desperation, Jake moved away from the team leader and joined Mat once again, hunkering down next to him. Although there was no way Mat could have heard Jake's verbal exchange with the captain, his friend nevertheless placed a consoling hand on his shoulder as if he had heard it all.

"Myers is tough," Mat whispered. "He can take-"

Both men jumped as the din of small arms fire suddenly erupted in the valley below. "Move out!" Sheridan bellowed. "We're going in."

Jake and Mat scrambled to their feet, following their leader down the slope along with the two other team members. With no need for radio silence any longer, Jake heard Sheridan speak into his lip mike. "What's your sit-rep, Six?" Six was Myers call sign. When no response ensued, the captain spoke again. "God damn it, Six, speak to me. Anybody down?"

Jake winced involuntarily as a sudden crackle of gunfire resonated harshly in his earpiece. Myers' voice suddenly cut in. "I'd love to chat with you, One, but I think we've got our hands full at the moment." A short pause ensued before Myers replied again, the cacophonous clatter of a firefight continuing to hang in the background. "Hold your position, One. We're coming back at you with a small package in tow."

Sheridan brought the team to a halt. "Come back to me, Six! Did you say you have a package?"

There was amusement in Myers' tone. "That's affirmative. Be ready to neutralize the hostiles climbing up our ass."

As Jake held his ground with the other Seals, he could have sworn Myers was actually having fun with this. Sighting over the barrel of his weapon through the NV goggles, he peered downslope and awaited the arrival of his teammates. Another minute passed before running footsteps could be heard.

"Hold your fire!" Sheridan ordered. "If that's you, Six, give me the password."

Almost immediately, the word "Copenhagen" blurted in Jake's earpiece.

"Let them pass!"

Jake watched as three forms burst into view on the terrain just below his position, the largest among them carrying something slung over his shoulder. The moment of anxiety passed as the threesome ducked down behind the temporary skirmish line formed by the team. Jake's relief was short-lived as a staccato of close-range gunfire cut the night air, sending a horde of rounds caroming angrily off some nearby rocks. In response, the team opened up on the muzzle flashes downslope of them, peppering the area with a withering storm of return fire.

Sheridan barked another command over the radio. "Grenades!"

Jake grabbed one of the four baseball grenades he carried and pulled the pin, letting the spoon spring off. Grenades like these had a four second delay, and he held it for a count of two before lobbing it in a high arc meant to shower the hostiles with an airburst of lethal shrapnel. Putting his head to the ground, he felt both the air and ground quake as five asynchronous explosions wreaked havoc on the pursuers. A prolonged scream echoed across the hills as someone cried out in pain, only to be followed by a pulsating silence.

Over the radio, Jake heard Sheridan mouth another order. "Pull back!"

With further pursuit discouraged, the team rose up and took off rapidly in the direction from which they had come. By the time they stopped to rest behind a mound of fallen boulders, they had traveled close to a thousand meters. With a steep cliff at their backs and a protective barrier of rock at their front, Sheridan posted two of the veteran Seals as lookouts to each side of their natural hideaway and once again implemented radio silence.

It was then that Raduyev set down the package he carried. Thoroughly winded from bearing such a load over the difficult terrain, he pulled back the heavy blanket that had covered what lay beneath. Through the NV goggles, Jake discerned the face of a young girl. The girl did not move, as though in deep slumber.

Sheridan kept his voice low as he addressed Sherkhan. "Are you sure this is the girl called Tesha?"

"There is no mistaking Noor Ghani's daughter. She has red hair and blue-gray eyes."

Sheridan placed a small penlight next to the girl's face, lifting one of her eyelids to confirm Sherkhan's claim. "Why is she unconscious?" Continuing with the examination, he answered his own question. "I think this girl's been drugged." He looked up sharply at the Pashtun and turned off the penlight. "What's going on here, Gullu?" he demanded.

Sherkhan shrugged as if mystified. "I am not sure. We found her in this condition."

Sheridan stared icily, awaiting something to sink his teeth into, something that would shed light on the mystery confronting him. When Sherkhan failed to offer more, Sheridan shifted his line of questioning. "How were you able to locate and make off with her so easily?" His manner was interrogative, his tone carrying the cutting edge of a machete.

Sheepishly, Sherkhan shrugged again. "Noor Ghani has a spy among the Kharotis. This man had informed him in advance when and where his daughter could be found. That is where I led your men."

With the aid of the night vision lenses, Jake was able to distinguish the imposing scowl that materialized in the captain's expression. "Why was I not told of this?" Sheridan growled. "Do you take me for a fool, Gullu?"

"Noor Ghani requested that I withhold such information. He considered it unimportant to this mission." The bland tone that had so far characterized Sherkhan was suddenly gone, his voice taking on a tenseness Jake hadn't heard before.

Jake sensed something altogether wrong with the current situation. Strange undercurrents were going on here that just didn't feel right.

The captain turned his attention to Raduyev. "Were you able to overhear anyone speaking Arabic back there, Seven?"

"I only heard two men speaking in the local Pashtu language."

Sheridan looked to Myers. "What about you, Six? Do you have anything pertinent to report?"

"It's pretty much like Gullu says. Slipping into that camp was fairly easy. Gullu seemed to know its exact layout, leading us to where the girl could be found. She was unguarded, almost as if she were a package set out for pickup by Parcel Post delivery. We didn't meet any resistance until we were on our way out."

"Who fired the first shot?" Sheridan asked.

"They did," Myers said.

"You're sure of that?"

"Yes."

"And did any of you return fire?"

Myers looked over at Sherkhan. "Gullu was the first to shoot back. Then we all began firing behind us as we ran."

The team leader nodded pensively. "Did the three of you remain in visual contact at all times?"

Myers gave the question some thought before replying. "That's affirmative, captain. We never lost sight of each other."

Sheridan let out a sigh of discontent. "What-"

One of the lookouts suddenly crowded up close to the captain, interrupting him. "We have a posse on our tail," Three blurted. "I counted twenty-six heads."

"How close?"

"About four minutes back. I could see their silhouettes coming up the rise."

From Three's vantage point, Jake knew the lookout would have had an unobstructed view of one area below them where the trail emerged over a ridgeline. With the team currently positioned along higher ground, they held a sizable tactical advantage over the men presently trailing them.

An old hand at this sort of thing, Three stared questioningly at his team leader, calmly awaiting a response. "What's your plan, sir? Do we stand and fight or do we keep moving?"

Sheridan turned his head, acknowledging Jake. "You feeling strong enough to carry the girl for the time being, Four?"

Jake knew the trail that lay before them would continue to wind its way considerably higher. What the captain was asking would challenge the limits of physical endurance of even the best-conditioned athletes, perhaps even reduce most of them to whimpering quitters as they gasped for air. The climb would be brutal under the harsh load he was forced to bear. "I think I can handle it, captain," Jake said stiffly, still unable to shake the uneasiness plaguing him.

The captain placed a hand on Mat's shoulder. "You'll be relieving Four of his burden, and then Five, once we reach the plateau above.

"Yes sir."

As the team prepared for a hasty departure, Jake reached down and, with little effort, hoisted the girl from the ground and gently draped her over his right shoulder. She was light, probably weighing no more than eighty-five pounds in his estimation. But with the grueling ascent that lay before him, the girl's weight in combination with the equipment and weapons he carried would grow progressively heavier.

With Sherkhan walking point and Three acting as rear guard, the team moved quickly up the rocky trail. They were strung out pretty good, making it difficult for an unseen enemy to take down more than one of them at one time should they walk into an ambush. Gradually they gained higher ground, and before long Jake's legs began to burn from the exertion. Forcing himself not to dwell on the pain, he ran other things through his mind. In a subtle way, the team had been steered away from its primary mission, and that was to locate the whereabouts of Bin Laden in these mountains. In helping Noor Ghani get his daughter back, they were led to believe an Al Qaeda presence might exist along the way. But so far, there was no evidence of such a connection.

As he thought about this, Sherkhan brought the team to a halt, motioning Captain Sheridan to his side. Though Jake was beyond earshot of what was being said, he sensed the team leader was being confronted with yet another decision. Standing fast, he saw Mat join the two men, and after another moment of discussion Mat came back to where he stood.

"What's going on?" Jake asked.

"The trail forks just ahead. Gullu recommends we take the branch we hadn't used before. The going will be longer, but he says there's less chance of an ambush if we go in that direction."

Mat scurried off toward the rear of the column where he conveyed this change in plans to the others. By the time the team began moving again, Jake's apprehension over impending danger had escalated several more degrees, and he kept his M4 assault rifle in low ready as he maintained a constant surveillance of the trail to each side.

The alternate footpath had less of a gradient than its predecessor, providing a more circuitous route around a cluster of nearby hills. With the uphill trek now less demanding, Jake found his legs rebounding and his strength quickly returned. The team trudged on for almost another twenty minutes before their Pashtun point man stopped the column's advance once again. Another short discussion ensued before Mat scampered back to Jake.

"Gullu's gonna take us through a cave that comes out the other side of the ridge," he said, holding his voice to a whisper. "We'll be able to pick up the original trail from there. The captain wants everyone to have their combat lights at the ready once we're inside. We're only to use them unless we absolutely have to."

As Mat moved back to inform the men to the rear, Jake checked the flashlight attached to his rifle. The device would be useful in probing the total darkness of a cave environment, illuminating any potential targets aligned with the barrel of the weapon. It would also come in handy if the NV goggles became ineffective. Unless there were sources of thermal emissions deep within the recesses of a subterranean cavern, infrared light would be minimal, rendering the night vision gear all but useless. But since all living creatures produced light in the infrared range, each member of the team would be able to see the thermal aura of the man directly in front of him, that is, all but Sherkhan.

To ensure visual contact with each other, the men stacked up closer together, one behind the other, before entering the dark maw set back in the hillside. Looking through his goggles, Jake followed Mat's glowing silhouette with no more than five feet separating them. About fifty feet beyond the entrance, Three's voice suddenly broke from Jake's earpiece, imparting a tone that dispelled any need for radio silence.

"We've got tangos coming up our rear, One. I'm still at the entrance looking back at them."

"Hold your position, Three, and keep them out of here!" Sheridan ordered, the words hissing harshly with static. "You know what to do."

"Indeed I do," Three remarked enthusiastically. "I'll catch up to you after I finish playing."

"We'll wait for you just outside the other end of the tunnel. Happy hunting, Three."

As Jake stayed on Mat's heels with the aid of his NV goggles, he wondered how Sherkhan was able to guide them through such ebony darkness without the use of such technology. The rocky passageway was not a straight run, consisting of numerous twists, turns and dead ends. Even lit, the cave would have been difficult to wend. Despite this, the Pashtun appeared to have no problems with the pitch-blackness, almost as if he had an intimate knowledge of the tunnel's precise layout. Navigating it without sight hinged on a complex sequence of memorized course adjustments, with each subsequent leg taking on a new heading followed by a specific number of paces. To do it by memory would have required making many practice runs through the dark confines with the use of a flashlight before doing it without one.

Turning left by almost ninety degrees to stay on Mat's tail, Jake felt the girl suddenly stir. He knew this was not a good thing, for if she regained consciousness in such a disorienting environment the consequences could be disastrous to the team, particularly if she cried out in panic. Her scream might carry down the length of the tunnel, alerting any unfriendlies to their presence. Much to his relief, though, the girl settled back down again, hanging listlessly across his shoulder like a wet dishrag.

Jake's relief was short-lived as the muffled sound of small arms fire from somewhere farther back brought all his senses on full alert. Sheridan was immediately on the radio. "What just happened, Three? Report!"

The question was answered with a brief burst of static, but an actual reply failed to come. Sheridan spoke again, his voice coming through Jake's earpiece hurried and tense this time. "Speak to me, Three! What's your sit-rep?"

A discomfiting silence seemed to saturate the air before all hell broke loose. The echo of sporadic gunfire resounded sharply as it was funneled through the tunnel. Sheridan's voice abruptly reverberated over the radio again, his tone ringing with confusion. "Does anyone see Gullu? Our guide is missing."

When no one responded, the captain's voice came back even more tense than before. "Somebody say something. I need answers, pe…"

Further communication was instantly cut off by a jarring blast that suddenly rocked the tunnel. Knocked off his feet, Jake lay dazed, his ears ringing like cathedral bells gone wild. Fighting his way through the cobwebs that muddled his brain, he managed to remove the night vision goggles and flick on his combat light. The air was thick with smoke and dust, and he groped blindly around him in an effort to orient himself. The inert forms of Mat and the girl he had been carrying lay nearby.

Mat suddenly stirred, letting out a low groan, and Jake lifted the NV goggles from his friend's face.

"What the hell hit us?" Mat moaned.

Jake probed the beam of his light through the dust-laden air, playing it against a mound of rock and rubble clogging the tunnel. "An explosion collapsed the cave in front of us," Jake rasped. His throat was now raw from the airborne grit he was forced to breath. "My guess is the only way out of here is back the way we-"

Jake pivoted his head at the sound of movement coming from behind them, and an instant later his eyes fell on another light bobbing toward him. Behind the light, a ghostly form materialized from the dust.

"Don't shoot!" a familiar voice blurted, causing Jake to ease up on his trigger-finger.

Myers crouched down between Jake and Mat and coughed lightly, his gaze finding the wall of collapsed rock blocking their way. "Oh, shit!" he exclaimed dismally.

"Where's Raduyev?" Jake asked.

"Gone!" Myers snarled. "I got suspicious when he started to lag too far behind me, and I followed him when he backtracked. That bastard snuck back near the cave entrance and killed Three. Shot him in the back. Sent a few rounds my way, but missed, then disappeared down a side passage."

"I knew that prick couldn't be trusted," Mat grumbled disdainfully.

Jake looked grimly from Mat to Myers. "My friends, it appears we've been set up."

Mat stared back. "You think Sherkhan led us into a trap?"

"Yeah, and Yeslam was in on it." Shifting his eyes to the girl, Jake said, "Somehow I get the feeling this girl is not Noor Ghani's daughter."

"How do you figure?" Myers asked.

Jake aimed his combat light on the girl's face. "Take a good look at her. Noor Ghani told us his daughter was thirteen years old. Does this girl look like she's thirteen?"

Under the light, the girl appeared considerably older, perhaps closer to the age of eighteen or nineteen. Unhampered by the NV goggles, Jake was able to scrutinize the girl's features more fully. Even with the dust coating her face, a serene attractiveness was all too evident. But then again, Jake recalled Noor Ghani having said his daughter was very beautiful.

"Looks can be deceiving," Mat offered. "Maybe she looks much older than she really is."

Just as Mat said this, the girl roused, opening her large eyes, and squinting into the light's harsh glare. Almost immediately she sat up and shielded her face, still groggy but clearly frightened.

Jake pulled the light away from her face and positioned it near his own so she could see him more clearly. "Don't be afraid," he whispered softly, unsure if the girl understood him. "No one is going to hurt you. Do you speak English?"

The girl nodded vigorously, her big eyes widening fearfully at the other two men hunkered next to Jake.

Jake kept his tone gentle. "Is your name Tesha?"

The girl nodded again, slower this time. "Where am I?" she said weakly, swiveling her head around apprehensively to assess the darkness beyond the light.

"You're in a cave several kilometers from Dandar Kili. I'll try to answer all your questions, but I'd appreciate it if you'd answer mine first."

The affright on Tesha's face slowly waned as she studied Jake's eyes, and again she nodded, her manner now calmer.

"Are you the daughter of a Wazir chieftain called Noor Ghani?"

A look of insult immediately gathered in Tesha's expression. "The Kharotis are my clan," she said, spewing the words out in anger. "Noor Ghani is a snake."

Jake shot a look at both Mat and Myers, noting the surprise on their faces before bringing his attention back to Tesha. "What's your father's name?"

"Guz Khalil is my father. He is a powerful Kharotis warlord."

Jake let out a dejected sigh, his throat and eyes continuing to burn from the dust still hanging in the air. He couldn't blame Sheridan for falling into the Wazir's deception, for Noor Ghani had seemed quite sincere. But the ruse had cost the Seal team dearly, and he had to assume three of his teammates were now dead, including his team leader. So far, the girl had given him enough information to conclude they had been severely tricked.

"Tesha, I'm sorry to say you have been drugged and abducted from your people," Jake said regretfully, deciding he at least owed the girl an explanation for her current situation. Though there was still a mystery to be sorted out, he knew that sooner or later he'd get to the bottom of it provided they didn't fall victim to any more of Sherkhan's treachery. "A man who calls himself Gullu Sherkhan was responsible for your abduction. Do you know him?"

The name seemed to strike a nerve within the girl, for her large eyes suddenly narrowed, pulled tight with petulance. "Sherkhan is another snake. Some say he works for Osama Bin Laden who is trying to gain control of land belonging to my people."

"What about Noor Ghani? Does he work for Bin Laden?"

"Noor Ghani has often provided sanctuary to Bin Laden and the Arabs that follow him."

Mat touched Jake's shoulder. "We better get moving, buddy. Otherwise, the posse coming after us is gonna have us trapped like rats."

"Good idea," Jake agreed, still looking at the girl. "Can you walk, Tesha?"

Wary concern crossed the girl's face. "Where are you taking me?"

"We have people after us that want us dead," Jake explained hurriedly, rising to his feet. "I'll try to get you back to your clan, but if we don't get out of here, the people pursuing us will get their wish."

The girl tried standing but faltered on unsteady legs, and Jake had to grab hold of her to keep her from falling back down. He pulled the NV goggles down over his eyes and turned off his combat light. "Lean up against me and try walking as best you can," he instructed the girl.

Tesha did as she was told and the group began backtracking the way they had come. With Myers leading the way and Mat following up the rear, they moved through the cave's ebony blackness using their night vision units to navigate. Between the weak thermal emissions left behind from the Seal team's prior passage and the heat from the explosion, there was sufficient residual infrared radiation for the NV goggles to pick up on. Jake was amazed, however, when they failed to encounter any hostiles waiting in ambush.

Five meters back from the entrance, Myers stopped, listening intently to the sound of movement coming from the rocky terrain just beyond. Turning, he moved close to Jake and pointed off to one side. "This is the passage Yeslam took," he whispered. "Whaddaya think?"

"I think we better use it before those tangos decide to send an RPG in here," Jake whispered back. "Sounds like they're preparing for a frontal assault. Either that or they're getting ready to blow the entrance."

Myers nodded in agreement, then slipped quickly into the side passage as Jake and Tesha stayed close behind. It wasn't long before Myers stopped again. "My NV unit's practically useless," he informed Jake. "I'm walking like a blind man. If we're gonna get out of here, I've got to use my light."

Jake pulled his own goggles to his forehead. "Alright," he concurred. "We'll follow your light, but Mat and I will keep ours off."

The group plodded on cautiously, aware that Raduyev could be lying in wait somewhere ahead of them. They had gone another seventy-five meters when an explosion rocked the tunnel some distance behind them. Immediately in its wake was a prolonged volley of gunfire, after which the muffled shouts of men could be heard. And then all was quiet again.

With Myers leading them higher through a seemingly endless succession of twists and turns, they finally reached a place where the passageway branched off in opposite directions.

Once again Myers stopped and looked back. "Do I flip a coin?"

Jake eyed the darkened maws, unsure which way to go.

"I know this cave," Tesha said, continuing to let Jake support most of her weight. "When I was younger I used to play with my brothers in here. If we go to the right, it will take us to the top of the rise."

"What about the left?" Jake asked.

"About fifty meters from here it becomes very narrow. Only a small child can fit through. It leads to the top of a cliff that faces the valley to the west."

Jake turned his eyes back to Myers. "You heard the girl, Flash. We go to the right."

It was ten minutes later by the time they emerged into the night air. Huddling low behind an outcropping of boulders, they were able to get a fix on their current location using the GPS coordinates provided by Mat's Magellan unit.

"I guess we better discuss our next move," Jake suggested.

"I think payback is in order," Myers announced angrily, holding his voice to a whisper. "I say we make a little visit to Noor Ghani and pay our respects."

Jake shifted his eyes to Mat. "What about you?"

"If Sheridan were still alive, he would've radioed us by now, assuming his radio is still working. I'm not sure the three of us can take on Noor Ghani's entire village by ourselves."

Jake sat silently for several seconds, taking the time to mull over these opposing viewpoints. "I think our next course of business should be getting Tesha back to her people." He glanced at the girl sitting quietly next to him. "We owe her that much."

"I don't think we'd be well received after what we did to them," Mat disagreed. "Perhaps dropping her off in Dandar Kili would be a wiser move. It's only a few klicks from here."

Jake brought his attention back to the girl. She was practically curled up against him, as if trusting his protection completely. "Do you have anything to say about this, Tesha?"

"If you please, I would like you to take me to Dandar Kili. There are people there that will send word to my father. He will come and get me."

Jake gazed stoically at Myers. "I'm also in favor of Kili." Sighing wearily, he added, "Sorry, Flash, but I guess you're outvoted three to one."

Myers nodded without complaint. "Then let's get to it. We can rehash the merits of payback once we drop Tesha off."

"Perhaps my father will help you once he learns what Noor Ghani has done," Tesha offered.

"We can always keep such an option open," Mat muttered. He rose to his feet and looked down at Myers. "I'll take point this time."

"To hell you will!" Myers shot back, standing to block his way. "A big lummox like you is too easy a target."

Mat gaped in surprise, words momentarily failing him. The lead man was always the most likely to catch a bullet, even under the veil of darkness, and Myers' more compact profile presented a smaller target.

Jake quickly interceded. "Oh, let the little man have his way if he's so eager to get shot."

"Besides," Myers added, his voice showing an overtone of cheerfulness. "Speed and grace always take precedence over slow and clumsy."

Jake could see that Myers was trying to lighten the situation. With three of their comrades now presumed dead and a fourth member of the team defecting, it was hard for any of them to project anything but a dark mood. Yet Myers, true to form, was doing just that, boosting their morale.

Mat finally found his tongue. "Forget about Noor Ghani, buddy; my first priority for payback has just shifted to you."

As they set off in single file again, Jake mulled the events leading up to their present circumstances. Gullu Sherkhan was obviously a double agent whose loyalties resided with Bin Laden. Noor Ghani was another Bin Laden sympathizer, and between them they had been able to pull off a ruse that had systematically led Sheridan into a trap. The Seal team had fallen victim to a scheme clearly hatched well in advance by unscrupulous minds, and now they were paying the price for failing to see through the deception. He was now convinced Raduyev was a mole, a one-man cell sent by Islamic radicals to acquire Seal training. With such training under his belt, he could teach others how to employ Seal tactics against American forces. And by coming here on this mission, he was able to abet a prearranged plot aimed at turning the Kharotis against their U.S. ally. What better way to do this than by making Guz Khalil think his daughter had been kidnapped by American troops?

Jake had to admit the ploy had been well thought out, a brilliant stroke of master planning. But for the plan to work, it had required the cooperation of a traitor among those who served the Kharoti warlord, a trusted follower of Khalil. Trust was needed to get close enough to the girl in order to drug her, thus preparing her for abduction. Sherkhan had not lied when he said Noor Ghani had a spy planted in the camp they had raided. And now that he analyzed it, it was highly probable that the people hot on their trail would be members of Khalil's clan rather than men aligned with Noor Ghani. That would explain why the rear entrance to the cave had not been sealed off with explosives as the front had been. With the forward exit now blocked and the Kharotis coming up behind them, they would be trapped. Noor Ghani and his cohorts wanted the Kharotis to find Tesha in the clutches of the Seal team. But the Wazir chieftain had miscalculated. He had failed to block the alternate escape route out of the cave.

An eerie chill suddenly raced up Jake's spine as he continued to dwell on Noor Ghani's blunder. No! Instinctively he realized the Wazir had not slipped up at all, and he now knew with certainty that an ambush was imminent.

"Everyone down!" Jake yelled. But even as the warning escaped his lips, he knew it was too late. Muzzle flashes lanced out of the darkness.

At close range, the staccato clatter of automatic fire assaulted his ears as he pulled the girl down to shield her with his body.

Tesha let out a horrid scream as several rounds tore through her petite form, and as they hit the ground, Jake felt her body go limp.

Jake stared dully as tracer rounds zipped overhead. With the girl so close to him, he found it hard to accept she was the one hit while he remained untouched. Reaching for the girl's carotid artery at the side of her neck, he could not detect a pulse. As if to confirm this, he became aware of the heavy smear of blood soaking the girl's chest, and he knew at once that Tesha's innocent life had been instantly snuffed out with a bullet through the heart.

A rush of adrenaline welled up deep within him as he looked down at the girl's lifeless body, and with it a wild surge of pained outrage. You bastards!

Catching sight of the muzzle flashes, Jake opened up, raking the nearby area with a savage hail from his M4. A short distance behind him, he sensed Mat doing the same thing. But up ahead, he heard no return fire coming from Myers' position.

Jake let up on the trigger and rolled to his left. Something seemed to brush his clothing, and he saw sparks fly from several rounds ricocheting off the rocky ground next to him. Arming a grenade, he held it for the count of two before flinging it. A heavy thump jolted the earth as the grenade detonated, and Jake had to hug the ground to avoid the spray of shrapnel slashing the air.

Jake lifted his head, searching out the shrieks that followed. His NV lenses were slightly askew, and he readjusted them as he scanned for movement. Rising to his feet, he spotted two distinct forms stumble and reel from behind some rocks. Drunkenly, they staggered forward, their silhouettes aglow in the greenish aura imparted by the lenses. Firing from the hip, he finished them off quickly.

Another glowing shadow materialized, rushing at him from the side, and Jake had to lean back to evade the point of the bayonet jabbed at him from the end of a Kalashnikov. Reflexively, he whipped his M4 around viciously, hewing his attacker squarely in the throat and almost taking his head off. Clotheslined, the man's feet left the ground and a dull thud resounded as he landed hard on his back. With his larynx crushed, the man let out a choking wheeze as he writhed snake-like on the ground, futilely trying to suck in breath. Unable to get air into hungry lungs, he clutched his throat with shaking hands.

"I've got your six covered, Jake." The voice was Mat's.

Jake hunkered down, unsure if any more threats were currently lurking in the dark. He glanced sharply in all directions before backpedaling toward Mat. "They killed Tesha," he hissed murderously, his rage almost pushing his voice above a whisper as he reached his friend's side. "Where's Flash?"

As if in answer, another voice rose from somewhere close by. "I finally got the little Jew." The tone was gruff and gloating, breaking off in a gush of laughter that chafed and goaded Jake with infuriating coldness.

"Show yourself, you fucking coward!" Jake bellowed.

More laughter came back at him. "I don't think so," the voice taunted delightedly. "Some visitors will be coming your way very shortly, and I am sure Guz Khalil will want to know why you killed his daughter."

Jake scanned the darkness, searching out Raduyev's position. He began reaching for another grenade, but before he could remove it, he heard Myers cry out.

"Ja…Jay…Jay!" The cry came to Jake's ears in a strained, whimpering gasp, as though uttering it required great effort.

Jake low-crawled in the direction of the sound, Mat right behind him. Myers lay on his back, one arm raised limply in the air, his head turned toward him. "Over…here!"

In seconds, Jake was on one knee cradling Myers' head and torso in his arms. Mat was beside him, lending support.

The light in Myers' eyes was fading fast, now faint as a flow of blood, black as ebony in the pale moonlight, welled up from his open mouth. "You…won't forget…our deal?" he croaked.

Jake nodded dumbly, suddenly remembering what Mat was asking of him. He had never considered it might come to this.

"Promise me!" Myers gasped, choking up more blood and focusing glazed eyes on the man holding him.

Jake could only nod, not trusting how he would sound if he spoke.

Myers groped for one of Jake's hands and squeezed, the grip surprisingly hard. "Say it!" he gurgled. "Promise me!"

For one fleeting moment, Jake forgot about Raduyev. "I...I promise," he vowed, afraid his tone would falter, but his voice suddenly firmed. "You have my word, good buddy."

The words seemed to satisfy Myers, for a smile came to his face. "You are the big brother I never had," he uttered weakly. And with that his grip went slack.

Jake gawked dazedly as Myers' head lolled to one side, the rage simmering within him like a pressure cooker about to explode.

"Jake..." Something nudged Jake's arm.

"Come on back to me, Jake."

Suddenly pulled back to the present, it took Jake a moment to realize where he was. "It never did work out quite the way that bastard planned it," he said acidly.

Mat sighed tiredly. "Cowards always run and hide." He was reminding Jake how Raduyev had scurried off into the night, disappearing completely. "But sooner or later fate catches up with them."

"Noor Ghani didn't hide."

"He'd probably still be alive had he done so."

Mat's reference evoked more memories to flash forward in Jake's mind. Leaving Tesha where she lay, they had moved as quickly as possible to elude the people chasing them. This had not been easy, for Jake would not leave without Myers. It was a Seal credo never to leave a fallen comrade behind, and in spite of Khalil's clan hot on their trail, there was no way he'd even consider it. There was nothing he could do for Sheridan and the other MIAs. In all probability, his team leader was buried under tons of rock back in the cave. But he could at least do something for Myers. Taking turns, he and Mat had carried Myers along a winding trail for several miles, eventually finding a place where they could hide his body, noting the location with Mat's Magellan unit. It had taken another five days before a Seal team was dispatched to the site, retrieving the body and sending it back stateside for full military honors.

Seeking retribution, Jake and Mat had made their way back to Noor Ghani's village just before dawn. Catching the Wazirs by surprise, they had succeeded in killing more than half of Noor Ghani's men while they slept, after which a fierce but swift fire fight had ensued. In the end, Noor Ghani and his followers all lay dead.

He and Mat had been severely reprimanded by their superiors for these actions, and they had narrowly escaped being court-martialed for going against the latest ROE protocol – Rules of Engagement. Fearful of being excoriated by a biased Liberal press for the conduct of one of its Seal teams, the Naval High Command had been harsh in its chastisement, practically throwing them under a bus. After all, innocent civilians in a peaceful Afghan village had been needlessly massacred without any provocation. Deeply embittered by this, Jake had promptly resigned his commission.

Both men reflected a moment longer before Mat broke the silence. "Well, good buddy," he said, scrutinizing his wristwatch as if suddenly aware of the time, "I've got work to do."

"I'll try staying in touch, Mat."

Mat grinned. "Yeah. Maybe we'll have a beer together later on. Don't forget about my offer. With us teamed up again, the bad guys won't stand a chance."

Jake returned the grin. "Like I said, maybe I'll just take you up on it."

Just before sailing away, Mat disappeared into the main cabin of Relentless, returning several moments later with something in his hands. Casually, he tossed it over to Jake, who stood leaning against the Angel's rail to see him off.

Jake hefted the small canvas satchel. "What's this?"

Mat stared back, smiling shrewdly. "It's a satellite phone, my insurance that you'll stay in contact. You can reach me at any time with that little gizmo. It's supposed to be encryption-secure, but then again, one can never be sure if that's actually the case seeing its government issue. Give me a call in a couple a days, okay?"

Jake looked back. "Nag, nag, nag."

Chapter 6

*T*he first rays of dawn filtered through the clear gray sky, outlining the mountains sitting in shadow to the east with brilliant hues of silver and orange radiance. A green Ford pickup, battered and belching wispy fumes of dark exhaust, made its way slowly up to the head of the wharf located in Port-au-Prince Harbor. Of the three men who got out, only one was smiling, displaying a shaggy mane of thick white hair that ran to his shoulders. He stepped forward toward a trim, tanned, and muscular individual who stood casually aloof with sinewy arms folded at the chest as if in challenge. With feet idly crossed at the ankles, the much younger man leaned up against a timber post, watching the approach of the grinning chap with the alert, intense look of a predator.

"Mister Javolyn, I presume?"

The younger man nodded.

"I'm Doctor Franklin Grahm," the older man said, extending a hand and continuing to smile disarmingly as if a frown would be impossible to achieve on so open a face.

Jake Javolyn disengaged himself from the post and clasped the offered hand. Grahm's grip was surprisingly firm and dry in spite of the early morning humidity, producing more strength than Jake would have expected from the aging zoologist.

Grahm turned and indicated his companions. "These are my assistants, Jeffrey Parker and Nicolas Henderson."

Jake assessed the others as additional handshakes ensued. Parker was short, stocky, and stoic, while Henderson, a thin, bespectacled, scholarly type, appeared somewhat brooding and pensive when measured against his amiable mentor. Both men were in their mid-twenties, most likely graduate students, he surmised. He immediately took to the older gent, automatically drawn to the man's intrinsic cheerfulness. For the time being he would withhold judgement toward the other two.

A moment of silence prevailed as all three men stared beyond Jake to the large vessel floating lazily beside the wharf, as if trying to gauge its suitability and seaworthiness.

"She doesn't look like much," Jake stated dryly, "but I'm sure she'll be able to help you fulfill any objectives you hope to accomplish on this trip."

The doctor's assistants looked skeptical, but Grahm remained enthusiastic, his deep-set jovial eyes appraising the vessel's stern. "An interesting name," he remarked. *"Avenging Angel.* I rather like the sound of it."

Jake smiled inwardly, remembering his first glimpse of the vessel. With Zimbola insisting it would be bad luck to change her previous designation, he had instead assuaged the Jamaican's superstitions by adding a prefix to the original name.

"She's a sturdy old gal and can take almost anything the sea can throw at her," Jake said, acknowledging his vessel proudly. "She and I have been through a lot together. To me, she is an angel."

The reverent affection in Jake's tone did not go unnoticed by Grahm. "Mr. Hennington informed me you have all the necessary dive gear, and you could provide the three of us with complete scuba rigs," Grahm said zestfully.

A broad smile blossomed on Jake's face, imparting a salient handsomeness to his features. All traces of his previous aloofness dissolved into an accommodating congeniality. "Everything you'll need is aboard this vessel. She's even equipped with surface-supplied air, complete with diver-to-surface communication and real-time underwater video recording capability. If you want to undertake especially deep dives, we also have various arrays of mixed gas available to extend your bottom time and reduce the duration of in-water decompression you would normally need on compressed air."

Parker's forehead wrinkled in interest. "I assume you mean nitrox."

"Both nitrox and heliox," Jake declared, taking pleasure at Parker's surprise.

Henderson frowned. The use of nitrox was rapidly gaining acceptance among members of sport and scientific diving communities who liked the challenge of going deep. But having heliox - a gas mixture of helium and oxygen - at their disposal was quite unexpected since it was primarily applicable to exceptionally deep salvage work or ocean-based oil wells where saturation dives were routinely carried out. "I don't think we'll have any need of helium in our breathing mixtures," he said, his tone supercilious. "We-"

Grahm cut his protégé off. "It seems you're better equipped than we had expected, Mr. Javolyn."

"You can call me Jake." He would reserve his preferred name once he knew Grahm better.

"As you wish, Jake. We had to pack rather hastily, so we only brought along the most essential gear. Is it all right if we bring these items aboard your boat?" Grahm pointed to an assortment of cases and luggage resting on the bed of the pickup.

"No need for you or your assistants to move them," Jake said. "I'll have Phillipe and Hector, two of my crew, bring it all aboard."

Fifty minutes later, the *Avenging Angel* was well underway, winding a course through one of the most difficult harbor entrances on the planet. Having safely stowed the gear of the passengers, Hector had remained up on deck with Grahm's two assistants while Phillipe stayed busy in the equipment locker preparing gear.

Parker and Henderson seemed content to linger in the mild sea breeze, glad to get some relief from the intense heat and humidity of Port-au-Prince's sweltering weather. Such conditions were palpable forces, causing every movement to take far more effort than they were accustomed to.

With Zimbola at the helm in the pilothouse, Jake and Dr. Grahm remained in the vessel's forward cabin. Jake followed the path Dr. Grahm's finger traced over the nautical chart laid before them.

"This is where I'd like to start," Grahm said. He pointed to a tiny teardrop-shape lying in the Windward Passage some forty miles west of Haiti.

Jake nodded knowingly. "Navassa Island, I'm familiar with it. It's a desolate hunk of limestone."

"Yes, but it's also a marine scientist's dream. The submerged coral shelf is one of the most intact and thriving ecosystems in the Caribbean."

There was something in Grahm's voice that made Jake look up. "Mind clueing me in on what you plan to do there."

The doctor remained silent for several seconds, seeming to weigh something of great significance. "Before I get to that, I think I should fill you in on a few things."

Jake didn't bother to divulge what he already knew about the man's work.

"Tursiops truncatus, better known as the bottlenose dolphin, is one of the most interesting creatures on the face of the earth," Grahm said. "The bottlenose has the second largest brain to body size ratio of any animal, topped only by human beings."

A smile crept onto Jake's face. "I've had more than a few encounters with the species."

"Then you know that they live in social groups that are highly structured in the way they function. Although there is major disagreement in scientific circles as to how intelligent dolphins are, particularly since it's difficult to define just what intelligence is, the collective opinion is that dolphins are exceptionally intelligent creatures. To survive in their groups, more precisely called pods, they must behave and communicate according to complex rules. A few scientists, myself included, have theorized that the complexity of this group interaction is the actual reason behind their highly evolved state of intelligence."

Grahm hesitated, collecting his thoughts. At that moment, the boat's intercom buzzed and Jake toggled a nearby switch. "What is it, Zimby?"

A disembodied voice filled the cabin. "We'll be clearing the harbor soon. What heading you want me to take?"

"Steer a course of two-seven-five," Jake said.

"Two-seven-five it is, Jay Jay."

"How long before we reach the eastern side of the island?" Grahm asked, seeming anxious to get there.

Scrutinizing the chart, Jake did a mental calculation. "The sea is relatively calm. ETA will be roughly oh eight three oh, give or take several minutes."

Grahm nodded and continued with his lecture. "Did you know that the bottlenose has a cerebral cortex about forty percent larger than a humans? Their cortex is stratified in much the same way as ours, with their frontal lobe developed to a level comparable to man's. However, their parietal lobe, the part of their brain which interprets the senses, is larger than the human frontal and parietal lobes combined."

The marine zoologist paused to study the puzzlement on Jake's face and grinned out of sympathy. "In other words, the dolphin brain has evolved to analyze sensory information to a much greater degree than our own. In addition, they have a higher neural density in some parts of their brain than humans, especially those areas that deal with such things as emotional control, objectivity, reality orientation, logically consistent abstract thought, humor, and creativity. This seems to be correlated with a dolphin's ability to maintain a healthy emotional state while in captivity. Humans in similar situations often don't fare as well emotionally."

Jake listened attentively. He had always been fascinated with dolphins. There was something about those amazing creatures that struck a resonant chord deep within him. He remembered quite vividly his first up-close encounter with these streamlined marine mammals while on maneuvers with Seal Team Six off Bermuda. The pod had been large, foraging and chittering away quite noisily just beyond his visual range as he flippered along at a depth of roughly thirty feet in the clear pristine water. Two bottlenose had suddenly burst into view, apparently inquisitive about his presence. They had darted and swooped in close, making a succession of rapid passes, emitting a series of clicks, whistles, and beeps as they did so. Finally, the larger of the pair had overcome its caution and swam to within arm's reach of him, remaining almost stationary as it surveyed him with that peculiar perpetual smile characteristic of the species. As Jake had stared into its black inscrutable orbs, something had moved deep within his soul, something akin to peace and bliss. In that instant of time, he had somehow perceived that he was gazing upon an evolved spiritual entity, and a profound though inexplicable connection transpired. An eternal bond had been born, not specifically with the creature floating before him, but a link that embraced the species and all its closely related cousins. From then on, he would forever be incapable of seeing any harm come to such beings, and instinctively he knew they would never bring harm to him.

Following that mystical experience, Jake had gotten the opportunity to work directly with a team of five specially trained bottlenose dolphins during a mine clearing exercise in the Iraqi port of Umm Qasr following the fall of Saddam Hussein. During that period, he had been loaned out to assist the Navy's Special Clearance Team One, a mine-clearing unit out of San Diego, California. He had been assigned to the unit in order to replace one of the unit's human divers who had impaled a leg on a sharp shard of metal jutting above the mud line in the area where the diver had been working. Jake had quickly learned about the astounding echolocation capabilities of these creatures, a kind of biological radar used for assessing their surroundings. By using both high and low clicking vocalizations, objects hidden from sight such as mines are revealed once the emitted sound waves are bounced back in the dolphin's direction. Developed over fifty million years of evolution, dolphin sonar was incredibly precise for locating mines or other objects in cluttered shallow-water harbors where electronic military hardware is rendered virtually useless.

Jake remembered the words of Lieutenant Gary Watson, the officer in charge of the M-7 series of mine-clearing dolphins. "They can distinguish and pick out objects like you wouldn't believe under the murkiest conditions, even down to detecting different types of metal." The memory of an M-7 bottlenose named Reno stuck with him. Upon locating a mine, the animal would return to its handler to be given a transponder, which was then dropped near the ship-destroying device so that divers like Jake, who were skilled in explosive demolition, could home in on and detonate with an explosive charge.

Based on that experience, Jake understood one thing for certain, that a dolphin's built-in sonar far surpassed the performance of any state-of-the art equipment produced by man. Not only could it clearly discern the size, shape, and texture of a submerged object, it could also gauge its density. Furthermore, according to Lieutenant Watson, no one had yet been able to jam or distort a dolphin's sonar. The lieutenant had demonstrated some of these remarkable abilities when he tossed a single air rifle BB shot a distance of perhaps seventy feet from their Zodiac. It had taken Reno less than thirty seconds to locate, retrieve and return it to Watson's hand. "They are exceptionally adept at directionalizing their sonar beams," Watson had explained.

"Are you with me, lad?" Grahm asked, bringing Jake back to the present. "You seem like you're a million miles away."

Jake suppressed his embarrassment. "So that big brain of theirs is designed to make sense of acoustic signals in such a way that they're able to see with their ears."

Grahm looked pleased. "Very good, Jake my lad. A dolphin gets the same input from its ears that we get from our eyes. Since their brain is much more acoustically oriented than ours, they are able to generate visual images based on auditory input, paralleling our own subjective experience of visual models. The neurological pathways and the brain area devoted to auditory processing in dolphins matches quite closely with that of the visual processing mechanism in humans. By means of its emitted sonar signals, a dolphin constructs a three-dimensional visual world around itself exactly as humans do with electromagnetic light waves reflected off their surroundings. Because of the reversal in the sizes of the human and dolphin visual and auditory brain cortices, one might say that the dolphin is able to hear as well as we can see and see as well as we can hear, or perhaps better on both counts.

Grahm glanced out a starboard window at the gentle heave of the sea as the trawler pursued a westerly course, then turned back to Jake. "Now here comes the interesting part, the part about how dolphins communicate with each other. Up until recently, most researchers attempting to analyze the sounds dolphins make have erroneously assumed that they communicate auditory information in the same linear, analytical form as humans do. Such an assumption, unfortunately, keeps leading to the same dead-end. A better approach to understanding their means of communication would be to assume that dolphins can reproduce or mimic the sounds they hear, or actually see. Let's call the process of a dolphin sending out sonar waves to see its environment as speak-see. In addition, let's refer to what they perceive through the signals bounced back to them as hear-see. By recreating the hear-see sounds, dolphins are then able to relate events from distant or remote time-space coordinates to other dolphins. Let's call this mimicking or recreating process, picture-speak. Based on this, a complete communication cycle or loop between dolphins would be something like the following. One dolphin performs a reconnaissance of its environment by speak-seeing. It then mimics the sounds reflected back from its surroundings by picture-speaking. A second dolphin hear-sees the message from its immediate environment and remembers it. That dolphin, in turn, picture-speaks these same arrangements of noise to other dolphins, ultimately creating a kind of virtual reality around its neighboring dolphins."

"Has such a hypothesis been proven?" Jake asked.

Grahm let out a great sigh. "Not conclusively. But there's a wealth of supporting evidence which makes such a theory plausible."

"For instance?"

"Well, the best example involves a pod of orcas swimming among a flotilla of fishing vessels. Orcas, better known as killer whales, as I'm sure you know, are another type of dolphin. Anyway, when one of the harpooners killed a member of the pod, the remaining whales began to avoid only those boats rigged with harpoon guns, continuing to approach the other vessels lacking such a killing device. Except for the harpoon guns, those other vessels presented the same exact overall configuration as the killing vessels. Yet the whales correctly perceived the non-harpoon vessels as no threat. That a verbal, linear analytical description of the potential killing vessels would suffice as an effective form of communication to keep the entire pod clear of just those particular vessels seems highly unlikely since the descriptions of the harpoon guns would have required a high degree of exactness for the whales to differentiate between boats. But by transmitting a visual image of the harpooning itself, the whales receiving the image would have no trouble distinguishing the harpoon vessels from the fishing boats that didn't have them. Such an acoustically sent message would be analogous to a holistic pictorial movie reel or TV news report."

"This is all very interesting," Jake said. "So, whereas one of us spinning a tale in words will cause our audience to conjure up images in their minds, a dolphin telling a story has the ability to bypass verbiage because it can project those images directly to its listeners."

Grahm appeared to be pleasantly satisfied with Jake's understanding of his discourse. "Yes, but whereas in humans the conjured images are internally visual, the images the dolphin receives will be externally visual."

"I see what you mean," Jake remarked thoughtfully, digesting this information, and searching for flaws in such a postulate. "But how does a dolphin distinguish the virtual presentation of a spoken picture from the actual picture of its current environment?"

"A good question," the scientist said, "and one that I haven't as yet been able to provide an explanation for. All I can tell you is there must exist some perceptual clues which would allow a dolphin to distinguish a spoken environment from a real one. A human can watch the comedian Rich Little impersonate Sean Connery and still know it's not Sean Connery. With dolphins, it's probably possible for them to become so enraptured in an unreal, virtual environment, one transmitted by a skilled picture-speaking member of their own or a neighboring pod, that they actually tune out their real surroundings for a time. Such a scenario, however, could be potentially detrimental to their safety. In safeguarding against this, their basic survival instincts would most likely cause some portion of their awareness to be attentive to the approach of predators or food."

Jake smiled in understanding. "So if we put an anthropomorphic spin on what you've just described, it would be like you or I watching and listening to a videotape and an actual speaker at the same time. In such a situation, we would alternately pay attention to one and then focus in on the other."

"That's a very good analogy, lad. Like humans, the architecture of the dolphin brain shows two distinct hemispheres. But unlike humans, each half has its own separate blood supply, a trait exclusive to dolphins. This may account for their independent eye movement, which has led many scientists to believe they are capable of sleeping one of the hemispheres, while the other hemisphere remains conscious and vigilant. In any case, there is strong evidence to show they use the two hemispheres completely separate. This allows them to produce clicks with one side of the brain, while the other side can simultaneously produce whistling. Because dolphins have a right and left nasal passage, with each passage containing a separate phonation apparatus, a given dolphin can have each hemisphere of its brain carry on an isolated conversation completely out of phase with the opposite hemisphere. Thus, if the left half of the brain is having a whistle conversation, the right side can be having a clicking conversation, with each half acting completely independent of the other. The reverse of this can also occur, but the two halves cannot both be whistling or clicking at exactly the same time. Such a dual communication mode is very efficient when two dolphins converse since it permits them to simultaneously speak-see and picture-speak. Therefore, letting each to see the other dolphin and to communicate with it all at once. The two kinds of sonic exchanges, that is, clicking and whistling, do not occur at the same time and there is a politeness involved on the part of the dolphins whereby the one receiving or listening will not interrupt the one sending or transmitting. If one dolphin transmits a click train, the other will listen and refrain from clicking, although it may emit whistles while it is receiving the clicks."

Jake suppressed a laugh. "No wonder it sounds so noisy when a school of dolphins is in the vicinity of a dive. I guess what you're saying is that one pair of dolphins communicating will actually sound like two pairs talking, one pair exchanging clickings and the other pair exchanging whistles."

Grahm gave an encouraging nod. "The need to take turns seeing and talking makes a pod sound much larger than it actually is even though the seeing and talking proceed concurrently."

"It kind of makes sense for them to be polite and take turns speaking," Jake agreed. "With each dolphin creating a picture-speak virtual reality, it would be rude to modify that picture while they were talking."

The marine scientist seemed to appreciate Jake's grasp of the subject. With a twinkle in his eyes, he went on to explain that the two phonation mechanisms in the dolphin's nasal passages can be linked to each other to produce a stereo-location process during execution of the speak-see channel. Dolphins also have a third sonar emitter in the larynx especially constructed for the projection of an ultrasonic beam. Grahm further indicated that if the speak-see process is, in fact, a stereo-location operation and the picture-speak process is a non-stereo operation, such a difference would allow dolphins to distinguish between the virtual and non-virtual realities. He pointed out that whereas in humans the process of seeing is an input operation only, with human eyes acting strictly as receptacles for visualizing the world around us. A dolphin's ears and phonation apparatuses, by comparison, provide it with both receptacles and transmitters of visual information.

Jake studied the garrulous doctor for an extended moment before replying. "This is all very intriguing, but what's your objective in telling me all this?"

The expression on Grahm's face seemed to indicate he had been anticipating such a question and he smiled effusively. "Don't you see," he gushed, "the processes by which a dolphin receives and communicates information are perfectly suited for computer modeling. Such a model would bridge the gap between the two most complex biocomputers on the planet, the mind of man and the mind of the dolphin."

Jake became solemn. "Somehow I get the feeling you've made some progress in this direction."

Grahm's face lit up like that of a child in a candy store. "Yes we have. Up until about eighteen months ago, progress had been exceedingly slow, moving at a snail's pace, you might say. Initially there were some major hurdles to overcome, primarily because we were dealing with a species that is acoustically oriented, as opposed to humans who are visually oriented. While a dolphin's visual system operates at one-tenth the speed of ours, their sonic and acoustic systems more than compensate for such a weakness by functioning at a rate ten times faster than our own. In other words, dolphins can absorb through their ears the same amount of information in the same amount of time that we are capable of taking in through our eyes. This presented my team with the problem of developing some highly complex algorithms that could solve the sonic picture language of the dolphin, algorithms that had the capacity to decipher various arrangements of acoustical noise by training a computer neural network to recreate those signals and convert them to recognizable visual images that we could understand. The process was incrementally tedious, to say the least, much like decoding the Rosetta stone. By reversing the process via the use of ultrasonic transducers with similar operating characteristics as the dolphins, we could use the neural net to picture-speak back to the dolphins. Henderson pretty much took care of the monumental task of programming a Mac OS X and Macromedia Director on a Mac G4 with Velocity Engine that would allow us to do this."

"You're getting a bit ahead of me, doc. You mentioned something about eighteen months ago?"

"That was when we found Natalie."

"Natalie?"

"An injured female bottlenose dolphin. We found her stranded on a desolate stretch of beach on the island of Jamaica during a previous research expedition. Seven others of her species had also beached themselves, but they were already dead. As best we could tell, the injuries sustained by Natalie and the others were consistent with those caused by a concussion-type pressure wave that results from detonating an explosive charge underwater. She was in pretty bad shape when we discovered her, but we were able to get her aboard our research vessel and bring her back to Miami. Somehow she survived the trip and once we got her back to our facility, we were able to nurse her back to good health rather quickly. As we would soon discover, finding Natalie was an unbelievable stroke of good fortune for us, for she not only proved to be exceptionally intelligent relative to her species, she became the key to greatly accelerating our program. In human terms, her intellect was comparable to that of an Einstein. Almost immediately, she seemed to figure out what we were trying to achieve, and within one month we had learned the equivalent picture-speak vocalizations of several hundred concepts which had meaning to both humans and dolphins alike, concepts such as food, help, up, and shark. In short order we learned how to effectively communicate with dolphins."

"That's incredible!"

"In more ways than you'd believe possible. Our database is now quite extensive, filled with numerous combinations of clicks and whistles. These are used as a baseline of comparison for sound recognition. The computer can then convert the sound trains into visual images and, in most cases, accompanying English language, making it fairly easy for us to understand. If we choose, we can reverse the process, using

English syntax as a means of conveying a certain concept and having the computer convert that concept into a delphine sound. This allows us to project a picture-speak sound train back to the dolphin."

"Have you been able to carry on an actual conversation using this method?"

Grahm's brow bunched like two white beetles, making the frown look out of place on his normally upbeat demeanor. "With the exception of only a few instances where the exchange consists essentially of a simple query followed by a snap reply, we haven't yet figured out when to pause our side of the conversation in order to be polite. And despite the super speed of the computer system we use, it's unable to process the signals fast enough to keep up with a dolphin's rapid-fire emission of complex picture-speak sonar which will convey multiple concepts during a conversation."

"It sounds like your system operates on the same principles as mechanical sonar."

The marine zoologist flashed another smile. "Lad, with that inquisitive mind of yours, you should have been a scientist." He drew a deep breath before continuing. "This system is far superior to the type of sonar found aboard most submarines. It can emit complex signals in the same way a dolphin does to assess its surroundings. But its true value lies in the way it can convert the reflected sounds into a holographic picture on a detailed level."

"So, what you're saying is it can both speak-see and hear-see."

"Thanks to Natalie, we've made great strides in that direction, but only on a very basic, rudimentary level. By rudimentary, I'm alluding to what a dolphin would probably consider it. But I believe most members of our own species would deem it a marvelous technological breakthrough. We've built our first stand-alone working prototype that houses such technology. It's considerably smaller and has far less capacity than the computer system back home, but it's portable and diver friendly. Henderson was instrumental in developing it. He's a brilliant electronics engineer."

Jake leaned back, clasping his hands behind his head in a lazy manner. "So that's what this trip is all about. Testing this unit of yours."

Grahm shook his head, and for the first time since meeting the man, Jake noticed a lugubrious sadness come over him. For several seconds the scientist stared dismally out the starboard window before turning back to Jake.

"The purpose of this trip is twofold. To investigate an anomaly we've discovered, but most important, to find Natalie," Grahm corrected.

"You lost her?"

"In a manner of speaking, yes." The words were spoken very softly. "We felt it necessary to get her back to her natural habitat and monitor how she communicated with other dolphins outside the artificial laboratory environment, so we radio-tagged her."

Grahm noticed Jake's puzzlement. "Dolphins have no prehensile extremities for manipulating their environment, and contrary to the human preoccupation with controlling the world around us, the dolphin's intelligence, it seems, has gone in a direction counter to ours. Their thoughts are quite different from ours and have been left to develop inwardly over more than fifty million years of evolution. Compare this to the paltry two million years during which the hominid mind has grown outward. Overall, dolphins appear to display an emotional stability that easily surpasses that of humans, and unlike us, rely heavily on one another for their survival. That their culture is totally different from our own cannot be denied. But I am even more convinced that they have an intelligence at least equal to our own, if not greater. As I've already indicated, Natalie is very unusual for a bottlenose dolphin. Among other things, her skin tone is albino, completely white over her entire body, a rare occurrence among her kind. She also had a long scarification along her left flank. But her most distinguishing feature..." Grahm hesitated and watched Jake closely. "Her most distinguishing feature was the prehensile extensions that jutted from beneath her pectoral fins."

At first Jake thought the doctor was putting him on, but something subliminal stirred in a back corner of his mind, and a troubling memory suddenly came to life.

"Hands!" The word leapt from Jake's mouth in a flash, and a sense of hopeful relief began to circulate within his brain. "You're telling me she had hands?" he pressed.

The doctor let out a small laugh, amused by Jake's enthusiastic outburst. "Oh, yes. Natalie had the equivalent of hands. The amazing thing was she could actually grasp and manipulate objects with them."

"A mutation?" Jake asked, finding it difficult to restrain his interest.

"I would call it more of an evolutionary jump," Grahm surmised. "What I didn't tell you earlier was that all of the other beached dolphins we found near Natalie exhibited the same set of appendages. Natalie, however, was the only albino among them."

Jake mulled this over. The memory lodged at the back of his mind continued to haunt him like a shadowy wraith.

"Surprisingly," Grahm went on, "all the appendages were retractable, forelimbs that folded up and came in tight against their bodies much the way the wings of a bird fold upon landing. They could be pulled in so as not to induce any drag on the pectoral fins. In this way, Natalie and her cousins were able to maintain a streamlined configuration when swimming fast. Anyway, scientific curiosity got the better of me and I thought if we released Natalie back into the wild, we might be able to track her back to her pod and possibly find more like her. Since most Caribbean bottlenose travel in relatively small groups, it's unlikely Natalie's pod would have exceeded more than twenty-five in number. And with seven of them already dead, it was doubtful we'd locate surviving members possessing those same anatomical irregularities. But it was worth a try. So, about three months ago, we brought Natalie back near the beach where she was found and attached a satellite linked radio transmitter to her. Radio telemetry linked to satellites is a marvelous tool for tracking a dolphin's movements, particularly when the unit is augmented with a microchip transponder that can record sequences of dolphin biosonar and then send it back to us in the form of compressed sound trains."

Once again, Grahm brought his signature smile to bear on Jake, searching for comprehension.

"So you could communicate with her from far away," Jake acknowledged.

"The communication was only one-way, from her to us. Although we couldn't communicate with her, we could actually see what Natalie's reflected sonar pulses brought back to her, the hear-see mode of her reflected transmissions once the Mac G4 did the processing. No matter what Natalie's position was in terms of latitude and longitude, her sonar transmissions could be received back in Miami for visual interpretation by the computer. The two-dimensional image could then be redirected back to the vessel we were aboard."

"Extraordinary!" Jake muttered, deep in thought. "Could this device also record and send pictures of what Natalie was seeing above the water?"

"Unfortunately, no. The Delphine Biosonar Transmitter, or Dee Bee Tee as I like to call it, was designed to record water-based sounds only. For the device to work correctly, it was essential that it be immersed in a hydrous medium to receive signals."

"So what happened with Natalie?"

"For seven straight days we were able to keep track of Natalie's movements, catching glimpses of her surroundings even though we couldn't keep up with her. On the open sea, she was an incredibly fast swimmer. Even among normal bottlenose dolphins, she would have been considered to be exceptionally fast, and unfortunately the vessel we were using had a top speed of only nineteen knots. So within a span of only two days, more than fifty miles separated us."

An intense sadness overcame the doctor once more. "Natalie was near the Haitian coast when we lost her signal."

Jake eyed the scientist intently. "And that was about three months ago, you say."

"Yes."

"And where precisely was Natalie when you lost her signal?"

"Well, I'd have to consult my notes to give you the exact global position, but I recall it was near the coastal town of Anse. Why do you ask?"

Now it was Jake's turn to smile. "Because I think I had an impromptu meeting with your dolphin."

Chapter 7

G rahm listened with enraptured attentiveness as Jake related his encounter with Natalie. The *Avenging Angel* had been sitting at anchor, quietly bobbing in the gentle swells that slowly rolled seaward above a coral reef of jagged, irregular topography, approximately one mile from the Haitian coastal town of Anse.

At a depth of sixty feet and hovering another ten feet above an outcropping of mostly dead coral covered in fleshy algae, Jake had been caught totally off guard as something grabbed hold of his left arm from behind and tugged with shocking, startling power, jerking him sideways. At first he thought it was Zimbola who had latched onto him and who had entered the water with him some ten minutes earlier to reconnoiter another section of reef, for Jake had heard no telltale clicks or whistles to herald the approach of a nearby dolphin. With a pounding heart and adrenaline surging, Jake could not mistake the torpedo-like shape that shot past and disappeared in the subaqueous gloom. Underwater visibility had not been particularly good during the dive, limiting his field of vision to perhaps forty feet at most in a water column that held considerable amounts of particulate matter moving laterally with the mild current. So close to shore, such organic pollution was not uncommon with a nation of nine million people having no sewage treatment facilities, nor sanitary landfills. Such human waste contributed significantly to the growth of fleshy algae, which tended to smother and kill off delicate corals and sponges.

Confusion engulfed Jake as he realized something still continued to clutch his arm. He spun and stared with disbelief at the ghostly apparition floating beside him. Except for an elongated indentation running along its left side, the skin was smooth, white and pliable as it brushed up against him. He glanced at the pectoral flipper that overlapped his arm and wondered how it could grip with such vice-like strength, then abruptly became aware of the finger-like appendages protruding from the base of the flipper. At least that's what he thought he saw a split second before the claw released him. In an instant, the creature turned to face him. The bottlenose dolphin let out a series of chirps as it peered through Jake's face mask, its permanent smile somehow giving Jake solace in the midst of his bewilderment. Jake looked again to the base of the mammal's pectoral flippers to confirm the impossible, but nothing jutted from the underside of the creature's lateral rudders. He must have been hallucinating. Then Jake noticed a small mechanical object strapped behind the dolphin's dorsal fin.

The dolphin suddenly let out with a loud piercing squeal, galvanizing Jake. He failed to spot the returning short-finned Mako until it was almost upon him. Possessing a length of twelve feet and a girth that suggested at least half a ton, the shark was about as big as a Mako gets and a good three feet longer than the white dolphin next to Jake. The large predator streaked to within arms-length before veering off, flashing a band of silver that separated a rich ultramarine dorsal surface and snowy underbelly as it shot past. Classically opportunistic feeders, this particular Mako radiated a mean-tempered aggressiveness, probably driven by hunger. This was understandable since overfishing in the vicinity of the island had greatly reduced fish populations. And although fishing permits were required by law, the number of active fishing boats dramatically exceeded the number with permits, causing fishing to become so intense that few fish reached reproductive size. Jake also knew that in warm tropical oceans, Makos notoriously liked to swim deep, preferring the cooler water below 650 feet. The fact that this one was hunting relatively shallow waters attested to its hunger, and it was not to be denied its meal.

Propelling itself stiffly through the water with short strokes from a thick, powerful tail, the Mako turned and swooped in again with muscular efficiency, its pointed conical snout rushing forward with the effortless thrust of a guided missile. Jake recognized the severity of danger confronting him and instinctively pulled the short bang stick from the scabbard strapped to a thigh. He had no doubt that he was in deep trouble.

Makos were the fastest of all sharks, let alone most fish in the sea. Although some shark experts maintained the isurus oxyrinchus was capable of speeds bordering on sixty miles per hour, more conservative estimates held them to top speeds of twenty-two. Short-finned Makos were known to leap as high as fifteen to twenty feet above the sea, making them the most spectacular game fish on the planet. And with their lower teeth always erect, Makos appeared as one of the meanest looking animals on earth. The teeth of a big Mako are huge in comparison to the more rounded pearly whites of smaller specimens. Resembling curved knives set in the jaw, they are flattened on the forward surface. When not in use, the teeth of most sharks remain in a laid-back position. Only when the mouth is opened do the teeth assume a vertical attitude. This phenomenon occurs to a limited extent with the Mako, but its lower teeth are perpetually bolt upright, serving to give such a shark a snaggletoothed and fearsome visage, the kind of which nightmares are made.

Time seemed to slow down as Jake watched the big shark bore down on him, as if the monster moved in slow motion. With his right hand, he held the 12-inch bang stick straight out, arm fully extended as the shark's jaws gaped wide to display its full arsenal of frightening weaponry. At the last second, a white blur slammed with crunching force into the side of the beast, deflecting its charge. The collision tumbled Jake backwards and when he regained his senses, he realized he still possessed the bang stick, its 12-gauge shotgun cartridge still not discharged. An inky cloud billowed around him, and he noticed the welling of blood emanating from the grisly gash in his left forearm where the Mako's teeth had raked him. Stunned and confused, the shark turned sluggishly. Almost too quick to follow by eye, the white bottlenose streaked in once more, ramming its rigid beak into the long gill slits of the monster. Jake saw his opportunity and kicked wildly toward the stricken predator wavering dazedly no more than fifteen feet from him. He readjusted his grip on the bang stick in preparation for an overhand strike. With the killing tip pointing downward, he jammed the cartridge into the head of the beast, between its black malevolent eyes. The stick bucked with brutal shock as the round exploded, causing Jake's hand to go numb. The fired slug tore through cartilage and brain matter, a killing thrust that rendered the shark a drifting hulk in an instant. Jake watched the creature slowly capsize and jerk spasmodically as it tumbled lazily toward the bottom.

The shark finally came to rest between two mounds of bleached brain coral where it remained motionless.

Jake looked around for his savior, but the albino dolphin was nowhere to be seen. A glint of metal near the dead Mako grabbed his attention, and upon swimming closer, discerned it to be the same mechanical device he had observed strapped to the bottlenose. He glanced hopefully about once more, and disappointed at not spotting his benefactor, he retrieved the fallen object.

"A most interesting story," Grahm said. The scientist's words pulled Jake back to the present. "That certainly explains why we lost the signal. Do you still have the unit?"

Jake nodded somberly and opened a nearby cabinet. He pulled out an oblong object that fit snugly into the palm of his hand, gleaming with the characteristic shine of stainless steel. A length of nylon strap hung loosely from an intact clip on one side of the device, but it was obvious that the opposing clip had been sheared away.

Grahm examined it thoughtfully before lifting it from Jake's hand, and then said, "If the microchip isn't damaged, Natalie's perception of the episode you just described will be stored in its data bank."

The statement surprised Jake. "Wouldn't you already have seen it?"

Grahm lifted his face from the contraption to acknowledge Jake. "This unit can only relay information when above the ocean surface. When submerged, the water greatly attenuates the signal."

Jake's expression flooded with understanding. "I get it. Natalie never breached the surface during the shark attack, so you wouldn't have received a transmission."

"That's correct. But the device has limited storage capacity. Once its bank is full, it will broadcast a compressed signal at the first opportunity in order to free up space for new information, and that would require the dolphin to come up for air."

Jake's eyes narrowed. "Wouldn't it have transmitted when I pulled it from the water?" he countered.

"It should have, but apparently it did not," the scientist said, retrieving a small kit of Allen wrenches from an accessory waistband and pulling one out. "I suspect the micro-transmitter may have been damaged from the impact." He began to unscrew the housing.

Jake eyed Grahm appraisingly. "There's just one other thing, doc."

Grahm raised an eyebrow, continuing to putter with the unit. "Yes lad, what is it?"

A short silence followed, just long enough for Jake to give his question special significance. "Could Natalie speak English?"

The scientist looked up sharply and locked eyes with Jake. "Why do you ask?"

"Because I could have sworn your dolphin yelled out a warning just before the Mako made a second run at me," Jake said, his voice conveying both skepticism and certainty all at once.

Grahm held his gaze, staring expectantly. "What do you think you heard her say?"

Jake sighed, feeling foolish in repeating something that should have been impossible. He realized if he uttered them, the professor might deem him an idiot. Yet the words he had distinctly heard suddenly reverberated within him with tenacious stubbornness, echoing inside the dome of his cranium with a furor that demanded a way out. But when he did voice them, they came out in close to a meek whisper. "She said 'Look out.'"

Chapter 8

Jake Javolyn was quite relieved when Dr. Franklin Grahm confirmed that Natalie could indeed speak English, for he had been doubting his own sanity ever since the female bottlenose had alerted him about the approach of the shark. When he had mentioned this fact to Zimbola shortly after the incident, the large Jamaican had looked at him as if he were crazy. Upon further describing the white dolphin's grasping appendages, Zimby's eyes went wide as he said, "Either one of Damballah's loas has taken over your brain, mon, or you been hittin' a little too much of that fine Jamaican rum behind my back."

So you taught her to speak in our tongue," Jake asked the doctor.

Grahm produced an enigmatic grin. "Hardly," he chortled. "She already knew how to converse in English when we found her."

Jake's mind floundered, leaving him momentarily speechless. "But… how's that possible?"

Grahm shrugged resignedly. "How is it possible she grew prehensile extensions? Both are mysteries I'm still trying to unravel." The scientist fell silent.

Jake was not about to give up so easily and came at the marine zoologist from another angle. "Didn't you tell me her appendages were caused by an evolutionary jump?"

"It's just a theory, pure speculation!"

"Then you must have a theory as to why she could speak English."

Grahm cleared his throat at the young man's persistence. "The fact that Natalie can speak is not so surprising when you consider that dolphins are capable of producing a seemingly endless variety of audible airborne noises, including a mimicry of humanoid sounds. In the wild, they primarily use water as a medium of exchange when communicating, and rarely if ever, resort to an airborne mode. Even dolphins in human captivity will initially attempt to communicate with us through waterborne whistles and various complex clicking patterns, the same as they do with one another, trying to induce us to use hydrosound. However, our consistent use of air-based sounds over a fairly extended period of close, kindly contact with them seems to cause a voluntary though radical shift in their behavior, prompting them to accommodate us in our own medium. When the shift occurs, they will mimic or at least try to approximate the sounds we make. Unfortunately, the noises they emit tend to get distorted by the limitations of their phonation apparatus and blowholes. The way they hear the airborne sound is also distorted since their hearing mechanism is much more attuned to a subaqueous medium. If they hear a sound differently from the way we perceive it, their reproduction of that sound may deviate markedly from the way it should actually be pronounced. They can easily enunciate vowels but have great difficulty producing consonants. Such a phenomenon is not unlike a deaf person learning to speak. In any event, when we speak to dolphins from above the water, they will lift their blowhole into the air and answer us. If we attempt to talk to them underwater, they will revert back to hydrosound emissions in response."

Jake was growing impatient and interjected. "Yes, but those dolphins are just trying to imitate the way we talk. While I admit Natalie's words were garbled and high pitched, they were clear enough to convey the meaning that she intended me to understand."

A contemplative, far off look was evident on Grahm's face. "She could articulate speech much more clearly out of the water," the scientist said. "It was as if she had experienced human companionship for most of her life. She was familiar with many human concepts."

"Such as?"

Grahm reflected on this for several seconds. "Love...if she liked a person, she could be very affectionate, very loving...she..." The scientist searched for the appropriate word. "She could be very empathic," he said at last. "She frequently spoke of others, all of whom she deeply missed."

"Dolphins?"

Grahm shook his head slowly, remorsefully. "I just don't know. Natalie never distinguished between people and cetaceans, even when asked to specify what type of being she was referring to."

"Did she have names for the others?"

The scientist nodded. "The names she mentioned the most were Apollo and Artemis." He paused momentarily. "But there were others she talked about. Aphrodite, Hermes, Hercules, Athena, and Amphitrite were other entities she often referred to by name."

"Correct me if I'm wrong doctor, but aren't those names from Greek mythology?"

A strange smile crossed Grahm's face. "Yes. Apart from Hercules and Amphitrite, the others are the names of five of the twelve gods the ancient Greeks called the Olympians. If you're familiar with Greek mythology, and it seems you are, you'll know the Olympians were the deities that overthrew the Titans. All of the Olympians were related in some way. They were so named because of the place where they dwelt, and that was Mount Olympus."

"Did she mention any other names?"

Grahm thought some more. "As I recall, she referred to another called Jacob. She also kept mentioning Coral and Reef, but I assume she was alluding to generics."

Jake's forehead wrinkled in confusion.

"You know, the animals that build submerged calcareous structures and the resulting formations." Grahm suddenly took on a distant look, then frowned. "One thing she frequently said was that the future of her kind was in the hands of destiny."

Jake pondered this before replying. "So you believe Natalie must've had considerable human contact to be able to speak English the way she did."

Grahm drew in a deep breath. "Yes."

"And the computer system you developed to communicate with dolphins...you didn't need that at all to talk to Natalie. She just helped provide you with a reference for talking to other dolphins...dolphins unlike her, dolphins without finger-like projections and an ability to speak English."

"Again, yes."

Jake thought some more. "Underwater visibility was not particularly good when I ran into Natalie...or I should say when she ran into me. Why didn't I hear any of her echo-locating sonar before she grabbed me? Shouldn't I have heard a series of clicks for her to find me so easily?"

The doctor scratched his chin pensively. "She probably emitted sound pulses above your hearing range."

"Okay, but why did the shark come straight for me? Natalie pulled me out of the way just before I became lunch. Most sharks will circle before striking."

"My guess is the Mako had been stalking Natalie for some time before your paths crossed. Because you were smaller and slower than Natalie, the shark perceived you as easier prey. You became a target of opportunity."

"Makes sense."

Jake stared silently out to sea as Grahm went back to puttering with the telemetric device. Without the transmitter strapped to her body, the likelihood of finding Natalie was extremely remote.

As an afterthought, Jake said, "Aside from trying to locate Natalie, you had mentioned a second item on your agenda."

Without looking up, the scientist continued to disassemble the unit. "The anomaly?"

"Yeah."

"Two days after we released Natalie, we received a rather startling transmission." Grahm fell mute as he detached the casing housing the unit, exposing a tight knot of electronic circuitry. "Just as I thought," he murmured distractedly. Lifting the device for Jake to see, he delicately prodded a tiny strand of loose wire within the mishmash of microchips and resistors with the tip of the Allen wrench. "There's the problem. A little solder and it'll be good as new."

Jake nodded. "What was so startling?"

With great care, Grahm gingerly placed the transmitter on the table and fixed his eyes on Jake. "As we tracked Natalie, she passed near Navassa Island. One sequence of transmitted signals we received showed a sunken boat."

Jake shrugged. "The seafloor throughout these waters is littered with sunken wrecks. What's so unusual about that?"

Grahm paused, suddenly appearing very solemn. "I was quite familiar with this particular vessel. My wife had been aboard it just before she disappeared."

The lingering hurt on Grahm's face made Jake look away. "Uh…I'm sorry for your loss," was all he could think to say.

"It happened a long time ago," Grahm added morosely.

An uncomfortable silence ensued. Grahm sat mutely, seemingly recollecting some deep memories, and Jake stood quiet, not wanting to intrude.

"*Tursiops* was a fifty-foot sloop owned by my wife and me," Grahm finally offered, taking control of his grief. "My wife…she was a heck of a sailor, better than most men. She loved the sea, sailing the Caribbean at every opportunity." He abruptly stifled a choke. "I should have been with her, but I was already committed to attend a conference in Chicago."

Grahm hesitated, once again composing himself before continuing. "Harriet was an extremely strong-willed woman, uncommonly independent and self-reliant. She was one of the strongest individuals I've ever known. So, it was no surprise when she insisted on taking the voyage without me…at least the initial leg of the voyage. We finally agreed that I'd meet up with her in Kingston, Jamaica."

Jake tried to phrase a question as tactfully as possible, but the words he chose seemed to betray any attempt at sensitivity as soon as he uttered them. "Did your wife sail alone?"

Grahm shook his head. "While she might have been called stubborn by some, by no means was she a foolish woman. She was five months pregnant at the time. Another scientist and two grad students made the trip with her. Like me, she was a marine zoologist. She had planned to do some field research during the outing, hoping to catalogue new species of coelenterates."

Jake's face clouded. "Coelenterates?"

Grahm looked bemused. "Jellyfish...that was her area of expertise."

Jake could not help but ask, "How long ago was it when she sailed?"

Grahm inhaled sharply. "Roughly twenty-three years has transpired since I last saw my wife or the people who made the trip with her."

"Are you certain the boat you saw was yours?" Jake prodded gently. "A lot can happen to a sunken vessel over time. In a tropical sea like this, they often become encased in coral and other marine growth. Their appearance can change drastically."

A deep introspection manifested itself on Grahm's face before he answered. "When I initially viewed the transmission, I didn't place much significance on it. Natalie's sonar reflections had revealed at least a dozen sunken vessels while we tracked her. She was a curious dolphin and always seemed to take special interest in objects not indigenous to the ocean bottom, typically making numerous passes to investigate them. The data containing the echo signature of that particular vessel ultimately became filed in my archives back in Miami. Believe it or not, it wasn't until a week ago that I had a most disturbing dream. In the dream I saw the wreck again, exactly as I had first seen it on the monitor during the transmission. I guess it was my subconscious alerting me to something I had previously missed. And like you said, a profusion of sponges and coral blanketed a good portion of the boat's hull and superstructure, effectively distorting its true configuration, but not enough to conceal the boat's distinctive bowsprit. You see, the *Tursiops* was uniquely outfitted with a six-foot bottlenose sculpted in bronze. Although the bowsprit I saw in the dream was covered in heavy growth, I was able to see beneath it, as if I had x-ray vision, and the image of the bowsprit the way I remembered it shone clearly through. When I awoke, I retrieved the stored electronic file and subjected it to a more thorough computer analysis, scanning the secondary sonar pulses echoing back at an ultra-frequency and culling them out."

Jake's expression clouded with puzzlement once again and Grahm quickly explained. "The use of this technique is analogous to that of using a real x-ray, and as we know, dolphins are able to penetrate objects with their tight beam laryngeal emitters which can produce sonar emissions at a much lower wavelength. They can turn this beam on any object and examine it in detail, and to a degree, see inside it. Once these particular wavelengths were converted to a visual, they not only revealed an underlying image of a dolphin, they also confirmed that it was composed of bronze. This discovery prompted me to make this trip."

Grahm paused momentarily. "I have no doubts that the vessel in question is the *Tursiops*. Maybe-"

The scientist realized he was raising his voice. "Maybe I'll learn what happened to my wife," he said softly.

Jake sat down, nodding slowly. "Do you have the precise coordinates of the vessel?"

"Yes. She lies near the southeast side of the island."

"Have you given any thought as to why your boat sank?"

A pained expression darkened Grahm's features and he sighed with the effort of answering. "Following the convention, I was to catch a flight from Chicago directly to Kingston, but a force-three hurricane near Jamaica delayed my departure for three days. When I finally got to Kingston, there was no record of Harriet ever having reached port. I notified the Coast Guard and a search was immediately undertaken. I remained in Jamaica for two weeks, hoping for the best, but the *Tursiops* never arrived, neither there nor anyplace else. Eventually, the Coast Guard abandoned the search."

"Was there any record of the Coast Guard or anyone else receiving an S.O.S.?" Jake pressed.

"None. The sloop vanished without a trace. My wife…she and the rest of the crew were never seen or heard from again. In those days, it was very hard for me to accept this. It still is. Harriet was a very resourceful woman, a true survivor. It wouldn't have been the first time she was caught at sea in a violent storm, especially one of hurricane strength. She was about as tough as they come, with a will of iron."

A wistful smile broke out on Grahm's face. "She was an exceptionally strong swimmer. Did you know that she was a member of the 1976 U.S. Olympic Swimming Team? In Montreal she competed in the five-thousand-meter crawl stroke. She had come in ahead of the rest of the field in all the preliminary heats, setting the best times. If not for a severe groin pull sustained in her pre-final heat, she probably would have taken home the gold going away. With such an injury, she could have easily opted to withdraw from the medal round and none of her teammates would have faulted her for doing so. Instead, she chose to race anyway, never once considering the prospect of dropping out and quitting. In spite of such a painful injury, she still managed to win the bronze."

Jake could not help but admire such a person, drawing from personal experience the full measure of such an injury. While with Seal Team Six, a groin pull had temporarily crippled him, making in-water mobility extremely painful and difficult. The fact that Grahm's wife had endured such suffering over 5,000 meters – more than three miles - while giving it all she had in order to medal bespoke volumes about the woman's grit.

"Sounds like she was a most courageous individual," Jake said, his voice tinged with both reverence and respect.

Grahm's expression suddenly brightened and he looked at Jake with appreciation in his eyes. "She was, lad…believe me when I tell you, she was."

With dark sunglasses shielding his eyes from the intense sun glare, Sebastian Ortega's focused stare in combination with his hooked beak of a nose gave him the look of an avian predator preparing to dive down on unsuspecting prey. Shifting his gaze forward, he continued to scan the ocean below, a vast expanse of indigo that stretched toward the horizon where a lone island jutted from the sea. Turning his head, a concentration of white lacy foam suddenly caught his attention.

"Ahi!" he barked, pointing furiously. There!

The pilot seated to his left noted the disturbance and tilted the cyclic stick hard to starboard, causing the Bell Ranger to swing rapidly in the direction Ortega had indicated.

"Lower! Bring us lower!" Ortega instructed in Spanish, speaking exuberantly into the microphone that protruded from his headset.

The pilot lowered the collective and the helicopter dropped to within 100 feet of the ocean surface where a huge shoal of fish congregated in agitated confusion.

Ortega smiled as the pilot hovered the chopper. The water was alive with the glimmer of scales extending in all directions just below the surface. "Alert the fleet!" he ordered. "Tell them we've got the mother of all tuna conventions."

With his side door having been removed before the flight, it was easy for Ortega to lean his torso out to get a better view. "Looks like a mix of blackfin and skipjack," he added.

Fascinated, he continued to watch the frothing turmoil as three vessels in the distance began to close the gap on his position. His smile turned to perplexity as he realized something must be herding the tuna into such a congested and stationary grouping. He scrutinized the water closely, finally spotting the sleek gray bodies moving along the outer perimeter of the mass, their dorsal fins slicing the waves as they encircled the multitude of entrapped fish.

Dolphins! He hated dolphins.

His lips curled in a savage sneer. Never taking his eyes from the darting forms, he groped behind him. From a box on the fuselage floor, he withdrew a cylindrical concussion grenade and pulled the pin. Extending his right arm out laterally, he released the spoon and let the grenade fall freely into the sea below. Several seconds passed before a tall geyser of white spray shot from the water, almost reaching the height of the aircraft. Almost immediately, the dense pack of fish bolted en masse, the water thrashed white in frenzied havoc as the shoal sped rapidly away.

Ortega cursed. "Stay with them!" he screamed, reaching for another grenade.

This was nothing new to the pilot. A veteran of many similar events, he kept pace above the heaviest concentration of churning pandemonium. Driven by the mayhem he was causing, Ortega dropped a second grenade, then another. Within a span of one minute, he detonated seven more concussion canisters into the fleeing throng. The explosions quickly took their toll and the water became littered with thousands of tuna floating sideways or belly up on the surface. Among their ranks, perhaps a dozen dolphins floundered lethargically, either stunned or dying.

Ortega laughed hysterically as he surveyed the scene. While spotting tuna was not his function within the Cardoza organization, he did it whenever he had the opportunity, taking immense pleasure in the thrill of blowing things up. And although the objective was to incapacitate as many tuna as possible for the fishing vessels to haul in, the fact that he got a few dolphins in the process only added to his enjoyment.

Like other Colombian and Mexican drug cartels, the Cardoza enterprise had invested heavily in a fleet of tuna vessels as a means of illegally transporting vast amounts of cocaine and other drugs. Hidden under huge loads of fish, hundreds of tons of cocaine could be smuggled with relative ease into the U.S. and Europe. And as a front for drug trafficking, the business became a legitimate vehicle for effectively laundering hundreds of millions of dollars in illicitly gained revenues.

One major pitfall in commercial tuna fishing, however, was the inadvertent killing of dolphins, which tended to get trapped in the huge seine nets of the fishing trawlers. When the U.S., Canada, and the European Union banned imports of dolphin-deadly tuna in the early 1990s, they literally crippled the major drug-smuggling pipeline of the crime syndicates. Cardoza's organization was particularly hard hit, and Ortega's percentage of the take had dropped considerably. With intense loathing, the Cardoza underboss recalled the costly bust of the 160-foot tuna trawler Don Miguel, boarded by the U.S. Coast Guard near Puerto Rico. A total of 9.5 tons of pure cocaine was found hidden in special compartments under tons of albacore. With a street value of nearly $500 million, the loss was staggering. The impounded vessel, valued at another $15 million, presented an additional financial setback to the organization. And all because of some overzealous passengers on a passing yacht. They had witnessed a number of dolphins being hauled aboard the trawler in its enormous seine nets and alerted the Coast Guard. The captain of the USCG cutter that was dispatched to investigate the incident just happened to be a dolphin lover. To Ortega, personally killing dolphins was payback for all the trouble they had caused him.

Continued reflection on the matter caused Ortega's upper lip to flare with outrage. On top of the lost profits dolphin-safety regulations had cost him, large amounts of money had also flowed from the cartel in an effort to overturn those mandates. One major coup was persuading the World Trade Organization to rule that the U.S. embargo was an illegal restraint of free trade. Additional bribes aimed at corrupting American, Mexican, and European officials were slowly weakening the International Dolphin Conservation Act which was originally enacted in 1997. Dubbed the Dolphin Death Act, its original intent to invoke strict standards for the Dolphin Safe label on American tuna cans was being systematically undermined, making the labels a farce.

Ortega had made substantial payouts to several high-ranking politicians within the U.S. Government to downplay the tuna-drug connection and to allay public outcries over dolphin deaths, attempting to kill two birds with one stone. Such avaricious individuals were key to getting an observer program implemented that would pacify environmentally conscious citizens. Using their considerable influence, the officials had pushed through legislation which implied that the IATTC, the Inter-American Tropical Tuna Commission, could effectively be used to deter drug smugglers while simultaneously ensuring the safety of dolphins by placing observers aboard tuna boats. Ortega smiled inwardly at the knowledge that the IATTC had never once levied a fine against a single member nation for killing dolphins. In fact, tuna imported from dolphin-killing countries could now be labeled dolphin-safe even if dolphins were chased, netted, injured, or even killed in the pursuit of tuna. But only as long as the observers aboard were willing to claim that no dolphins were seriously harmed.

The ruse had given Ortega some satisfaction. Intimidation was a most useful tool in coercing observers to falsify dolphin mortality records when bribery failed to work. The image of one uncooperative observer came to mind. The obstinate dolphin lover had been dragged behind the *San Carlo*, another Cardoza-owned vessel, as a pack of maddened sharks induced to frenzy by the scent of blood in the water tore his body to pieces. Even now, the memory of the man's intense screams of terror continued to gratify, producing a perverted arousal within Ortega. Reported as an unfortunate case of a man falling overboard in a shark infested sea, the incident had accomplished the desired result. When word of it had gotten out, no further problems had emerged within the ranks of IATTC observers.

Environmental blackmail also had its uses. The governments of Colombia, Venezuela, and Mexico all but threatened that their fishing fleets would go out and intentionally slaughter more dolphins unless the U.S. changed its laws and redefined the dolphin-safe label.

That was all well and fine with Ortega. He would certainly continue to do his part in swaying the U.S. stance. But right now, he had another important matter to attend to.

"Head for the island!" he ordered.

Glancing sideways, the pilot acknowledged the command with mild stoicism before banking the aircraft hard in the direction that would take them to the massive outcropping of rock and green vegetation jutting above the sea.

Chapter 9

*E*ven at a distance of several miles, the girl could sense the physical distress and suffering of the creatures. Impatient to reach them, she conveyed her intent to Jacob merely by pointing. At that moment, there was no need for words. Without hesitation, she slipped the goggles over her eyes and launched herself gracefully from the side of the small boat as it continued its slow plod, its single antiquated engine laboring in a steady, coughing chug. Her plunge was clean and precise, hardly making a splash as she disappeared beneath the surface with the deftness of a seabird diving for fish.

Jacob well knew there was no need to be concerned as the girl was joined by one of her companions. In moments she was quickly carried away from him. He would follow, eventually catching up and doing whatever he could. The girl had known him her entire life and had come to depend on him in the familiar way a child might come to depend on a parent. Inherently inclined toward the philosophic, he lived simply, never requiring much, and possessing only those things that gave him sufficient shelter and the means to eke out an existence. Yet he was a happy man by nature, but more so because the girl gave him endless joy.

He lifted his eyes to the indistinct band of what appeared to be white mist squatting low on the horizon, judging it to be no more than five miles distant. Both he and the girl had visited it countless times in the past, but never with the urgency that consumed them now. The girl was currently far ahead, her escort of six surrounding both her and the one she rode in a symmetric formation, their coordinated movements in synchronous harmony so precise that from afar they appeared as a single entity.

The bond that existed between Jacob and the girl was strong, almost as strong as the bonds she had formed with her companions, and he was continually elated with the knowledge that his face was one of the very first the girl saw when she came into the world. Though he was biologically unrelated to her, he smiled the way a proud father would as he watched the ebony sheen of the girl's wetted mane glimmer in the early morning sunlight as she distanced herself from him. Exhibiting extraordinary abilities shortly after her exit from her mother's womb, the girl had kept him in a constant state of wonder as he witnessed those abilities develop and mature over the succeeding years. A Christian by conviction, Jacob truly believed the girl's special gift had a divine purpose, one that had come about not by chance but by the will of God, and it gladdened him that he was able to convene routinely with so unique a person, for it imparted meaning to his life as well.

Jacob listened to the monotonous chug of the diesel as it struggled to push his dilapidated pinnace forward, the sound of it giving the misguided impression that the pistons were always on the verge of missing a stroke. But they never did. The pitch of the motor had changed little since the girl's birth some twenty years earlier, and lulled by it, his mind drifted back to that strange milestone in his life.

He had lived alone, preferring the solitude of the cove rather than the nearby village. Serene and beautiful, the place was enclosed by rugged, heavily-vegetated outcroppings of limestone. The craggy terrain rose steeply in a series of steps from the thin strip of white sandy beach that skirted its base. It was more of a narrow chasm that had been gradually carved out of the rock over eons of time. On one side high above, a natural spring sent an endless torrent of freshwater cascading down the rock walls until it joined the normally crystal-clear water of the cove in a tumultuous spray.

There had been no gray in his beard in those days and his body, at age thirty-six, still retained the lean hard lines of youth before the ravages of unrelenting sun and wind in unison with the passage of time would slowly take their toll.

The storm had been exceptionally brutal, the worst one he had ever seen. All the warning signs heralding its approach had been there, the peculiar tufts of cloud, the subtle change of wind, the unusual behavior of the songbirds seeking refuge in the rocky crags above his home, and the reddest dawn he had ever gazed upon just hours before it hit.

And though it held no significance that he could correlate to the impending storm, he also remembered the twin-engine seaplane as it raced out over the ocean on that morning, no more than two hundred feet above the water. Had it been another precursor of the storm to come? Why such an event would stay indelibly ingrained in his memory, he had no inkling. Perhaps it was the odd drone of its engines that struck a subliminal chord within him, subtly reminding him of the imperfect engine that powered his own craft. But somehow he had detected an abnormal tempo within them as they strained to keep the fixed-wing aircraft aloft as it disappeared over the western horizon.

Sadly, he remembered the other fishermen from the nearby village who had ventured out to sea, never to return. He had given them ample warning of what was to come, virtually pleading with them not to go, but they just laughed and told him how foolish he was. For some inexplicable reason during that period in his life, weather reports were inaccessible to the locals as radio and television transmissions in the area were always garbled, incessantly distorted by static. Everyone assumed it was because of the steep terrain hugging the coastline that blocked the signals. Then again, most villagers had no electricity available to power such devices anyway, although several of the more affluent, as he recalled, did have generators at the time. And batteries had been awfully expensive and hard to get.

The hurricane had struck like a colossal demon, vengefully pummeling the coast with merciless wind and lashing rain, pushing monstrous waves before it. Miraculously, the small cove where Jacob lived provided just enough lee to allow both his boat and rundown abode to remain relatively undamaged as the pernicious cyclone tore past unabated.

It was nearly two days later while pulling tree branches from the roof of his shack that something had caught his eye. It had entered the cove on a low roller, floating torpidly along the surface of the turbid water. From his elevated vantage point, it looked like a thick tree trunk that had been ripped free by the recent blow. At first he gave it no more than a passing glance and went back to removing sprigs lodged in the crown of his home. Moments later, movement drew his attention back to the object and he suddenly became aware of the person clinging to it. By the time he had climbed down, he knew that what he was seeing was a dolphin with a woman hugging its back, a white woman, her head barely above the water and draped to one side of the dolphin's dorsal fin.

The unusual event in all its detail would stay lucently etched in his mind for the remainder of his days. After the dolphin had beached itself, Jacob was amazed to discover that both beings were not only female but pregnant, their midriffs swollen in the latter stages of procreation. The extreme exhaustion of the strange pair was evident, however, and the profusion of crisscrossed angry raw welts blistering both bodies jarred his senses. Relieved of its burden, the dolphin had managed to squirm off the sandy shore in the creaming backwash of a diminutive breaker, swimming sluggishly out to the center of the cove where it lingered idly, as if awaiting how the woman fared.

The woman was rather small and scantily clad, wearing baggy Bermuda shorts and a bikini top. With the exception of her protruding belly, she was thin and appeared to be badly dehydrated. She groaned in agony as Jacob gently lifted her from the light surf foaming around his ankles, carrying her to his home nestled against the rock wall of the cove where it overlooked the beach. And although she initially seemed conscious of his presence, she soon became delirious and lapsed into coma, remaining in that condition for two days as he periodically administered his own specially prepared salve to her wounds. He recognized the welts to be the nasty by-product of severe jellyfish stings and knew his home remedy would speed up the healing process and ease the pain. Every so often, he lifted the woman's head from the pillow as she lay on his bed, squeezing drinking water out of a dampened cloth so that it trickled into her mouth.

By the third day, the unconscious woman was beginning to show signs of improvement. Her breathing became less labored and the severity of her burns appeared to be subsiding. As Jacob was applying more of the soothing embrocation to her arms, she abruptly opened her eyes. Though seemingly alert, she stared at him in confusion.

"Who are you?" she croaked weakly, her question spoken in English.

"My name is Jacob," he answered cheerfully, producing a warm smile in an attempt to show the woman she was in safe hands. He rarely conversed in any language other than Creole since leaving the university where he had studied philosophy. The locals from the nearby village were the only people he spoke with these days, and that was only occasionally, but the Christian Bible he possessed was the King James version and most of his books were written in English, all of which he read regularly.

The woman's eyes darted about the small room in alarm, as if searching for some sign of familiarity. "Where am I?"

"You are just south of the tiny village of Malique."

"Where is that?"

"It lies midway between the cities of Gonaives in the north and Saint-Marc to the south. You are in Haiti."

She tried to rise, but flinched from the effort, shrinking back in obvious pain.

"It would be unwise to sit up just yet," Jacob advised tenderly. "Your body is still not healed." He scooped some more of the ointment from the jar he held, a concoction of various herbs he had gathered from plants growing in the narrow gorge that towered above his home.

The woman lay momentarily still, then asked, "How did I get here?"

"A most gracious and concerned friend carried you here." He watched her face closely. "You do not remember?"

Slowly, the woman shook her head.

"She still waits outside. You are extremely fortunate to have such a devoted friend. Most people are not so lucky."

Jacob stopped spreading the ointment. "You have not told me your name."

A blank stare fell across the woman's face and suddenly her eyes went wide. "I...I don't know." There was the residue of panic in her voice.

"You are still very weak," Jacob said sympathetically. "Perhaps your memory will return after more rest and some nourishment."

He reached behind him and lifted a jug of water laced with more medicinal herbs, pouring the water into a glass. "Please drink, it will speed up your recovery." He placed a hand under the woman's head, helping her to sip from the glass. Gulping greedily and breathing hard, she coughed and nearly choked as she quaffed down the liquid. After a second glass, her thirst seemed to abate and she lay back wearily as if to sleep. But when Jacob brought a tray full of baked grouper fillets and various tropical fruit, the aroma of the food seemed to reawaken her, and she hungrily ate every hand-fed morsel given her. After that, the woman dropped off into a deep slumber.

Jacob stepped outside and scanned the water. He quickly located the female dolphin, her dorsal fin poking above the water on the far side of the cove. On impulse, he hefted the bucket containing the remaining portions of the twenty-pound Nassau grouper and strode down to the beach, placing the bucket in the tiny dory he had set back from the water. Dragging the dory across the sand, he pulled it out through the low surf until the water was at knee level, then stepped over the aluminum gunwale. As he rowed toward deeper water, the dolphin swam in his direction until it came alongside the small boat. The permanently smiling face rose to scrutinize him.

Jacob stopped rowing and smiled back. "Good deeds deserve good rewards," he said as he lifted a chunk from the bucket.

The dolphin's head rose higher, as if in anticipation of Jacob's intentions. She was a big female, longer than the eight-foot dory he sat in. When the creature was within a foot of the boat, Jacob extended his arm out over the gunwale and dropped the chunk into the waiting jaws. The food was immediately swallowed and the animal looked expectantly for more. Jacob was happy to comply. Hefting another four-pound chunk, he brought his hand to within inches of the dolphin's powerful beak, unconcerned about the potential danger to which he was exposing himself. He had been around the sea all his life and understood the bite of a rumbustious dolphin was something to be avoided, but he made no attempt to pull his hand back. As ravenous as she was, the female plucked the morsel from Jacob's grasp with the delicate precision of a surgeon before gulping it down. The process was repeated several more times until the pail was emptied of its contents.

Feeling a close kinship with the animal, Jacob reached out and gently rubbed the female's forehead. Like the woman, the welts on its skin had diminished considerably, but to a much greater degree. He had often heard about the remarkable ability of these creatures to rapidly heal themselves following an injury and had previously dismissed such talk as the idle exaggerations of over-imaginative minds. But as he studied the docile female, he was now convinced that such outlandish assertions were actually true.

"I am very sorry, my sweet girl, but I have no more food for you right now," Jacob said, keeping his voice soothing as he continued to stroke the dolphin's head and snout. "Perhaps I can catch you some more fish to eat."

There was appraisal in those dark, mysterious eyes, almost as if the creature had understood his words, and as he stared into them he suddenly sensed an unfathomable intelligence. In that instant he was certain the animal trusted him and that an accord had been struck. There was something else.

Jacob's smile quickly gave way to comprehension. "If you are wondering about your friend, she is slowly regaining her strength." With those words, the dolphin nuzzled his hand affectionately before gliding away toward the far end of the cove.

In the days that followed, Jacob had a succession of moderate successes in netting fish whenever he sailed his pinnace out into the open sea. Each time he brought back the catch, the dolphin ate most of it, devouring each fish given it with insatiable intensity.

Just before sunup on the fifth day since discovering the woman, Jacob awoke to find her missing. Upon arising from his bedside vigil, he soon located her standing motionless on the sandy shore with her back to him, tiny wavelets washing around her feet. Something held her attention, and as his eyes adjusted to the dawn twilight he discerned the head of the dolphin staring back at her from the water. As he watched with growing fascination, both woman and dolphin continued to contemplate each other with the eternal reverie of statues frozen in time. Then as if a silent signal had passed between them, the woman suddenly waded into the nearly flat surf. When she was waist deep she pushed off in an overhead stroke that brought her to within arm's length of the marine mammal. For a few moments she tread water before grabbing hold of the dolphin's dorsal fin. As the light grew stronger, the strange pair moved out across the water, slowly at first, then with increasing speed.

For the next several hours, the dolphin circled the cove with the woman in tow, most of the time along the water's surface, and Jacob became uneasy whenever the duo would disappear into the depths, now pristine and clear, only to reemerge at some other corner of the cove. The duration of each submergence seemed longer than the last, and yet the woman's face glowed with unrestrained elation each time the pair came up for air.

Later that morning after the woman strode briskly ashore, her spirits seemed to flag when she still failed to remember her past. "I don't know who I am," she stated morosely as Jacob prepared the morning meal. Sighing with frustration, she sat on a boulder fronting Jacob's tiny dwelling and surveyed her surroundings with a critical eye. After a few minutes, her manner brightened. "I love this place, Jacob. It's like a tiny little paradise, a microcosm of all the good things life has to offer."

Jacob nodded in agreement. "I have always been able to think clearly in this cove. It is the reason I have chosen to live here and not closer to the village."

The woman peered in awe at the kaleidoscope of pigmentation highlighting the vegetation lining the craggy rock walls rising steeply above her. Various species of wildflowers, predominantly hibiscus, bloomed everywhere, their multi-hued effect spanning the entire spectrum of a rainbow. Palm trees and jumbled arrays of fruit-bearing trees further added to the hodgepodge of living matter growing from the tiered ledges. The thriving plant life teemed with brilliantly tinted butterflies and brightly plumed tropical birds flitting and nesting among the dense flora. The proliferation of biota with its explosion of pigmentation dazzled the eye. "Nature wears many colors," she said offhandedly.

Jacob smiled. "A noted philosopher and poet once wrote something very much like that. Did you ever read the work of Ralph Waldo Emerson?"

From the expression on the woman's face, Jacob could tell he had dislodged some shred of memory from the woman's previous life. "Didn't he say that nature always wears the colors of the spirit, that a person laboring under calamity will know sadness from the heat of their own fire?"

"Yes. And do you know what he meant by that?"

Something registered with sudden clarity in the woman's eyes. "Nature is the symbol of the spirit. We are connected to the landscape and as we turn, so does it. As our moods change, so too do our perceptions of the hues and shapes of nature."

"I see you have obviously studied Emerson." Jacob looked thoughtful. "It is very likely you are an educated woman. Maybe you had attended a university at one time," he hypothesized encouragingly. "You seem to have a bit of the philosopher in you."

"Do you think?"

"Another wise man once wrote 'Nature is the art of God' when he attempted to reconcile religion and science. If you were truly a scholar of philosophy, you would surely remember his name."

The answer came easily. "Sir Thomas Browne said that in 1635 in his Religio Medici."

Jacob grinned again, pleased with the answer. He thought some more. "The famous Greek scientist and philosopher, Aristotle, gave philosophy a definition. Any student of philosophy would remember it."

The words were out of the woman's mouth before she realized she had uttered them. "Philosophy is the science which considers truth."

Jacob was enjoying the woman's company. "I think we have taken the first step in unraveling who you are."

The woman looked up at the profusion of colorful plant and avian life overlooking the water, seemingly mesmerized by the magnificent panorama. Like the dolphin, the unsightly blemishes that had marred her skin when he had found her were now gone, with no trace of scarring anywhere. Her complexion was now beginning to take on a smooth, robust glow, further enhanced by her developing pregnancy. Still slightly damp from her earlier swim in the cove, her dark brown hair hung limply to the middle of her back. He knew that when it dried completely, it would be thick and wavy, much like a lion's mane, tinged with streaks of reddish-gold that gave it a lustrous sheen when the sun reflected off it. He judged her to be somewhere in her late twenties. She was a petite, pretty woman, with large and expressive dark brown eyes that seemed to take in everything with measured interest. If not for her jutting belly, he could tell she would normally be athletically trim and lithe, and when she walked along the beach she carried herself in the determined posture of the achiever, the type of person that seemed to constantly strive for purpose.

Jacob handed the woman a plate of exotic fruit consisting of sliced mangos, apricots, and papayas and glanced out over the water. "Does your friend have a name?" he asked, indicating the dolphin floating lazily near the base of the waterfall.

The woman broke from her reflective mood. "I have decided to call her Athena."

Jacob ran his fingers through his beard, crinkling his eyes with amusement. "Ah, yes, from Greek mythology. The daughter of Zeus." He popped a piece of mango into his mouth. "She sprang full grown in armor from his forehead, and therefore, has no mother. She is fierce and brave in battle, but fights only to protect the state and home from outside enemies. She invented the bridle, which allowed man to tame horses. Other things like the ship and chariot were created by her. She is the embodiment of wisdom, purity, and reason. Among his children, Zeus considered her his favorite and allowed her to use his weapons, including his thunderbolt."

"You seem like a very learned man," the woman said between bites. "Your little house is stuffed with books."

"I have a hunger for knowledge. Many things interest me. I enjoy reading."

"Yet you live very simply."

"I do not require anything more than what you see all around us. I am very happy here." Jacob studied the woman thoughtfully. "Would you mind if I gave you a name to call you by…at least until your memory returns?"

"That depends on what it is."

"Amphitrite. I would like to call you Amphitrite."

"Wasn't she another Greek goddess?" It was more of a statement than a question.

"Yes. The circumstances that brought you here parallel to a certain degree the story of Amphitrite. She was the queen of the sea, variously given as the daughter of Oceanus and Tethys, or of Nereus and Doris. The sea god Poseidon…" He abruptly hesitated and lowered his eyes, trying to conceal his sudden embarrassment by stuffing more fruit into his mouth but nearly choking.

The woman looked at him expectantly. "Yes, go on. What about Poseidon?"

Jacob found himself tongue-tied as he realized the faux pas of using such a comparison. "He, ah…he wanted her as his bride, but she declined from the honor and hid from him in the Atlantic Ocean," he said, unable to hide the fluster in his voice. "A dolphin not only located her, but also brought her back to him and he married her. As a reward, the dolphin was granted a place in heaven."

The woman laughed. He could tell she was not offended.

Jacob quickly recovered his poise but avoided looking at the woman's belly. "Thereafter, Amphitrite gave birth to Triton, the fish-man."

The woman kept smiling. "That's an interesting story."

"Greek amphoras often depict Amphitrite riding a sea creature surrounded by Tritons. Like the queen she is, she is shown decorated with her waving hair covered with a net, and sometimes with the pincers of a lobster attached to her temples."

"How do you remember all these things?"

"For some unknown reason, God has given me an eidetic memory. Whenever I see, hear, or read something, I never forget it, down to the most minute detail."

The woman eyed Jacob with envy. "Such a talent must be a blessing."

Jacob shook his head. "It is more of a curse. Never being able to forget anything can sometimes be cumbersome. The more I learn, the more things I realize I don't know. This makes me hunger to gain more knowledge, and because of it my head gets filled with all types of information and correlations."

Jacob sighed wearily. "Sometimes I wonder if knowing less would make life so much simpler."

The woman listened with interest, but consumed her food as though she had not eaten in several days. "Didn't someone once say knowledge is power," she said between mouthfuls. "Such a statement leads one to the conclusion that most people who strive for knowledge are either consciously or unconsciously seeking power in some form. With what you know, you could probably be a rich man within Haitian society, yet you live the life of a simple man."

"I have no desire for power or riches. Didn't you ever hear the phrase 'Power corrupts?' Most of the ills of this world seem to be caused by those who seek power." Jacob let out another sigh, deeper than before. "Anyway, I am very happy to live here in this cove and read my books. It has been my observation that most people of ambition who succeed in achieving power and wealth ultimately yearn for communion with nature. They buy country estates with gardens and luxury yachts, looking for a place that offers peace and tranquility. I have all of that right here."

The woman gazed at Jacob with undisguised admiration. "You're an unusual man, Jacob. I guess I'm very fortunate that you found me." She continued to eat, seeming to ponder something, then said, "Your choice of name for me…Amphitrite will do just fine for the time being."

For a long moment, Jacob remained silent and withdrawn, caught up in the midst of a heavy decision. "The American Embassy in Port-au-Prince may be able to pinpoint your identity. You have the look and speech of an American. A bus comes by the village each week bound for the capital. I can take you there if you like," he offered unenthusiastically.

The suggestion seemed to startle Amphitrite. She glanced apprehensively in the direction of the dolphin. "If it's all the same to you, I'd like to stay here a while longer." She turned back to Jacob, her eyes revealing both a profound confusion and a plea. "You've been very kind to me, and it isn't my intention to impose on your gracious hospitality by overextending my stay, but…"

"Yes."

"Athena needs me right now and I can't leave her after what she's done for me, not just yet."

The vibrant smile that blossomed on Jacob's face was not unlike one of the hibiscus flowers adorning the cove. "Both you and your friend are welcome here as long as you wish to stay."

The next week went by quickly. Early every morning Amphitrite took a long swim in the cove with Athena, frolicking playfully for hours at a time. Jacob noticed that on each of these occasions before Amphitrite entered the water, the same strange ritual would occur. As had happened the first time he had witnessed it, Amphitrite and her dolphin friend would stare fixedly at one another for several minutes, as if some covert communication transpired between them on an unknown level. Each time the woman would stand immobile on the sandy beach, her face frozen with the inscrutable expression of a statue sculpted from marble. And each time Athena would float nearly motionless, with unfathomable anthracite eyes locked on Amphitrite. Then without a word uttered, Amphitrite would wade out into the water with the vacant gaze of a sleepwalker.

Sometimes Jacob would sit on the sand and watch the interplay with the fascination of a child seeing something new and unusual unfold before its eyes. At other times he felt distantly removed from the abysmal bond the woman and dolphin shared and would turn away to attend some chore or sail beyond the cove to net more fish.

Later each day, Amphitrite would return from her swim refreshed and exuberant, always eager to engage in conversation with Jacob. In spite of her memory loss, she soon revealed an intelligent, sagacious mind, seeming to be well versed in a surprisingly broad range of subjects. While she failed to remember any portion of her former life, she was able to draw upon substantial blocks of both general and specialized knowledge retained in her brain. This tended to support Jacob's initial supposition that she was educated. Often their confabulations were intellectually stimulating, and Jacob quickly found himself appreciating the woman's company more and more.

When not swimming with the dolphin, the woman was now spending most of her waking hours with Jacob, opting to accompany him whenever he went fishing or brought Athena food.

One day while feeding the dolphin a particularly meager catch of fish, he looked soulfully into the creature's eyes and apologized for not having more. Amphitrite appeared momentarily distant as if listening to some inner voice, then said, "There is no need to explain yourself. Athena knows you do the best you can."

"Is that your assessment or Athena's?"

"It's what she told me." Amphitrite noted Jacob's skepticism. "She knows only that you're a kind man and that you are deeply concerned about her welfare. That is all she needs to know."

The following day as Jacob prepared his pinnace for another bout of fishing, Amphitrite displayed an enigmatic grin. "I think there's a sizable school of striped mullet that awaits your net today," she announced happily.

Jacob smiled back politely, enjoying her jovial mood but keeping the absurdity of such a proclamation to himself. He knew that striped mullet were not commonly found in the Caribbean. Either she was grossly naïve or jesting, particularly in light of the fact that overfishing in Haitian coastal waters had decimated populations of mullet decades earlier.

"I do not think that is possible," he said seriously. "Such fish vanished from these waters long ago."

Amphitrite retained her cheerful smile. "Athena and I are going to show you they're still around," she replied optimistically.

As the pinnace chugged from the protection of the cove, Jacob was surprised to note Athena knifing through the low swells on the craft's port side. As far as he knew, this was the first time the dolphin had ventured beyond the cove's rocky confines since he had discovered her.

After the pinnace had cleared the narrow channel through the reef, Jacob began steering a wide arc that would take them on a northerly course to the spot he deemed the most promising for harvesting fish.

"South will prove to be the better choice today," Amphitrite recommended. To Jacob's puzzlement she still wore that strange enigmatic smile.

"Why do you say that?" questioned Jacob. "The better fishing has always been north of here."

Amphitrite directed her gaze behind Jacob. "See that promontory jutting out into the ocean." Jacob turned around and noted the headland she was looking at three miles distant. "If you take this boat just off that point of land, good fortune will befall you."

Bemused, Jacob laughed aloud. "Translated into its English equivalent, the place you are referring is called the Devil's Horn. The currents near the Horn are unpredictable and the fishing has always been a disappointment to all the fishermen who have tried their luck there. No one fishes the Horn anymore."

Amphitrite remained unmoved by Jacob's lack of faith. "If you go there, I promise your luck will change."

"It will be a waste of fuel," Jacob objected wearily.

Amphitrite just kept smiling encouragingly, and his resolve began to waver. Against his better judgement he turned the boat around. "Okay," he conceded, "but only for a short time. If no fish come into my net within one hour, then we will go to the place of my choosing with no arguments. Agreed?"

"Fair enough."

With Athena leading the way, they were soon positioned off the Devil's Horn and drifting with the current. "Here!" Amphitrite cried jubilantly. "Drop your net here. Athena will herd the fish into it."

Begrudgingly, Jacob flung the net and Athena disappeared beneath the surface. Within seconds he felt a heavy resistance on the drag lines, and as he began to pull, the effort of hauling in the net took all his strength. As he heaved the net to the surface, it became obvious it was filled with a squirming mass of fish, most of them averaging one foot in length. Mouth agape, he stared at Amphitrite strangely. The net was glutted with striped mullet.

With Athena's assistance, Jacob swiftly succeeded in hauling aboard eight more loads of fish. Each time the net bulged voluminously with hundreds of striped mullet.

Jacob had outfitted the pinnace with several large holding tanks a few years earlier, but it had been quite some time since they had been used. Now the tanks were filled to capacity with the sudden windfall, and with the aeration pumps keeping the catch alive and the gunwales substantially lower in the water, Jacob put the boat on a heading that would take them back to the cove. Along the way he tossed Athena fish after fish until she was sated and could eat no more. With her belly gorged almost to the point of bursting, she swam sluggishly as she re-entered the rocky domain that served as Jacob's home.

In one corner of the cove Jacob had installed a fish pen, and he filled it with most of the captured mullet. There would be enough live fish on hand to keep Athena well fed for several weeks to come.

Sunset was always a wondrous sight in the cove from October through March. Framed by the steep sides of the chasm, the red solar disk provided a surrealistic vista as it dipped below the rim of the rock wall towering above the cove's west side like a molten ball of magma.

"It was a beautiful day," Amphitrite remarked blithely as the light began to fade. "It's been many months since Athena has eaten so well."

Jacob mulled this and frowned. "So you are starting to remember events prior to coming here?"

Amphitrite held his gaze momentarily and shook her head. "Athena told me this. She wanted me to thank you and tell you she'll try to reciprocate your act of kindness."

Jacob sat still, looking out over the water as darkness descended to engulf them. He knew that darkness fell much more rapidly the closer one got to the equator. "How did you know?" he asked. He kept his tone casual.

"Know what?"

"How did you know where to find the fish?" Like a pesky gnat buzzing relentlessly about his head, the riddle had plagued him most of the day.

Amphitrite pondered the question as if examining some hidden truth from several different angles. "I know it sounds crazy," she said at last, "but I saw it in a dream. Just as it happened today, I saw it in a dream last night. It seemed so real that I knew it would actually happen, and it did."

Jacob's mind raced. Even as a young boy, his grandmother, now deceased, had instilled in him never to ignore events which unfolded in dreams. Because of it, he had made it a priority to read up on any information that dealt with the subject whenever he could find it.

"You experienced precognition," he said, trying to restrain his excitement and succeeding. "It occurs predominantly in dreams for most people who experience it, although it can also take the form of a waking vision, flashing thoughts entering the mind, or a sense of just knowing. There is much scientific evidence to support that some people are able to see certain future events, although there is currently no accepted explanation as to how or why it occurs. It may be possible you have such a psychic ability, one that enables you to have visions of things to come."

Amphitrite appeared stymied. "I have no memory of having experienced visions before the one in my dream last night," she replied stiffly. "Try as I might, I can't seem to picture any past at all. It's as if I never existed anywhere else other than in this cove."

There was a profound sadness in her words, and Jacob placed a consoling hand on her shoulder, a gesture of sympathetic understanding. "It may be that your inability to remember your past has somehow given you the power to glimpse the future…at least some portion of it." He thought about it some more. "In a way, what you saw became a self-fulfilling prophecy."

"Does that make me some kind of freak?" There was the hint of weary resignation in her voice.

"Hardly! Precognitive dreams are quite common. Many people have them without realizing it, perhaps because they do not recall the details or fail to properly interpret the symbols within the dream."

"There were no symbols in my dream. I saw the future exactly as it occurred this morning."

"What you experienced was a prophetic dream. It predicted the future with a high degree of accuracy, what some might call an unchangeable future. Prophetic dreams are much rarer than most other forms of precognition. By definition, all prophecy is considered to be precognition. However, not all precognition can be classified as prophecy."

"How's that?"

Jacob found himself regurgitating some of the things he had read on the subject. "There are basically two types of precognitive dreams. One involves a perception of the future that cannot be altered. That is what you saw. It predicted what would happen, and was therefore, unchangeable. Whatever happened in the dream occurred because it was already etched in the great cosmic plan, what most people would call destiny or fate. The other type of precognitive dream involves a look into a possible future, but one that can be changed. Such a dream allows someone to change the future outcome. This apparent ability to alter the perceived future makes precognition difficult to understand since if it is truly a look into the future, then the effects are witnessed before the causes. Such conditions do occur in quantum physics, however."

"I'm not very familiar with quantum physics," Amphitrite said, tilting her head to survey the velvet tapestry of the heavens that had so rapidly replaced the last glimmers of daylight. The stars twinkled spectacularly with remote indifference.

A look of intense satisfaction broke out on Jacob's face. He was in his element. Maybe he should have become a teacher, he thought. He was a veritable storehouse of information and he enjoyed disseminating it. "It is one of the foundations of modern science. Quantum physics focuses on studying matter at the subatomic level. It was developed to explain various anomalies observed in classical physics. At its core, classical physics is a flawed theory, but only dramatically flawed when dealing with extremely small particles on the atomic scale or exceptionally fast velocities that get close to the speed of light where relativity takes over. For everyday things, which are much larger than atoms and much slower than the speed of light, classical physics does an excellent job at predicting what will happen, at least with a high degree of approximation. Plus, it is much easier to use than either quantum mechanics or relativity, each of which requires a more extensive amount of mathematics to compute the end result. Recent discoveries in quantum physics and also in cosmology, the branch of astronomy that deals with the universe taken as a whole, have shed much light on how the mind interacts with the universe. These findings compel acceptance of the idea that there is far more than one universe and that we constantly, but unconsciously, interact with other unseen or hidden universes and higher dimensions. Unfortunately, most books on quantum cosmology are written in mathematical language that few people understand."

Amphitrite remained quiet, intent on listening, and Jacob elaborated further. "Anyway, to avoid digressing on the nuances of quantum mechanics, I will simply say that some scientists believe it holds the key to revealing the precise process by which precognition works."

Jacob inhaled deeply, savoring the sweet aroma of hibiscus before continuing. "To date, two theories have emerged which may explain it, but they are rather general in nature. The most popular theory holds that precognition is a glimpse of a possible future that is based upon present conditions and existing information, and which may be altered depending on acts of free will. Such a theory implies that the future can cause the past, a phenomenon called backward causality or retro-causality. However, a different and much more controversial theory contends that the precognitive experience itself unleashes a powerful psychokinetic energy, which directly influences the state of matter. This then brings the envisioned future to pass, and therefore your self-fulfilling prophecy."

A heavy cloud of introspection seemed to wash over Amphitrite. "It was a marvelous vision, my prophetic dream. Only good came of it." She hesitated briefly. "But what does one do if the dream were to contain something horrible. Having such an ability to prophesize something bad like that would be a terrible thing, would it not?"

The happy air that had accompanied Jacob's lecture a moment earlier vanished abruptly. "Only if the final outcome could not be altered to result in something beneficial or benign," he stated solemnly.

Late that night Jacob stirred groggily from a sound sleep. Something had awakened him and as he sat up he became aware of cries coming from Amphitrite's bunk. The woman thrashed about wildly in the throes of some nightmare, her face glistening with sweat in the dim moonlight. He immediately rose and gently prodded her. With a start she jerked awake, letting out several short gasps.

"It is all right," Jacob said comfortingly. "You are safe here." Amphitrite looked about dazedly. "You were having a bad dream."

Teetering on the verge of panic, Amphitrite stared at him with wide, fearful eyes. "The village! How far is the village?" she demanded.

"Not far," Jacob said calmly. "Maybe a thirty-minute walk through the hills. The climb out of this cove is difficult and treacherous. By boat it takes a little longer, but the journey is much safer and less strenuous." Jacob was perplexed. "Why do you want to know?"

The answer came back in a barely audible whisper as Amphitrite trembled uncontrollably. "There is no time to explain." As if in empathic synchrony with Amphitrite's despondency, Athena chittered mournfully from the nearby water.

Jacob's soothing presence did little to alleviate Amphitrite's fright. He lit a candle to bring more illumination inside the dwelling. With tears trickling down her cheeks, Amphitrite's face was a waxen mask, her eyes clouded with misty shadows that foretold of chilling horrors lurking in her mind. "We must hurry!" she implored, rising hastily from the bed and slipping on the sandals Jacob had made for her. "Please take me to the village by the quickest route." There was a latent tension in her voice.

Jacob studied her expression intimately a moment longer. He sensed something dark and terrifying to the spirit, something that was all too real to the woman. He pressed the matter no further, springing to his feet and striding to the door of the dwelling. "Follow me!" he blurted. If there was an explanation for Amphitrite's request, he was certain she would tell him on the way to the village.

Under a gibbous moon, Jacob led Amphitrite up the escarpment, steep in areas and shelved in others. Although faint, there was just enough light to distinguish the nuances in topography they had to negotiate, and Jacob was thoroughly familiar with all of them. Years earlier, he had set about making the climb out of the cove easier when he had planted various types of flowering plants and fruit-bearing trees along the broader ledges where sufficient topsoil existed. A series of strategically placed guide ropes, railings and handholds allowed them to pull themselves along those rocky pathways which were less precipitously sloped, while wooden ladders fastened along fissures in the limestone provided the means to scale the worst portions of the chasm. As they made their way up, Jacob kept close to Amphitrite, reaching out from time to time to hold her arm. Her gravid condition made him nervous and he focused on keeping her safe. Near the uppermost region of the ascent, a narrow trail opened up and wound its way through a dense thicket of thorns and underbrush. The ground underfoot was still soggy from the recent storm and their feet became mired in mud at intervals as they trudged along the path.

"Does a man by the name of Emmanuel Baptiste live in the village?" Amphitrite suddenly asked, huffing heavily from the climb.

Jacob almost stopped in his tracks, but then decided to keep going. "Yes," he said. "There is such a person with that name." The mention of Baptiste was strangely disturbing to him, for he knew that the man was a fierce and outspoken opponent of the current dictator that ruled the population.

"His life is in terrible danger," Amphitrite uttered hoarsely, gasping for breath as she tried to keep up with Jacob. "Some men are coming this very night to kill him. We must warn him before they get there."

Jacob stopped and turned sharply. "You saw this in a dream?" Dreams that involved death could not be ignored under any circumstances. His thoughts scurried ahead, suddenly filled with foreboding apprehension. And if it was a precognitive dream, could murder be averted?

"It was another of those dreams," Amphitrite answered, her voice shaking. "It was so real, so terribly evil."

Prodded by her words, Jacob resumed walking again, his legs moving more hastily this time. "How can you be sure it was a precognitive dream?"

"I can't explain it, I just know." Though still shaken, her tone held a trace of indignation. Jacob had no desire to offend the woman and he offered no argument.

After moving another twenty paces Amphitrite asked, "What does the phrase 'Tonton Makout' mean?"

Yes, Jacob thought, it made sense. "It is a Creole term that translates to bogeymen in English. The Tonton Makout are the bully boys of "Baby Doc" Duvalier, the president of Haiti. They are very evil men."

When Jacob was a young boy, Baby Doc's father, Francois Duvalier, had ruled Haiti with an iron fist. A physician by profession, he came to power in 1957 with the full support of the Haitian army behind him. "Papa Doc," as he came to be called, was overwhelmingly reelected president in 1961 in a military-controlled sham election. And in 1964 he declared himself dictator for life. His regime, the longest in Haiti's history, was a brutal reign of terror in which all political opponents were either jailed or summarily executed. Under Papa Doc, the populace was kept in a constant state of abject fear by his personal secret police force, the notorious Tonton Makout. These were unpaid volunteers who were directly responsible only to Duvalier and who were given a virtual license to torture, kill, and extort in order to achieve Papa Doc's political objectives. Under Francois Duvalier's administration, the Tonton Makout had murdered hundreds, maybe thousands, of opponents, sometimes publicly hanging the corpses as warnings to the rest of the citizenry. While the economy of Haiti had been slowly declining prior to Duvalier's succession to power, it continued to deteriorate under his rule, and the illiteracy rate of the nation remained at about ninety percent. Papa Doc nevertheless maintained control over the nation, and his practice of voodooism encouraged rumors among the people that he possessed supernatural powers. Before his death in 1971, he arranged for his son, Jean-Claude, to succeed him.

Jacob recalled that the first few years of John-Claude's installation as Haiti's ninth president-for-life were a largely uneventful extension of his father's rule. Baby Doc, however, did change the name of the Tonton Makout to the Volunteer Security Nationals, though they continued to terrorize the citizenry. To most of the population the VSN were still referred to as the Tonton Makout. Under Baby Doc, the balance between the VSN and the armed forces changed. He realigned these competing power bases, if only to ensure control over Haiti's security apparatus.

In a half-hearted attempt to open Haiti to the outside world and to secure renewed foreign assistance from the United States, Baby Doc initially curbed the abuses of the VSN. Unfortunately for the nation, Jean-Claude limited his interest in government to various fraudulent schemes and to outright misappropriations of government funds for which no balance sheets were ever kept. Baby Doc's kleptocracy, along with his failure to back with actions his rhetoric endorsing economic and public-health reform, left the regime vulnerable to unanticipated crises that were exacerbated by endemic poverty. With public services already minimal, the ineptness of government further deteriorated as Jean-Claude and his ruling clique continued to abscond with funds from the national treasury.

Jacob remembered the widespread discontent that began to manifest itself in March of 1983 when Pope John Paul II visited Haiti. During the visit, the pontiff had openly declared that the economic and social climate within the poverty-stricken nation needed change. He called for a more equitable distribution of wealth, a more egalitarian social structure, more concern among the elite for the well-being of the masses, and increased participation by the ruling party in public life. The message had revitalized both laymen and clergy, and it contributed heavily to a sudden rise in political and social activism.

A short time after the Pope's visit, the Haitian Bishops Conference launched a nationwide but short-lived literacy program in the midst of mushrooming discontent with the Duvalier regime. Anti-government riots quickly ensued and the VSN stepped in to quell the disturbances. Two hundred peasants were massacred at Jean-Rabeau after demonstrating for more land. A revolt began in the provinces two years later. Raids on food-distribution warehouses occurred in the coastal city of Gonaives and quickly expanded in a sequence of riots that spread to six other cities. As his power began to wane, brutal excesses by the increasingly desperate VSN further eroded Duvalier's position. With the military no longer supporting him, he relied heavily on the VSN and on limited local police capabilities to restore order, but to no avail.

Jacob had heard rumors that altogether as many as 60,000 people had been killed and tortured by the VSN during Baby Doc's reign in order for him to retain his dictatorship. But he also knew that it was only a matter of time before the government collapsed completely and Baby Doc was forced to flee the country, particularly if the Haitian army wanted Duvalier ousted. So far, though, Duvalier was stubbornly hanging on to the reins of power and was even resisting pressure from the United States government to step down.

As he brought Amphitrite along the path that led to Malique, Jacob well understood the consequences of what they were trying to do. He made a decision and abruptly stopped, turning to face Amphitrite and speaking gravely. "If the men you saw in your dream are truly Tonton Makout, then we will be killed if they catch us trying to warn Baptiste. He is a potent adversary of Duvalier and has been inflaming the local citizenry to revolt against the government. Baptiste commands a great amount of respect and support from the population."

Amphitrite's face was an indistinct shadow against the backdrop of subdued moonlight. "It isn't just Baptiste I'm trying to save. These men are coming to kill everyone in the village, even the women and children. We must do whatever we can to keep that from happening."

Jacob was momentarily at a loss for words. He had lived a simple existence for most of his life, generally keeping to himself and doing his best to prevent the rest of the world, with all its problems, crises, and miseries, from touching him. Rarely, if ever, had he been confronted with a situation that placed him in extreme peril.

"You will be putting both yourself and your unborn child in unnecessary danger," said Jacob. "There is no reason for you to come. I will go on ahead and alert the villagers. You will do much to ease my mind if you return to the cove and wait for me there."

When Jacob turned to leave, Amphitrite grabbed his arm. Her grip was surprisingly strong and tenacious. "It's crucial that I go with you."

Jacob shook his head stubbornly. "No!"

Amphitrite maintained her hold on Jacob, her voice urgent. "You don't understand. I see it clearly now. I think I know how we can stop these men, how we can keep them away from the village."

"How?"

"Is there not a road that leads to Malique from the south?"

"Yes. This trail overlooks that road on the other side of the village."

"The Makout will be taking that road, Jacob. They will be coming in a convoy of four trucks led by a jeep."

"I still do not see-"

"This trail runs by an ancient stone wall. The wall is crescent-shaped and stands to one side of a huge tree high above the road. The slope there is steep and barren of other trees. Isn't this so?" There was resolute conviction in her words.

The hair rose on the nape of Jacob's neck and a chill crept down his spine. The place Amphitrite described was a voodoo shrine, established two generations earlier by the locals. Candles, carvings of wood, and the blood and bones of sacrificed animals were scattered in the immediate vicinity of the towering tree. The villagers believed the tree was protected by the maître du grand bois – the master spirit of the great woods.

"Yes, there is such a place," Jacob acquiesced. "Some of the villagers go there to get drinking water. There is a well near the tree. The tree you speak of is a giant mapou tree. It draws precious spring water to the surface from deep underground."

Amphitrite rushed on hastily. Lives were at stake. "The ground, Jacob. The ground that slopes toward the road is very unstable. If we can cause a mudslide, we can block the road."

Jacob had some understanding of soil mechanics and had once read a book on the subject. What Amphitrite was suggesting meant that the torrential rains brought by the recent hurricane had saturated the soil to the point where the load of elevated overburden started to exceed the shear strength capacity of the underlying earth and rock. If inordinate amounts of rainwater collected on top of a slope before it was able to drain, the substratum could no longer support the added weight by frictional resistance. Eventually the instability would cause the overlying mass of earth and rock to shear away and plunge to lower ground. Mudslides were common on the Island of Hispaniola and were often attributable to the deforestation of hillsides by locals who needed the wood from trees for cooking and building.

"And how do you propose to accomplish this?" Jacob asked. He tried his best to keep any trace of skepticism from his voice.

"If we can collapse the rock wall, the ensuing avalanche will do the rest," Amphitrite stated with certainty. "The hill will slide down."

Jacob hesitated a moment longer. "You saw the hill come down in the dream? You saw a landslide?" He needed confirmation. He had to know if the dream was prophetic in nature.

The question seemed to discombobulate her, and she wavered with uncertainty before ascertaining the full meaning of his query. "No! I did not see a landslide," she countered in agitation. "But I believe the dream contained a clue how we can save the village."

"What? What did you hear? What did you see?" Jacob demanded, refusing to go another step. "I will not take you to the tree unless you describe the contents of the dream exactly."

Exasperated, Amphitrite spoke quickly. "There was a man, the one in charge of the convoy. He rode in a jeep leading four trucks. In his left hand was a sickle, in his right a machete. In the dream his face turned into a skull, and the skull yelled the words, 'The Tonton Makout has come to harvest Emmanuel Baptiste and all of Malique, and only a river of mud can stop the slaughter.' Then the skull smiled horribly and turned to stare up at a steep hill. Except for one enormous tree that stood at the top of the hill, the slope was barren. A partially collapsed stone wall stood in front of the tree. I heard the screams of women and children in the background and the machete and sickle held by the skull began to drip with blood. The screams turned to thunder as the skull changed back into the face of the Makout leader. The man opened his mouth and said, 'If the wall fell, so would the hill, but now we are free to do what we will. The maître du grand bois has no power over us.'"

Amphitrite drew breath before going on. "As soon as he said it, the convoy entered the village just as a tidal wave of blood swept in from the sea to engulf everything, including the mapou tree."

Amphitrite stopped and stared at Jacob, as if the weight of what she was telling him was too much to bear. Her lips quivered and she spoke again in a low, subdued voice. "When the sea of blood receded, the tree and village were gone. There were bodies scattered everywhere along the shore."

"If the dream was prophetic, then we cannot stop it from happening," Jacob said despondently.

"No! There still may be a chance."

"What do you mean?"

"There was more. The dead suddenly disappeared and Malique was whole again. I saw the mapou tree firmly rooted in the center of the village."

Jacob stood as if mesmerized and Amphitrite had to push him hard to jar him from the grip of horror she had just described. "We are running out of time!" she screamed.

Even though Jacob had grown up in the midst of a society dominated by superstition and a fear of the unknown, he rarely let himself become influenced by such things. He was a learned man and left such nonsense to the illiterate masses that clung steadfastly to such beliefs. Yet Amphitrite's precognition of future events was something that bordered on the supernatural. Somehow he trusted her, sensing there was at least an inkling of truth to the things she had foreseen. Two questions hung heavily on his mind. Could they reach the mapou tree in time? And how would they collapse the wall?

In that moment Jacob made a decision. "I will take you to the mapou tree," he said, turning to follow the trail.

They continued along the path, gradually gaining higher ground as it wound through rock outcroppings and thorn scrub. Eventually the moderate upward grade gave way to more level terrain, and as they walked around a bend the dark mass of the ocean came into view like a vast sheet of polished slate. Under the glow of a crescent moon, the village of Malique hugged the hillside of an inlet. A dense cluster of houses and shacks nestled above a rocky beach where several piers jutted obtrusively into the sea. A fleet of small fishing boats abutted the piers, perhaps thirty in all, with several larger vessels dominating the group. With the exception of a few lighted windows, it appeared that most of the citizenry was asleep. A heavy silence pervaded the air, belying the possibility of any impending calamity that might befall the slumbering community.

As they moved on a little further, the trail abruptly forked. Jacob halted and faced Amphitrite. "The path to the left leads down to the village," he said. "The one to the right will take us to the mapou tree."

"How much farther?" Amphitrite asked in a strained voice.

"Almost two kilometers."

Even in the semi-darkness Jacob could discern the toll their journey was taking on Amphitrite. Her face glistened with sweat and it was becoming increasingly difficult for her to maintain the pace she had set earlier. Jacob intentionally slowed to accommodate her growing fatigue. "Perhaps we should rest a minute," he suggested.

"There is no time for that!" she protested breathlessly, plodding past Jacob and taking the trail to the right.

As they trudged on, the trail began a rapid descent through a rugged landscape, falling away steeply in a few places. Jacob kept a firm grip on Amphitrite in areas such as these lest she stumble and fall. Within minutes the trail meandered down to a narrow dirt road and traversed it.

"This is the road that leads to Malique," Jacob said.

Immediately beyond the road, the trail rose quickly and Amphitrite began to gasp for breath. They ascended higher. Amphitrite's step began to falter but she refused to quit. Suddenly she stopped and doubled over. A stifled cry revealed her agony. In the midst of her spasm, something flashed in her mind.

"You must rest!" Jacob ordered. "Think of your baby!"

"I can't!" she groaned.

"The mapou tree is not much farther. I will go on ahead and topple the wall. I can do that by myself. I do not need your help."

Amphitrite's face relaxed as the pain eased. She straightened up, but her speech was labored. "You will need me to show you the weak spot on the wall. There is one stone that will bring down the others. If it is moved even a little, the rest of the wall will collapse."

"You saw this?"

"Yes. It came to me a moment ago."

"Tell me where it is and I will find it," Jacob pleaded.

Amphitrite began walking again. "The location is indistinct. I'll know it when I see it."

A short time later, the immense bulk of the mapou tree loomed over them like an ominous shadow, its trunk rising to a dizzying height and blocking out the stars overhead as it reached for the heavens. A jumbled semicircular formation stood to one side of the tree, the stones comprising it leaning precariously over the incline of the hill. The formation was the remains of an antediluvian well, its wall becoming exposed as the hill eroded away from deforestation. Stones that had once comprised the portion of the well closest to the hillside littered the slope below. The dark shapes of various objects could be discerned scattered near the outer rim of the wall or hanging from the branches of the tree. Jacob knew that daylight would reveal them to be symbolic wood carvings and the bones of sacrificed animals. The ancient voodoo shrine had always made Jacob feel uneasy whenever he had ventured near the site, and because of it, he generally avoided the place.

As they approached the wall, Amphitrite let out a gasp, a sound born of surprise rather than pain. "They're coming, Jacob!" she blurted apprehensively. "I can feel them."

Jacob took several steps back to command a better view of the base of the slope to the south. He knew the closest portion of road that led to Malique was roughly 300 meters southwest of the old well and almost 120 meters below their position vertically. The location where the road would be showed nothing in the scant moonlight.

"I do not see anything," replied Jacob in frustration, but he somehow trusted her senses. He scampered back near the wall. "Show me the spot where the wall is weakest," he instructed.

The silhouette of Amphitrite's darkened form seemed unreal in the dimness of night. "I need light, Jacob. I cannot point out something I can't see."

Jacob noted the wall's convex side. Shielded from the dull light cast by a waning moon, it was obscured in shadow. An idea came upon him and he strode cautiously to the crude altar fronting the tree. He knew that a cluster of candles was usually placed there, and as he drew closer to it an involuntary shudder coursed through him like a jolt of electricity. He shrugged aside the feeling and groped beneath the dais in a sheltered alcove hewn from coarse wood until his fingers located a small box. As a small boy he had witnessed a few of the ceremonial voodoo rituals venerating the master spirit purportedly residing in the great mapou tree. From experience he knew the box would contain matches with which to light the candles, but there was an implied warning to his trespass. No one ever took any of the artifacts surrounding the tree. Although religious custom forbade the tampering or removal of any objects from the site, it was actually superstitious dread that prevented it. If the custom were violated, the wrath of the master spirit would descend upon and devour the offender. Only a mambo or houngan was allowed to touch the tree or the ornaments adorning the holy site.

Jacob hurriedly opened the matchbox and struck a match. The sudden burst of light illuminated a row of candles in various states of deformed consumption, their waxy bases bonded with the altar's wooden surface. Jacob lit the largest candle and broke it from its perch, then walked swiftly back to the rock wall.

"Hurry, Jacob!" Amphitrite shouted anxiously. "I can see them."

Jacob craned his head around the wall, careful to keep the candlelight concealed behind the rock formation so as not to alert anyone of their presence. Five pairs of headlights pierced the night, strung out in a single column at the far end of the valley below them. Like the implacable yellow orbs of nocturnal predators, they crept slowly forward with leisurely patience, as if there was no doubt that quarry would soon be snatched between serrated jaws.

Ducking back behind the convex side of the rock formation, he looked up at its highest section standing nearly four meters above the uneven ground. Some of the boulders comprising the stack were huge, judging them to weigh as much as half a ton. Raising the candle to illuminate the wall more clearly, he surveyed the interlaced chunks of rock intently. What remained of the stonework appeared quite stable and immovable.

He glanced at Amphitrite questioningly. "Where?"

Under the candle's flickering glow, her eyes flittered over the structure like hummingbirds in search of nectar. Jacob could see a growing alarm in them. "I don't see it!" she cried. "I can't visualize it anymore."

Jacob moved the candle further along the wall, changing the way the light reflected off the stones. "Maybe you are trying too hard," he suggested soothingly. "Visions cannot be forced, nor a remembrance of all their details." Everything he had ever read about precognition pointed to such a fact. He shifted the candle some more, as if it might help her recall the key to toppling the wall. On an impulse he told her, "Touch the stones! Touch them and clear your mind of any thoughts, as if it were an empty vessel." Based on what he had read on the subject, the human mind had little control invoking precognitive events. Conscious effort rarely worked.

The wildness in Amphitrite's eyes steadied as she comprehended Jacob's words. She nodded and reached out to place a hand on the stonework, then closed her eyes. She remained still for many seconds before stirring. She opened her eyes again and stared at Jacob, her expression resounding with hopelessness.

Jacob lowered the candle to the ground and peered around the wall. The headlights were much closer now, bobbing erratically as the vehicles bounced along the pothole-ridden road. Turning, he took Amphitrite by the hand and led her to the mapou tree. The trunk was enormous, at least twenty-three feet in circumference. Jacob envisioned the way it looked during the day. Under a bright tropical sun, the trunk was a startling pale gray, rising straight up and branching only near the top where it unfurled a broadleaf canopy.

Coming to within arms-length of the tree, he stopped. Never had he come this close to the mapou. That he still retained a shred of his ancestral beliefs revolted him. As learned and rational-minded as he was, it was difficult for him to discard completely the last vestiges of superstitious dogma that had been so thoroughly ingrained in his people and passed on to him. Black magic and mysticism were for the illiterate and weak-minded, he often chided himself. But as he stood before the tree, he could not help but sense its awesome energy.

Esmerelda's essence abounded in that tree, at least some vestige of her spirit. That was what his grandmother had once told him. "There will come a day, Jacob, when you must cast aside your fear, for within this tree lies the salvation you will surely need. Esmerelda had read the expression on his face and smiled. Do not impede yourself with logic, Jacob. To do so will only discourage you from drawing on that which I leave behind." With his mind teetering on the cliff of doubt, he had watched as his grandmother had placed her palms upon the mapou's trunk.

Jacob pulled Amphitrite beside him. She came docilely, seeming distant and preoccupied with her own dismal failure. "Put your hand on the tree!" he urged. His voice was tight, betraying the fear that was inbred within him.

The proximity of the tree seemed to polarize Amphitrite's awareness. She stepped closer as if drawn to some unseen force and extended a hand. Jacob blinked. He could have sworn he saw sparks fly as her fingers made contact with the mapou's bark. Abruptly her body stiffened and she let out a small, startled cry. His instincts were right. The tree was a reservoir of mysterious energy and had triggered something in Amphitrite.

Jacob avoided touching the tree himself. He rose up on tiptoes instead to look beyond a rift in the hill's crest. The ground elevation at the tree was higher than the top of the wall, and it afforded him a view of the valley floor from where the convoy approached. He could see the lights of the lead vehicle were almost even with the base of the hill closest to their position. In another minute Duvalier's thugs would be beyond the reach of any possible avalanche.

Jacob turned his head back to Amphitrite. She suddenly flinched, drawing in a sharp intake of breath as if something stabbed deeply into her flesh. She cried out again, letting a prolonged scream escape her lips, a scream that grew in shrillness and conveyed intense pain. In panic, Jacob tried to pull her away from the tree, but it was as if her body was a rigid extension of the wood comprising it. He could not budge her. In disbelief he used both his hands to grip the wrist of her lone hand making contact with the mapou and tugged hard. He could not free it. Her palm remained flattened up against the trunk as if fused with the timber at the molecular level.

A strange rhythmic humming seemed to flow beneath his fingers as they clutched her wrist, and as he puzzled over it, a gentle rumbling could be felt underfoot. The rumble escalated rapidly, moving like rolling thunder through the soil until the earth trembled and shook violently. The sound of splintering rock drew his attention back to the wall. Fragments of stone caromed into the air as the exposed remnants of the ancient well crumbled away and toppled down the incline of the hill. Like an approaching earthquake, the rumble became a deafening roar. The ground pitched and vibrated and a jagged split in the earth began to materialize all at once, not more than five meters from where they stood. The rift widened swiftly like the hideous jaws of some titanic beast gaping wide to swallow anything near it.

Jacob stared in awe as the outer edge of the hill trundled away, breaking up and tumbling in a cataclysmic cascade of rock and muddy soil. The view down the hill broadened as the slope collapsed, and the headlights of the approaching convoy came fully before his eyes, its occupants unsuspecting and oblivious of the danger hurtling down to meet them. Jacob could not bring himself to look away, enthralled by the magnitude and ferocity of the spectacle. The immense mass of mud and debris surged on and gathered momentum, its leading edge a barrier of impending destruction, and it tore into the column with devastating force. One of the trucks flared, erupting in flames and sending a churning, expanding fireball soaring high above. A swath of fire spewed forth, trailing away on top of the moving wall of mud.

The inferno lit the night in vivid clarity, and Jacob knew that it was the severe impact and heat of collision that had caused the truck's fuel tank to rupture and ignite. The powerful rush of mud and rock bent and twisted the metal frames of the trucks as if they were flimsy paper toys. Under the deadly press, men and steel disappeared, crushed and buried as the pull of gravity compressed the onslaught of flowing rubble into a tightly compacted hodgepodge that was fast becoming a graveyard.

The lead vehicle was more fortunate. As the tsunami of earth swept over the road, it carried the smaller transport with it like a kayak caught in a surge of foaming whitewater. The beams emitted from its headlights rotated skyward as the wave of mud pulled it along, partially engulfing it. Within seconds the torrent of debris slowed, finally coming to rest on the far side of where the road used to be, the rear half of the remaining vehicle embedded in a thick slurry of earthen matter, its lights pointing vertically at the stars as though they were signal beacons.

Almost immediately, the ground ceased shaking and the train-like rumble abruptly abated. The patter of a few pebbles trickling down the newly carved slope was the only sound to mark the aftermath of the impossible event. Sometime during the avalanche, Amphitrite's cries had died away, and as Jacob tore his eyes from the scene of destruction, her hand came free of the tree. Illuminated by both the distant flames and modest moonlight, her face was ashen and glazed. Released from her ordeal, she was now drained and exhausted, no longer possessing the strength to remain standing. She slumped backward listlessly and Jacob extended his arms, cradling her body before it hit the ground.

He stared back at the re-arranged landscape below the mapou tree, his mind speeding along in analytical amazement. Somehow he and the woman had stumbled upon a hidden portal of the mind and spirit where few people ever journeyed.

Chapter 10

*T*he buzz of the trawler's intercom jolted Jake from his focused reverie with the piercing acuteness of a pistol shot. He had been mulling over all the things Grahm had told him, and one item troubled him deeply. He had turned that item over and over, examining it minutely from every angle much the way a jeweler might examine a rare gemstone for crystalline flaws under a magnifying glass. Reaching for the intercom, he toggled the switch and put aside the thought.

"What is it, Zimby?"

"I think you better get up here, Jay Jay. I want to hear you tell me Damballah is not playing tricks with my eyes." Zimbola's deep voice seemed to quake with awe.

Dr. Grahm looked up sharply from fiddling with the electronic gadgetry in his hands.

"Excuse me, Doctor," Jake apologized, hiding his annoyance, "but I better see what's troubling my overgrown friend."

Jake made his way forward and climbed the ladder leading to the pilothouse. "What?" he questioned with more than a little testiness. He hated it whenever Zimby made reference to the voodoo snake god. It often meant that strange or unwanted events were about to befall them.

Zimbola extended a huge arm and pointed off the starboard bow. "There! Are you seeing what I am seeing?"

It took several seconds for Jake's vision to adjust to the sun glare reflecting off the sea before he spotted it. His initial perception was that he was looking at some gigantic but unknown sea monster. As his brain continued to process the sight, he realized what he was actually seeing.

A small group of bottlenose dolphins clove their way through the water on nearly the same heading as the *Angel*, no more than forty feet from the side of his vessel. All were albino…all except for the one in the center of the pack. That one also displayed white skin, but something was astride its back.

Jake closed his eyes, then opened them again, only to witness the same thing. A human female clung to the dorsal area of the creature at the pod's hub. Sunlight shimmered off a mane of long flowing hair with the consistency of burnished anthracite as it trailed down her back in the wash of waves.

As Jake watched, the dolphins began to pull away, switch-backing swiftly through the sea in perfect unified synchronization, the speed of the group much greater than anything the *Angel* was capable of. From what he could discern, the dolphin on which the female rode appeared to be the largest of the pack, its dorsal fin jutting higher than the others. For one brief moment the human female turned her head to glance in Jake's direction, seeming to look directly at him. A set of goggles was strapped firmly over her eyes, effectively concealing the full extent of her facial features. With the exception of her head, neck, and hands, her body was completely clad in a one-piece, form-fitting wet suit, its color precisely matching the skin tone of the creature she rode. Her body was lithe and tiny, exhibiting the feminine lines indigenous of a healthy young woman. The girl swung her head forward again as the group raced hurriedly away toward some obscure destination, and Jake could not help but sense a measured purpose emanating from the pack.

The entire episode left Jake reeling in amazement. As if he had suddenly lost his voice, he stared mutely at Zimbola who stood frozen at the helm gazing at the rapidly fading pod with the glazed look of a sleepwalker. For several more seconds neither man spoke. Only then did Jake become aware of Grahm standing behind him. Apparently the scientist had followed him up to the bridge out of curiosity and had witnessed it all, for his eyes continued to track the strange procession of creatures in the distance.

Jake was the first to break the silence. "As I live and breathe, I've never seen anything like that."

Grahm's introspective manner suddenly changed gears and he became animated with excitement. "I think we've just seen some of Natalie's cousins," he said effusively.

Jake noted the faint outline of white limestone cliffs floating on the horizon, appearing insubstantial and ethereal rather than something comprised of rock and earth. Navassa Island was dead ahead. "Seems their destination may be the same as ours," he uttered. The way the group had surrounded the girl reminded him of a military escort, the kind assigned to guarding an important dignitary. "Those creatures appeared to be very protective of that girl, whoever she is." He looked inquiringly at Grahm. "You don't suppose she's the person who taught Natalie to master human speech?"

"Who is Natalie?" Zimbola asked in bewilderment.

A subtle smile broke out on Grahm's lips and he turned to address Jake, his eyes alive with the implications of the discovery. "Possibly!" He stared back thoughtfully toward the receding pod as it seemed to merge and then blend in with the misty bluffs in the distance. "The only way we'll know for sure is to speak to her."

"Who is Natalie?" Zimbola repeated.

Looking up at him, Jake said, "I'll explain it all to you later, but right now I need you to follow that pack!"

The small helicopter set down on the southeast side of the island like a falcon coming to roost, its skids finding purchase on the only available patch of flat terrain clear of scrub and jagged bedrock within the immediate area. All around it low-growing poisonwood trees predominated in dense clusters, with scattered cactus and thorn scrub adding to a hodgepodge of vegetation capping the island's broad plateau. With the throttle eased, the main rotor blades slowed rapidly, swishing through the air in a mild but deadly whisper. Hopping down from the co-pilot's side of the cockpit, Sebastian Ortega ducked his head and ambled over to the lone individual who stood watching him.

As Ortega drew closer, he took careful stock of the man awaiting him. The man was large and trim, exuding an air of haughty arrogance. A neatly trimmed shock of course, dirty blonde hair carpeted the lower half of his youthful face, the skin the color of unpolished bronze. His brow was wide and deep, his gaze dark and penetrating like that of a mesmeric cobra, cold as obsidian. Taking in the full measure of the persona before him, Ortega had difficulty tearing his eyes from the prominent scar marring the skin just above the man's right cheekbone. Somehow such a blemish seemed in character with the underlying savageness the man represented. Though subtle in nature, he thought he recognized the disconcerting gleam of the fanatic burning within the depths of the man's pupils, much the way hot embers might continue to smolder beneath spent ashes in a seemingly extinguished hearth. He looked at the shoulders and arms and saw the telltale signs of muscular development underlying the sweat-stained long-sleeved shirt that clung snugly to a lean but powerful torso. The dark haft of a long-bladed Bowie knife jutted from a sheath of black leather strapped firmly to his right thigh, and a shoulder holster containing a 9mm Browning P35 rode under his left armpit, both weapons appearing as if they were permanent bodily fixtures. In many ways, here was a man much like himself, tough, ruthless, and when circumstances called for it, cruel and without mercy. He had no doubts the man was exactly what he appeared to be, a warrior.

"Allah akhbar!" the man greeted him in Arabic.

When a look of incomprehension manifested itself on Ortega's face, the man quickly reverted to English. "God is great, is he not?" he said, then added, "I trust your flight went well."

Although Ortega possessed little patience for idle small talk, nor religious convictions of any significance to acknowledge such pious reverence, the fact that he was now face to face with a supposed ranking member of the Afghan drug trade caused him to curb any impulse toward sarcasm. Except for divergent ideologies governing each of them, and that was only speculation on his part, he instinctively sensed a similarity in their core natures. For the time being he would refrain from sardonic replies or mocking comments, something he normally had no compulsions against directing at most people with whom he did business. While a show of sarcasm would generally indicate a total lack of trepidation on his part, it often conveyed a disrespect or contempt of that same person. Such self-styled interaction had a way of invoking fear, and fear made others subservient and eager to please, discouraging the temptation to swindle or deceive.

Though Ortega had a history of doling out insults, his reputation was such that he did not handle barbs well when on the receiving end. Habitually bad-tempered, there had been times when he was in a particularly foul mood, which was often, that he had been known to eradicate an offender for even a misperceived slight, and in a most brutal manner. For some strange reason, he was certain the man standing before him had a violence of temper akin to his own and could not be intimidated. But because he valued the man's affiliation as potentially useful, he preferred keeping him an ally rather than an adversary through unwarranted offense. After all, an Afghan connection would ultimately prove rewarding and most profitable to the Cardoza organization, assuming the man was who he professed to be.

In studying the fierce individual standing before him, Ortega wondered if the fat little broker had purposely withheld any other relevant information. According to Hennington, this meeting had been arranged at the request of the Colonel, who claimed the man to be a representative of an international drug consortium controlling a multi-billion-pound supply of heroin stockpiled in Afghanistan. From what he had been told, the man had come to Haiti seeking to provide exclusive rights to the enterprising Colombian drug lord willing to take on the task of distributing huge amounts of white heroin, a type of narcotic that is eighty percent pure. Going by the name of Omar, he was looking to do business with only serious-minded people having the available resources to effectively handle vast quantities of such a drug.

Ortega had concurred with Hennington's assessment that only Al Qaeda operatives had enough clout in that part of the world to keep a firm grip on such an enormous stockpile. Smelling rich profits to be had, Ortega readily agreed to meet with Omar at the prescribed place and time, not even bothering to notify his boss, Rafael Cardoza, about the planned rendezvous. Before apprising the drug lord about the meeting, he wanted to ferret out the legitimacy of the offer. For reasons known only to Omar, the man had chosen this desolate chunk of rock.

Ortega realized Omar was studying him intently, expecting some kind of courteous reply to his greeting. "My flights are always enjoyable whenever I am able to mix business with pleasure," he remarked in

English, thinking back to his recent grenade-dropping escapade. He beamed with genuine heartfelt delight at the memory. "But tell me," he questioned, continuing to keep his manner cordial, "what is the nature of this meeting?"

Omar seemed a little taken back. "Did your good friend, Mr. Hennington, not inform you?"

Ortega feigned ignorance. "My schedule was such that I was unable to get any details. Perhaps you can elaborate on what you had told Mr. Hennington."

A cloud of suspicion suddenly arose from Omar, and he surveyed his surroundings with the wary, alert eyes of a man expecting an attack from any quarter before focusing his gaze on three ships many miles away along the southwest horizon. "Those ships, they belong to you?"

"To my organization, yes."

"I understand them to be tuna vessels. Is this not so?"

Maintaining his patience, Ortega nodded.

"Your boats, their holds are large enough to accommodate sizable cargo?"

"Yes."

"They are outfitted with heavy duty winches capable of lifting ten tons or more?"

Ortega's brows furrowed with impatience. "Yes."

A deep somberness overcame Omar as he seemed to digest this information with the analytical demeanor of a billionaire deciding where to invest his wealth. His black serpentine eyes flicked over to the helicopter pilot who sat alertly at the controls while keeping the engine idling, the aircraft's main rotor continuing to slice the air in a low whooshing pitch. Though Omar's right hand hung loosely, seemingly casually near the haft of the Bowie knife riding his leg, it was all too evident to Ortega that he was prepared to draw it at the slightest hint of danger. Ortega could tell he preferred the use of the blade over the pistol he carried, making him think of Pedro, Cardoza's truculent and all too often fractious nephew. Here was an individual who lived always on the edge, a risk taker. An existence based on subterfuge was a natural way of life to the man.

Satisfied with the answers for the moment, Omar appeared to make a decision. "I represent an Asian group that maintains control of most of the poppy fields in that part of the world. As I am sure you know, processed correctly, poppies can be converted into opium and heroin."

Omar paused to observe Ortega's reaction to his words, but the Colombian remained stolid. "A recent bout of bumper crops during the past several years and improvements in the way the poppies are processed have allowed us to produce excessive amounts of high-grade Heroin Number Four, what you might call white heroin."

Omar's eyes never left Ortega's face as he spoke. "My people are looking for a buyer that can undertake the distribution of substantial amounts of this drug." He let the last sentence hang in the air, awaiting a response.

The corners of Ortega's mouth rose in a shrewd grin. Normally he was exceptionally adept at reading people, but it was still possible Omar's proposition was not authentic, that he could very likely be an agent working undercover for the U.S. Drug Enforcement Administration or the ATF. It would not be the first time such agents attempted to entrap him. His instincts, however, told him otherwise, and although he felt he could trust what the man had told him so far to be valid, he would refrain from tipping his hand just yet. "Mr. Hennington may have misled you. I am in the business of catching and exporting tuna, a legitimate enterprise that keeps within the boundaries of international law governing commercial fishing and trade, nothing more."

As if perceiving the preposterousness of Ortega's declaration, Omar did not look the least bit perturbed or disappointed. He reached into a pants pocket and produced a small plastic bag containing a white powdery substance, then held it before him as if dangling an apple before an obstinate donkey. "Perhaps you would be willing to change your mind once you sample the product."

Narrowing his eyes, Ortega stared at the packet with fascination, then abruptly met Omar's penetrating gaze. The man was practically leering at him. "I would think drug trafficking would go against the teachings of Islam," he tested.

The statement seemed to catch Omar off guard and he flushed with irritation, a crazed glint in his eyes.

Emboldened, Ortega decided to probe deeper. "Why would your spiritual leader, Bin Laden, resort to what most Muslims would call a vulgar display of unholiness?"

From the look on Omar's face, he could see that Hennington's assessment had been right on the money. Omar seemed to have great difficulty composing himself and Ortega half expected him to draw the blade at his side out of frustration. Surprisingly, the denial of such an affiliation never left Omar's lips. "Yes, it is true that our great leader has had to advocate the use of such a blasphemous activity, but it is a necessary evil that can only help us achieve our goals."

"And they are?" Ortega pumped.

A humorless smile materialized across Omar's countenance. "Why to raise money to fund our operations. Ridding Muslim lands of Americans and Jews is our primary aim."

"You mean Westerners, don't you? All those you consider to be infidels?" Ortega tested him further. "What makes you think an infidel such as me would be foolish enough to consider doing business with the organization you represent?"

"Non-Muslims who aid our cause will not be harmed. The will of Allah forbids it."

The way the words were uttered made Omar appear ostentatiously pompous, and Ortega almost burst out laughing, but caught himself. Instead, he reached for the bag still clutched by the Islamist. The bag was already open and he dabbed a tiny portion of its contents on his tongue. Although extremely bitter in taste, he suddenly smiled as if assessing a sweet succulent fruit.

Omar did not return Ortega's smile. Ortega could still detect the faint glimmer of the religious zealot emanating from the man's eyes, making the Colombian feel uneasy. It was becoming increasingly difficult for him to remain outwardly affable.

Glancing briefly around him, Ortega wondered how the man had gained access to the higher inland plateau. On the flight in he had ordered the pilot to make one complete low-altitude pass along the fortress-like cliffs skirting the island's 8-kilometer perimeter. There were no sandy beaches and the cliffs, ranging in height from six to twenty meters, dropped directly into the sea and were often undercut, making landings by water impossible in most places. He had not seen any boats near the shoreline or any signs of human habitation, judging the place to be deserted. With the exception of transient Haitian fishermen occasionally using the island as a camping stopover, or a fact-finding scientific expedition, visitors to the island were few and far between, and the place generally remained unoccupied.

The island was actually the remains of an ancient coral reef, a clump of irregular karst protruding above the sea and covering an area slightly over five square kilometers in the shape of a teardrop. Extensive stretches of undulating topography defined by dogtooth limestone made the island inhospitable and perilous to walk along in many locations. Above the encircling escarpments was a lower terrace that had once been mined for phosphates back in the latter half of the nineteenth century, giving the terrain there a crater-pocked landscape, hosting only meager vegetation in the bottoms of the pits. Farther upland there was another set of cliffs that defined an upper terrace, and within the upper terrace dense stands of poisonwood trees predominated.

While reconning the island, Ortega had instructed the pilot to make one low-level pass over the interior, and he was certain he had spotted a footpath that wound its way through the vegetation. The path seemed to run from east to west along the southern side of the upper terrace, terminating in the clearing where he now stood. Only in one area was there a relatively gradual slope between the upper and lower terraces, and that dropped down to the old landing spot where the phosphate ore had once been loaded onto boats, a place designated as Lulu Bay on nautical charts of the island. The name was a misnomer, for it did not resemble a bay at all. From the air Ortega had noticed the ruins of the abandoned workers' settlement at the base of the slope below him, the only location where a determined individual could make their way up a deteriorated ladder consisting of rusted steel and weathered rope in order to reach the higher elevations. If anything, the island seemed uniquely equipped to repel human visitors.

Before this trip, Ortega had taken the liberty of familiarizing himself with the island's past. Its recorded history began in 1504 when

Christopher Columbus, stranded on Jamaica, sent some crew members to Hispaniola by canoe for help. Along the way, the men had stumbled upon the island and stopped in search of fresh water. Finding none, they resumed their journey and for the next 350 years mariners avoided the place.

It wasn't until 1857 when the United States claimed the island under the Guano Act. Prized as a powerful fertilizer, *guano* was actually petrified bird dung, which was in big demand by agriculture before the advent of artificial fertilizers. The Guano Islands Act had been intended to spur American entrepreneurs to seek out and exploit sources of *guano*. At the time of its enactment, American agriculture was clamoring for this new and much sought fertilizer, particularly Maryland and Virginia farmers whose soil had been decimated by decades of rapacious tobacco and cotton production. This congressional wisdom dictated that any uninhabited, unclaimed island on which a U.S. citizen mined *guano* would automatically become U.S. property. Under the Act, mining rights could be awarded to any explorer who discovered *guano* on an uninhabited and otherwise unclaimed island. In other words, once some procedural paperwork had been completed, one could essentially hoist the Stars and Stripes over any desolate island, cay, atoll, key or reef covered in bird droppings.

The Haitian government had protested the U.S. claim, sending a pair of vessels a year later to proclaim that the island and its *guano* belonged to Haiti, especially since it was located only forty miles west of Hispaniola's southern peninsula. Upon such encroachment, several U.S. naval vessels were summoned to chase them away. Up to the present-day, Haiti still continued to claim sovereignty over the island. The thought that both the wealthiest and poorest nations on the planet would contest an island with its only worth being tons of petrified bird shit had made Ortega laugh aloud when he had first researched it. The fish-filled waters near the island had attracted vast flocks of seabirds, mainly Red-footed Boobies, which roosted and defecated for tens of thousands of years to ultimately produce rich layers of solidified bird dung more than one hundred feet deep in places along the island's perimeter.

Looking eastward, Ortega caught sight of the highest point on the island, an aged lighthouse towering forty-six meters above its base and slightly over 120 meters above sea level. Two circular turrets were visible near the top of the structure, the lower one a walk-around observation deck. Built in 1917 by the U.S. Lighthouse Service in response to the opening of the Panama Canal three years earlier, the tall concrete and glass spire had remained essentially unmanned since the time of its automation in 1929. Prior to the automation, a keeper and two assistants had lived on the island in quarters adjacent to the tall structure. Situated in the Windward Passage between Cuba and Haiti, the island presented a hazard to ships plying the waters from the American eastern seaboard to the Canal; thus, the installation of a lighthouse had been necessary to warn shipping away. The U.S. Coast Guard had serviced the automatic beacon twice each year since taking it over from the U.S. Lighthouse Service in 1939. During World War II, the U.S. Navy had established an observation post in the lighthouse, but since then the facility had remained essentially unoccupied with the exception of occasional Haitian fishermen passing through.

In 1996 the U.S. Coast Guard had decommissioned the lighthouse in the face of widespread usage of global positioning systems which rendered the beacon obsolete, and a year later the U.S. Department of the Interior assumed control of the island and placed it under its Office of Insular Affairs. Ortega well knew that while the OIA still retained direct authority for the island's political affairs, it was in 1999 that the U.S. Fish and Wildlife Service assumed administrative responsibility for the island, which then became a National Wildlife Refuge. Technically, he was violating the jurisdictional laws of the United States by trespassing on it without the explicit permission of the Fish and Wildlife Service.

Ortega knew the U.S. Coast Guard paid little attention to the waters in the immediate vicinity of the island, patrolling them only infrequently. And when it did, a well-paid informant embedded within its ranks always gave him sufficient advance warning as to when and from what direction one of its cutters or aircraft would be coming. Several other high-ranking individuals representing a few other branches of the United States military were also on the Cardoza payroll, greatly reducing the risk of having their activities compromised. Such knowledge made Ortega dizzy with pleasure, for it allowed him to operate in this region of the Caribbean with near impunity.

Shifting his gaze to the broad expanse of sea below him, he could not help but wonder why the fishing near Navassa was so good. From experience he knew that this had not always been the case. Over the last several decades, the great shoals of edible fish within the Caribbean Basin had been decimated by overfishing, forcing the large commercial tuna enterprises to venture into both the Pacific and Atlantic in search of more fruitful fishing grounds. To Ortega, more fish meant increased amounts of legitimate product that was crucial in concealing large quantities of illegal drugs. Greater tonnages of harvested tuna equated to being able to transport vaster amounts of heroin and cocaine more quickly. In Ortega's estimation, he would require huge catches of tuna to effectively hide the magnitude of white heroin that Omar was offering for sale. The record hauls he had seen of late gave him a certain degree of assurance that he could undertake the distribution of such huge drug shipments. For some unknown reason, the local environment abounded with enormous schools of tuna, the largest he had ever seen. Somehow this discovery had eluded competing fishing fleets which were busy elsewhere, thereby giving his organization a monopoly over what the adjacent waters could produce.

Aside from the abundance of tuna plying the immediate sea, Ortega puzzled over another peculiarity he had stumbled upon close to Navassa. It had occurred during a fishing excursion near the island almost six months ago. Just as he had done earlier on this day, he had resorted to the use of concussion grenades during that trip, dropping them into swarming masses of Yellowfin and Skipjack. Upon hauling in its net, the *San Carlo* had brought aboard three dead bottlenose dolphins, their gray-toned carcasses intermingled with an incredibly large catch of tuna. The strange thing was, they were unlike any bottlenose he had ever seen before. From all outward appearances they seemed to exhibit all the traits characteristic of their species, with the exception of one striking anomaly. All of them displayed finger-like appendages protruding from the underside of their pectoral flukes. A close examination of those appendages had shown them to be retractable. The significance of the find had stunned him and, never one to miss the smell of potential profits, he had carefully measured and photographed the creatures, documenting details of the odd protuberances from every angle before storing the bodies in deep freeze within the *San Carlo*'s hold.

The unusual find had taken place just before he had decided to dispose of the stubborn IATTC observer stationed aboard his vessel. As of yet the IATTC had failed to provide a replacement for the murdered observer, which was quite all right with Ortega, and the *San Carlo* was still without one.

Considering it important that he keep the *San Carlo's* participation in the discovery of the freak dolphins anonymous, he had given the photos of the creatures to Hennington, instructing the broker to find a buyer for their frozen remains. Amazingly, and to Ortega's intense satisfaction, Hennington had succeeded.

Standing before Omar, Ortega stifled a grin thinking about how quickly Hennington had found a prospective purchaser, an individual that went by the name of McPherson. According to Hennington, the man was willing to offer the equivalent of a king's ransom for a live and fully intact specimen of this new type of dolphin. McPherson was a high-ranking U.S. Naval officer. Yes, Ortega thought, things were going exceptionally well lately.

And if he could capture just one of those creatures alive, he might have a most useful bargaining chip for further and more lucrative transactions.

As Ortega pondered all this, he became aware of Omar's penetrating stare. The Islamist was awaiting an answer.

"Perhaps we can do business," Ortega said, managing to suppress his excitement by keeping his manner and tone neutral.

Chapter 11

*T*he small pod of white dolphin slowed as it came to within three miles of the squat mount jutting above the sea, the lone human female riding its center fully sensing the pain of the pod's injured cousins. Like a homing beacon, the distress of the wounded was easy to follow, emanating steadily from a point directly ahead. As though they were of one mind, the girl and the pack attuned their thoughts further, thus reducing the possibility of missing their intended target in so vast an ocean. Fleeting visual images continued to impinge on their consciousness, intertwined with intermittent twinges of suffering and panic that rose and fell like the ebb and flow of a rapidly moving tide, pulsing stronger as they neared their destination. While the sensation greatly dispirited the group, they pushed on with tenacious resolution.

Within a short interlude a sonic holographic picture was sent their way from one being in particular, its familiar signature whistle identifying itself and providing the pod with additional information on the calamity that had befallen its comrades. Although unnecessary, the pod answered back in kind, millions of years of evolutionary conditioning causing instinct to override and frequently conflict with newly developed abilities. A sudden burst of rapid-fire speak-see clicks triggered at frequencies approximating 160,000 hertz was suddenly sent forth in a tightly directed beam by the laryngeal emitters of every member of the group ringing the girl. Almost instantaneously, the returning echoes were processed by highly sophisticated brains. Deciphering the complex sounds into symbols and pictures, they confirmed the presence of seven other bottlenose dolphin, five males and two females. Among these creatures, four were physically impaired, two severely. All were adults except for a juvenile male which remained unharmed.

Once again, the use of such old-fashioned biophysical processing was unnecessary. The girl and every member of her pod would have seen and felt the plight of their laboring cousins anyway.

On a microscopic structural level, the brain of each animal in the pack was at least as advanced as the human brain, with cell counts just as high per cubic millimeter and the number of layers in their brain cortex equally as great. However, in the last four generations of this new breed of dolphin, the number of cells interconnected to one another had increased by one-third over the average human brain, giving them extraordinary powers of the mind. Strangely, the girl's brain also manifested this same anomaly, something passed on to her from her mother, providing her with a telepathic link not only to the creatures surrounding her, but to others with similar genetic traits. Such an attribute had made it possible for her and her companions to align their thoughts and emotions into harmonic resonance, allowing them to achieve a mental synergy well beyond the grasp of scientific explanation.

As the other dolphins came into visual range, two paired teams of adults could be seen supporting the two most injured, each team using their heads and snouts to buoy up one of the badly wounded creatures high enough so that its blowhole remained clear of the water. If they failed to do this, the creatures would drown.

Both of the succored dolphins were grays. Each of the assisting pairs contained one albino dolphin. Although one of the albinos was mildly injured, the other was unscathed. Altogether, the adults consisted of two albinos and four grays, all bottlenose. One of the assisting grays displayed a lacerated pectoral fluke and was teamed with an uninjured albino. The injured albino was teamed with an uninjured gray. The girl could sense that both dolphins being supported were fending off unconsciousness from internal trauma. Her heart went out to the juvenile albino, little more than four years old, flitting among the adults in confusion and panic.

The girl opened her mind to the eddies in time and space swirling about her, currents caused by past events and events yet to come. A powerful malevolence had passed this way and would soon come again, and she intuitively knew they had little time with which to lend assistance.

Breaking formation, the two dolphins leading the girl's pod shot forward to help. Hermes was a male, Aphrodite a female. Both grays being kept afloat were in critical condition, and like all cetaceans, their respiratory mechanisms were totally voluntary. Unlike most land-based mammals whose breathing systems were automatic and involuntary when unconscious, dolphins could not afford to have such a mechanism. If they did it would cause them to breathe water while submerged in an unconscious state. For a cetacean, passing out for any reason in the open sea was dangerous and usually fatal if left unattended. They needed to be awake to breathe. And because of it, a voluntary breathing system created an interdependency among dolphins and among whales if they were to survive. A seriously incapacitated cetacean had to rely on his fellow creatures to bring him to the surface and keep him awake in order that he inhale, otherwise he dies.

The girl watched the rescue unfold as Hercules, the abnormally big male she rode, dipped below the surface in the crystal-clear water. One of the endangered grays, a female, appeared to be slipping into coma. Hercules' fine beam sonar verified that the gray had ceased breathing. Inconsolable, her young calf shot back and forth close by, squealing forlornly at the physical distress of its mother.

Continuing her mind meld with those of her companions, the girl sensed the parlous condition almost as quickly as did the albinos. Ultrasonic scans of both supported creatures revealed significant hemorrhaging among their internal organs, particularly in the lungs, and every so often, a fine pink mist would spew forth from blowholes bubbling with red froth. But now nothing emanated from the nostrils of the female. Hastily, Aphrodite squeezed deftly between the two dolphins supporting the unconscious gray, raking her dorsal fin across the anal region of the comatose creature. The contact caused an involuntary reflex contraction of the gray's pectoral flukes and seemed to revive her. Persisting in keeping the ailing dolphin conscious, Aphrodite kept nudging the female with her rostrum.

Something further out caught the girl's attention, just a faint nudge on her consciousness. Coral and Reef had detected it, a minuscule trace of unpropitious presentiment wafting in like the aroma of rotting flesh. Apollo and Artemis were the first to assess its significance. Several large tiger sharks were being drawn inexorably to the scene by the scent of blood and the physical distress. Though they were still several hundred meters off, she sensed them as if they were within arm's reach. Abruptly, Apollo and Artemis, the brother-sister twins forming the rear guard of the albino pod, veered off sharply in opposite directions to discourage and divert the advancement of the pelagic predators.

The girl was not concerned about the safety of the duo as they disappeared from sight into the submarine murk. From firsthand experience she knew they and the rest of the albinos displayed exceptional athletic abilities that surpassed those of the common bottlenose strain. Superior muscular development and greater natural speed coupled with enhanced cerebral intelligence and a heightened physical endurance over and above their gray cousins made them a formidable match for any large and ferocious oceanic carnivore. According to Jacob, if not for the environmental abuses proliferated by man, and barring any cataclysmic natural disasters, the new breed would, in all likelihood, survive and continue to proliferate under any other circumstances.

The beings that comprised the girl's pod were implausible creations of nature. Superbly sleek and marvelously agile, Hermes was the fastest of the lot and could explode through the sea with an acceleration unequaled by his companions. It was not unusual for him to leap to a height of twenty meters above the sea when frolicking exuberantly with the others of the group or when seeking a bird's eye view of the sea around them. His graceful and energetic displays of aerial acrobatics were fantastic sights to behold, and the girl never tired of watching, always awed by each performance. Whereas Hermes was the personification of blazing speed and unparalleled agility, his twin sister, Aphrodite, was the embodiment of empathic clairvoyance and psychic healing. Her extraordinarily loving and compassionate nature gave her a distinct aura that resonated to all members of the pod like a lambent jewel, and the girl constantly delighted in the gentle and disparate caress of her astral presence, which was always the most soothing among any of her kind.

The youngest members of the pack, Apollo and Artemis, were the most analytical and calculating among them, and their healing prowess was only surpassed by that of Aphrodite. They were always the quickest to interpret the meaning of psychic anomalies that occasionally permeated the fabric of four-dimensional space surrounding them and which drifted just beyond the boundaries of physical awareness.

Coral and Reef, the flanking members of the pod's traveling formation, were the holistic thinkers within their ranks, providing philosophical guidance to the clan whenever it was confronted with a moral dilemma. They were always the backdrop of reason and wisdom to those of their ilk. The two of them were the only ones that could read Jacob's thoughts with any degree of consistency. They were the oldest of the three pairs of twins comprising the immediate group and the most adept at being able to sense impending danger. Coral was the female of the pair and Reef her brother.

The most prodigious among them, Hercules, was the manifestation of awesome strength and raw power, exhibiting inordinately thick muscular development throughout the length of his massive body. Incredibly, the albino bull was considerably larger than his counterparts and stronger than any orca having a body size twice his length and thrice his weight, measuring slightly over five and a half meters from the tip of his beak to the end of his tail fluke. The extra drag the girl caused him was no more than an afterthought. Known as the gentle giant of the pod, his characteristically mild temperament would transform radically to one of cold, measured belligerence at the slightest threat confronting the group, most particularly one directed at the girl.

The girl had hoped the rescue would go unimpeded, but all her senses told her otherwise. Jacob still lagged far behind and the pinnace would be needed to bring the incapacitated dolphins to safety. She felt deep compassion for her ailing friends, understanding completely their fear and revulsion of drowning at sea or becoming a meal for the predators that abounded in it because they were too weak to escape or defend themselves. When sick or significantly injured, or when death was inevitable, a deep-seated primeval calling always drew them unrelentingly to the land, the place of their primordial origins where their ancient ancestors once flourished. They would much prefer to perish under the light of the sun or moon on a remote sandy shore rather than in the cold, dark depths of the ocean. The land always beckoned under such circumstances and accounted for the beaching of untold numbers of dolphin ever since they first ventured into antediluvian seas in eons past. By beaching themselves or entering the very shallow water of a protected estuary or lagoon, they at least had a chance to recover from their illness, secure from the threat of sharks and other predators. But out here in these waters she knew there was no immediate safe haven where they could bring the enervated dolphins. She was quite familiar with the nearby island, knowing that its surrounding cliffs rising directly from the sea provided no shelves, beaches or inlets. What the island did hold, however, was the key to the ultimate salvation of the dolphins. That it might also benefit the future welfare of the human race was also a strong possibility, for the secret it held was truly a blessing.

As Hercules breached, the girl looked around hopefully. Although she could feel Jacob's presence, there was still no sight of him. The outline of another vessel in the distance caught her eye. Different in configuration from the pinnace and much larger in size, she realized it was the same vessel the pod had overtaken a short time earlier. Although the proximity of a strange vessel would typically make her feel uneasy, she sensed that it posed no threat. Under normal circumstances, the pod would have exercised caution and steered clear of marine traffic, knowing that a human observer might consider the sight of it highly unusual considering a human female rode one of the creatures in its midst. Such an event might induce a curious sailor to pursue the pack for a closer look, something Jacob had warned her about. According to him, one could never be fully sure of the intentions of strangers since they might potentially bring harm to members of the pod. Therefore, it would be prudent to avoid contact with unknown humans at sea altogether. But this was an emergency, and the pod had felt it necessary to take a direct route to its stricken cousins if they were to have any chance at all of saving them. Although passing in full view of the strange boat's crew had been a risk, it had nevertheless been one worth taking.

A strange feeling had come over her when the pod had come close to the other boat. She remembered the name painted on its stern. It was an odd name, a contradiction. Angels were supposed to be endowed with goodness, perfect spiritual beings that were kind and loving. Avenging implied a retaliatory punishment or payback for harm received, an act of evil, of wickedness. How could an angel harbor such a malicious trait? Wouldn't it be incongruous with a morally pure nature? Didn't Jesus tell everyone to turn the other cheek? Wasn't he the one who promoted the golden rule: Do unto others as you would have them do unto you?

She momentarily puzzled over these fleeting thoughts, vaguely aware that her musing didn't go unnoticed by the other members of the clan. Her mind was still linked synchronously with them and she sensed their confusion over the diametrically opposed and conflicting concepts, particularly the latter idea. Such turpitude went against the grain of their inherent makeup.

She recalled that there had been six men aboard the *Avenging Angel*, three of them gawking oddly at her from the open doorway of the pilothouse. Other than her mother, Jacob, and the villagers of Malique, she had seldom run into others of her kind. Jacob had instilled in her that most of the world's ills were caused by human greed. Was it not man who was slowly but methodically killing off the dolphins and whales, he had often reminded her. Were not humans responsible for overfishing the oceans with vast nets and poisoning the waters with toxic wastes, garbage, and organic pollution? Man was an out-of-control virus that, if left to his own vices and thoughtless actions, would eventually consume the earth, ultimately destroying all its beautiful wonders.

During her young life, the girl had seen many of her aquatic friends injured and killed by the abuses of man, most often due to carelessness and ignorance, but sometimes because of a thing Jacob referred to as sadism. Although it was a trait indigenous to some human beings, it was something she was ill prepared to conceive of, a notion totally alien to her. Jacob had tried to explain it to her but it was a concept that escaped her like water slipping through her fingers. The idea that a person could experience pleasure by deliberately inflicting pain or death on another living creature was a notion she had trouble grasping. But as she glanced over at her debilitated comrades, a dawning comprehension took hold of her and she suddenly knew they had been disabled by such an act.

As the girl watched the approach of the strange vessel, Jacob's words rang clearly in her head. We humans are still fighting each other, destroying more than we are creating. There are some people who want to gain, not only at the expense of other humans, but other living things. Mankind has evolved to the point where it has made great strides in many things. It has sent men to the moon and the deepest part of the ocean, it has made tremendous breakthroughs in physics and medicine, yet it has failed miserably in mastering its own human nature. Humanity is using its abilities incorrectly and causing terrible damage to our planet and all its inhabitants in the process. Man is still insufficiently developed to protect and care for the world we live in. She was only six years old when he told her this, but the words stayed with her as if he had uttered them yesterday.

She vividly remembered the place where he had given her this moralization. She had been sitting in the pinnace as it chugged along the coast many miles south of the cove. She had looked questioningly at Jacob. "What is that?" Jacob had shielded his eyes from the sun and followed her gaze. A vast quantity of plastic containers and garbage littered the nearby beach, most of it washed in with the tide. A look of distaste crossed Jacob's features as he eyed the waste. "This is Haiti, little one. If the land could speak it would tell of tragedy and abuse, of power and greed, violence and bloodshed." She realized then how ugly the world could be beyond the beautiful sanctity of the cove.

It was shortly thereafter that her real education had begun, but it wasn't until she turned ten that they had initiated the project. "You and your playmates were put on this earth to fulfill a profound and far-reaching purpose," Jacob had told her solemnly on her birthday. "Mother Nature is a wise old lady. Perhaps in her infinite wisdom she has seen fit to place the care of this planet in the hands of more responsible creatures." He had paused and let out a great sigh. "And I believe she has chosen you and your friends. The time for intervention has arrived." Even then, at so young an age, she had instinctively comprehended what he had meant.

With the exception of her mother, she was certain she was the only human on the planet that truly understood the mind and soul of the dolphin, to revel in the joy of simply being. She was completely aware of their dual existence, knowing that these incredible creatures simultaneously dwelt within two realms, one of the mind and one of the spirit. For some inexplicable reason, this duality was also indelibly ingrained in her, and like her companions, she understood the multifaceted light of love, the most powerful force in creation. She fathomed its pure energy that was capable of transcending all barriers, both material and ethereal, perceiving its endless flow from an eternal, infinite waterfall. It was a ceaseless, all-encompassing radiance that set no conditions or boundaries, streaming forth unconfined and without limits. And it was firmly rooted in who she was, integrated into her soul, her very essence.

She could feel this same energy, its purity and simplicity, emanating outward from all the pod members, blanketing and imbuing the stricken dolphins, and she added that which was a part of her astral being into the discharge. On a spiritual level, unconditional love radiated forth and intensified, becoming greater than the combined total of their individual outputs. But on a physical level, the biosonar wave emissions originating from those closest to the wounded creatures created a cavitation, a rippling effect in the matter comprising the damaged flesh. The resonance of the impaired tissue changed and healing suddenly accelerated. Even Jacob could not provide a satisfactory scientific explanation as to why it worked, but she knew it did.

On both planes of existence, spiritual and physical, the girl and her clan avoided absorbing the greater portion of the pain of the injured, for a requisite amount of detachment on their part had to be exercised if their ministrations were going to be effective. She knew the danger of integrating too much pain and suffering into the minds and souls of the healers. Doing so could easily overwhelm, pulling the potential healer under tumultuous emotions that should not be their own to bear. This was a lesson carried down and expanded upon over the ages among cetaceans, and then further refined by the new breed. She understood that neither the healer's soul nor the one for whom they are absorbing the pain is ultimately served by such actions, for no soul can do this for another since we are all here to journey our own path. If this tenet were overlooked or ignored, then the assisting soul risks being pulled down and drowned in a quagmire of suffering, and the one they desire to assist is denied the life lessons they were sent here to learn. Thus, the need for an adequate level of restraint to take on the full brunt of the pain of another.

The girl was proud of her relationship with these noble beings. She knew it was unique, that a special bond existed between them that transcended time and space. Their boundless sensitivity and awareness continually amazed her. Her companions were fully awakened creatures who knew themselves to be one with all things and they experienced this through the power of love at all times. Their minds transported them into unlimited consciousness, carrying them beyond earthly restraints. Their physical bodies resonated with unconditional love and limitless energy, filling them with ecstasy and unconstrained joy. They understood the key to oneness and harmony. They shared love at all times and held no judgements. Their use of sound went well beyond current medical technology, making them able to alter frequencies to create the most appropriate healing actions for the sick and injured in the water with them, seeing inside the being and manipulating the required energies perfectly. She knew without a doubt their blissful presence and loving nature was capable of healing wounds of the heart and opening the spirit to portals of boundless freedom. On spiritual planes, they were powerful and creative guides, using geometry, sound and light to inspire higher awareness, clear consciousness, and pure wisdom.

The girl's awareness was suddenly brought back to the strange vessel as it neared, and she studied it with a mix of uncertainty and ... something else. A transference of psychic warning echoed from Coral and Reef simultaneously. Hercules turned sharply and the girl looked below her. A dark shadow glided through the depths far below, holding to a course bearing directly at the island. Too deep for the sunlight filtering into the void of inky hydrospace to provide definition to the object, it remained indistinct to her human eyes as it traveled on a straight and level heading. Her current position was a significant distance from the island and the underlying water was still quite deep.

Biosonar emissions from her companions were quickly directed at the strange object and an image of the thing suddenly flashed into her mind. It was large, very large, having an overall length almost as great as that of a fully-grown blue whale and a configuration just as streamlined. But it lacked the characteristics consistent with living flesh. Rather than being soft and pliant in texture, the object was rigid and metallic, a thing fabricated by human hands, a submarine. The girl had never seen one before and wondered what such a machine was doing out in these waters. A thought suddenly galvanized her. What if the people piloting the strange craft were to find the undersea cavern and discover its secret? A feeling of dread began to engulf her and she quickly shook it off. Her eyes followed the shadow a few moments longer before all traces of it vanished into the dark blue murk.

By the time Hercules again breached, the girl found herself looking up into the faces of several men leaning over the side of the surface vessel that had followed her pod. Sensing no menace from them, she stared silently back, not knowing what to do next.

"I believe you and your friends can use some help," the man in the middle called to her, a thick shock of white hair cascading down to his shoulders from beneath a baseball cap and a smile parting his lips.

Something about the man struck a chord deep within her, perhaps the lilt of his voice. Somehow it conveyed solace, reassurance. Without immediately realizing what she was doing, however, her gaze was drawn to the face of the man standing to the left of the older gent. She found it difficult to pull her eyes away from those penetrating green orbs.

"Are you a friend of Natalie?" the white-haired man asked.

The question stunned the girl and she stared back intently at the elderly man, sitting up straighter as Hercules floated docilely beneath her. Only a handful of people knew the names of her friends, including the man who had saved Natalie.

"Are you the man who rescued Natalie and tended her injuries?" the girl queried in a mellifluous voice. The man fit the description Natalie had given her and she studied him with newfound respect.

"Yes. My name is Franklin Grahm...Doctor Franklin Grahm," the scientist said exuberantly, looking hopefully to the other creatures floating close by. "Is Natalie with you now?"

Pivoting her head, the girl took inventory of the other men perched on the deck above her, her eyes flitting from one face to the next, seeming to gain some insight as to the true essence of each persona aboard the vessel. Her gaze came back to linger on Grahm for several more seconds before settling on Jake once again. "Natalie is not among this group," she said at last, her voice containing an unmistakable sadness.

It was then that she lifted the goggles from her eyes, letting them rest on her forehead. Jake noticed that the goggles were actually a low-volume face mask with a nosepiece that allowed the wearer to equalize the air pressure behind the two separate eye plates with the surrounding water pressure. He also noted that even after prolonged immersion in the sea, there was a healthy glow to the girl's creamy complexion, which was smooth and unblemished. Amazingly, the goggles left no temporary imprint on the skin surrounding a large pair of doe-like eyes that glistened a sparkling brown and which stared back serenely as if regarding the world beyond from a strange and alien perspective. Gazing into them was like focusing on a revolving prism subjected to the light, mesmerizing the beholder with a variegated spectrum of endless mystery. On the whole, however, it was her eyes that gave definition to a face of protracted innocence and limitless compassion, uncorrupted by cynicism or the darker side of man's nature.

Silence hung heavily in the air a moment longer before Grahm spoke again. "If you'll allow us, my dear, we can bring your injured friends aboard and treat their wounds."

The girl continued to stare steadfastly at Jake, appearing inattentive to the offer. "Thank you, but that will not be necessary. Help will be here shortly." As if to emphasize this, she withdrew her eyes from Jake and glanced over her shoulder.

In unison, Jake, Grahm, and Zimbola looked in the direction of the girl's gaze. A tiny white dot sat on the eastern horizon, still a considerable distance away.

"Is there anything we can do for you?" Grahm persisted, disappointment apparent in both his tone and manner.

The girl shook her head, her eyes now fixed on the approaching boat.

"What is your name?" Grahm continued to press.

The girl brought those doe-like eyes to bear on Grahm once again. "My name is of no importance." Her voice was soft and melodious, almost childlike in timbre.

Grahm smiled warmly. "Sometimes names can be very important," he said tactfully, touching Jake's shoulder. "This gentleman, here, goes by the name of Jake Javolyn. He is the captain of this vessel." He looked to his left. "This rather large fellow is Zimbola, Captain Javolyn's first mate." Looking aft, Grahm indicated the other members of the crew, introducing Hector, Phillipe, and his two assistants. Turning back to face the girl, Grahm's manner became imbued with alacrity. "Now that I've introduced everyone, good social etiquette can only be satisfied if you introduce yourself, as well."

The girl studied Grahm with renewed interest before replying. "I'm called Destiny."

The name did not surprise Jake. As a matter of fact, it provided the missing piece of the puzzle he had been mulling over concerning Grahm's conversations with Natalie. The future of her kind was in the hands of Destiny, Natalie had told Grahm. This had not gone over Jake's head and he had not ruled out the possibility that the reference to destiny might involve a person. With mild amusement, Jake watched the expression on the doctor's face unfold. The false assumption Grahm had previously harbored lifted like a curtain on a Broadway stage to reveal a hidden truth, and the doctor nodded at the girl with sudden understanding.

Grahm let his eyes drift over the other nearby sea mammals. "Tell me, my dear, did you teach all of these dolphins to speak English as fluently as Natalie?"

Destiny's face turned passive. "I didn't teach them anything."

A cloud of confusion swept across the scientist's countenance. "Then how did Natalie acquire this ability?"

"She...," the girl started to say, but stopped abruptly. Her eyes seemed to glaze over in that instant, as if listening to an inner voice. Although she continued to stare directly at Grahm, the doctor had the impression she was not seeing him at all, that she was looking right through him.

"Natalie's in trouble," she said suddenly, her voice carrying an edge of urgency. "I must go to her."

As Jake and the others watched, the large white dolphin the girl rode began to turn away, but Destiny glanced back at the three men grouped together next to the pilothouse. "A man will be here shortly. His name is Jacob," she cried out, her tone almost pleading. "Please help him recover my injured friends." Her eyes singled Jake out as she said this, as if speaking to him alone. Refitting the face mask over her eyes, she hunched forward and reached down on each side of Hercules broad body to grasp a rein looped over the base of each pectoral fin. She quickly sped away on a southwest heading, unattended by her previous retinue.

Jake ducked into the pilothouse and retrieved a pair of binoculars, bringing them to his eyes and aligning them with several objects far away. He didn't need the spyglasses to distinguish the outlines of the three ships hanging on the horizon, estimating the nearest one to be only two miles distant. The binoculars, however, confirmed something else. Satisfied, he lowered the glasses, handing them over to Zimbola while continuing to keep his gaze locked on the closest vessel. "You recognize anything about that ship?" he said.

Zimbola lifted the binoculars to his eyes and scanned the vessel, the instrument looking ridiculously small in his huge paw. The big man nodded. "It is the Colombian tuna trawler we saw in the harbor yesterday. Her crew is just beginning to drop her net."

Without wasting another second, Jake craned his head over the gunwale and shouted aft, calling to Hector and Phillipe. Both men stood gawking at Destiny's receding form. "Prepare the Kawasaki," Jake ordered.

"With everything?" Hector shot back, clearly perplexed. The crew knew that Jake only used the Kawasaki during a Code One which, based on experience, always occurred at night. Code One implied fully armed.

"Everything!" Jake growled. "I want it fully locked and loaded."

Zimbola appeared taken aback, and he stared down at Jake questioningly.

"What are you doing?" Grahm asked.

Jake halted in mid stride. "I don't know what's going on, but something tells me I better help that girl before she buys herself a whole heap of trouble she's not ready to take on." As an afterthought, he turned back toward Zimbola. "After I launch, stay here on station."

Eyebrows rose up on the big man. "You do not want me to follow?"

"You heard the girl," Jake bellowed. "She wants us to assist a guy called Jacob."

Chapter 12

As the pinnace crept closer to the distant island, Jacob's thoughts continued to drift back to earlier times. Subsequent to the landslide that had thwarted the Tonton Makout raid on Malique and Amphitrite's ensuing collapse at the ancient mapou tree, he had been confronted with carrying her limp body to safety. At first he had sought to move her back to the cove but then realized her gravid state ruled out such an endeavor. Attempting to move her by himself down the ladders anchored to the cove's steep walls would have been too risky for her and her baby.

Having lifted her from the ground and cradled her in his arms, he knew the only logical place to bring her would be the nearby village. Trudging along with her inert form up and down the hilly trail had been an undertaking that had taken him to the absolute limits of his endurance, and every so often he had to stop to rest, lowering her body gently to the ground. The last thing he wanted was to stumble and drop her. Wearily, with biceps, shoulders and back burning with fatigue, he had eventually made it to the village. Staggering with his burden to the front door of Baptiste's humble abode, he had kicked at it loudly with his foot. A good ten seconds of hushed silence had prevailed before Jacob was forced to repeat the action, and then he had heard movement inside.

"Who comes to my home in the middle of the night?" a groggy but wary voice had questioned in French from the other side of the door.

"It is me, your cousin Jacob," he had answered in the same language, his tone faltering and all his reserves nearly gone.

Baptiste had opened the door a crack and peeked outside. Seeing Jacob with the comatose white woman, his eyes had widened with surprise and he had hastily ushered them inside. Baptiste's wife, Lucette, had been at Jacob's side in a flash and, with her and her husband assisting, they quickly had Amphitrite lying comfortably in a cot.

So vibrant was the memory that Jacob became lost in the full range of its scope, and he was suddenly reliving it once again and correlating the experience with other items of significance. Baptiste turned his full attention back to Jacob. "Who is this woman, Jacob? What has happened to her?"

Jacob found a chair and seated himself, too exhausted to speak as yet. He was still breathing hard from his physical ordeal.

"Have you no eyes, Emmanuel?" Lucette interceded. "Can you not see your cousin is trying to catch his breath?" She ran from the room and returned several moments later, handing Jacob a tall glass of water. Greedily, he quaffed it down.

Both Emmanuel and Lucette eyed him expectantly, their gazes implacable as owls in an aviary waiting to be fed succulent mice by the keeper. "Your village has been targeted by Duvalier's thugs," Jacob wheezed, his speech barely understandable. "This woman managed to stop them."

Baptiste and his wife looked at one another, their expressions muddled.

Jacob felt his strength returning and he found his voice again. "The hill where the sacred mapou tree sits has partially collapsed and blocked the road leading to this village. It triggered a mudslide that prevented the Tonton Makout from coming here."

Baptiste still appeared confused. "A moment ago, you said this woman stopped them." He turned to glance at Amphitrite's still form. She seemed to be sleeping peacefully. He swiveled his head back and his mouth took on the shape of a silly smile. "Did she cause the mudslide?" his query saturated with doubt.

The directness and simplicity of the question rocked Jacob. Both he and his cousin were analytical thinkers. Growing up in a society characterized by superstition and antiquated beliefs, the two of them had refused to accept such indoctrination at fairly early ages, considering such credence to exceed the bounds of reason and belonging to another time and place. Emmanuel had long ago cast off the shackles of such dogma, proclaiming that such thinking belonged to the ignorant.

Jacob was suddenly at a loss for words. Here he was, about to describe something inexplicable, something seemingly miraculous. How did he explain that Amphitrite had simply placed her hand on the tree and caused the hill to come down? Was it mere coincidence? How improbable was such a two-sided happening. In this case logic was ambivalent towards supporting a relationship between the two distinct and what could be considered mutually exclusive incidents. On the one hand Emmanuel could argue that the recent heavy rains wrought by the hurricane had made the hill unstable, thus setting the stage for the inevitable mudslide, a condition that would remain unconnected in any way with Amphitrite's contact with the mapou. He wondered what the odds were for such a confluence of supposedly unrelated actions, the touching of the tree and the collapse of the hill, to occur at nearly the same time. Jacob was certain Emmanuel would reject any suggestion of causality. In an orderly universe, logic dictated that an interrelationship between both events was contrary to nature, a cause-and-effect duality that defied the impossible. But he had seen it with his own eyes and could not refute it. The woman's precognition he could accept as lying within the realm of possibility, and therefore, would have no difficulty elucidating upon. There was a wealth of scientific evidence to support it. In retrospect, there was no satisfactory explanation for initiating a mudslide by placing one's hand upon a tree…unless. He looked sharply at the unconscious woman. Unless one accepted the premise that Amphitrite was endowed with telekinetic powers. From experience, he knew Emmanuel would consider such a possibility as being absurd.

Jacob found himself nodding slowly in reply to Emmanuel's question, a gesture laden with diffidence. He was not fully prepared to shrug off the skepticism his words were sure to prompt. "I cannot account for how she was able to do it," was all he offered, his tone betraying the reticence he felt.

Emmanuel absorbed this information quietly, peering owlishly over his glasses at Jacob. "Who is this woman, Jacob?" he finally asked. "She is unfamiliar to me."

Jacob's mind changed gears. "A dolphin brought her to the cove where I live. She-"

A stifled cry left Lucette's lips and she brought a hand to her mouth, her eyes huge and penetrating, staring at Jacob as if he were a ghostly apparition.

Agitated, Emmanuel turned to face her. "What is wrong, woman?"

"Esmerelda's prophecy!"

"What are you talking about?"

Lucette pulled her eyes from Jacob and took hold of her husband's arm, glancing behind her at the sleeping woman. "It is just as Esmerelda prophesied."

Emmanuel's expression went blank. "I do not understand."

Swallowing hard, Lucette said excitedly, "The day before your grandmother's death, she told me a white woman would come from the sea riding a dolphin. She said that once this woman arrived upon our shore, life as we knew it would change forever."

Jacob was stunned. This was a revelation that caught him totally by surprise. But he was sure Lucette would not mislead Emmanuel with such a story for she had been very close with Esmerelda and would have been privy to many of her thoughts.

Emmanuel suddenly appeared angry. "My grandmother was both the practitioner and victim of archaic cultural beliefs rooted in witchcraft. Her predictions of the future rarely amounted to anything more than generalizations that could be applied to any situation under most circumstances."

Jacob listened to the diatribe with analytical interest, understanding Emmanuel well enough to know that his words lacked sufficient conviction.

Emmanuel refocused his attention back on Jacob. His countenance remained clouded. "Please go on. Pay no mind to the ravings of my wife who still insists upon holding onto primitive tenets and outmoded consuetude. The prognostications of Esmerelda held no significant meaning."

A play of emotion rippled across Lucette's face. "How can you say such a horrible thing?" she decried. "Your grandmother loved you." Her gaze swept back to Jacob, her eyes glistening with moisture and foreshadowing tears. "She loved all of us." She spread out her arms. "She loved this village. She protected Malique with her vaudun."

Emmanuel's petulance turned to exasperation. "Did her vaudun warn of the storm that nearly wrecked our village?" he countered, the sting in his voice abating a notch. "Did it save five of our fishermen that perished in it?" Pausing for effect, Emmanuel brought more venom back into his tone, slamming home a final point like a hammer blow. "Did it save her?"

The first tears trickled down Lucette's cheeks. "Her magic spared us from Duvalier's assassins when others were not so fortunate. Even now we are still protected. Did not your cousin just tell you the Tonton Makout were stopped from reaching this place?"

Emmanuel threw his arms up in frustration. "Why must you be so bullheaded, woman?" Abruptly he turned back to Jacob. "Are you sure the Tonton were coming here?"

A wave of heat surged up the back of Jacob's neck, its flame threatening to climb onto his face. An intense feeling of discomfort washed over him and he looked away to conceal the chagrin that was rapidly eating away at his composure. "I cannot substantiate that," was all he could bring himself to say.

"Then how can you be certain this village was in any danger?" Emmanuel grumbled with annoyance.

"She saw it in a dream," Jacob riposted, gesturing toward the still unconscious Amphitrite.

Two years Jacob's senior, Emmanuel grew momentarily quiet, his eyes filled with reprobation, magnified further by his owlish spectacles. His reply was cold and harsh. "I would have thought that you of all people would have known better. You-"

"Her dream was precognitive in nature," Jacob interrupted, spitting out the words in protest. "This woman never met you or had any previous knowledge of you, yet she heard your name in a dream, a dream that told her the Tonton Makout were coming to kill you this very night."

"Most dreams never equate to reality. Their contents rarely transpire in the real world, and hardly ever the way we remember them when they do. Nightmares are especially unlikely to play out the way they were dreamt. Could it be that you had mentioned my name in conversation and it reemerged in her nightmare? How can you be sure Duvalier's assassins were coming here at all?"

Too tired to become argumentative, Jacob kept his voice level. "Would you have preferred me to ignore her vision altogether and do nothing. The value I place on your life and this village is too high for me not to have taken any action at all."

Jacob paused, letting the full impact of his words sink in. "No, your name was never brought up in conversation prior to her dream. You know as well as I that dreams can often foretell the future. Sometimes they are prophetic. But sometimes they act as a warning against approaching danger, often providing us with a course of action to follow in order to avoid the threat. Earlier on this night, the white woman awoke from a sound sleep in a highly emotional state. She was very concerned for your safety and the safety of this village. She saw the men and the trucks traveling along the road that leads here and described them to me. She referred to them as the Tonton Makout and asked me what the name meant. She even described the sacred mapou tree as well as the remnants of the old well next to it."

A scowl broke out on Emmanuel's face. "There is nothing sacred about that tree."

Jacob disregarded the remark, noting Lucette's dismay before continuing. "Though she had never laid eyes on the tree nor had any awareness of its existence before the dream, she knew the hill from which it grew was unstable enough to cause a mudslide capable of destroying the convoy of trucks."

"You saw this convoy?"

"Yes. Even before we reached the hill, she told me four trucks led by a jeep would be coming. My own eyes confirmed her description to be accurate."

Emmanuel pursed his lips and nodded, a slow, almost imperceptible acknowledgement of Jacob's story. Although his cousin's previous testiness was rapidly evaporating, Jacob could tell he was not entirely convinced about the dream's accuracy or validity. "Then tell me, cousin," Emmanuel continued to probe, a shrewd gleam in his eyes, "how this woman was able to cause the mudslide at just the right moment?"

Jacob mentally winced. Emmanuel was a master at locating the pivotal point in any argument. Like a bloodhound, he always seemed to sniff out the possible flaws in the fabric of truth, the areas where the subtle scent of controversy was strongest and could be exploited.

Remaining steadfast, Jacob refused to alter what he had witnessed. "Just before the convoy passed the hill, the woman reached out and placed a hand on the mapou tree. It was then that part of the hill tumbled away and buried the trucks."

A broad smirk suddenly spread across Emmanuel's face, compounded further by a rumbling laugh that burst forth from deep down in his belly.

"Forgive me, my cousin, but I find such an assertion to be highly amusing," he cackled. "Either you were hallucinating or that exceptionally bright mind of yours is starting to revert back to ancient beliefs." Abruptly, he stopped hooting, seeming to consider something. "I just hope this alleged mudslide did not injure or kill any innocents. Maybe we should go there to see if anyone is still alive," he ridiculed.

"Attempting to provide any aid would not be a wise course of action," Jacob objected wearily. "If there are any survivors, only misfortune can result in trying to render assistance." A vision of the lead vehicle remaining only partially buried came to mind, its headlights aimed at the firmament.

Emmanuel sobered markedly. "How can you be so certain of this?" he challenged, looking closely for any signs of doubt in Jacob's face. "It is unlike you to accept such a supposition without absolute proof. I would think it is quite possible that the people trapped in this mudslide of yours are not members of the Tonton Makout at all."

Jacob remained unwavering. "Everything points to the premise that the men in that convoy are Duvalier's assassins. Who else would be traveling toward this village in the middle of the night in a military-type convoy? That road ends here and goes no farther." He shook his head. "No, cousin, any survivors you find will, in all probability, be armed and dangerous. As a precautionary measure, I strongly recommend you post some villagers with weapons in concealment along the trail leading here."

Emmanuel absorbed this logic thoughtfully for several moments. His demeanor slowly changed, and a look of deep-seated respect seeped into his eyes. "Tell me about this woman, Jacob," he requested, turning to view the sleeping woman on the cot.

"She was delirious and in poor physical condition when I found her. She was suffering from a combination of severe jellyfish stings, dehydration, and exhaustion. As of now, she is afflicted with an extreme case of amnesia. Because she has no recollection of who she is or where she came from, I have taken the liberty of naming her Amphitrite until her memory returns."

"When did you find her?"

"Almost eleven days ago."

Like Jacob, Emmanuel Baptiste was one of the few locals to have received a college education. Both men had graduated the university in Port-au-Prince together in 1975. Gaunt and scholarly-looking by virtue of a set of tiny spectacles clinging precariously to the bridge of his nose, Emmanuel had distinguished himself at the university as an outspoken proponent of environmentalism. "Haiti is an ecological disaster," he had often said. "If all our citizens banded together, it is within our power to make Haiti a more beautiful country, not the garbage ridden eyesore the rest of the world sees. The land is ours, and if we fail to give it the respect it deserves, we should not expect other people to love and respect it for us."

Both men shared the same but now deceased grandmother, Esmerelda Brisson, a renowned priestess of vaudun, the branch of voodoo considered to be white magic. Widely venerated for the potency of her powers, she had become a formidable adversary of both the Papa Doc and Baby Doc regimes. Many believed that she, and she alone, had been able to invoke a spell that had allowed Malique and its inhabitants to escape the brutal reign of terror perpetuated by the Duvalier government. In fact, some of her staunchest followers had credited her with causing the death of the senior Duvalier in 1971 at the age of 64.

It was Papa Doc who had initiated the use of vaudun, the evil branch of voodoo, to sustain his regime over the peasant culture that dominated the nation. His practice of black magic and sorcery encouraged rumors among the people that he possessed dark mystical powers, further bolstering the abject fear he spread as a means to controlling the populace. Often seen dressed in a black top hat and coat reminiscent of the outfit worn by Baron Samedi, the powerful spirit of the cemeteries, Papa Doc had recruited many practitioners of the black occult into his network of spies and informants.

Although Catholicism was made the official religion of Haiti in 1860, the majority of people, living as peasant farmers and fishermen, had developed a system of beliefs drawing on African traditions. While ninety-five percent of all Haitians were Roman Catholics, voodoo was considered the country's national religion, which most voodooists believed could coexist with other religions. Through personal experience with his grandmother, Jacob well understood that adherents of voodoo did not perceive themselves as members of a separate belief. Paradoxically, most Haitians had conjoined the two religions, claiming that you could not serve the spirits unless you were Catholic.

As a means of self-defense against outright opposition to its practice, most predominantly by those of the Protestant faith and to a lesser extent by the Catholic Church, voodoo had come to be shrouded in mystery and secrecy. It existed as a semi-underground religion, with ceremonies taking place at night and its temples hidden away. Unlike structured formal religions, voodoo had never been codified in writing, lacking a fixed theology or organized hierarchy, making it extremely difficult to pin down exactly what it was. As did Esmerelda, Jacob knew each practitioner developed his or her own reputation for either helping people or causing harm to others.

Although he had deeply loved his grandmother, both he and Emmanuel could never bring themselves to embrace her beliefs, considering them to fly in the face of reason. Born with superior intellect, their minds were encumbered by too much rational and analytical thinking, as Esmerelda had put it, to fully grasp the dimensions of spirituality that plainly existed just beyond the constricting boundaries of reality as they perceived it. We are mirrors of each other's souls, she had preached. The universe is all one. No event has a life of its own, and each thing affects something else. Nature knows this. A strange visceral smile would further broaden Esmerelda's characteristically wide face whenever she sensed Jacob's struggle to accept her teachings, for she had implied that deep rational thinking was not conducive to understanding such concepts. Since we all serve as parts of one, she had said, what you do unto another, you also do unto yourself, because you are the other. Voo doo, view you. The creator is manifest through the spirits of ancestors who can bring good or harm and must be honored in ceremonies. Do not strangle your mind with limitations, she had frequently warned. Do not question everything. The mysteries voodoo holds have no room for ambivalence or skepticism. You must open yourself and let your mind soar to untold heights if you are to achieve divine wisdom.

Esmerelda Brisson had been the most powerful mambo in the land, able to diagnose illnesses with the touch of a hand, frequently revealing the origins of another's misfortune. An accomplished herbalist who had successfully treated a wide variety of ailments and injuries over her lifetime, she had imparted some of this specialized knowledge to Jacob.

When Jacob had attended the university, he had been a quiet and reserved student in stark contrast to his outspoken cousin, who did not go unnoticed by those within Baby Doc Duvalier's administration. Emmanuel had frequently ridiculed the government for its unrestrained corruption and its dismal failing to implement environmental policies that would improve the country. A gifted orator and skilled debater, Emmanuel had rapidly garnered a following, and because of it, the junior Duvalier saw him as a potential threat. But fearful that he might provoke the wrath of Esmerelda if he attempted to silence the voice of this rising star, Baby Doc refrained from dispatching his henchmen. Instead, he had his acolytes search the land high and low for the most powerful adept of vaudun, hoping to counter any spell invoked by the powerful Esmerelda through such a person. It did not take them long to find such an individual, a woman that called herself Erzulie, so named after the mistress of Damballah. In order to strengthen his hold on the population, Baby Doc had brought the woman into his inner circle, often showcasing her by his side during public appearances. It soon became evident that the woman was the epitome of pure evil. Dissidents of Duvalier's dictatorship began to mysteriously disappear.

Not long thereafter, Esmerelda had been summoned by several Malique fishermen to improve the fishing in the waters close to the village. While she was performing an incantation, the sky suddenly darkened and a black ominous cloud scudded low over the water belching thunder and bolts of lightning and unleashing a torrential downpour. A towering wave had abruptly risen up and swept over the vessel upon which Esmerelda stood, upending the boat and washing overboard all those riding it. Eyewitnesses who had been closest to the event swore they had seen the jaws of a monstrous shark close over Esmerelda's body as she thrashed about in the water. Her remains still had not been found.

That ill-fated event had taken place little more than two weeks earlier, and it had left the village of Malique bereft of its beloved mambo. Lucette had taken Esmerelda's death especially hard, and much to her husband's revulsion, it was she who had tried to fill the void left behind by the parting of Emmanuel's grandmother. As Esmerelda's apprentice, it was only natural that she do so, but unfortunately she was greatly lacking in the powers or insights of her highly regarded predecessor.

A sudden loud rapping jarred Jacob from his fleeting thoughts. Someone was knocking on the front door.

Emmanuel visibly paled at the intrusion but quickly overcame his unease and stepped close to the door. "Who comes to my door at this hour of the night?" he said with annoyance.

"It is Jimenez," a disembodied voice answered.

Cautiously, Emmanuel opened the door a crack, then peeked through the gap. Satisfied at the identity of the intruder, he allowed the man entrance.

Middle-aged and of medium build, Jimenez displayed a face with the weathered consistency of mahogany subjected to excessive amounts of sun, wind, and sea. Having spent his entire life hauling in fishing nets from the local waters, his forearms gave the appearance of fluted black stone.

"What is it?" Emmanuel asked.

Jimenez looked grave. "Two boats have entered the harbor."

"So."

"I am unfamiliar with these boats. They have made no attempt as yet to come ashore and appear to be holding to positions a stone's throw from our docks."

Emmanuel abruptly stiffened and glanced apprehensively at Jacob before turning back to Jimenez. "Who-"

A sharp obtrusive gasp cut Emmanuel off. Amphitrite was now awake and standing on unsteady feet. Her eyes were wide and unfocused, as if seeing something beyond the room. Her mouth parted in an attempt to speak but no words escaped her lips.

In an instant, Jacob was at her side and lending support. "You must rest," he said.

Amphitrite's eyes rolled back, then focused. All at once she became aware of the others occupying the room. "The people aboard those boats are intent upon doing this village much harm," she said in a voice low and trembling.

"Who are they?" Jacob questioned.

"More Tonton Makout." Amphitrite seemed to look inwardly again. "But there is one among them who is much more dangerous than the rest. The only way I can describe this person is that she pulses with pure evil."

"Erzulie! Erzulie is with them!" Lucette screeched hysterically. "Esmerelda warned me about her. She is the most evil witch in all of Haiti. Black magic is her source of power. She will put a vile curse on us all." Lucette immediately made the sign of the crucifixion, but from the look of her Jacob thought she was on the verge of fainting.

"Stop your gibbering at once, woman," Emmanuel scolded. "How can you let yourself believe such nonsense?"

"We will all die!" Lucette wailed. "Without Esmerelda we are doomed."

Jacob scrutinized Emmanuel's reaction carefully. In his cousin's manner he could sense the glowing embers of both confusion and indecision. And though subtle, there was something else...a growing sign of fear. He could tell Emmanuel was truly fearful of this sudden turn of events.

"Do you not see what is going on?" Jacob blurted. "Duvalier wanted to hit this village from two sides simultaneously, one by land and the other by sea. Those vessels floating idly out there await a land-side attack. They are positioned to stop and destroy anyone from attempting to escape by sea."

"Maybe you are assuming too much," Emmanuel said hastily. "You have no way of being certain of this."

Jacob glowered angrily at his cousin. He was beginning to lose patience with such ridiculous obstinacy. "Do you think so? Baby Doc views you as one of the few people in our land capable of garnering widespread rebellion. He sees the seeds of insurrection firmly rooted in those loyal to your cause, which is essentially everyone in this village. He perceives Malique as a bastion of resistance and prefers that all its inhabitants permanently disappear. When Esmerelda was alive he was too caught up in his own superstitious convictions to believe it possible that this village could be wiped out, a prisoner of the very tool he has consistently used to keep political unrest at bay. With our grandmother now gone, he is convinced Malique is now vulnerable to attack, no longer under the protection of a once powerful mambo. Do you not see that Duvalier believes a retaliatory strike or spell invoked by Esmerelda against him is no longer possible?"

"Erzulie would never have come here when Esmerelda was alive," Lucette chimed in meekly, giving support to Jacob's argument. She now seemed ashamed of her previous craven outburst. Staring demurely at Emmanuel, she added, "Even Erzulie knew she would be no match for your grandmother, not against what Esmerelda possessed."

"Esmerelda's untimely death is not common knowledge," Emmanuel countered. "Only the people of this village know about it. How would Duvalier have learned of this recent circumstance?"

"Perhaps you have a spy within your midst," Jacob offered. He threw his hands up in the air. "What does it matter now anyway? Apparently Duvalier is fully aware of Esmerelda's demise and seeks to put an end to the threat you pose."

Jacob paused as another thought struck him. He looked at Jimenez. "These strange boats in the harbor. Were you able to estimate their size?"

"Each has a length of about nine meters. Under the moonlight their shapes were nearly identical."

Jacob nodded reflectively. "Taking an informed guess, I would venture those are government gunboats, most likely Montauk motor vessels. The Haitian Navy has only five such gunboats and most of the time they are in a state of disrepair. They are rarely seen because they are frequently inoperable. However, they all possess a .50 caliber machine gun. Such a weapon has the capacity to wreak much damage on anything within range."

Jacob noted a stubborn trace of skepticism still lingering on his cousin's face and quickly added, "I know this because I once read a block of material that provided facts about Haiti's limited navy. The article was published by the Combined Arms Research Library, an institution located in Fort Leavenworth in the American state of Kansas. You know as well as I do that I am able to retain and regurgitate any such trivia."

Emmanuel's expression appeared to give ground, and Jacob could tell his cousin was close to being won over, but not just yet. "If, as you contend, these boats are armed with such firepower, why have they not already destroyed our fishing fleet and eliminated any possible escape by sea?"

"Because the only incentive Duvalier's secret police have for carrying out his orders is the looting they can partake in. Remember, rumor has it that Baby Doc does not pay the Tonton Makout. They do not enjoy monetary recompense for their services, that is, other than what they can plunder and ransack. They see the fishing vessels of this village as valuable assets and will avoid damaging them unless they absolutely have to."

Emmanuel sagged heavily into a nearby chair, seemingly caving to Jacob's logic. "What do you suggest we do?" he said helplessly.

Jacob gave the question careful consideration, then looked to Amphitrite. "This woman you spoke of, you are sure she is on one of those boats?"

Amphitrite produced a weak nod. She was still wobbly and Jacob kept his arm firmly around her waist until he had her seated. Kneeling down beside her, he held her gaze for several seconds before addressing her in a quiet comforting voice. "I am not sure what powers, if any, this woman you described possesses, but somehow I believe you have a profound purpose in all of this."

Jacob's mind was speeding along, continually searching for answers to the situation confronting them. It didn't make sense for Erzulie to accompany Duvalier's thugs in raiding the village...unless. He stared at Amphitrite curiously. "Do you sense any motive this woman has for being here?"

"She seeks to gain possession of a valuable but ancient artifact, a charm she perceives as having great power." The exhaustion in her speech and manner made Jacob nervous.

Lucette drew in a sharp intake of breath. "Esmerelda's amulet. She wants Esmerelda's amulet."

Jacob visualized the trinket Lucette spoke of, a garish pendant about the size of a U.S. silver dollar that had often been worn around Esmerelda's neck. His grandmother had greatly cherished the object, claiming that it had been handed down from generation to generation from a long line of ancestors. This extensive ancestry dated all the way back to the pharaohs of Egypt where one of her Nubian forebears had been a slave to a high-ranking priestess in the Temple of Hathor. The amulet was a bronze disc with a symmetrical, exquisitely cut crystal of blue quartz embedded in its center and seven slivers of yellowed ivory radiating outward from the central gem, a relic from a bygone era of human history. According to Esmerelda, the amulet had been originally worn by the priestess as a symbolic ornament during religious rites, but had been given to the slave as a tribute for many years of faithful service. For the next three thousand years, the ancient heirloom had made its way through the heart of the African continent, moving among various tribes where it had been frequently used in rituals and religious ceremonies.

"There is a wealth of untold history and power in this charm," his grandmother had once told him. "The spirits of all your ancestors have left some of their essence in it. In the hands of a true believer in whose veins flows the blood of our ancestors, it can be used to invoke much good or great harm."

At the time, he had dismissed her allegation as utter nonsense. And although the amulet held substantial historical value, to him it was just a worthless piece of timeworn junk.

"Esmerelda's amulet was lost at sea with her," Jacob reminded Emmanuel's wife.

Lucette shook her head vigorously. "No. You are mistaken. Your grandmother gave it to me for safekeeping." A gloomy sadness crept into her eyes. "For some unknown reason she refrained from wearing it on the day of her demise. She told me if anything happened to her, I was to hold onto it until the day came when I would know what to do with it."

"That day may have already arrived," Jacob said. "But how does this woman know of the amulet?"

An icy dread seemed to take hold of Lucette's persona. "I do not know."

"Esmerelda and this woman come from the same African lineage," Amphitrite suddenly explained, her voice reduced to a dull monotone.

Everyone's gaze fell on her in disbelief. Oblivious of the stares, she seemed to search inwardly as if trying to grasp some elusive shred of knowledge before continuing. "They both descended from common family roots, but their genealogy separated four generations ago. They share the same great-great-grandmother. Knowledge of the amulet has been passed onto this woman by traditional family lore."

Emmanuel scowled, staring at Amphitrite as if she were insane. "How can you possibly know this?" he challenged.

Amphitrite did not look at him. "I have no explanation for it." Her manner appeared distant, almost trance-like.

"If this is true, it is little wonder Erzulie never openly tried to match her power against Esmerelda's," Lucette interposed. "Because she shares a common origin with Esmerelda, she felt the older spirits of her African ancestors, the rada, would favor the descendant that possessed the amulet. Erzulie was afraid she would displease them if she attempted any confrontation with your grandmother. If she had done so, she would have risked bringing great harm to herself. With Esmerelda now gone, she has no such fear."

"But you are now the possessor of the amulet," Jacob pointed out.

"I am a family member only by marriage, not bloodline. The Loa of Esmerelda's ancestors cannot protect me."

Jacob well understood that voodoo was a family oriented belief, revolving around ancestral spirits who were inherited through maternal and paternal lines. Voodoo was actually a derivative of the world's oldest known religions that originated in different parts of Africa long before the Europeans started the slave trade in the Americas. It was the enforced immigration of enslaved Africans from different tribes and ethnic groups that provided the setting for the birth of present-day voodoo in Haiti. In the abject misery of slavery, various transplanted Africans began to integrate and fuse differing beliefs until a new religious structure evolved.

"She comes ashore," Amphitrite stated dully.

"Erzulie?" Jacob asked.

"If that is her name, yes."

"Are there others with her?"

"Yes, there are two others."

"Are they armed?" Jacob pressed.

"It is difficult to determine."

"Do you see them in a vision, a waking dream?"

"No. It is what Athena tells me."

This revelation surprised Jacob. "Athena is in the harbor?"

"Yes."

Jacob had completely forgotten about the dolphin. The fact that Athena was currently conveying information to Amphitrite about the interlopers in the harbor only further substantiated the mysterious communication that existed between them. It suddenly struck him that the dolphin would have little or no concept of what a weapon was, and therefore, would be unable to identify one as such.

From the way the others in the room looked at him, it was understandable that they would be confused, but he had no time to explain. Even he was mystified. There was something going on here that defied reason, extending way beyond the boundaries of what should actually occur in a logical, orderly universe. In any case, either Athena had sensed the present danger on her own and swam up the coast to Malique by choice or Amphitrite had summoned her earlier on. Was it possible Amphitrite had glimpsed the woman and her two-man escort through the eyes of the dolphin?

Rising from his chair, Emmanuel said, "If, as you say, this planned land-side raid has been neutralized, then perhaps the people aboard those supposed gunboats will eventually leave when…" His words were abruptly cut off and he sank to his knees clutching his throat.

Lucette jumped to her husband's side, grabbing him by the shoulders. "What is wrong?"

Emmanuel looked up into her face, his eyes filled with a strange mix of shock and panic.

"He cannot breathe! He is choking!" Lucette shrieked. She looked to Jacob for help. "Do something!"

"The witch senses the proximity of her distant cousin," Amphitrite said, speaking with a detached air. "She has conjured a spell and will not release it until the amulet is brought to her."

Like a man being slowly strangled, Emmanuel's tongue lolled from between convulsing lips and his eyes began to bulge in terror. "Do not let her do this to you!" Lucette cried, hugging him fiercely.

Jacob put a hand on Lucette's shoulder to get her attention. "You must give me the amulet," he instructed, urgency in his voice. He was desperately trying to keep the alarm he felt from showing in his tone. "I will bring it to this woman."

Lucette hesitated for one brief moment, then beheld Emmanuel's dreadful expression once again. He was close to suffocation. "Yes, yes," she suddenly agreed. She bolted quickly from the room, returning several seconds later with the ancient charm and handing it over to Jacob. "Please hurry!" she begged. "Give the witch what she wants so that my husband may live. There is little time to lose."

Emmanuel let out a strained, quavering wheeze, holding out his arm in a futile bid for Jacob not to go.

Jacob ignored the gesture, running past a stunned Jimenez and throwing the door wide to expedite his departure. He sprinted rapidly toward the docks, expecting to see Erzulie and her escort at any moment, but the witch failed to appear. Continuing on, he ran out onto the main pier, noting the dark shapes of the vessels described by Jimenez floating about fifty meters further out to sea on each side of the structure. A varied array of local fishing craft lined both sides of the aging wooden platform, their differing sizes and configurations contrasting sharply in the moonlight. Puzzled that no one stood before him he slowed his pace, then stopped altogether. In the late night breeze, the sound of creaking timbers and the chafing rustle of mooring lines seemed to charge the air with a foreboding energy. Jacob advanced a little farther along the deck planks, now fully wary and anticipating the worst.

"You will give the amulet to me!" a voice suddenly said, hissing out the command like red-hot steel being plunged into cool water. Spoken in Creole, the words came from behind him.

Jacob spun and immediately froze. Not more than three meters away a dark figure stood in the center of the pier, its features hidden under a hooded cloak. The unexpected appearance made Jacob take a step backward, and as he did so, the figure seemed to float closer.

"Give me the amulet!" the figure repeated in the same serpentine tone.

As if to comply, Jacob extended the hand holding the amulet, but was not ready to relinquish it just yet. "You will first release my cousin from whatever dark power you have unleashed upon him."

"You will give me the amulet now!" the figure ordered shrilly. "I have waited all my life for what you hold in your hand and I will not be denied it now."

Jacob felt his throat constricting. It was as if a cord had been looped around his neck and tightened. He gasped for air as the witch appeared to hover still closer. She dangled something conspicuously before him.

"Do you remember this?" she cackled gleefully.

Jacob studied the object as he strained for more breath. A small black doll hung from a necktie cinched snugly around its neck. In the faint glow of moonlight, he recognized the tie almost immediately. He had worn it during his graduation ceremony at the university in Port-au-Prince, a delicate hand-stitched strip of cloth made by his grandmother and given to him as a gift shortly before he had earned his college degree. The design depicted a pod of white dolphin embroidered on a cobalt-blue backdrop. The focal point of the artistic layout, however, was unusual and automatically drew the eye. It was an ivory-skinned girl with long-flowing black hair streaming behind her. The girl sat astride the largest dolphin positioned at the center of the pack.

As Jacob looked on, the witch fumbled briefly under her cloak and produced another strip of cloth knotted tightly around the throat of a second doll. It was another of Esmerelda's beautifully handcrafted neckties, but this one portrayed a mix of colorful yet odd-looking jellyfish interspersed among a group of sea cucumbers. The second tie was similar to the first in that it displayed the same cobalt-blue background. Both neckties had turned up missing subsequent to the graduation of the cousins. Someone had broken into their dormitory room and taken not only the ties, but several other items of clothing.

In spite of his pain, Jacob tightened his grip on the bronze medallion. If the witch could do this to him with such seemingly insignificant objects, he wondered what horrors she would be capable once she had the primordial charm in her possession.

"You and your cousin have always amused me with your pitiful rejection of ancient beliefs," the witch continued in that sibilating tone of hers. She lifted the doll representing Jacob so that it dangled only inches from his face. "And yet the strangulation you are experiencing would not work unless some part of you, whether you are consciously aware of it or not, actually did accept what you have so insistently refuted as being nothing more than ineffectual sorcery." She suddenly cinched the dolphin necktie tighter.

Jacob began to reel dizzily as he felt himself beginning to black out. Managing to keep his feet under him, he backpedaled drunkenly away from the woman as he clutched his throat. He tried to speak but no words were able to escape his larynx.

Erzulie shadowed him, keeping close. "Your grandmother was a worthy adversary, a powerful practitioner of vaudun, but only because she possessed what you presently hold in your hand."

Jacob continued to stagger backward with Erzulie following. "With Esmerelda now gone, it is I, Erzulie, who is the natural heir of the amulet, the one most deserving of it. The rada must have foreseen the merit in helping me invoke the forces of nature that took your grandmother from this world so that someone more worthy should take charge of it." Erzulie cackled raucously at Jacob's futile stubbornness.

An intense feeling of torpidity was beginning to consume Jacob. His previous steadfast belief in a world based on rationality and logic was being severely challenged on this night. Aside from his physical distress, he felt like a man viewing a lush oasis from afar in the midst of a hot sandy desert, only to discover that what was assumed to be a sanctuary of life-giving sustenance was nothing more than a mirage. For the closer he got to it, the more the vision crumbled away to reveal only more of the same desolate hellhole in which he now found himself stranded, a place devoid of the beauty and harmony which he so dearly cherished, a realm where only evil and misery flourished. He was a man fast sinking in the quicksand of self-doubt. It was only at this moment as he was inexorably being drawn toward death that he was now beginning to grasp the true essence of reality and he suddenly understood that the three-dimensional space of ordinary experience was simply an illusion, a thing created by the mind. But try as he might, the forces assailing him were much too powerful for even his superb intellect to fight, let alone comprehend. He felt himself rapidly weakening, buckling under the witch's onslaught.

He realized he had collapsed onto the wooden deck of the pier, and as he looked up, the witch loomed over him. Too weak to resist any longer, he watched listlessly as Erzulie abruptly stopped cackling, her fingers prepared to impart a final wrench on the necktie's knot. He knew she was about to terminate his life.

"You will now learn of the ultimate penalty that others who have defied me have wrought upon themselves." Erzulie said, her words dripping with contempt and hatred.

Even with the prospect of death now imminent, Jacob continued to withhold the amulet. The witch would have to take it from his inert corpse. With an abruptness he did not immediately perceive, the pressure on his throat relaxed and, reflexively, he inhaled deeply, inundating his lungs with sweet Haitian air.

A piercing howl suddenly knifed its way through the night as Erzulie inspected the doll representing Jacob. The doll had somehow fallen away from the necktie's noose.

"My spell has been broken." she squawked incredulously. "How can this be?"

"You cannot bring harm to the people of this village," a familiar voice said.

Though Jacob knew who had spoken the words, there was a strange new quality in the way they were uttered, a calm authority behind them. Freed from his painful stupor, he watched Erzulie's dark form go rigid before turning to face the unanticipated intrusion behind her.

"I have felt your presence earlier," the witch said venomously. She cocked her head, remaining still for several seconds as if listening for something in the air. "You are an outsider...yet I sense something familiar about you."

"You were never meant to possess the amulet," Amphitrite said. "Even if you hold it in your hand you will be unable to draw on its power."

"That is not possible," Erzulie countered angrily. "The rada have already chosen me to take charge of it."

Amphitrite looked beyond the witch to Jacob. "Give her what she wants, Jacob. Let her see for herself."

The remaining traces of Jacob's incapacitating suffocation fell away, leaving him clear-minded and alert. Although stunned by Amphitrite's directive, he instinctively trusted her. He nevertheless hesitated. "My cousin, Emmanuel...he is alright?"

"He has been released from the spell," Amphitrite assured him.

Erzulie gasped loudly, realizing the necktie had fallen off the doll representing Emmanuel. "You will pay for your insolence," she screamed.

Jacob thrust the amulet in front of the witch, letting it dangle invitingly before her. Though Erzulie's face still remained hidden within the shadow of her cowl, he could tell she was working herself into a maddening rage. "Here! Take it and leave us alone, witch," he spat irritably.

Erzulie's hand snaked out and snagged the talisman, clutching it tightly. Seemingly pacified for the moment, she caressed the charm lovingly with her fingertips, enjoying the feel of it. "Without this ancient artifact, Esmerelda would never have been able to protect this village from me. I find it most strange she chose not to wear it at the time of her death. Had she done so, it is possible she would still be alive and this village spared from the wrath it is about to suffer."

"Your plan has failed," Amphitrite said. There was an unconquerable confidence in her voice. "The motor convoy you have sent to attack this village has been crushed in a mudslide. There is nothing else you can do here."

As Amphitrite addressed the witch, Erzulie appeared to concentrate her attention briefly on the small gathering of villagers led by Emmanuel and Lucette that was beginning to congregate at the foot of the pier. Her cowled head swiveled back toward Amphitrite. "The fate of Duvalier's main force is of little consequence now that I possess this," she intoned in a sibilating hiss, indicating the amulet. "I have no need of an army to destroy all those who live here. Malique is about to be bathed in its own blood."

With those words, Erzulie's cloaked visage seemed to swell, looming closer to Amphitrite. "I will start with you."

The witch began to recite a low rambling chant, repeating the litany over and over, each redundancy rising in volume and fervor. Though the phrases did not conform to any language in which Jacob was fluent, their meaning was all too clear. All at once the mild breeze changed into a swirling turbulence and whitecaps began to form in the water on both sides of the pier, the disturbances gaining more violence with each rendition of the mantra.

Jacob looked on, overcome with alarm as lightning flashed overhead and the sky rumbled in protest. The witch threw her arms wide, slowly raising them to the heavens as her incantation reached a fever pitch, then abruptly stabbed the fist holding the amulet toward Amphitrite who held her ground with impassive defiance. Erzulie held that position for a short interlude, then let out a sharp guttural cry.

In unison, the swiftly forming vortex of wind quickly died away and the churning sea rapidly subsided. Erzulie held her hands stiffly before her in the now intensified moonlight, standing with the rigidity of a mountaineer frozen in the icy grip of a Himalayan gale. Her gaze lingered on the dark liquid oozing from both palms before letting the blood-drenched talisman slip from her fingers. The ancient charm hit the wooden platform with a dull clunk, then disappeared between two of the deck planks, dragging its chain with it.

"I told you the amulet would be useless in your hands," Amphitrite reminded the witch. "In attempting to use it to destroy others, you have only managed to bring injury upon yourself."

Erzulie's bloody hands clenched, then shook uncontrollably. Jacob watched the spectacle with amazement, noticing the witch's dark form was quaking violently as if in seizure. He had the distinct impression that the paroxysm was caused by colossal humiliation rather than pain.

"You will pay for this," Erzulie screamed as she studied the blood dripping from her palms. She was beside herself with rage, swearing profane obscenities and gruesome vengeance on all those nearest her.

"You will be unable to hurt any of us," Amphitrite insisted, cutting into the witch's ravings. "Your power has been neutralized."

Erzulie suddenly sobered. Appearing to gain some semblance of control over her emotions, the witch lifted her gaze to Amphitrite. "You think you have won," she said, hissing out the words like a cornered reptile. "But you are wrong. You and all these people will die anyway." She looked behind her and called loudly. "Antoine! Dervin! Show yourselves."

From opposite sides of the pier, two figures suddenly emerged from hidden positions aboard the nearest berthed fishing vessels. They hopped quickly onto the dock and stood shoulder to shoulder, staring implacably at those before them. Erzulie scrambled to meet them, taking refuge immediately behind the men. It was then that Jacob became aware of the assault rifle each man wielded.

"Kill them all!" Erzulie shrieked. "I want them all dead."

At the witch's command, each man chambered a round, bringing his gun barrel to bear on Amphitrite and the villagers grouped behind her. Jacob looked on in horror at this sudden turn of events, but before a single round could be unleashed, a large glistening object flew from the water on one side of the pier. With blinding speed, it cleared the tethered boat immediately in front of it and rose still higher, following a low parabolic trajectory. Awestruck, Jacob tracked its flight as it turned sideways in mid-air, closing in on its intended targets. Erzulie and her cohorts became aware of it only a split second before it struck. But by then it was too late. The tail of the hurtling object flicked laterally, slamming into the three assassins with uncanny precision and sweeping them from the pier. With arms and legs flailing crazily, the witch and her accomplices hit the water with a resounding splash.

Side by side, Jacob and Amphitrite stepped to the edge of the deck. Looking down, their would be attackers floundered in agitated confusion. Athena surfaced moments later off to one side, then submerged again.

"It appears Athena has saved us for the moment," Jacob said with admiration. He made no attempt to hide the affection he felt for the dolphin. "But those gunboats standing by out there are another matter we must concern ourselves with."

Amphitrite glanced seaward. "The village will be spared," she said, her tone carrying unbridled conviction. She lowered her gaze to the water below the pier and her expression hardened as she watched Erzulie and her cohorts struggle to stay afloat. "You must leave this place at once," she cautioned the witch. "Should you direct any further aggression toward the people of this village, that aggression will only flow back at you tenfold."

Erzulie appeared to heed the warning, for within moments her companions were towing her toward the nearest gunboat coming forward to meet them.

As Jacob observed their departure, Athena suddenly popped her snout above the water. Something glinted in the moonlight. Curious, Jacob jumped down onto the deck of the adjacent fishing boat for a closer look. Esmerelda's amulet was clutched gently between Athena's jaws. The dolphin raised herself higher out of the water and tossed him the charm with a flip of her head. Jacob caught it, then climbed back onto the dock.

"I think you should hold onto this," Jacob told Lucette, handing the trinket over to her.

Lucette took possession of the ancient medallion with undisguised reverence, cradling it so gently in her outstretched hands that one would think it was comprised of fragile glass rather than hard metal. She studied the charm intently, periodically gazing over at Amphitrite, her eyes harboring a far off look as if something weighed heavily on her mind.

Emmanuel joined Jacob, watching Erzulie and the two men assisting her being pulled from the sea by the gunboat's crew. "Power held by a ruthless dictator through the use of violence is an aberration and will only last as long as people are willing to obey him," he said off-handedly. "With political unrest now widespread in our land, Duvalier's reign may be coming to an end."

Jacob kept his eyes fixed on the gunboat. Now less than twenty meters away, he could clearly hear Erzulie's rantings. The witch berated the men aboard with a steady stream of rabid scolding, venting her frustration and rage on them and every so often threatening some grisly form of mayhem. Within a short time, the second gunboat joined the first, after which the two vessels slowly turned away, following the coastline on a southerly heading. The sound of Erzulie's ceaseless tirade gradually tapered off as the boats gained distance from the village.

Glancing around him, Jacob noticed the way the villagers closest to Amphitrite gawked at her. It was as if they were witnessing some strange yet benevolent white goddess that had suddenly come into their midst without warning, and in a way it was not far from the truth. To most Haitians, whites were regarded with suspicion, a carryover from Haiti's violent past when the black population rose up and liberated itself from its chains of bondage. But for reasons unknown to Jacob, it was apparent the locals were accepting her.

With a look of genuine awe on her face, Lucette walked over to Amphitrite and held the amulet before her in offering. "Esmerelda told me I would know what to do with this when the time came. Although you are not of her ancestry, I think she would have wanted you to have it." Other villagers standing behind Lucette nodded their agreement.

Amphitrite stared at the amulet as if recognizing an old friend, and as Jacob watched, he could have sworn something had changed in the white woman's manner, some profound transformation that somehow imparted a regal aura to her persona. A heavy silence seemed to hang in the air when Amphitrite did not immediately respond. She continued to contemplate the amulet in quiet consideration for a full ten seconds before lifting her eyes to Lucette, whereupon she gave a slight nod and lowered her head. Smiling broadly, Lucette draped the chain holding the artifact around Amphitrite's neck, letting the charm settle gently above her breasts as if it belonged there.

The moment passed swiftly. Amphitrite stared vacantly off into space, then abruptly turned to Jacob and sighed deeply. "I am tired, Jacob. Please take me back to the cove."

The recent events had taken a tremendous toll on her, both physically and emotionally, and it suddenly showed in the way she carried herself.

Jacob could still feel the effects of the adrenaline that had driven him on since the collapse of the hill at the mapou tree and he was willing to make the journey, if only to satisfy Amphitrite's request. She had done Emmanuel and the people of the village a huge service on this fateful night and he felt indebted to repay her for her sacrifice in whatever manner he could.

Emmanuel, however, would hear none of this. "The two of you are welcome to spend the remainder of the night with Lucette and me," he offered. He looked at Amphitrite with renewed interest, his expression inquisitive and searching. "Forgive me for not introducing myself earlier. I have been extremely impolite. I am Emmanuel Baptiste, Jacob's cousin." He hesitated momentarily, pulling Lucette to his side. "And this is my wife, Lucette. Both you and Jacob have endured through much in the last several hours. Perhaps a good rest will revitalize you before you go back to Jacob's home."

Amphitrite eyed him tiredly. "That is most gracious of you, but I don't wish to impose on your hospitality."

"It is no imposition at all," Emmanuel replied. He regarded the white woman appraisingly with an owlish stare. "Jacob tells me you have no recollection of your previous identity, that you suffer from amnesia. Your accent leads me to believe you are an American, but I find it strange you can speak Creole. Visitors to this land generally have great difficulty in learning such a dialect, particularly when it is much more practical to communicate in French. Oddly, you seem to be fluent in both tongues."

It suddenly dawned on Jacob that Amphitrite had spoken both French and Creole ever since she had regained consciousness in the village. He frequently alternated between the two languages without any forethought, and with the threat of Erzulie and the gunboats confronting them, he had failed to notice Amphitrite's use of colloquial French in Emmanuel's home and her subsequent withdrawal into the more common Haitian pidgin during her encounter with the witch.

Because his very first conversation with her had been in English, he had made the foolish assumption she was monolingual.

As Jacob listened he noted that his cousin was speaking to Amphitrite in French. He knew that Emmanuel generally avoided the use of pidgin, considering such an idiom to be too simplified to adequately express oneself in a rich, stylistic manner.

Amphitrite nodded wearily. "If I knew where I learned these languages, I would know who I am," she said, replying in Emmanuel's tongue. She suddenly swooned.

Jacob had been standing ready for such a possibility and caught her as she collapsed, cradling her in his arms once again. The villagers that had crowded out onto the pier parted to open a path as Jacob carried her forward. With the throng following, Emmanuel and Lucette took up a position on each side of him as he moved in the direction of his cousin's abode.

"This woman is in need of rest," Jacob huffed, turning his head to face Emmanuel as he walked with his burden. "If you have not noticed, she is with child."

"Forgive me, cousin, for being so inconsiderate," Emmanuel apologized. "I should have been more observant."

No further words were exchanged until Jacob had Amphitrite gently positioned back on the cot in his cousin's house.

"She seems to be sleeping peacefully," Emmanuel said. Jacob detected a subtle trace of contrition in his tone. He knew Emmanuel only too well, sensing that his cousin was ashamed of his earlier skepticism over Jacob's mudslide story, particularly after witnessing something he would have otherwise deemed impossible.

Lucette laid a hand on Jacob's arm. "You should get some rest yourself. I will watch over this woman while you sleep."

Jacob suddenly had great difficulty keeping his eyes open as an overpowering drowsiness crept over him. Whatever reservations he had against Lucette's offer quickly faded and he let Lucette lead him to the bed she shared with Emmanuel. Within seconds he dropped off into a deep slumber and did not awaken until late the next morning. As he opened his eyes, a vague remembrance of the nightmares that had haunted his dreams continued to swirl in his head, visions of dark demonic figures relentlessly chasing him down winding passageways. The pursuit terminated at the end of a dank, dismal hallway where, seemingly by itself, a corroded steel door abruptly swung open to admit him. Within the room beyond, a cloaked shadowy creature awaited, rising up at him with malicious intent and pulsing with pure evil. He had no doubt that the creature was Erzulie.

Rising from the bed, it soon became apparent to Jacob that the house was deserted. Rubbing the sleep from his eyes, he left the lodgings and wandered out along the waterfront.

A small crowd was assembled on the beach, and as Jacob got closer he could see that all faces were enchanted by something out on the water. Amphitrite was riding Athena again, and as he looked on, it was plain that the twosome were following a course that would take them down the coast. Perplexed, he kept his gaze riveted on them until they disappeared from sight around a rocky promontory jutting from the shoreline south of the village.

Emmanuel separated himself from the onlookers and approached Jacob with a spring in his step. "You have missed much here this morning, my cousin." There was a rare gleam of appreciation in his eyes as he said this, something Emmanuel seldom exhibited as far back as Jacob could remember. "Your woman and that dolphin of hers are a strange pair, indeed."

"She is not my woman," Jacob corrected, desperately fighting back the offense he felt. The loose comment implied a sexual relationship. And although he was almost certain Emmanuel had not meant it that way, the unintended innuendo somehow diminished Amphitrite's rectitude. He stared back toward the promontory, anxiously wondering where the woman and dolphin were going.

Emmanuel stopped in his tracks and studied Jacob carefully for several seconds. "What is the name you have given her? I have forgotten it already."

"Amphitrite." Mouthing the word, it sounded appropriate to Jacob, a befitting designation to a most unique individual.

"Amphitrite awoke early and left the house while Lucette was still asleep," Emmanuel informed him. "Jimenez and several others discovered her and the dolphin swimming together near the docks. It would appear that the white woman takes great pleasure in riding that dolphin. Being that Jimenez was preparing to get underway to go fishing anyway, he followed the two of them out to sea. They led him to a bonanza of fish. His boat came back filled with striped mullet."

Jacob nodded distractedly. This did not surprise him at all.

"Two other fishermen also came back with full boatloads after the woman and dolphin showed them where to cast their nets," Emmanuel said, his voice light and cheerful. "Amphitrite rode the dolphin back to the beach after the boats returned. Louwanda happened to be there with her son. The white woman led the boy out into the water until he was chest deep, whereupon the dolphin circled him several times before nuzzling up against him. It was then that the woman placed a hand on the boy's head."

Emmanuel hesitated and a small laugh left his lips, causing Jacob to turn back and face him. He was suddenly intrigued. "And?"

Emmanuel broadened his smile. "Samuel can see again. His sight has returned."

To Jacob, the implications of such a revelation astounded him. Two years ago, Samuel had struck his head on a submerged rock while spear fishing. A freak wave had swept him into an outcropping of jagged coral. The boy had been blind ever since.

As Jacob recounted the history of Samuel's catastrophic injury, Louwanda strolled up to him with the twelve-year old boy next to her. "God bless you, Jacob," she said, hugging him with a rapturous fervor and planting a huge kiss on his cheek. "May the spirits of your ancestors bestow good fortune upon you." Tears of joy streamed down her face. "Thanks to you my boy is able to see the beauty of the world around him once again."

Jacob was nearly speechless. "I...I did nothing for Samuel," he stammered awkwardly.

"You brought the dolphin woman to our village. That is enough."

Jacob continued to stare in amazement as Louwanda led Samuel away. The boy turned his head, looking back at him with hero worship evident in his eyes. The ugly scar Samuel had carried on his forehead ever since the tragic accident was now almost gone. Jacob suddenly became aware of others regarding him with similar looks. Glancing around, he found himself to be a focal point of attention.

Emmanuel's manner became more somber. "Earlier this morning I visited the mapou tree and confirmed everything you had told me to be true," he confessed. "All the trucks were crushed, mostly buried under tons of mud and rubble, but the jeep was only partially covered."

Such verification made Jacob feel better, for he had begun to question his own sanity. "Did you find any survivors?"

"None. I had several others from the village accompany me and we found the soil to be very soft in many places. It was easy for us to become bogged down up to our knees. Next to and leading away from the jeep, it was evident that two people had struggled through the mire trying to reach firmer ground. They left a trail of sunken footprints heading west toward the coast. We followed their tracks into the hills where their spoor vanished on the exposed bedrock."

Jacob absorbed this information thoughtfully. "Perhaps it is better that you did not encounter these people. As I told you before, it is likely that they carry firearms."

Emmanuel nodded gravely. "That is probably true. And with the safety of our people possibly at risk with armed assassins running loose around the countryside, it is necessary that we be equally armed. Fortunately for us, the two men who assisted the witch lost their weapons in the water when they were knocked from the dock." Emmanuel paused, suddenly displaying a broad smile. "Those weapons were recovered earlier this morning and are now in our custody. We dried them off and oiled them. The cartridges appeared to be watertight, but just to make sure, we test fired one round from each gun and they seem to function perfectly. I have given your prior suggestion careful consideration and decided to post two sentries in concealment with those weapons along the trail leading here as a precautionary measure."

"That may prove to be a wise course of action," Jacob agreed, growing increasingly uncomfortable as more of the locals began to stare in his direction. An introvert by nature, he had always been regarded as a recluse by his neighbors. In the past, they had normally taken little notice of him during his infrequent visits to the village. But the scrutiny he was now drawing was becoming disconcerting and he found himself suddenly yearning for the cove's solitude.

"Did Amphitrite say where she was going?" Jacob asked, struggling hard to keep the anxiety he felt from showing itself in his voice.

Emmanuel peered at him owlishly before replying. "No, cousin, she gave no indication as to where she was going."

Lucette made her way through the crowd of onlookers and came up to Jacob. "This belongs to you," she said, placing something in his hand. Jacob stared dumbly at the necktie depicting the ivory-skinned girl amid the pack of white dolphins. She held his gaze with solemn reverence. "There was purpose in everything your grandmother did. Maybe time will reveal what this tie signifies."

Jacob folded the tie carefully and slowly turned away.

"Where are you going?" Emmanuel wanted to know.

"Home," Jacob muttered. "I wish to go home."

Emmanuel was aghast. "Did we not just discuss the possibility of Duvalier's assassins roaming the nearby hills?" He shook his head in horror. "I do not want you walking the trail by yourself. I will take you back by boat."

Jacob hesitated. He desperately needed to get away from the village and its people, to be alone to mull over all the extraordinary things he had seen and heard over the past ten hours. He needed to rationalize past events, to put everything in perspective. A long walk by himself, undisturbed, would give him the time he needed for such meditation. Traveling back to the cove on foot, however, had potentially dangerous consequences. He turned fully and met Emmanuel's eyes.

"As you wish," he acquiesced.

Chapter 13

*T*he boat ride down the coast was slow and uneventful. Emmanuel's vessel was similar in construction to Jacob's, pushed along by a listless diesel far past its prime, a mechanical conglomeration of cannibalized parts that, if pushed too hard, protested with a hammering chorus of ear-splitting pings as it coughed occasional wisps of black smoke. Lucette had accompanied both men for the short trip, taking up a position near the bow and sitting quietly as she stared directly ahead.

Emmanuel seemed to sense Jacob's need for reflection, refraining from conversation and piloting the pinnace with a steady hand. With eyes squinted behind spectacles that rode low on the bridge of his nose, he periodically shifted his gaze, alternately scanning the open sea and the waters adjoining the coastline.

Gaining access to the cove was a difficult undertaking, even for a skilled seaman like Emmanuel, and if he did not pay careful attention he could easily miss the narrow break in the reef. With the tide now low, it was the only place within several miles that would allow passage for even a shallow draft boat to the leeward side of the coral barrier. As Emmanuel guided the craft through, imposing but perilous fangs of calcareous growth loomed up on each side of the hull only inches from the water's surface. Once through the treacherous opening, Emmanuel swung the vessel sharply back on a heading opposite the way they had come down the coastline, paralleling the rocky shoreline for nearly a hundred meters.

From the seaward side of the reef the entrance to the cove was almost impossible to spot. The natural topography of eclipsing rock formations rising steeply from the water presented an optical illusion that kept the gorge well hidden. Angled into a jagged bluff of bedrock, the cove entrance was deceptive to the naked eye even at close range.

As they entered the narrow opening, a feeling that something was amiss suddenly engulfed Jacob like a tsunami crashing down on a calm shoreline without warning. Emmanuel steered the boat past the last outcropping in the confined inlet, giving Jacob an unobstructed view of the small structure that served as his home. Amphitrite stood in the doorway with her back facing him, seemingly preoccupied with something in the cabin. Close to the beach, Athena could be seen knifing rapidly through the water and throwing out a wake. She seemed to be in a highly agitated state. As the pinnace glided closer to the beach, Athena began to slap the water violently with her tail. Up to now, he had not seen this type of behavior in the dolphin.

Emmanuel reversed the throttle and slid the bow of the craft gently onto the sandy shore, whereupon Jacob jumped out. Amphitrite was still facing away from him, but as he moved closer she backed out of the entrance to his home.

Jacob abruptly froze as two men emerged from the doorway. Each was clad in blue denim with a red necktie, the typical dress of Duvalier's private militia, the Tonton Makout. One man carried a revolver holstered at his hip while the other brandished an assault rifle. Jacob recognized the rifle to be similar to the weapons carried by the men Athena had swept from the pier, and from photographs he had seen of such firearms, knew them to be Kalashnikov AK-47s. He immediately presumed the men to be the mudslide survivors Emmanuel had talked about. The dried mud covering much of their clothing further supported this presumption.

The man sporting the rifle darted past Amphitrite and came on at Jacob, his eyes filled with malevolence. "Do not attempt to flee," he grunted in Creole. He prodded Jacob forcefully with the muzzle of the weapon. "Lie face down in the sand with your hands behind your head and do not move or speak, otherwise I will kill you."

Jacob considered resisting but quickly abandoned the idea upon studying the man's face. A hair trigger temperament clearly manifested itself there. If irked even slightly, he was certain the assassin would have no compunctions about squeezing off a few rounds.

Lying chest down in the sand, Jacob heard the man order Emmanuel and Lucette from the boat and, in a harsh, belligerent tone, force them to lay prone next to him in the same manner in which he had been instructed to assume.

Jacob lifted his head and looked forward. The other man grabbed Amphitrite roughly by the arm and walked her over to where he lay. Shoving her down into a sitting position next to Jacob, the man strutted slowly off to one side with his hands clasped stiffly behind his back in a smug, authoritative manner. He was a solidly built individual and from all outward appearances seemed to be the leader of the two-man squad.

"Tell me," he said, "have any of you noticed any unusual flotsam drifting in the local waters?" The man spoke in crisp, impeccable French. He turned around and swaggered back toward Jacob and the others, raising an eyebrow. "Is it possible you might have seen some odd wreckage wash up on the shoreline, what could be identified as the remains of a seaplane?"

The man halted and leveled his gaze at Jacob, expecting some kind of response. When Jacob did not answer, the man shifted his eyes to Emmanuel. "You…you are a fisherman. Perhaps you have observed some of these things."

Jacob had not seen any plane wreckage, nor did he anticipate that Emmanuel had, either. He was surprised, however, when his cousin chose to respond. "We have had many sightings of debris and wreckage. It is common after a powerful storm like the one that recently passed through here."

The man stared hard at Emmanuel. "You did not answer the question to my satisfaction. I will ask you again. Did you see what might be considered the wreckage from a seaplane?"

"I have seen no such objects," Emmanuel said.

The man riveted Emmanuel with a baleful glare, punctuated by crazed, chilling eyes. He suddenly turned, his hands still clasped firmly behind him. He held that position for a prolonged period before spinning back around and displaying a shrewd smile. "A rumor has reached my ears that some wreckage from an airplane was discovered near here." He looked once again to Emmanuel for an answer.

"As I already told you, we have found no plane wreckage," Emmanuel spat with annoyance. "What significance does a wrecked seaplane hold for you?"

"You will address me as Captain Henri Ternier, a soldier in the service of President Jean Claude Duvalier, the leader of our country." The man gave Emmanuel a few seconds to digest the name, then went on speaking. "I should think you would remember my name. Like you and your cousin, I had attended the university in Port-au-Prince during the same period when both of you were students there."

Yes, of course, Jacob thought. The memory of the man came flooding back with brutal clarity. During his studies, two factions had comprised the student body at the university: pro-Duvalier and anti-Duvalier, with those against the current regime predominating by a ratio of three to one. Ternier had been the leader of the group supporting the policies of Baby Doc.

As Jacob scrutinized Ternier he understood why he had failed to immediately recognize him. The man's features had changed considerably. No longer the gangly youth, Ternier's physique had filled out substantially, his shoulders broadening to an impressive width and his frame gaining solid muscle in all the right places. The transformation gave him an imposing bearing of strength and power. Even the structure of his face had changed, maturing into a stately, almost handsome countenance. It was the eyes of the man that had remained the same, however. When Ternier was irked, they burned with a wild intensity that tended to unhinge anyone unfortunate enough to look into them. Jacob also knew the man harbored an exceptional intellect, for Ternier had been one of the top students at the university while he was in attendance there.

Jacob swiveled his eyes and read his cousin's face, seeing the outrage about to erupt. Emmanuel arched his head up in a bold show of defiance, unable to contain his anger. "Duvalier is a murderer and a thief," he spat furiously. "He has plundered the national treasury and stolen most of the government assets. He holds power at the end of a gun. Instead of seeking change and positive ends, he seeks to destroy the very fabric of Haitian society. He-"

Emmanuel's outburst was abruptly silenced as the man with the Kalashnikov slammed the butt of the weapon forcefully into the back of his head. Lucette let out a terrified scream as Emmanuel's body instantly went slack, his face slumping into the sand.

"Do not attempt to try my patience again," Ternier warned, his demented eyes flaring and falling back on Jacob. "The consequences will be most unpleasant."

Ternier tilted his head and looked at Lucette who sobbed quietly, then turned his gaze on Amphitrite. "Your survival amazes me," he said. "It appears the sea has not taken you, after all. I applaud you for having beaten tremendous odds." He shook his head in a mendacious display of commiseration. "What a pity you have endured the worst the storm could throw at you, only to fall into my hands a second time."

Ternier's words threw Jacob off balance and he shifted his head in an effort to gauge Amphitrite's reaction. Bewilderment blossomed in her expression. He could see that she was having great difficulty trying to make light of what Ternier was saying. As he continued to watch, the water thrashed wildly behind him, and droplets of water began to rain down on all of them. The disturbance seemed to escalate in direct proportion to Amphitrite's growing frustration at failing to remember past events.

The sound of the commotion drew Ternier's attention and he smiled with wry amusement. "I have to assume the dolphin over there is the reason you did not drown. Too bad it cannot save you now."

Amphitrite stared at Ternier, her face revealing intense inner confusion.

"The woman has no recollection of what you speak," Jacob found himself saying. "She has lost her memory." He heard Ternier's underling move behind him, half expecting to be clouted in the same manner as his cousin.

Ternier held out a hand, keeping the other man at bay. Studying Amphitrite intently, he said, "You do not remember our previous encounter?"

Amphitrite did not acknowledge the question. She seemed to be lost in a quagmire of deep introspection.

Ternier grew angry. "Answer me, woman! Do you remember what happened?"

"I have no remembrance of my life prior to coming here," Amphitrite stated. "I draw only a blank when I attempt to recall it."

"Then I will refresh your memory," Ternier snapped back, his face contorting into a twisted, sadistic grin. He seemed to glean some perverted joy in what he was about to divulge. "Several weeks ago, I had been given the responsibility of delivering a valuable cargo for President Duvalier. With a small contingent of men under my command, the cargo was loaded aboard a seaplane about thirty kilometers south of this location. The flight was bound for Grand Cayman Island. The cargo was quite sizable, and unfortunately, may have put too much of a strain on the aircraft engines. As a result, the plane lost power and the pilot had to execute an emergency landing into the sea. While descending, the pilot spotted a sailboat in the water below and he was able to land the plane safely near the boat's position."

Ternier paused, fixating widened, unnerving eyes on Amphitrite, watching her closely to assess the effect his words were having. "You were aboard that boat, you and three companions. In your eagerness to provide assistance, I commandeered your vessel. It was my intention to remove all of the cargo from the plane and load it aboard your boat, then complete my assignment by sailing on to the Caymans. The pilot of the seaplane had received weather reports that a hurricane was on the way and informed me that we had precious little time to transfer all the cargo. To expedite the process, we managed to lash the plane and boat together."

Ternier stopped talking, waiting for some kind of reaction. When Amphitrite failed to respond, he continued. "As it turned out, you were not very cooperative and proved to be a constant thorn in my side, consorting with your friends to thwart my mission at every turn. Because of you, I found it necessary to put an end to the resistance your companions posed by shooting each of them and throwing their bodies overboard. You were spared because you were needed to operate the boat and navigate it to my planned destination. Your boat was equipped with a state-of-the-art global positioning system, which neither the plane's pilot nor I knew how to operate. As a precautionary measure, I ordered my men to bind you to a chair in the boat's main cabin. While my men were transferring the cargo, the sea began to build, eventually making it impossible for us to complete the transfer to your vessel. Only a few items still remained aboard the seaplane, but this nevertheless created a most serious dilemma for me. You see, Duvalier is a most unforgiving individual. Had I lost even a small portion of the cargo, he would have been very displeased. Therefore, the only available course of action for me was to attempt to ride out the storm, keeping the plane and boat tied together. As it turned out, the ferocity of the storm surpassed my expectations, and the boat and plane began to slam together with such force that I was afraid both would eventually sink. At that point, I had no alternative but to cut the plane loose. I attached a towline to it and trailed it behind the boat, leaving the pilot and two of my men aboard the aircraft to do what they could to keep it afloat. That plan also failed. After playing out the entire length of towline, a large wave flipped the plane upside down, snapping off one of the wings. Within moments it took on water and began to submerge. Had I not cut the towline, the weight of the plane would have pulled the boat under as well. Unfortunately, three of my men went down with it."

Ternier lifted his gaze from Amphitrite and glanced out over the water, his expression remote as if reliving the incident. Jacob still had his hands clasped tightly behind his head, not wanting to provoke the man holding the rifle. His neck and upper back began to burn painfully with the effort of keeping his eyes trained on Ternier's face. To relieve the discomfort, he rested his chin in the sand and watched Ternier's booted feet as they took several paces beyond where Emmanuel lay. His cousin was still unconscious, the glasses on his face askew and partially buried in the sand.

"It was most dispiriting, seeing that plane go down like that," Ternier said. "But at least I had instructed the pilot to record the plane's last known position just before we landed in the sea. Our geodetic coordinates were written down on a scrap of paper and placed within a waterproof briefcase which I carried with me. After hijacking your boat, I noted the water to be less than a hundred meters deep, as indicated by the depth sounder aboard the vessel. With such information I was confident I could return to the area and, with a little luck and the right equipment, locate the plane again. The cargo aboard it could then be recovered. Misfortune, however, has a way of continuing once it comes your way. I soon learned that the boat was taking on water at a rate greater than the bilge pump could handle. An inspection of the inside hull revealed a jagged hole with seawater pouring in. My guess was that one of seaplane pontoons had punctured the hull. The intensity of wind and sea had reached dangerous levels, and with the waves surging, the sailboat had taken a terrible pounding from the seaplane when the two had been tied together. It was inevitable we were going to sink. I quickly realized I had to abandon the vessel if I was to survive. The boat was equipped with an inflatable life raft, the type that is enclosed and provides shelter from the elements. Launching it was exceptionally difficult, particularly since I had only one man left to help me carry out such a task."

A muffled groan suddenly interrupted Ternier's recount as Emmanuel stirred. Powerless to do anything, Jacob watched with dismay as one of Ternier's booted feet abruptly pivoted and impacted viciously against the side of Emmanuel's temple. Lucette wailed loudly once more as Emmanuel lapsed back into silence a second time. Jacob tensed and peered upward, straining hard to catch a glimpse of the intense hatred that flamed in the countenance hovering above him.

Ternier cast cruel, accusing eyes on Amphitrite. The promise of depravity-ridden reprisals for all his ill-gained misfortune flowed from him like searing heat from a furnace. Paradoxically, his voice remained calm. "You proved yourself to be a most resourceful woman. You managed to free yourself from your bonds and arm yourself with a spear gun while the life raft was being launched. I had just climbed aboard it and had reached back to take possession of my briefcase handed me by my assistant. This was no simple task because the raft was bouncing wildly in the surge. While my assistant was handing me the case, you fired a spear into his back. He fell into the sea and disappeared from sight."

There was a moment's hesitation as Ternier let Amphitrite absorb this last bit of information. Athena was now slapping the water with a renewed frenzy and Jacob felt another spray of water, heavier than before, rain down on him. He could see some of the droplets fall on Ternier, but the man seemed not to notice.

Amphitrite stared up at Ternier stoically. "What happened after that?"

A brooding scowl materialized on Ternier's features. "The force of the wind pulled the life raft away, and as I looked back, your boat was beginning to flounder. It was awash in whitewater and began listing to one side. You stood at the railing, watching me. I found it rather strange that you showed no fear."

The frown Ternier wore changed into a twisted smile at the memory. "Until today, that was the last glimpse I had of you just before a large wave took your vessel." He scanned Amphitrite's face closely. "Has the event I just described caused your memory to return?"

Amphitrite's features remained devoid of all emotion. "I remember none of this."

Ternier went rigid, the whites of his eyes suddenly appearing bloodshot and bulging grotesquely. The sight made Jacob think of stories told by his grandmother about zombies risen from the dead. Clearly this was not the answer Ternier wanted to hear. Jacob had seen this same reaction in the man during his days at the university and knew Ternier was on the verge of bloodlust. He remembered an incident in which Ternier had suddenly attacked another student without warning, exhibiting the same behavior just before plunging a knife into the chest of his victim. Even though the other student had died, Ternier had not been charged with any wrongdoing. It was his political clout with Duvalier that had exonerated him of any crime. Even back then, rumor had it that Ternier was a spy for the Haitian dictator.

"I must have the geodetic coordinates of the area where the seaplane went down," Ternier said calmly, his tone belying the madness consuming his face. "You will search your memory and give me the position of your vessel when you first saw the plane."

Amphitrite met his frightening gaze, appearing unfazed and sitting mute.

Ternier suddenly reached out, grabbing Amphitrite's shirt and tugging hard. "Do you hear me, woman? You..." A metamorphosis seemed to take hold of his expression as he became aware of the amulet that popped out from under the shirt. In one swift motion, his hand shot out and yanked the medallion from Amphitrite's neck, snapping the chain from which it dangled. "Where did you get this?"

Amphitrite's eyes narrowed and she rose up from the sand. "It is ill advised for a man such as yourself to hold what is in your hand. Only pain can come of it."

Something sizzled and Ternier flinched, letting out a thunderous bellow. He dropped the amulet as if it were a burning chunk of coal. His eyes widened again, but this time out of shock and awe. "You are a witch of the vaudun, a white mambo!" he roared accusingly. "How is such a thing possible?"

Amphitrite reached down and retrieved the amulet from the sand. Jacob perceived the crystal at its center emitting vivid bursts of blue fire as she stepped close to Ternier. "You cannot hurt any of us anymore," she said, holding the charm in such a way that the light emanating from its jewel danced up into Ternier's face. To Jacob, her tone matched her expression, a countenance in which all traces of emotion were absent.

Ternier took a step backward. "How can such a thing be?" he said, his voice lowered to almost a whisper. "Whites have no knowledge of the secrets voodoo holds." He stared down at the amulet, then gazed back at Amphitrite in disbelief. "No. You are a cheval. A Loa has taken possession of your soul," he bayed. "It is the only explanation why you are here now, why the storm did not take you."

"You cannot hurt any of us anymore," Amphitrite repeated.

"You have already died," Ternier insisted, his voice rising again. "It explains why your memory fails you, why you have no recollection of your former life. You are not alive. You cannot be."

"You will leave this place at once and never return," Amphitrite commanded, crowding closer to Ternier and holding the amulet near his face.

Ternier drew back, reaching for the revolver at his hip and drawing it from the holster. "You are an accursed thing, a vile corpse with the spirit of a Loa inside you," he yelled, bringing the barrel of the pistol to bear directly between her eyes.

Jacob sprang to his feet, no longer mindful of the man at his rear. He was by no means an athletic individual, but he nevertheless summoned all the strength and speed he could muster and channeled it into one fleeting movement, slamming into Ternier's blind side with jarring force.

The collision drove the hand gripping the gun off its intended alignment a split second before the weapon discharged, the sound cracking the air as if caused by a whip. Jacob felt his shoulder go numb from the impact as both men went sprawling. Ternier was a big powerfully built man and Jacob felt as though he had tackled a tree.

As Jacob wrestled with the larger man, Ternier glanced over at his accomplice. "Shoot her!" he howled. "Shoot her before she uses any more of her magic against us."

Knowing he could not stop the inevitable, Jacob looked up in horror at the sight of the man wielding the assault rifle. Preoccupied with this, he suddenly became airborne as Ternier placed a foot against his chest and pushed hard. He felt the wind knocked from him as he landed on his back near the water's edge, a good twelve feet from where Ternier had launched him. With dazed vision, he watched the nightmare unfold as if in a dream.

The man with the rifle stood frozen for several moments, refraining from pointing the weapon. His eyes were filled with fear and indecision as he faced Amphitrite. "It is unwise to provoke a loa," the man said, an obvious slave to superstitious dogma. Keeping his gaze trained on the amulet in Amphitrite's hand, he added, "We invite great misfortune upon ourselves by doing so."

"Then you are a fool," Ternier spat venomously, rising from the ground. He still retained custody of the pistol, but the gun was now covered with a coating of damp sand. He cocked the hammer, bringing a sickening smile to his face.

Jacob quickly gathered his wits about him. He had a gambit to play that just might drive the wedge of controversy still further into the opposing views. "It was this woman who caused the mudslide that destroyed your truck convoy," he announced, spitting out the words in time to make Ternier look over at him before the pistol was fired. "She was able to invoke such an event simply by willing it. She does not want to harm you, she just wants you to go away and leave us in peace. If you try to hurt her or any one of us, the repercussions will be disastrous for you."

"I will take my chances," Ternier snarled, bug-eyed once again. He turned back in Amphitrite's direction.

Jacob played one more card. "Her powers are greater than you can imagine. She defeated Erzulie last night."

Ternier froze in his tracks. He turned back fully to face Jacob. "Such a feat is not possible. Only one mambo was powerful enough to oppose Erzulie and she is dead. You are a liar!"

Jacob forced himself to laugh. "I have been called many things by people who truly know me, but never a liar. The amulet held by this woman was taken from the hand of Erzulie in the same manner by which she took it from you."

For the moment, it was becoming clear that Jacob's revelation was keeping the situation temporarily in check, for Ternier's expression became contorted with an equal mix of caution and the need for retribution. "That is impossible," he persisted uncertainly. "Erzulie has likely laid waste to Malique by now."

"Erzulie has left Malique undamaged and all its citizens alive," Jacob chuckled. "She has already fled down the coast, fearful of what this woman can do to her." The words spoken by Amphitrite during her confrontation with the witch suddenly came to mind and he grasped at them in desperation, hoping to neutralize Ternier's thirst for vengeance. "If you direct any further aggression against any one of us, that aggression will only flow back at you and your companion tenfold."

Ternier continued to vacillate for several seconds longer before scowling darkly. "You are lying!" he growled savagely. He raised the revolver and aimed it at Jacob. "Tell me you are lying!"

Jacob ignored the threat and looked over at the second man. "Only an idiot would fail to heed my warning. This woman was able to destroy your assault force because of what they intended to do to the nearby villagers." He brought a measure of sternness to his voice and manner. "Either leave us in peace or the Loa inside this woman will bring an agonizing end to you. Harm us and you gamble with the lives of your children as well. Incessant misfortune and suffering will plague your families for generations to come."

A contemptuous laugh sprang from Ternier as he took careful aim at Jacob's head. "I have no children," he sneered.

"Stop!" the other man screamed, suddenly pointing the barrel of his assault weapon at Ternier. "Do not do it. I do not wish to have the wrath of a powerful Loa befall me or my descendants."

Ternier glanced back in surprise at the lone soldier under his command. "Do you presume to question the judgement of your commanding officer?"

The man remained insubordinate. "Anger has clouded your judgement. You do not see what you are doing. I have a wife and three children and will not risk bestowing a life of torment and misery on them by offending a goddess of the underworld."

Ternier's eyes bore into the man. "You will lower your weapon at once, sergeant," he ordered.

The sergeant shook his head lugubriously. "I cannot, I have my family to consider."

Ternier's brow bunched questioningly over this sudden turn of events. "You would shoot me?"

"If I must, yes."

"Very well," Ternier said, seeming to concede the argument. He sighed deeply and extended his arms wide in a show of compliance. "Maybe you are right." He turned away from his mutinous subordinate, lifting the flap on his holster and appearing to slide the handgun back into its leather case.

"Begging your forgiveness, sir, but you gave me no choice," the sergeant lamented apologetically. He dropped the muzzle of his weapon so that it pointed at the ground. "You know I have never before hesitated to carry out your orders without question, but this woman has shown us powerful magic. She-"

Two sharp reports suddenly cut through the air, startling Jacob. The sergeant's mouth hung open in a silent 'O' of shocked amazement as he looked down at the merging twin stains spreading rapidly across the front of his shirt. Slowly, he lifted glazed eyes to bear dully on Ternier, taking an unsteady step forward and dragging the tip of the assault rifle through the sand before letting it slip from his fingers. Taking another step, his left knee gave way under him, causing him to totter sideways to the ground where he rolled onto his back and stared sightlessly at the sky.

To Jacob, the moment was surrealistic. Ternier stood immobile, his dark pupils contracted to the size of pinpricks within the swollen white orbs surrounding them. His gun arm was still fully extended, gray tendrils of smoke drifting lazily upward from the barrel of the pistol gripped tightly in his hand.

Ternier looked down at the fallen man, his demeanor suddenly changing and exhibiting infatuation over the spectacle of death sprawled before him. "A pity he feared the cheval more than me," he said, almost as if talking to himself. He glanced quickly at Jacob but tilted his head to keep a wary eye on Amphitrite as well. "Had he not challenged my authority, he would have seen the absurdity of your story, though it seems the woman here is able to exert some small measure of magical power."

Ternier took several paces to his left until both Amphitrite and Jacob were within his line of sight, keeping Amphitrite closest to him. "But now I must end the threat you pose, whatever you are." Thumbing back the hammer on the revolver, he pointed the gun at Amphitrite and squeezed the trigger.

Nothing happened!

Though the firing pin clicked noticeably, the pistol failed to fire. As if in panic, Ternier depressed the trigger several more times with the same result. His composure seemed to be disintegrating rapidly. Hurriedly, he examined the weapon, bringing it close to his face, then opened the cylinder for an inspection of the cartridges. With practiced hands, he removed the four dud .38 caliber bullets plus the two spent casings, replacing them with spare rounds from his belt. Expertly, he spun the reloaded cylinder and clicked it shut.

Amphitrite remained standing before Ternier, not attempting to move during the reloading process. "The weapon will not work," she said calmly.

Ternier's lips curled into a sadistic smile. "We shall see," he said, the words coming out in a sick, demented laugh. Once again he targeted Amphitrite and pulled back on the trigger.

Still nothing!

Ternier let out a string of profanity. Thoroughly enraged, he hurled the pistol away and reached down, snatching from the sand the Kalashnikov that lay near the dead sergeant. Examining the weapon's safety, he flicked it to semi-automatic firing mode. Satisfied, he brought the stock of the weapon to his shoulder and sighted over the barrel, aligning it on Amphitrite.

"The weapon is useless in your hands," Amphitrite said, displaying not the slightest bit of fear.

Ternier growled insanely before squeezing back on the trigger. A single earsplitting clap resounded, sending out a shock wave that reverberated off the confining cove walls before fading away into a throbbing silence. Ternier staggered back, stunned and bleeding, the assault rifle torn from his hands, its barrel ripped asunder and laying in shattered pieces on the ground in front of him. Falling to his knees, he moaned lethargically, his arms drooped pitifully at his sides. A gush of blood flowed profusely from an open gash along his cheekbone and lower jaw where the stock of the weapon had abutted the side of his face just before exploding. Dazedly, he stared up at Amphitrite with glazed, uncomprehending eyes as she stepped close to him.

Amphitrite placed a hand on his injury. "You were forewarned, but you did not listen," she said softly. "Your hatred has come back at you full circle."

Ternier opened his mouth to speak but abruptly collapsed into the sand, now unconscious.

Jacob was immediately at Amphitrite's side, trying to make light of what he had just witnessed. Intrigued, he reached for the remains of the gun barrel, discovering the wet sand clogging the muzzle. Enlightened with understanding, he looked questioningly at Amphitrite. "You knew the rifle barrel was blocked and would explode?"

Amphitrite stared back with soulful eyes. "I only knew we could not be harmed." She looked over at Emmanuel, still out cold, his head resting in Lucette's lap. Lucette was stroking the side of his head soothingly where blood had congealed from the vicious kick Ternier had delivered.

"We must heal Emmanuel's injury before there is permanent damage," Amphitrite said. "Help me pull him out into the water, Jacob."

A minute later, Jacob, Amphitrite, and Lucette had Emmanuel in waist deep water, careful to keep his head propped above the surface. Athena swam in close and nuzzled her beak against the nape of Emmanuel's neck, emitting strange sounding creaks as she did so. Jacob noted the severity of Emmanuel's injury, an ugly laceration in his cousin's left temple.

Holding the amulet in her left hand and placing her right over the wound, Amphitrite closed her eyes, appearing to focus her full concentration on some image of the mind. Almost immediately, the quartz jewel at the center of the talisman began to pulse slowly with an eerie blue light, dimly at first and then growing in brightness as it blinked with escalating frequency. Reflexively, Jacob closed his eyes at the blinding flash that suddenly erupted from the jewel, a light so intense that it seemed to penetrate to the very core of his being.

As Jacob opened his eyes, a multitude of spots danced before them, and several moments passed before he was able to see clearly again. Emmanuel abruptly stirred and his eyelids fluttered wide to full awareness. "What has happened?" he asked weakly.

Lucette let out a small joyful cry and a cascade of tears flowed down her cheeks as she clung to her husband.

"You were hurt, and Amphitrite revived you," Jacob said, awed by the sight of Emmanuel's almost fully healed wound.

Jacob shifted his gaze to the white woman's face, amazed at her strange abilities, but his manner changed swiftly to one of concern as he studied her. Amphitrite appeared physically drained and paler than usual. Athena drifted to her side, letting the woman clutch her dorsal fin for support.

"You must rest!" Jacob found himself saying. "You have been subjected to more than any woman in your condition should be put through." He reached out and placed a hand on her shoulder. "Come! I will help you from the water."

Within minutes, everyone was settled into Jacob's small cottage. Unsure if Ternier was alive or dead, Jacob decided to go back outside and check on the man. Ternier was still out cold, but his pulse was steady and the open wound on the side of his face had ceased hemorrhaging. He wondered if Amphitrite had been responsible for stopping the bleeding when she had laid a hand on the injury.

Not wanting to take any more chances, however, Jacob retrieved some spare rope from his boat and hog-tied Ternier, binding his arms and legs behind him while the man remained unconscious and leaving him where he lay. He would let the Tonton Makout captain stay in that position for the time being, still considering the man to be extremely dangerous despite Amphitrite's belief that he could not hurt any of them. Though it went against his core nature to treat another human being this way, he would rather be harsh than foolhardy, and besides, he was just too tired to attempt to move the big man at this time.

Rising from the prostrate form, Jacob looked over at Ternier's dead underling. He would bury the man a little later, but right now other things weighed heavily on his mind.

Distractedly, he wandered along the beach, and as he did so his eyes fell upon the discarded handgun lying in the sand directly in front of him. On impulse, he picked it up, carefully inspecting the weapon and determining that the muzzle was free of any sand or debris and that the firing pin was intact. Thumbing the cylinder open, he removed the cartridges one by one, examining each round carefully for any flaws before placing it back in its chamber. Puzzled, he aimed the gun at the far end of the cove and pulled the trigger, expecting the firearm to remain dormant. The weapon abruptly jumped in his hand as a shot rang out. Even at a distance, he could discern a burst of rock fragments where the bullet had struck, a stark testament to the gun's lethal power.

Dumbfounded, he examined the pistol again. The recent string of events he had been witness to were rife with phenomena that could not adequately be explained in the universe he had come to know and understand, a place where certain proven physical laws supposedly governed and could not be violated. Yet here he was again, observing still another paradox that slipped through the net of reasonable explanation.

Thoroughly confused, he tossed the gun aside as though it were some repugnant, hideous thing. Wearily, he sat down in the sand and stared long and hard out over the water, his mind churning with a myriad of previously uncharted possibilities. Like a tangled mass of worms, they swarmed and ceaselessly intertwined, each segment in constant motion, interminably disappearing and reemerging. One thought in particular kept rising to prominence within their midst, however. Was it conceivable that Ternier had been correct about Amphitrite? Was she a cheval, possessed by the spirit of a Loa? And even more importantly, if this were somehow true, did this sufficiently rationalize all the improbable happenings he had observed?

Jacob continued to sit and meditate deeply on these matters for such a prolonged period that by the time he arose, the sun had set, replaced by the grandeur of countless pinpricks of light twinkling majestically above on a velvet carpet of night.

Chapter 14

S kimming over the ocean at full throttle, Jake had no idea what he was going to do next. What he did know, however, was that the crew of the closest tuna trawler were not the type of people that would act kindly towards the girl, assuming that was where she had gone. And if Natalie was truly in trouble as Destiny had said, then he had a debt to repay. He owed the female dolphin that much. The girl was another enigma. There was something about her that automatically made him want to protect her, some intangible arcane quality that was too elusive to grasp.

As Jake approached the fishing vessel floating ponderously before him, he could clearly see its immense net being deployed. A small workboat was working in concert with the vessel and currently in the process of hauling the purse seine back to the ship to complete the entrapment circle. Weighted at the bottom and having a continuous series of floatation buoys strung together along its upper edge, the purse seine was like a gargantuan drape that was moved along an invisible circular curtain rod, ultimately positioned to close off a huge volume of ocean. Once fully deployed, a set of cables acting as draw strings were used to pull the bottom of the net together much like the jaws of an enormous purse, thus closing off any possible escape to fish and other creatures trapped within its confines.

Through the binoculars aboard the *Angel*, he had noted the ship's name. The *San Carlo* was a modern tuna trawler, the majority of its hull and superstructure standing out a bright white in stark contrast to the dark blue sea upon which it rode. Angled so that its bow was nearer to Jake than its stern, the ship's orientation was such that its port side faced him, a hulking barrier of steel that seemed to portend an aura of extreme menace the closer he got to it. A sixteen-foot runabout with a lone driver cruised further out from both the ship and workboat. Jake was familiar with the tactics being used in such an operation, knowing the noise from the runabout's engine would tend to keep shoals of fish herded toward the net until the circle was completed.

Judging the trawler to be just over 280 feet in length, Jake understood that a vast amount of fish could be stored in its refrigerated holds and that it carried enormously powerful winches. He also knew that once the catch was trapped and the seine drawn into a tighter circle, the crew would remove captured fish from the net's confines by dipping a large collecting basket into the squirming mass, then dropping the catch into a chute leading to a freezer compartment. Organisms unfortunate enough to remain entangled in the net's mesh would be ripped apart once the winches hauled the net through the elevated power block, which was suspended from a gantry straddling the ship's rear superstructure. If left in the net, remnants of shredded and crushed fish would decompose and produce the unpleasant smell of rot and decay.

As if confirming this, a slight breeze sprang up, blowing off the ship directly into Jake's face and bringing with it a sickening stench. The loathsome odor did not surprise him. In fact, he had expected it. He knew that many Colombian fishing vessels were used as drug runners. True fishermen generally took pride in their vessel, often taking the time to keep their ship free of rotting organic matter following a catch. A vigilant power block operator was responsible for monitoring the net as it was being hauled back aboard, often stopping the net to remove fish caught up in the mesh. On the other hand, putrefying organic matter would make the vessel particularly offensive to approach, thus discouraging shipboard searches by crews of the U.S. Coast Guard.

Jake continued to scan the water between him and the ship but failed to spot the girl or the giant bottlenose that carried her. He had lost sight of Destiny and her mount shortly after she had left the vicinity of the *Angel*, and since she had seemed to be holding to a course aimed straight at the *San Carlo*, he had naturally assumed that was where she had gone. He suddenly wondered if she had purposely decoyed him in the wrong direction in order to avoid being pursued. Although he couldn't rule out such a possibility, he still trusted his instincts that she had headed toward the Colombian ship.

Coming closer to the vessel, Jake discerned seven crew members on the trawler's stern and three more individuals aboard the workboat. He could see that the ends of the net were being drawn inexorably closer together. Acting as a small tug, the workboat only had to travel perhaps another six hundred feet in a clockwise direction before the leading edge of the net was brought back to the ship. The net was immense, encompassing an area which he estimated to be at least fifteen hundred feet across.

As yet, the trawler's crew had not taken any notice of him. Nearing the vessel, he could see that something else had grabbed their attention. All heads on both ship and workboat appeared to be drawn to the same focal point, which was out near the center of the area girded by the net's floatation boom. Whatever it was, it seemed to distract all hands from their assigned tasks, creating a mild confusion among their ranks. Mouths agape, men on the ship's deck ran to the rails to get a better look, while the crew of the tug ceased all activity as they too sought a more distinct view of something in the water.

The diversion was short-lived. One of the men on the trawler's stern began gesticulating wildly and shouting orders. Within moments all hands were scrambling back to their stations. The workboat abruptly ceased its aimless drift and immediately resumed its bid to complete the enclosure. With renewed and fervid energy, the entire crew went back to work, but now with the objective of keeping the thing they had seen from escaping. Harvesting tuna was now secondary.

With all eyes continuing to stay riveted on the object, Jake was able to slip to within a hundred feet of the ship's stern before bringing attention to himself. The rear of the ship no longer blocked his view and he could now see the cause of the uproar. Off to one side of the ringed enclosure, Destiny's petite form sat astride the huge albino bull. The bull was assisting a smaller white dolphin in keeping a gray bottlenose afloat, both albinos nudging the creature toward the slowly diminishing gap in the net.

Leaning his weight to starboard, Jake brought the waverunner on a new heading, streaking toward the opening separating the tug from the ship's aft section, the area the net had not yet closed off. As he raced past the trawler's stern, one of the crewmen looked his way, the same individual who moments earlier had been shouting at everyone.

Jake recognized the man immediately. It was the one called Pedro: the vicious Colombian fisherman Zimbola had knocked unconscious outside the Port-au-Prince tavern the night before. Even at a distance of thirty meters, Jake could make out the heavy bruises on the man's face and neck. Sporting two ugly black eyes and a huge purple contusion where Zimbola's banana-size fingers had gripped his throat, it was a wonder Pedro was standing on his feet at all, let alone moving about.

As Jake shot past, it was apparent that Pedro did not know what to make out of Jake's presence, evidenced by the unmistakable surprise etched on the Colombian's face. Jake was certain the man could not possibly have noticed him while in the grasp of a crushing stranglehold applied by Zimbola.

A moment later, the Kawasaki roared through the gap in the net, still three hundred feet wide, but shrinking ever smaller with each passing second. His first impulse was to steer directly for the girl, but a sudden idea made him swerve toward the tug.

Having an open deck that lacked any kind of pilothouse or cabin, the workboat was outfitted with two powerful diesel engines capable of towing the massive purse seine. Possessing a raked bow with a slight taper, the craft was wide and squat, with an overall length of approximately thirty feet and a fourteen-foot beam. Bearing down on the vessel, Jake let off the throttle, letting the Kawasaki coast into the path of the on-coming tugboat. The three men working its deck stared back at him as if dumbstruck. Drifting at idle, Jake drew his fingers across his throat, gesturing that he wanted the tug operator to cut his engines.

Instead of reducing power, however, the workboat kept coming on at a relatively slow, steady pace. Either the tug operator had failed to read the sign or Jake was being ignored. If Jake failed to move, the Kawasaki would be overrun and swept back into the tug's churning propeller blades where he would be torn to pieces.

Jake decided it was time for a little persuasion. Up to now he had kept the Kawasaki's guns concealed under a small tarp tied down snugly over the weapons. Yanking on the slipknot that held the tarp in place, he lifted the canvas covering from the guns, bunching it quickly and stowing it in the rear compartment. With a flick of the throttle, he turned the waverunner sideways so that the crewmen aboard the workboat were given a broadside glimpse of the automatic weapons, then swung the small craft towards the on-coming vessel, both gun barrels trained on it.

With a broad smile on his face, Jake yelled the word, "Pare!" He knew little Spanish and doubted the workboat's crew would hear the command to stop above the din of the tug's diesels. But the gun barrels turned out to be a most effective communicator, and the eyes of the tug operator went wide at the threat they posed. Cowed for the moment, the man abruptly put the engines into neutral, staring back at Jake, his face bloated with fear and uncertainty.

Unfortunately for Jake, the driver of the small runabout had seen the situation unfold and apparently had other ideas. With reckless abandon, he swept past the ship's stern, racing toward Jake's rear as if to ram him. Coming to within sixty feet of the Kawasaki, the boat veered sharply and began to speed away, but not before the driver tossed something into the air. As if in slow motion, the object flew end over end in a lazy arc, following a trajectory that sought the Kawasaki.

As the small cylinder reached its apex, the blood in Jake's veins turned to ice as he realized what it was. Reflexively, he twisted the throttle gripped in his hand with such savageness that he was afraid it would shear away. Like a thoroughbred racehorse bolting from a starting gate, the Kawasaki leapt forward, but to Jake's now heightened awareness it accelerated with all the sluggish inertia of a thousand-ton barge.

Glancing over his shoulder, he caught a final glimpse of the thing as it fell into the sea. As if attesting to the skill of the man who had hurled it, the object hit the spot where he had been only an instant earlier with chilling accuracy. He was nearly flung from the waverunner as the sea erupted violently behind him, lifting the small craft clear of the water for one brief moment. Falling back into the sea, the craft slammed down with bone jarring force. Dazed, Jake had the vague impression the Kawasaki had been severely damaged, but the familiar vibration of the engine beneath him seemed to contradict this. Still managing to clutch the throttle, Jake felt the waverunner race forward as a tumultuous spray washed over him. With a detached lucidity, he noticed a tall geyser mushroom overhead, then plummet to rejoin the sea. By the time he fully regained his senses, the remnants of the water column began to dissipate into a fine mist, dispersing rapidly on the wind. It was then that the tug loomed up at him and he had to lean the Kawasaki heavily on its larboard side to avoid a head-on collision.

Missing the tug's bow by mere inches, Jake righted the waverunner, bringing it back on an even keel and scanning the sea for his assailant. He caught sight of t-he motorboat racing away rapidly in the direction of the girl. He quickly realized he had a dilemma on his hands, one that offered only two options to choose from, neither of which would do much to remedy the present situation. Deeming the driver of the runabout to be the more immediate threat, he tore after him. He had no idea what these men would do to the girl and her companions should they be captured, but knowing what he did of their cruel natures he could only assume the worse. As far as he was concerned, the girl and the dolphins were in big trouble if he did not intercede at once.

With the modified STX-12F engine now running wide open, he began to overtake the runabout like a cheetah running down a rabbit. As he closed in, the driver glanced back at him in obvious surprise, alarmed at how fast the Kawasaki was closing the distance separating them. The man suddenly turned and reached for something as the craft under him bounced over the waves. Hunching his shoulders, the man looked back again, tracking Jake's approach. Without warning, the driver lobbed another canister behind him. This time Jake was ready and he swung the waverunner wide of the grenade's path, veering away almost laterally. Once again the water erupted in a towering geyser, but Jake was well clear of the blast.

Putting the Kawasaki into a steep bank, Jake angled the small craft back to head off the runabout, giving it full throttle. He literally exploded across the water and quickly outflanked the driver, effectively cutting him off from the girl. All at once, the runabout veered away and Jake pulled in behind him, much the way a fighter pilot might come up behind an enemy aircraft during a dogfight. He had all he was going to take from the man in front of him. Without taking his eyes from his quarry, he thumbed aside the safety guard on the M-60's arming switch and flicked the toggle. He had the advantage now, and as he closed in on the driver he could see the man stare back into the gun barrels mounted atop the Kawasaki, the expression on his face seeming to quail at the deadly power they represented. The man was swarthy, burned dark from too much time spent in the sun, but his skin seemed to suddenly pale and in his demeanor Jake sensed the panic of a routed foe.

In an attempt to shake Jake off his tail, the man took the boat into a sharp right turn, sliding out from under the sixty's sights. Jake had anticipated the move and reacted with the swiftness of a mongoose taking down a cobra, sticking to the runabout's tail like a Louisiana tick. The driver was now running a zigzag course, but one that was taking the racing pair ever closer to the purse seine's floatation boom.

With sudden abruptness the driver veered acutely, tracking back in the opposite direction. Jake mimicked the maneuver, pulling to within thirty feet of the runabout's stern and lining up the sixty on the Evinrude outboard engine that powered the craft. Looking beyond the runabout, Jake made sure the girl and her companions were currently out of his line of fire. Satisfied, he triggered the machine gun. A shudder swept through the Kawasaki as a burst of rounds poured from the weapon and tore through the Evinrude. His spirit lifted as the outboard cowling flew apart a brief nanosecond before the cylinders flared into a fireball. The explosion sent the driver hurtling through the air and into the sea as the boat spun sharply toward the floatation boom defining the net's boundary. Continuing on with unspent momentum, the boat plowed into the boom, nearly gliding over it before the remnants of its outdrive got hung up in the mesh. It was then that its fuel tank ignited, setting off a monstrous secondary blast that sent a huge fireball swirling skyward. The concussion from the explosion nearly toppled Jake from the Kawasaki, forcing him to turn his face away from the ensuing heat. He realized he had initiated a chain reaction that had triggered the unused grenades aboard the runabout.

Jake looked back at the boat driver. Shaken up and a little scorched but otherwise none the less for wear, the man floundered aimlessly about, kept afloat by an orange life vest strapped to his chest. Shifting his gaze in the direction of the runabout, Jake realized it had sunk from sight, pulling a small portion of the net below the surface. Steering closer to the breach, he stared down into the clear water. The boat was caught up on the seine, no more than fifteen feet below him, a gaping hole in its keel. The weight of it had compromised the positive buoyancy of the floats in the immediate area, causing the edge of the net to sag downward.

To Jake, this was an enormous stroke of good fortune. With adrenaline still coursing through him, he located the tug. As expected, its operator had recommenced towing the net and was now only moments away from reaching the ship. His pursuit of the runabout had almost taken him to the far side of the entrapment circle where he presently sat, a good twelve hundred feet from the ship's stern. As his eyes continued to survey the enclosure, he spied the girl's form bobbing midway between his position and the ship. He quickly fathomed she was moving away from him, albeit slowly.

Twisting the throttle, he pivoted the Kawasaki and raced over the open water like a man possessed. The driver of the runabout glared up at him as Jake flew by, a look of intense hatred screwing up his features. Jake ignored him, leaving the man in his wake and steering directly toward Destiny and the three dolphins. He couldn't help but notice clumps of dead fish littering the water, the bulk of the carnage seeming to be tuna.

The Kawasaki covered the distance to the girl in less than fifteen seconds, and as Jake throttled the craft down, the girl glanced up at him distractedly. Though her face mask was still strapped firmly in place, he detected the faint glimmer of sadness in her eyes as they gazed back at him from behind the lenses.

Jake shouted stridently. "You've got to stay away from that ship. The…"

A spray of water suddenly sprang up twenty feet away, cutting off Jake's warning. They were taking fire from the direction of the ship. In spite of it he kept his outward demeanor calm, locking his gaze more fixedly on Destiny's face.

"There's an opening in the net," he yelled, pointing to the distant break in the white line delimiting the net's periphery, some five hundred feet away. "You must go there at once!"

Jake turned and indicated the ship as the water erupted again in a series of mini geysers, this time several feet closer. "The men aboard that vessel will do great harm to you and your friends if you don't get out of here now." He swung the waverunner around, positioning himself between the girl and the ship, shielding her from the deadly salvos.

"Go!" he bellowed.

Destiny studied him for a brief moment longer before the giant bottlenose bearing her began to move away, nudging and pushing the incapacitated gray in unison with its small albino partner. Through the pristine water, Jake could discern the lengthy lateral scar running along the flank of the shorter albino.

Water continued to kick up in sporadic bursts in front of Jake, and he knew it was only a matter of time before the shooter zeroed in on him. In response, he turned the throttle lightly, causing the Kawasaki's nose to rise in alignment with the level of the deck at the ship's stern. The sixty was still armed and he sent a short burst of 7.62mm rounds streaking toward it.

Another storm of gunfire roiled the sea, this time impinging simultaneously on opposite sides of the Kawasaki. Staying low behind the console, Jake spotted gunmen. He was now being targeted by more than one shooter. Giving the engine more gas, he answered the in-coming salvo with another burst. Heads aboard the vessel abruptly hunkered down as the glint of steel sparked briefly along the ship's railing. For several seconds there was no return fire, and Jake glanced behind him quickly, taking the momentary respite to track the girl's progress.

She still had the length of a football field to cover in order to reach the area where the boom sagged. Although he was certain that the albinos were capable of leaping over the barrier at any point along the net's perimeter, he also knew it was unlikely the pair would leave the stricken gray, which was too weak to perform such a feat. Thus, it was crucial the group reach the opening if they were going to escape.

Jake snapped his head back, taking in the ship before him. A few gun barrels began to poke out from above the railing. Gunning the throttle, he brought the nose of the craft higher above the water, leaning the Kawasaki to larboard and peppering the upper edge of the trawler's hull as he did so. The effect was almost instantaneous. Gun muzzles were suddenly withdrawn, disappearing beyond the edge of the deck as he unleashed a withering enfilade of suppressive fire. He kept his strafing run short, letting off the trigger and veering sharply to his left. As he raced away, a curtain of water suddenly rose up on his starboard side. Something zinged close to his scalp a split second before he felt a hot sting on his left triceps. A trickle of blood running down his forearm told him he had been hit, possibly a graze, but he had no time to assess the wound.

Leaning the Kawasaki hard left, he shot away from the ship, building distance between himself and the weapons tracking him. Circling in a wide arc, something caught his eye and, reflexively, he turned his head to see what had drawn his attention. Another runabout, almost identical to the first one, was skirting clockwise along the outside perimeter of the net. Jake chastised himself for not anticipating such a possibility. When he had initially approached the trawler, he had taken note of the small boat suspended from davits situated on the ship's forward port side.

Sometime during the firefight, members of the fishing crew had launched the second runabout covertly from the opposite side of the ship, driving it along the vessel's port side hull, completely hidden from Jake's view. By the time he had spotted it, the boat was way beyond the ship's bow, having already circumvented one-third of the floatation boom. Four men could be seen occupying the boat, three of them bearing firearms. As the runabout raced along the outside edge of the net, it suddenly dawned on him that its passengers were seeking to block the opening in the seine. If they succeeded, Destiny and her retinue would be trapped.

Seeing this, Jake hastily adjusted his course. Though he was still within range of the ship's weaponry, the marksmanship of the gunners was too inept to be effective, and the gunfire quickly abated. The girl was still plainly visible before him, and he estimated her group had only another hundred feet to go before gaining access to the open sea. Unfortunately, the burden of the injured dolphin was making progress exceedingly slow and cumbersome, making it possible for the men in the boat to reach the breach in the net ahead of them.

Only moments elapsed before Jake overtook the three dolphins, and as he sped by he could see Destiny watching him. Rocketing through the gap in the net, he leaned the Kawasaki hard left, nearly laying the craft on its side before cutting the throttle and facing the on-coming boat head on. A steely resolve took hold of his emotions. It was all consuming, pushing against his gut like the icy thrust of an arctic glacier, relentless and unstoppable. He recognized the danger of it, a total disregard for self-preservation. He had experienced it only a few times in the past, each occurrence transpiring while on dangerous Seal missions.

When it swept over him like this, he felt omnipotent and invincible, but a surviving thread of remaining rationality within him understood the utter recklessness of being in such a state. It was as if a portion of his being stepped aside, a neutral observer that was both amazed at his stupidity and powerless to stop it as the feeling came on with all the momentum of a runaway freight train. Helpless in its grip, he threw all caution to the winds.

Less than two hundred feet away, the runabout's crew opened up on him, sending a hail of bullets screaming past the waverunner and kicking up the sea behind it. Undaunted, Jake watched the rapidly approaching threat with cold, unflinching eyes, any thoughts of personal safety as remote as the far reaches of the cosmos. He was immune from harm, invulnerable, his body cast from some unknown, indestructible metal forged from the deep interior of a distant star.

As the boat continued to come on, weapons blazing, Jake armed the starboard torpedo a split second before triggering the sixty. The sixty belched, spewing a storm of rounds directly into the bow of the runabout. Abruptly the boat veered sharply to port, no longer firing. As it swung wide of him, Jake could see the gunners aboard it holding on desperately to keep from being flung overboard with the sudden course change. Flicking the throttle slightly and leaning his weight, he gave the Kawasaki just enough power for the STX-12F to pivot, allowing the torpedo launch tube to lead the bow of the passing boat by ten feet. With the runabout's broadside now totally exposed, Jake depressed the firing button. The Kawasaki kicked, yawing slightly right as the torpedo leapt away, a streaking blur just beneath the water.

A half-second elapsed before the missile and runabout converged in a horrendous explosion. Hurled skyward, the boat somersaulted end over end, savagely ejecting the men aboard before plummeting upside down into the sea where it abruptly sank. Fortunately, all four men were wearing life vests, allowing them to remain afloat. Surveying the damage, Jake realized how potent these torpedoes could be when allowed to retain their full charge.

Jake looked behind him. Destiny and the dolphins had finally succeeded in reaching the net's breach and were now clear of the enclosure. He half expected them to immediately head off in the direction of the *Angel*, but was surprised when the girl and her mount suddenly veered toward him, leaving the smaller albino to support the disabled gray. As the twosome came upon the nearest floating casualty of Jake's attack, the girl leaned her torso sideways, reaching out laterally with one arm and grabbing hold of the injured man bobbing listlessly in the water. Maintaining a tight grip, she held on as her mount towed its newfound burden to the seine's buoyed perimeter where she dismounted and floated beside the stricken individual. The large bull turned, whereupon it gently nudged the comatose man with its snout as Destiny placed a hand on the man's forehead. A few seconds elapsed before the man stirred, awakening with a start and appearing unnerved by the proximity of the huge albino.

Seemingly satisfied with the man's condition, the girl pulled herself onto the dolphin's back and headed to the next victim, leaving the revived man holding onto the net's boom. Jake looked on with interest at the girl's show of compassion, watching her repeat the procedure three more times as she resuscitated each man in silence. Occasionally she would glance in his direction, her eyes peering stoically at him from behind the face mask before refocusing her attention back on the task at hand.

Within a short period, all four Colombians were left floating together as Destiny rejoined the smaller albino and its charge. Mystification flooded the expressions of the revived men as the girl and her mount departed, but Jake noted the lingering hatred on several faces whenever they stared his way. As he studied the men, however, he sensed no ill will emanating from the youngest among them. He could now hear the thrum of the trawler's winches in the distance, causing the stranded men to recede more quickly behind him as the powerful machinery began to haul in the seine.

Jake removed the headset from the Kawasaki's rear compartment, jacking it into the waterproof Motorola before folding it over his cranium. "Arrow to Goliath." Several seconds passed as he awaited a reply. When none came, he repeated the call, but this time a response came back almost immediately.

"This is Goliath," Zimbola answered, the static garbling his tone unable to hide the concern it harbored. "Where you been, Arrow? We beginning to worry."

Jake's countenance eased into a smile. "Arrow back to you. Seems our Colombian friends wanted to throw a little farewell party in my honor. Tell you all about it later. Has the girl's friend arrived yet, over?"

"His boat is tied alongside. He wants to know if you found the girl."

"Affirmative. She's got two more friends with her, one of them in pretty bad shape. I'm on her six and following her back now, but the going is slow. ETA will probably be another hour. See you then. Arrow out."

A nefarious smile lit Ortega's face. An informal accord had been struck. All the rudiments of a loosely knit working arrangement had been made with the man called Omar. The initial terms of the transaction had been laid out and agreed upon with minimal negotiation. Sitting cross-legged in the shade of a poisonwood tree, the two men had parlayed for almost an hour.

From Ortega's perspective, it had all seemed easy, so natural that the two men would do business. And though he made it a habit never to trust anyone, he instinctively sensed that Omar was cut from the same ilk as he himself, a man whose very existence was characterized by violence, a man not to be crossed. Omar seemed to sense a similar trait in Ortega, and because of it, a common bond of begrudging respect had quickly developed between them.

Ortega was more than satisfied with the terms of the deal, and he wondered if Omar had any business sense at all. From his perspective, it seemed that the Islamist had been far too accommodating, seemingly giving away far more than what he would receive. Initially, no money would change hands. For starters, Omar would provide Ortega with three tons of white heroin. Three tons!

The amount staggered the Colombian, and he found it difficult to believe he was in a position to become the Caribbean's sole distributor of such a highly prized narcotic. In exchange, Ortega would place one of the Cardoza tuna trawlers at Omar's disposal for a period of one day, to be used for the retrieval and delivery of a cargo whose nature was to remain undisclosed. One other stipulation was placed on Ortega to cement the deal, and the requirement caused the Colombian to grin even more wickedly than before. As far as he was concerned, satisfying that end of the bargain would be exceptionally simple, particularly since he had at least a dozen crew members aboard the *San Carlo* who would take great pleasure in following through on it.

Ortega was suddenly pulled from these thoughts, summoned by the voice erupting from the walkie-talkie clipped to his belt. Fernando was calling him. Swiveling his head, he looked back at his pilot sitting at the controls within the helicopter cockpit twenty meters away. He knew there were no Coast Guard reconnaissance flights scheduled over the island today, but he had made it a standing practice to keep his pilot stationed in the aircraft, prepared for a rapid takeoff during times like this.

Holding back his annoyance over the interruption, he brought the walkie-talkie to his mouth, making an effort to keep his tone bland. "What is it?"

Fernando's voice was urgent. "A call has come in from the *San Carlo*. Pedro tells me the ship has come under attack. Both runabouts have been destroyed and several crew members injured."

Omar noted the way Ortega's face abruptly clouded. "There is a problem?"

Ortega did not answer as he jumped to his feet, raising a set of binoculars to his eyes and aiming the instrument seaward. Although the lenses were powerful, the *San Carlo* was still too distant for him to discern anything amiss, though he could tell that most of the seine had been hauled in. The net's white boom had a tendency to stand out even at great distance, contrasting sharply with the blue-gray mantle of sea upon which it floated.

Scanning the ocean between the ship and the island, Ortega's eyes were suddenly drawn to a tiny black dot slowly traversing the water. He was able to track it for a few seconds before losing sight of the object. Realizing a nearby rise in the land was blocking his view, he moved to a better vantage point and looked through the glasses again. He cursed silently when the lenses revealed an empty sea. He had to shift the binoculars around before locating the strange object a second time, but as he studied it he could only conclude that it was too insignificant in size to have any type of attack capability.

Ortega lowered the spyglasses in frustration and lifted the portable radio to his mouth. "Hail the *San Carlo*, Fernando, and ask Pedro what attacked them."

While Ortega waited for a response, he continued to scan the ocean surrounding the trawler. With the exception of the other two Cardoza fishing vessels floating much further out to sea, the waters proved to be devoid of any other watercraft within striking distance of his flagship. Failing to find any other boats, he checked the sky for signs of aircraft.

The radio blurted again, alive with Fernando's voice. "Pedro informs me that a man on a waverunner attacked them. He said the watercraft had a machine gun mounted on it and that it was able to maneuver at a high rate of speed. He is not certain, but he thinks one of our boats was hit by a torpedo."

Fernando started to say something else, but Ortega cut him off. "Does Pedro have any idea why this man attacked us?" he screamed, unable to control his temper, yet aware that Omar was watching him closely.

Ortega looked through the binoculars once more, locating the distant black dot again. The object was now closer. Straining his eyes, he could see it was trailing behind something in the water…no, there were other objects out there, a small cluster of them grouped tightly together. Estimating the group's direction of travel, he moved a few paces closer to the edge of the island's upper terrace and traversed the glasses slowly across the vast panorama of ocean, following a projected heading of east by southeast. Another vessel suddenly came into view within the circle of magnification. Focusing the lenses, he was able to distinguish not one but two boats tethered together, one much smaller than the other. Compared to the distant black dot, the vessels were close enough for him to discern the anchor line angling away from the bigger boat. As he studied the scene, it became evident that a fairly large floatation device was being used to support something on the water's surface, but the larger vessel partially blocked his view. Even without the aid of the binoculars, he could see the boats clearly.

"Pedro said several dolphins were trapped within the net," Fernando's disembodied voice came back, his speech buzzing with radio static. "A girl was riding one of them. It seems this man was trying to protect the girl and the dolphins."

Ortega lifted the glasses to his eyes again. He could now see what was taking place.

"Crank up the bird," he yelled into the radio, now totally enraged. "We have some business to attend to." He met Omar's eyes. "Care to go for a ride?"

Omar hesitated only briefly before nodding. Intrigued by the situation rapidly developing before him, he would be a fool not to accept the offer. A bird's eye view of the island might prove useful down the road, particularly since the place was to become his primary base of operations in the Caribbean.

Chapter 15

Volunteering himself as acting rear guard to the small contingent of dolphins, Jake pondered the strange girl riding the freakishly oversized bottlenose. To him, the sight was totally alien to anything he had ever previously seen, and Jake had seen plenty of odd things during the past twenty-nine years of his life.

As he drove the STX-12F behind the slowly plodding group, he could not help but wonder how such a partnership had evolved. The girl seemed completely at home in the ocean, somehow giving the impression that she could easily survive out in the open sea, far removed from the proximity of land. Yes, he concluded, as long as she had her dolphin friends to accompany her, she would remain immune to the hazards indigenous of an ocean environment. The presence of man, however, somehow complicated the picture. With the introduction of man into the equation, both the girl and her dolphin companions would be defenseless against the dangers man represented, vulnerable to perils not typically associated with the briny depths. Humanity, plain and simple, was an interdicting element, a careless constraining blight within the hydrosphere, posing a lurking threat to the girl and these strange albino mammals.

Studying the group before him, Jake realized he was witnessing a symbiosis of completely dissimilar but highly evolved organisms, a psychological connection of spirits that appeared to harmonize in a way that benefited both species.

Jake continued to dwell on this seemingly mystical alliance, noting the girl's concern for the injured dolphin the other two creatures were supporting and pushing along. He was certain she would have ridden the huge bull hundreds of sea miles in the harshest weather if it meant saving just one of these amazing creations of nature.

Jake was glad he had helped this odd union of beings, deriving pleasure in the way the girl would glance over her shoulder to stare back at him every so often, but uncertain whether she was condemning him for his aggressive actions toward the trawler crew. He was beginning to relax, enjoying this small journey back to the *Angel* in spite of the painfully slow progress the group was making.

Jake suddenly tensed. His awareness shifted to full alert at the sight of the girl lifting her head to gaze skyward. The drone of the approaching aircraft over the purr of the Kawasaki caused his pulse to quicken, and he knew immediately that it had been a mistake to assume they were out of danger.

Scanning the haze above him, Jake spotted the helicopter as it swooped rapidly toward them like an angry bee intent on stinging. Though there was no overt sign of a threat, all his instincts told him otherwise, that they were being pursued by people hell-bent on doing them harm.

Leaning the waverunner hard to port, Jake swung the nose of the Kawasaki less than ninety degrees so that its guns aligned with the oncoming aircraft. Better to be cautious than sorry, he thought. He had to be prepared to counter any hostile moves the aircraft might make.

Searching his memory, he didn't recall seeing a helicopter aboard the tuna trawler he had recently opposed, but now that he thought about it he remembered the vessel had a raised platform nestled among its superstructure, what could easily qualify as a helicopter landing pad. A vision of the throngs of dead fish floating belly-up within the perimeter of the seine net abruptly came to mind, and he suddenly understood how the dolphins had been injured.

Almost instantly, a cold rage swept over him like a blast of arctic wind, besieging him with an intense desire for retribution. Automatically, his fingers found the arming toggle to the sixty as he cast frigid eyes on the swiftly approaching target, still too distant to bring down. Here was an opportunity to wipe some of the slate clean of the wrongs man had wreaked on dolphins. If he were to have any chance of hitting the aircraft at all, it would have to descend still lower. As if his mind had been read, the helicopter suddenly veered right, gaining altitude rapidly and presenting a target that was currently above the maximum elevation his guns could achieve. And with the fixed mounting of his weaponry, he knew that his guns would only be effective against a moving target at fairly close range. Beyond that it would be a waste of ammunition.

Jake followed the helicopter's flight path, keeping the nose of the waverunner aimed in the general direction of the aircraft as it began to circle cautiously some distance away. He was familiar with many types of helicopters from his days in the military, and he recognized this one to be a Bell Ranger. Uneasily, he watched as it began to climb, taking on a new heading until it was several hundred feet almost directly above him. With the aircraft in such a position, the people aboard it would be able to exploit the current limitations of his weaponry. It was then that he had an inkling of what was in store for him, and a moment later that thought was confirmed.

The sight of the tiny object hurtling down from the sky caused him to gun the Kawasaki to get clear of its path. Keeping his gaze locked on the object, he calculated that it would land a tad wide of him and the girl, but close enough for concern. Even before it reached the water it detonated sharply, quaking the air with a deafening boom and dusting him with a thin cloud of gray smoke.

Jake craned his head around, relieved that the girl and dolphins remained unscathed as they continued to maintain a heading toward the *Angel*, now less than half a mile away. Reaching out in front of him, he removed two locking pins and a cable fixture from the upper weapon emplacement, quickly disengaging the Stoner from its mounting and taking it off safety mode. Looking above him, he sighted the gun on the whirlybird hovering high overhead and squeezed off a quick burst, bracing himself against the hard recoil of the weapon. Several red tracers streaked away, disappearing rapidly from sight as they merged with the aircraft.

The figure of a man leaning out of the cockpit withdrew sharply back into the open cabin. Like a frightened pigeon, the helicopter abruptly broke from its near hover as its pilot realized he was being fired upon. Breaking right, the pilot dipped the rotor blades low, taking the Bell Ranger into a shallow dive in an effort to gain air speed.

Jake sighted the Stoner again and let off another short burst, giving the pilot little respite in eluding the unexpected counterattack. With the Stoner having only a limited supply of ammunition within its magazine, Jake would have to maintain a strict firing discipline. One hundred fifty rounds were all that had been available for the rapid-fire weapon prior to using it. Already he was likely down by thirty rounds in his estimation. And if the temperamental weapon ended up jamming, he always had the Heckler and Koch USP-9 submachine pistol riding his thigh to fall back on as a last resort.

As Jake tracked the aircraft, it seemed like the people aboard it were uncertain about what they were going to do next, for the helicopter withdrew to a safe distance where it proceeded to turn several circles in the sky. Then, all at once, it leaned over in a steep bank before heading off in the direction of the *Angel*.

Jake gripped the Motorola headset and spoke rapidly, literally yelling into the lip mike. "Arrow to Goliath."

Zimbola's reply was almost instant, the natural rumble of his tone higher than usual. "Jeez mon, you tryin' to make Zimby go deaf, Arrow?"

"A Code One is headed your way, Goliath," Jake warned, his tone brisk and conveying the urgency the situation warranted. "That bird coming straight at you from the west is not a friendly. Break out the firearms and be prepared to fend it off. It's armed with concussion grenades."

Zimbola's voice was all business. "I read you, Arrow. Goliath Out."

A sense of dread took hold of Jake as he watched the Bell Ranger grow smaller as it shot for the *Angel*. Thinking quickly, he weighed his limited options, redirecting his gaze to Destiny as he did so. The girl stared off in the direction of the helicopter, seemingly aware of the lethal capability it posed but, as far as he could tell, appearing calm and unperturbed about its presence. Her tranquil disposition somehow galvanized him further, and suddenly he knew what he must do. Clenching the Stoner firmly between his upper arm and right side, he managed to clutch the Kawasaki handgrips awkwardly before bracing himself for the rough ride ahead. Gunning the engine to full throttle, he took off in pursuit of the whirlybird, leaving the girl and dolphins behind.

Chapter 16

O rtega had not anticipated the man on the waverunner to be capable of firing straight up at him. Such an erroneous expectation had been based solely on information conveyed to him by Pedro, who had indicated the machine guns carried by the small watercraft were fix-mounted and could only fire straight ahead. Supposedly they would be unable to line up on an aircraft flying high above. He should have known better, he thought. Pedro had the judgment of an idiot. Unfortunately, he was stuck with Cardoza's irksome nephew for better or worse, although it was the latter case which seemed to prevail most of the time.

Lifting his eyes to the roof of the cockpit, he surveyed the two diminutive holes where small caliber bullets had punched through, narrowly missing him in the process. The sight of the perforations maddened him to the brink of insanity, causing him to envision the various heinous tortures he would dole out on the man below if ever he got his hands on him.

Upon instructing Fernando to keep out of range of the unknown sharpshooter, he was relieved to find that the Bell Ranger had not sustained any critical damage. Apparently nothing vital had been hit. A quick scan of the gauges fronting the aircraft's instrument console told him that all mechanical and electrical systems were functioning normally and that there was no immediate danger of an ensuing malfunction. Carefully assessing the sound of the engine, he neither heard nor felt any unusual noises or vibrations, certainly a telltale sign of no serious impairment to the power train.

Checking the rear fuselage behind him, Ortega was also relieved to find his passenger unhurt and none the less for wear. Omar appeared not the least bit unhinged by the close encounter, providing further proof that Ortega's original assessment of the militant Islamist was correct, that the man was used to close brushes with death.

The state of Omar's health was now very important to Ortega. From his point of view, Omar represented a potential windfall of newfound wealth. The fact that Omar had not been killed meant that their budding business relationship would now be able to grow and prosper. A dealing of such magnitude would allow him to be able to skim some of the immense profits right out from under Cardoza's nose, something he had managed to get away with from time to time in the past. Perhaps he would eventually be able to stash away enough cash to buy the right loyalties. Then he could usurp Cardoza and take over the organization. But right now, he had other business that demanded his attention.

Assessing the situation at hand, he knew it would be too risky to attack the rider of the waverunner again, particularly since the helicopter presently lacked the necessary firepower he would need to attempt such a stunt. Aside from the ineffective short range of the handguns both he and Omar carried, the grenades were all he had available in seeking retribution. And unfortunately, he would have to place the aircraft in too compromising a position in order to use them. If anything, the foe below was a skilled marksman, having hit the airframe with his opening volley. With this in mind, the Colombian could not help but wonder what other damage the Ranger might have taken.

Just before he had dropped the grenade, Ortega had gotten a good look at the other objects in the water. The sight of the white dolphins had astounded him, one so big that at first he thought he was looking at an albino pilot whale or small orca. At seeing a human riding the back of the larger creature, he was reminded of what Pedro had said about a girl. Something most strange was going on here.

Recalling the odd scene, he pulled the binoculars he carried to his face and trained them on the water in front of the waverunner, steadying the spyglasses as best he could. Focusing binoculars on even a stationary target from a moving aircraft was not easy to do, and because the objects below him were on the move, the task was made all the more difficult. As he stared through the lenses though, he realized Pedro had been correct. There was a girl down there. Continuing to study the creatures, he discovered that there were actually three dolphins and that two of them did indeed possess a white skin tone.

Lowering the glasses, an image of the mutant bottlenose dolphins he had previously discovered suddenly came to mind, their carcasses still in deep freeze aboard the *San Carlo*. He was scheduled to deliver them to Hennington during his next stopover in Port-au-Prince. While they were not albinos like the ones below him, they had nevertheless been caught in these waters. Dwelling on it, he began to see a weird connection between the two, a link that could not possibly be coincidental in nature as far as he was concerned.

Ortega continued to seethe as he mulled over the state of affairs confronting him. The present situation was personal in nature and demanded some form of retaliatory action, something that would give him satisfaction. Yet he dared not get too close to the rider of the waverunner who seemed to be protecting both the girl and the strange dolphins.

There was, however, another course of action open to him. Looking east, he eyed the two vessels sitting at anchor less than a mile distant. Yes, he thought, a feral grin suddenly replacing the dour expression that had dominated his features only an instant earlier. Revenge was a most pleasant undertaking if you went about it the right way.

Chapter 17

*J*acob had nearly completed deploying the specially fabricated floatation devices that buoyed up the two most seriously injured dolphins, getting assistance from several people aboard the vessel called *Avenging Angel*. When he had first spotted the boat from afar, his initial inclination was to steer clear of it. A subtle inner flicker, however, had beckoned him on, causing him to hold to a course directly toward the unfamiliar vessel.

Over the years, Jacob had grown accustomed to such flickers infringing on his consciousness, and these days they seemed to be stronger than ever, coming upon him at the oddest times. Sometimes they gave him a fleeting glimpse of something felt or seen by the creatures, even when they were far removed from him. In any event, he had learned to trust such inward stirrings whenever they invaded his awareness or, as happened today, whenever they interrupted his daydreams. Even before he had become mindful of the vessel, it was one of those strange flickers that had pulled him from his deep reminiscence over events that had taken place years earlier, bringing him back to reality.

The people aboard the vessel had been awaiting his arrival, forewarned by Destiny that he would be coming to attend the injured dolphins. While all the other albinos in her escort were on hand to meet him, the girl, much to his surprise, had gone off somewhere with Hercules and was still missing. According to one of the people assisting him, the white-haired individual called Doctor Grahm, Destiny had left to find Natalie who she said was in trouble, but that the captain of the *Avenging Angel* had followed shortly after her departure to help.

About ten minutes after his arrival, Jacob was relieved to learn that Captain Javolyn had radioed the *Angel*, reporting that he was currently on his way back with Destiny and three dolphins. But now, another radio transmission had just come in, this one seemingly urgent and blaring, causing the black giant presently in charge to shout orders at two others of the crew. All at once he sensed an orderly panic as these crew members scrambled forward to retrieve what he distinctly heard to be guns.

Trying to fathom exactly what was going on, Jacob was suddenly struck by another flicker, making him heedful of a growing buzz. Looking toward the sound, he lifted his eyes to the west to observe a helicopter bearing straight at them, the aircraft rapidly slowing and descending quickly as it approached.

At that moment, Jacob knew they were vulnerable. Coral and Reef were currently maneuvering the floatation mat into place beneath the second incapacitated gray, each albino grasping a side with their unique appendages. Once the mat was positioned correctly, Jacob would throw the valve that would inflate it, thus raising the injured mammal above the water. The oldest and wisest among the new breed, Coral and Reef would not leave their posts until the task was completed.

Out of the corner of his eye, Jacob vaguely perceived that no weapons capable of repelling the aircraft were currently on deck. Knowing that it was now too late to avoid an attack, he turned to face the on-coming helicopter just as it flared into a near hover almost directly over the *Avenging Angel*. Something small glinted in the sunlight on the right side of the whirlybird for one brief moment, then fell.

Something much larger exploded from the water in that same instant, rising on an intercept course with the falling thing. Spellbound, Jacob realized that something was Hermes. Leaping to a height of fifteen meters, the athletic albino snagged the object in midair with its beak, seeming to hang suspended in defiance of gravity. With a deft flick of his head, Hermes whipped the object skyward, launching it back the way it had come just before he fell off into a lazy seaward plunge. Jacob stared in amazement as the albino clove the water cleanly a split second before the surrounding atmosphere was shaken by a powerful airburst.

Buffeted by the blast, the helicopter yawed violently, sliding sideways overhead as its pilot fought to regain control. Jacob kept his gaze fixed on it as it fluttered upwind and abruptly stabilized. He could see three men aboard it, two of them poking their heads from the aircraft's open doorways as they looked back at the scene below. It was then that the loud stutter of a machine gun assaulted his ears, causing the aircraft to veer rapidly away.

Turning his head, Jacob spied the black giant firing an assault rifle from the hip, the weapon appearing like a toy in his hands. Another sound caught his attention above the staccato din, adding to the cacophony. As he turned to investigate the source, he noted a small watercraft racing around the side of the larger vessel, its driver unleashing intermittent bursts from another rapid-fire weapon snuggled tightly to his side by one arm. As Jacob took in the spectacle, the driver of the watercraft tore off in pursuit of the helicopter, chasing it across the water and continuing to fire upon it with sporadic volleys.

With the heavy barrage put out by the two weapons, Jacob was certain one of the shooters had scored a hit, for a thin plume of gray smoke suddenly streamed away from the aircraft. The helicopter made a wide turn, swinging low over the water and heading off in the direction from which it had come. Seeming to have difficulty maintaining its air speed, it labored on, all the while with the small watercraft tenaciously dogging it. From his perspective, it appeared that the helicopter was making for the distant white ship. As he watched, the two foes began to recede into the distance.

With the threat now gone, Jacob went back to finishing the job he had started. He noticed that Coral and Reef had completed their task, and he could see that the injured gray was ready for lifting. With a turn of the valve, he sent a stream of compressed air into the floatation device. With relief, he watched the mat inflate, buoying the dolphin cradled within its cushioning folds. Satisfied, he pivoted his head to study the other injured gray and the air mat upon which it lay. In tandem, both floatation rigs would be towed behind the pinnace for the long trip back to the cove. But right now, he had to await the arrival of Destiny before he headed back.

Chapter 18

*T*he Bell Ranger set down heavily on the landing pad aboard the *San Carlo*, and not a second too soon. Fernando immediately shut down the overheating turbine, hoping the engine was not too extensively damaged. He had been monitoring the temperature gauge for the last several minutes of flight, cringing when it had gone into the red. The turbine had taken on a vibration, and he had avoided putting any more strain on it than was necessary, shunning the temptation to put more pitch into the main rotor blades and climb higher for fear that the power train would come apart.

The unknown assailant chasing after them on the waverunner had been relentless, continuing to fire upon the helicopter every so often as it struggled to stay aloft. They had been lucky, he knew, for their air speed had begun to drop enough for their attacker to gain on them. Had the man not decided to break off the attack, he would have nailed them for sure.

Fernando was eager to exit the aircraft, wanting to effect whatever repairs were necessary to get the helicopter back up and flying again. Within the holds of the tuna trawler, they had enough spare parts to practically build a second helicopter. Of greater urgency, however, was a need to keep busy and out of Ortega's way. The Cardoza lieutenant was one step away from a neurotic outburst that might seriously injure or even kill one of the crewmen. Fernando had been witness to Ortega's homicidal rages, and anyone within striking distance of him was potential game. That is, anyone except for Pedro. As always, Ortega would refrain from harming a single hair on the head of Cardoza's favorite nephew.

Far as Fernando could tell, the only thing presently keeping Ortega's fury in check was the presence of the passenger who had accompanied the flight and who was, by necessity, still with them. Fernando had worked under the Cardoza lieutenant long enough to know that only one thing would supplant Ortega's need for vengeance, and that thing was greed. Though Fernando hadn't been privy to the discussion that had taken place between Ortega and the other man, he had seen the plastic bag containing the white powder and was confident the meeting was the initiation of a drug deal. Ortega, he was certain, would keep a tight rein on himself if he thought a display of temper would turn the stranger off to doing any further business. Side ventures outside normal business channels indigenous of the Cardoza monopolies gave Ortega the opportunity to siphon off additional profits into his own pockets.

And while Fernando feared Ortega, the stranger made him feel even more uneasy, much like the way he felt when he had gotten a glimpse of Cardoza's pet tiger back at the drug lord's compound in Colombia. Though the tiger appeared to be well fed, there was that lurking yet unmistakable measure of uncertainty about one's own safety hanging in the air like the promise of death should one get too close to the creature. Fernando had made eye contact with the man only once, just before the stranger had stepped aboard the helicopter, but it was enough to make him avoid looking directly into that face again. Like the tiger, there was the ready challenge of the predator that lay within the man's eyes…and something else. Yes, it was a deep-seated streak of maliciousness, cold and unyielding to any influence not within the man's sphere of belief.

As the main rotor came to a stop, Fernando climbed up onto the airframe, noting the two bullet holes in the engine cowling and several others in the main rotor. Removing the cowling, he winced when he saw the damage to the turbine.

Ortega scowled up at him. "How long before you have this bird flying again?" The tone of his voice was strained and curt, as if he were having great difficulty holding back the temper tantrum building behind the stiff exterior he presented. The fact that Ortega's composure hadn't cracked already was something new to Fernando, but he nevertheless expected the man to erupt at any moment. He likened Ortega to an ocean dike that gave no indication it was ready to burst, structurally unsuitable to hold back the pressure pushing against it.

Fernando did not like having to disappoint his boss, knowing the potential consequences of such negative news, but he had no choice.

"It doesn't look good," he croaked, shaking his head disconsolately and trying to mask the nervousness he felt. "At least a day."

Ortega spun and stared out to sea, letting his gaze linger hatefully in the direction of the waverunner. The unknown rider was still within sight, heading toward the two vessels positioned near the southeast side of the island. Grumbling to himself, he turned his eyes to Pedro who had just come up the steps to the heliport.

Pedro opened his mouth to say something but stopped short when he saw the blond stranger standing off to one side.

"What is it?" Ortega said irritably.

"I have called both the *San Diablo* and the *San Pinto* and told each of them to send a runabout this way," Pedro informed him, his eyes shifting to the distant waverunner. "We will catch that bastard before the day is out."

"You idiot!" Ortega bellowed scornfully, unable to contain himself any longer. "Small motorboats will be useless against our attacker." Walking to the edge of the landing pad, he pointed disgustedly at the remains of one of the destroyed runabouts. The ruined boat hung suspended from the trawler's power block, still caught up in the seine net. "Look at what he's already done. Do you want the rest of our boats wrecked as well?"

Pedro frowned darkly at the insult but said nothing.

"Get back on the radio and tell the other vessels not to send any boats," Ortega growled. "I'll not have any more of our equipment damaged."

Pedro hesitated momentarily as if to question the order, then nodded. Briefly, he cast curious eyes on the stranger once again before climbing back down the steps leading from the landing pad.

"I have a suggestion," Omar said quietly, speaking for the first time since arriving at the *San Carlo*, prompting Ortega to turn and face him. "Is there someplace we can go to talk privately?"

Chapter 19

*T*he girl and the three dolphins rendezvoused at the *Angel* only a minute ahead of Jake. Leery of another attack, Jake felt it prudent to keep the Kawasaki tied alongside the *Angel* rather than stow it back aboard the vessel. As an added precaution, he made sure the other weaponry was at the ready, including the second M-60, which was left mounted on its pedestal at the *Angel's* stern. Stationing Hector behind the special Plexiglas shield that was brought up from below deck, he posted him as lookout for the approach of any other unwanted guests.

With these measures now in place, Jake was able to feel more relaxed. Focusing his attention back on the marine mammals, he observed how the last of the severely impaired dolphins was being assisted. The sight of two of the albinos employing those remarkable appendages of theirs drew his interest as the creatures used them to position an inflatable mat under the third stricken gray. The man called Jacob gave him a brief smile just before injecting the mat with air. Within moments the mat expanded, then bobbed to the surface with its burden secured and cushioned atop it. Almost immediately, the closest albino extended one of its claw-like appendages and removed the air hose from its quick disconnect fitting attached to the side of the mat. With this accomplished, Jake watched Jacob tie a tow rope to the float, attaching it to one of the other floatation devices. The three mats would form a line towed behind the pinnace.

Gathered at the swim platform of the *Angel*, Jake noted Grahm and his two assistants taking in the proceedings with scientific curiosity. When Jake had first arrived back at the *Angel*, he had seen the way Grahm had been preoccupied with one albino dolphin in particular, leaning over the water in greeting. "Good to see you again, old girl," Grahm had said close to tears, stroking the mammal's snout affectionately in the manner of old friends. "You don't know how much I missed you."

To Jake, the reunion was touching. And although he had been forewarned about it, he was astounded when he heard the dolphin reply, "I, too, have missed you." Distorted by the medium of air, Natalie's speech had sounded garbled and close to incomprehensible, but the words were enunciated clearly enough for him to decipher their meaning.

As he ran such a seemingly implausible exchange over in his mind again, he had the vague impression he was being watched. Turning his head, he spied the girl studying him intently as she continued to sit astride her mount less than twenty feet away, her face mask now resting against her forehead. Jake found himself staring back as the girl drifted closer on the huge albino.

"You have been injured," she said softly, her voice dulcet and enchanting. She pointed at the coagulating blood dribbling slowly down his left arm. "If you let me, I can stop the bleeding."

Jake had completely forgotten about the wound, lifting his arm to scrutinize the extent of the injury. It was more than a graze. A bullet had sliced deep enough to furrow the flesh across his triceps, leaving it bloody and swollen. In the tropics, infection would set in rapidly if such a wound were left untreated for too long.

"Come into the water," the girl invited in that soothing mellifluous voice. "I will heal your injury."

Jake remembered the way the girl had revived the men he had routed back near the tuna trawler and knew there might be a shred of truth in what she was offering. Nevertheless, he found it difficult to stop the sardonic grin that crossed his face. "I think it will take more than good intentions to fix this little inconvenience," he replied matter-of-factly. "More likely a good antiseptic and a few stitches."

Jacob looked up from the pinnace berthed alongside the *Angel*. "Good intentions are not what the girl is proposing," he interposed, smiling wryly. "If you let her treat the wound, the result may surprise you."

Grahm wandered to Jake's side, motivated by curiosity. "My lad, why don't you take her up on the offer," he suggested solemnly. "Perhaps she can do what she says."

Jake eyed Grahm in surprise. "I would think a true scientist like yourself would doubt such a thing is possible."

Grahm suddenly chuckled. "One must always keep an open mind when it concerns scientific inquiry." He stared at Jake a moment longer, coaxing him with an encouraging smile. "Go on lad, you've nothing to lose."

Jake looked back at Jacob. Though the man was grizzled and weather-beaten, his eyes danced with a warmness not altogether different from Grahm's. As he searched the man's face, he sensed a deep reservoir of underlying intelligence that seemed totally at odds with the simple outward appearance the man exhibited. Jacob was a contradiction. There was more to the man than met the eye, as if he and he alone were privy to some cryptic cosmic joke humanity was in the dark about.

Jake found himself suddenly laughing, deciding to play along with this absurd notion, if only to get closer to the girl. "Oh, what the hell," he muttered, removing the submachine pistol strapped to his thigh and tossing it to Phillipe who stood nearby. Grabbing hold of the boat's railing, he vaulted over it into the sea.

Not sure what to expect, he treaded water as the giant bottlenose brought Destiny abreast of him. The girl seemed ready to dismount from the huge bull but stopped just short of doing so, suddenly appearing shy and confused. She clung to the dolphin for several more seconds before sliding off, then floated beside Jake. Three more albinos abruptly broke the surface near the girl and crowded in close, surrounding Jake and brushing him lightly with their rostrums. Reaching out, Destiny placed a hand on the injury.

A strange sensation suddenly took hold of Jake. He was abruptly suffused with a feeling of immense happiness, simultaneously taken to glimmering oceanic depths and the farthest reaches of the cosmos, the vastness of both making him feel insignificant. All at once an ineffable peace swept over him, nearly taking his breath away. Images danced before him, some lucid, others vague. It was as though he were being borne by a gentle breeze to a distant place, another dimension. He was not a religious man by nature, but if God truly existed, he was being held in the palm of his hand. Spellbound, he glanced sideways into the orbs of the unique creatures surrounding him, then fell into the eyes of the girl at the far end of the universe. There was no discernible difference. It seemed he was looking into their very souls. The girl and her companions were unified by swirling threads of energy, bound together as tightly as the matter comprising a neutron star, matter that was paradoxically as lose as the wind. A profound wisdom shone within each of those dark orbs, transcending the barriers of flesh and form. He could feel their rhythmic breathing, deep inhalations that seemed to draw from the wellspring of time and space, followed by exhalations that fell in crashing crescendos like waves against craggy rocks and sandy beaches, purifying everything they touched. And then he understood. All life was to be nurtured and loved.

Lacey patterns of sunlight shimmered on the water's surface as Jake found himself back in the sea, immensely refreshed as if awakening from a deep, satisfying sleep. The adult albinos had pulled away and the girl had remounted the large bull. Looking up, Jake found Grahm staring down at him from the *Angel*, his expression inquisitive.

Jake was about to climb back aboard the vessel when the water erupted next to him. An albino juvenile bounded from the sea, turning slightly in mid-flight to make eye contact just before disappearing with a tail flip. The smaller bottlenose leapt from the water several more times, spiraling and pirouetting before splashing down less than two feet away.

"I think he likes you."

Jake turned in the direction of the pinnace, realizing it was Jacob who had spoken.

The Haitian exuded a wry grin. "Achilles usually keeps his distance from humans."

Jake took in the words distractedly, still marveling over the incredible rush he had just experienced. He spun in the water to look at Destiny again. The pensive expression she had previously worn had now changed over into a shy smile. He studied her for several more seconds, awed by the girl's loveliness. There was a radiance to her that went way beyond physical beauty, an elusive mystique all too alluring that made him want to reach out for her. Moments ago, he had only gotten a brief glimpse of it and yet he was still confused. She had made a connection with something deep inside him, though he wasn't quite sure what it was. The girl was an enigma, harboring some unknown quality that was obscure and esoteric in nature. Not knowing who she was triggered a fountain of curiosity within him.

Jake's reflective mood was suddenly interrupted, and he became aware of Zimbola calling out to him. He pulled his eyes from Destiny and turned his gaze to the black giant who stood next to Grahm on the *Angel's* deck.

"A boat approaches from the direction of the ship," Zimbola grunted.

Jake followed the giant's gaze. A small vessel appeared to be making for the island. Quickly, he propelled himself to the side of the *Angel* using a few powerful overhand strokes. Zimbola reached over and grabbed his hand, pulling him up onto the deck with little effort.

Taking the spyglasses from the Jamaican's other hand, Jake stared through the powerful lenses. The vessel presented a low profile.

"It's the tug that pulls the net," Jake commented. "Probably the only vessel they have left besides the ship." He continued to study the tug, able to discern four men aboard it. Even with the binoculars, the distance was too great to clearly make out their features. As Jake watched, the tug continued on a slow steady course toward the island.

Jake handed the spyglasses back to Zimbola. "They don't appear to be a threat at the moment but keep your eye on them. I'd like to know what they're up to."

Casting a sideways glance in the direction of the girl, Jake noticed she had climbed aboard the pinnace and was standing next to Jacob. He couldn't help but wonder about the relationship between the two.

"Your wound!" Grahm uttered in astonishment. "It's almost fully healed!" His tone was racked with emotion.

Jake had completely forgotten why he had gone in the water. Reflexively, he ran his fingers over the injury. Feeling no pain and only smooth skin, he craned his head over the area that had been lacerated. All the blood had washed away, revealing only pink scar tissue in the final stages of healing. Awestruck, he looked back at Destiny. How was such a thing possible?

"We'll be on our way now," Jacob said, throwing a knowing smile in Jake's direction. "We thank you for your assistance."

"Wait," Grahm shouted, his expression rife with consternation. "There's so much we have to discuss, so many questions that need answers. My life's work has revolved around dolphins. You...you can't just leave."

Sympathy showed on Jacob's face. "I'm sorry, my friend, but I must get these injured creatures to a place where we can better take care of them."

"Let us go with you," Grahm persisted. "I'll help you any way I can."

Jacob fidgeted uncomfortably before turning to the girl beside him, looking to see how she was reacting to all this. Destiny stared at Grahm searchingly before shifting her gaze to Jake. A strained silence hung in the air as Grahm waited for an answer. The silence was finally broken when Achilles suddenly bolted from the water, executing a spectacular triple somersault, and reaching a height of at least eight meters above the surface. Reentering the water in a perfect dive, the juvenile disappeared from sight. As if responding to the antics of the young bottlenose, Destiny turned to Jacob with an approving smile and nodded.

"Your offer is accepted," Jacob said gravely, looking to Grahm. "But I must warn you, the trip will be slow and time consuming. The maximum speed this old boat will give me is about seven knots and we have about forty-five nautical miles to travel. You can follow if you like, but we will take no offense if you should decide to leave us during the trip."

Grahm could not hold back his excitement, his expression overflowing with joyous exuberance. "You don't have to worry about that, we'll be right behind you every step of the way," he gushed, looking to Jake for his concurrence.

Without even realizing it, Jake found himself nodding in agreement.

Chapter 20

*T*wo hours had gone by since pulling anchor. To Jake, the voyage was agonizingly slow and tedious as the *Avenging Angel* continued to hang behind the pinnace as it plodded along directly ahead. At Grahm's request, Jacob had allowed the scientist to board the smaller vessel where he could better utilize the time to carry on discussions and ask questions of the girl and her companion.

Jake had consulted his charts. Based on their heading, he knew they were running a course that would take them just south of the tiny village of Malique on the Haitian coast. The Kawasaki had been brought back aboard the *Angel* and secured. Not wanting to leave his rear unprotected, however, he continued to keep the auxiliary M-60 mounted at its rear station with Hector manning it. His days in the military had thoroughly honed the importance of vigilance into him, and every so often he would scan the surrounding sea to look for the approach of any other vessels or aircraft.

Just before their departure near the island he had observed the tug from the tuna trawler through his binoculars. According to a chart of Navassa Island, the tug had made landfall at a place designated as Lulu Bay. A lone individual had been dropped off and had quickly disappeared, vanishing into the rugged terrain rising up from the shoreline. After that, the tug had chugged back the way it had come. As of now, both the tug and its mother ship were long gone from sight, having been left over the horizon more than an hour ago.

To busy himself, Jake had disassembled both machine guns carried by the Kawasaki, wiping away the salt water residue and oiling all the parts before reassembling them. He had expended more than three hundred rounds from the Stoner and was diligent in replacing the missing ammunition, refilling the gun's magazine to maximum capacity. The Kawasaki's remaining torpedo was then removed from its tube and also wiped down and oiled. This accomplished, he stowed each of the weapons in their concealed hiding place below deck. In these waters he had to be prepared for a fight at all times. It was ingrained in him, an integral part of who he was.

Jake came back out on deck and stretched, then climbed up to the pilothouse. Zimbola was at the helm, and as Jake entered the cabin his first mate eyed him oddly.

"What?" Jake asked, somewhat taken back by Zimbola's strange manner. There was something on his friend's mind.

Zimbola opened his mouth as if to say something, then abruptly shut it and cast his eyes on the smaller vessel leading the way. His expression was somber.

"What's going on?" Jake pressed.

Zimbola turned and looked down at Jake's left arm. "Your wound…it appears to have healed completely."

Jake ran his fingers over the area, then scrutinized the remaining thin line of pink scar tissue in amazement. It was hardly noticeable. "This is a bad thing? Why should this bother you?"

"The way your injury has healed is not what concerns me."

"Then what's bugging you?"

The black giant shook his head dismally. "There is evil lurking about… very powerful evil."

Jake let out a laugh. "We chased away the bad guys, didn't we?" He glanced at the pinnace in front of them. "We helped these people. Whatever evil you feel is far behind us now."

Zimbola's expression remained bleak. "The girl…she is a witch."

"A witch, huh." Jake was starting to get annoyed. Here he was again, listening to his first mate spouting off on superstitious belief. "You're telling me she's evil?"

"No!" The Jamaican shook his head emphatically. "The girl has the power of white magic within her. She is not evil. Only a white witch can heal such a wound so quickly."

Jake was floundering in confusion. He threw his arms up in frustration. "Well, if you don't think she's evil, then just what are you getting at?"

"White witches are like magnets. They have a way of attracting evil. The forces of evil are always at odds with goodness. Evil will always challenge virtue."

"So by being around these people you feel we're placing ourselves in great danger?"

"It is what I sense, a premonition of things to come."

"You were never one to shy away from danger, to show fear. I've never seen you run from anything."

"It is not myself I fear for," Zimbola said, bringing doleful eyes to bear on Jake.

"Who then?"

Zimbola's expression hardened. "You should not trouble yourself with the worries of an overly cautious black man."

Jake punched Zimbola lightly on the arm. "I've never considered you overly cautious, big guy. Perhaps a bit headstrong, but never too cautious." With that said, he wandered out onto the deck, not wanting to press his oversized friend any further. He was glad to end the discussion. He hated it whenever Zimby indulged in island cultural beliefs. It sometimes tended to put the man in an emotional funk as it did now.

Climbing down from the pilothouse, Jake walked forward to the bow and made a surveillance of the sea all around him. Satisfied that they were not being followed, he studied the scene immediately in front of the *Angel*. Trailing behind the pinnace, eleven bottlenose dolphins knifed their way slowly through the sea on each side of the floatation mats being towed, nine of them albinos.

Jake abruptly frowned. Two albinos were missing from the pack. Keeping his eyes glued to the procession for several more minutes, he performed a mental recount five additional times to see if he had overlooked any. When no others breached the surface, he was certain he had not miscounted. He ran over in his mind the number of bottlenose he had witnessed earlier on. When he had first spotted the girl, seven albinos were in her escort, including the giant upon which she rode. Destiny's pod had joined up with seven more dolphins, three of them proving to be this new breed of white bottlenose with the claw-like appendages. That brought the count to fourteen dolphins, with only four in the mix being the more common grays. Two additional bottlenose were later discovered within the tuna trawler's seine net, one of them Natalie. Altogether, that added up to sixteen dolphins, including five grays. With three injured grays towed along on the mats, a total of thirteen bottlenose should have been in the water, eleven of them albinos. And yet all he could see were eleven, nine of which were this new breed. Two albinos were missing.

Jake couldn't help but wonder what had become of the two white dolphins. He looked over at the girl, attempting to get a read on her, trying to determine if she was aware of this. She was sitting at the stern of the pinnace, withdrawn and contemplative, monitoring the incapacitated creatures being towed on the mats. Every so often she would glance his way, resting her eyes on him for several seconds before bringing her attention back to the injured dolphins.

The swimming dolphins remained close to the floats, periodically splashing water onto their wounded cousins. It soon became obvious to Jake why they were doing this. Although Jacob had secured blankets over the injured creatures to shield their skin from the intense tropical sun, the protective fabric had to be kept both damp and cool to prevent the blanketed dolphins from overheating and their skin from dehydrating.

As Jake continued to watch, he could see Grahm and Jacob in deep discussion. From where Jake stood, Grahm's manner differed sharply with that of Jacob's. The scientist appeared quite animated and jovial, seeming to throw a non-stop series of questions at the islander, whose attitude looked to be pensive and guarded by contrast.

Jake let his gaze fall on the girl once again. In his mind, he revisited the moment Destiny had climbed aboard the pinnace. From where he had stood aboard the *Angel* he had had an unobstructed view of her. It was the first time he had not seen her hunkered forward astride the huge bottlenose or treading water. He had noted how slim the girl was and how graceful she walked. She was so young and lovely, so pure and innocent. The skintight wetsuit clinging to her body only tended to emphasize the long coltish legs, the small buttocks and the subtle feminine curves she possessed. She was tiny, barely five feet in stature and probably well under ninety pounds. Were it not for the thrust of her breasts, which were full and round, and her long black hair fluttering in the breeze, she might have been taken for a boy at a distance.

As Jake pondered this, he couldn't help but dwell on the words Zimbola had used in assessing the girl, White witch. He couldn't refute the girl's unusual ability, having had a firsthand taste of it. And while it was true she had a mysterious bond with the most incredible creatures he had ever come across, the word witch just didn't seem quite appropriate. No, he decided. Destiny was anything but a witch. Continuing to think on it, he concluded that only one word seemed befitting enough to describe her.

Angel!

Jake had a special fondness for the word. After all, didn't his own vessel go by such a name, at least in part? Angels, he knew, were selfless spiritual beings that looked out for the welfare of others. They were protectors, altruistic to the core.

Destiny met his eyes as he stared over at her. Yes, he suddenly realized. He had no doubts, no doubts whatsoever that he was looking at an Angel.

To find out what happens next in this on-going saga, read
Part Two of The Dolphin Riders Series -
The Girl Who Rode Dolphins, 2nd Edition
Gaia's Heartbeat.

ACKNOWLEDGMENTS

No one deserves more credit for their support in the writing of this tale than my wife and soul mate, Harriet, my biggest fan. Her indomitable spirit and encouragement was indispensable in keeping me focused on completing a work that could have otherwise gone unfinished, a story that could have conceivably transpired in an alternate universe closely paralleling our own. As the novel progressed, it was always a delight to gauge her reaction, which was never disappointing as I read proceeding entries to her over breakfast each and every Saturday morning.

But the thing that finally compelled me to actually write it was the way Harriet was able to cope with her illness. Harriet is tough as nails and since the year 2000 she's been battling CML - chronic myeloid leukemia - and so far she's put up one hell of a valiant fight, absolutely refusing to yield to what most doctors would describe as a devastating, life-threatening malady. Thus, she made up her mind long ago to live out a normal existence, avoiding hospitals completely and refraining from seeing doctors as much as possible. Consequently, it was her grit and determination that inspired me to take pen to paper and flesh out an adventure imbued with these admirable qualities of the spirit. In its basic subliminal form, I wanted to honor her with something unique, essentially a literary work that came from the deepest part of me, something only I could give her, but something which would reflect her iron will and indomitable strength. This is initially mirrored in the book's opening scene where we find a woman adrift and marooned in a thunderous, tumultuous sea. She is alone and clinging to a piece of flotsam, and the reader finds the woman to be pregnant. By all rights, she should accept her fate and succumb to the elements, but she continues to fight on in the face of overwhelming odds, clinging to life and refusing to quit until she has nothing left within her to resist the battering forces of a sea gone mad. Later in the book we learn the woman survives with the help of a dolphin and that her name is Harriet Grahm. And although she has no recollection of her former life, she ends up taking on a new identity, becoming Amphitrite, one of the cornerstone characters of the story. During her ordeal at sea, something incredible has happened to Amphitrite, and her failure to remember her past has somehow given her the power to glimpse the future. Henceforth, she becomes an arrant believer in this power and what the future holds, convinced her visions are real, and it is this ability that spills over and infects the reader to make the story palpable and real.

Writing the novel was a labor of love that took four years to complete. In creating it, I had to constantly challenge myself to come up with new ideas, not always knowing where the story was headed since some of the characters within the developing plot started taking on a life of their own. I only knew I wanted to take the reader on a journey to high adventure, an escape from the often mundane routines of everyday life most of us encounter, and in adhering to this I kept imagining what I'd like to see on the big screen if the novel was ever made into a blockbuster movie. My heartfelt appreciation also goes out to my daughter, Melissa, for her added encouragement to keep me moving forward with this project. And I certainly would be remiss if I left out her three little progenies, Troy Jacob, Solomon, and the latest addition to the family, Jayna Jocelynne, each of whom provided me with the personality traits and inspiration to create the mischievous impish characters which have now come alive to play an integral part within the sequel to this tale.

And lastly, I want to thank my sister, Barbara, in showing an enthusiastic interest in my creativity. Whenever she picked up the uncompleted manuscript, she always seemed to have trouble putting it down, totally absorbed and fascinated by the plot's intrigue and explosiveness.